MW00573351

Also by the Author

The Erin O'Reilly Mysteries

Black Velvet
Irish Car Bomb
White Russian
Double Scotch
Manhattan
Black Magic
Death By Chocolate
Massacre
Flashback
First Love
High Stakes
Aquarium
The Devil You Know
Hair of the Dog
Punch Drunk
Bossa Nova
Blackout
Angel Face
Italian Stallion
White Lightning
Kamikaze
Jackhammer
Frostbite (coming soon)

Tequila Sunrise: A James Corcoran Story

Fathers
A Modern Christmas Story

The Clarion Chronicles
Ember of Dreams

Jackhammer

The Erin O'Reilly Mysteries
Book Twenty-Two

Steven Henry

Clickworks Press • Baltimore, MD

Copyright © 2023 Steven Henry
Cover design © 2023 Ingrid Henry
Cover photo © 2023 under license from Shutterstock.com (Credit: Dmitry Kalinovsky/Shutterstock)
Additional cover photo © 2023 under license from Shutterstock.com (Credit: CynthiaL04/Shutterstock)
NYPD shield photo used under license from Shutterstock.com (Credit: Stephen Mulcahey/Shutterstock)
Author photo © 2017 Shelley Paulson Photography
Spine image used under license from Shutterstock.com (Credit: Olga_Shestakova/Shutterstock)
All rights reserved

First publication: Clickworks Press, 2023
Release: CWP-EOR22-INT-P.IS-1.0

Sign up for updates, deals, and exclusive sneak peeks at clickworkspress.com/join.

Ebook: 979-8-88900-014-3
Paperback: 979-8-88900-015-0
Hardcover: 979-8-88900-016-7

This is a work of fiction. Names, characters, places, organizations, and events are either the products of the author's imagination or used in a fictitious manner. Any resemblance to actual persons, living or dead, is purely coincidental.

For the builders, who pick up the pieces
of our broken world and rebuild it.

We've got a bonus story for you!

We're so grateful for the love and support you've shown for Erin and Rolf. As a special thank you, we want to give you a free bonus story starring Vic Neshenko and Zofia Piekarski.

Keep reading after Jackhammer to enjoy

Screwdriver

A Vic Neshenko Story

Vic and Zofia are apartment hunting.
But the Manhattan real estate market is killer.

Jackhammer

Fill an old-fashioned glass with ice. Pour 1 oz. Jack Daniels and 1 oz. amaretto into glass. Serve with a stir straw.

Chapter 1

"This is unbelievable. It's impossible."

Erin O'Reilly leaned back in her chair and rubbed her eyes. She was tired, depressed, and had a headache that felt like somebody was trying to crack her skull open.

"I assure you, darling, it's the simple truth," Morton Carlyle said.

"We're only scratching the surface, love," James Corcoran added. "It gets ever so much worse as you go deeper."

"We've been here for hours," Erin complained.

"Three hours and forty-seven minutes," Charles Markham said. The District Attorney had a reputation for precision, along with complete and perfect self-control. After almost four hours in the man's presence, Erin believed every bit of it. He had yet to raise his voice or show any emotion whatever. Rumor had it, he could face down a child-murdering serial killer as politely and calmly as if he was talking to a bank teller.

"Feels longer," Erin muttered. She was being surly and knew it, but was rapidly getting to the point where she didn't care. She wondered whether this was why her partner Vic Neshenko acted the way he did. If so, it explained his liking for vodka.

"We're at a point in the investigation where it's important you understand the particulars," Markham said.

"That's why we're having this meeting," Phil Stachowski said gently.

Erin nodded. She understood; she just didn't like it. A four-hour meeting was a form of slow torture, no matter what your career might be. For a street cop who thrived on action, it was like holding her forehead against a belt sander.

The meeting was being held in an NYPD safe house in Brooklyn, a brick two-story building that had been seized from a crooked contractor a few months earlier. It was in a good neighborhood, far from any known gang activity; an excellent place for a low-profile get-together of cops, city officials, and semi-reformed gangsters.

They were in the dining room, sitting around a nice hardwood table. On one side of the table sat Lieutenant Stachowski and Captain Holliday, representing New York's Finest. Opposite them were Corky and Carlyle, the criminal contingent. DA Markham held court at the head of the table. Erin sat at the other end; cops to her left, gangsters to her right. Rolf, her K-9, snoozed under the table. The tabletop was littered with stacks of papers, photographs, and laptop computers.

"I know why we're having the meeting," Erin said. She gestured to the papers on the table.

"What I don't believe is what I'm seeing here."

"You didn't know all of this?" Captain Holliday asked. One side of his mustache quirked up in surprise.

She shook her head. "I'd never actually seen Evan O'Malley's ledger," she said. "All I know is what I've been told. I thought..."

"You thought he was naught but a jumped-up street hoodlum," Carlyle said.

"I knew he ran a lot of criminal shit," Erin said. "And shady things like union racketeering. But there's all sorts of stuff here on top of the gambling, prostitution, money laundering, smuggling, and drugs. Legitimate businesses. We're talking construction, service industries, garbage collection, real estate, you name it."

"You did know about the garbage business," Carlyle said.

"Yeah, I guess." After Carlyle had immigrated from Northern Ireland, he'd put his IRA bomb-making expertise to work in Evan's service, blowing up the competition's garbage trucks in what had become known as the New York Garbage War.

"It's a lot to take in," Phil said.

"That's what's so insidious about organized crime," Holliday said. "They get their fingers into everything. They corrupt everything they touch."

"And that is precisely why this ledger is invaluable," Markham said, tapping the tallest stack of papers. "The money trail outlines every bit of O'Malley influence in New York. Every crooked business, every associate and earner, every dirty civil servant."

"We've got three State Representatives in there!" Erin said.

"We nearly had a Senator, too," Corky said cheerfully. "But you and I scotched that when we scuttled his reelection campaign. Marcus Ross was buyable; it seems Senator Locke is made of better stuff. She's proven resistant to all overtures thus far."

"We're all glad to hear it," Holliday said dryly. "The point, Detective O'Reilly, is that this is a sprawling, complicated investigation touching on numerous Areas of Service and levels of government. It's been very difficult to collate all the necessary data and coordinate our response, particularly while keeping the O'Malley leadership in the dark."

"However, I think we have everything we need," Markham said.

"That's it?" Erin said eagerly. "We're done?"

She couldn't quite believe it. Not after so many months of careful, dangerous undercover work. She'd expected more fanfare, somehow; some Hollywood-style pyrotechnics, or maybe a triumphant musical chord.

"We'll fetch the champagne," Corky said. "Cars, you've a few bottles in your cellar, aye?"

"Not quite," Holliday said.

"What do you mean, sir?" Erin asked.

"We've played this operation very close to the chest," Holliday said. "Outside of the people in this room, only one other man knows about it."

Erin said nothing. Holliday was talking about Lieutenant Keane, Precinct 8's Internal Affairs commander. But Holliday was wrong; at least three others knew what Erin had been up to. Vic Neshenko, Lieutenant Webb, and Erin's dad had all tumbled to the truth. But telling Holliday about them wouldn't do any good; it would just make him nervous.

"We need to expand," Holliday continued. "We're approaching the tactical stage of the operation."

"We've identified seventy-three key individuals," Markham said. "Together with a further eighty-five peripheral targets. We need to take them under close surveillance and prepare for a massive wave of simultaneous arrests."

"We can't take them a few at a time," Holliday said. "If we try, the rest of them will spook and go to ground or flee. It's got to happen like clockwork, within a fifteen to thirty-minute window."

"That's pretty tight," Erin said.

"It gets worse," Holliday said grimly. "There's the financial aspect to consider."

"We need to freeze all their accounts," Markham explained. "We'll lock down as many of their assets as possible. We can't do that early, or we'll tip them off."

"And we'll need a full report for the Commissioner," Holliday said. "The PC will want—he'll *need*—to hold a press conference within a few hours of the takedown. This will be front-page news all over the country and the Department needs to be ready for the follow-up and fallout."

"Who gives a damn about image?" Erin blurted out. "That's just political crap. Can't we sort that out after?"

"Not if we all want to keep our jobs and advance in them," Holliday said. "Do you want to be a captain someday?"

"God spare me," Erin muttered. Everyone but Markham laughed. Even Holliday chuckled.

"I'm serious, Detective," he said. "This is a career-making case. It's commendable that you're not thinking of yourself, but it wouldn't hurt to spare a thought for your future. The PC won't thank us if we blindside him. It would be inappropriate, unwise, and in direct violation of departmental guidelines."

"Can I let you worry about the politics, sir?" she replied. "Since I'm not a captain yet?"

"That's what I'm there for," Holliday said. "But we do need to coordinate it, along with the rest of the operation. We're talking, at minimum, three to four hundred officers."

"Four hundred?" Erin repeated hollowly.

"That's not counting multiple ESU teams," Holliday went on relentlessly. "And a dozen or so ambulances with EMTs on standby, in case some of these guys don't come quietly. Then there's DA Markham's people, writing up all the charges. We have to have most of that done ahead of time."

"Otherwise my office may not be able to charge everyone within the proper window of time," Markham said. "Captain Holliday is neglecting to mention the other legal personnel we'll need."

"All told, we're going to have over five hundred people directly involved," Holliday said.

"Some of whom will be compromised," Carlyle said quietly.

"We'll make sure nobody in the ledger is in on it," Holliday said.

"All respect, Captain, that won't matter," Corky said. "Some of your lads are going to be bent, you can wager on it. They may not be directly beholden to Evan O'Malley, but they'll be working for someone in the Life. It's simple mathematics. Suppose, optimistically, two percent of your lads aren't to be trusted."

Holliday bristled at the suggestion. "Optimistically?" he repeated in ominous tones.

Corky ignored him. "That means, out of five hundred, at least ten lads will run their mouths. I'd wager word will get to Evan within six hours, eight at the most."

"He's right," Phil said, forestalling the protest he saw forming on Holliday's face. "As the number of people involved in an undercover op goes up, the probability of it being blown increases exponentially. Five hundred? As they say on the street, forget about it. It'll get out as fast as Mr. Corcoran says."

"Which is precisely why we need to move slowly and circumspectly," Markham said. "We will conceal our preparations as much as possible. Only a very few people need to know our specific objective. The rest will only see little pieces of the puzzle until the very end."

"How long will this take?" Erin asked, fearing she already had a good idea.

"A month, minimum," Markham said.

Holliday nodded. "That's reasonable," he said. "In the meantime, proceed with business as usual."

"With pleasure," Corky said with a grin. Holliday scowled at him. The scowl bounced off the irrepressible Irishman without effect.

"Back undercover," Erin sighed. "I guess I'm used to it."

"Erin?" Phil said. "Can you handle this?"

"Absolutely," she said. "It won't be a problem."

"One month," Holliday said.

"Minimum," Markham said. "It may be longer."

"Don't let it go too long," Phil said. "Every day is a risk, and the risk is cumulative."

The buzz of Erin's phone made everyone jump. Even Rolf raised his head and perked his ears.

"Are you on call, Detective?" Holliday asked. It was about 9:30 in the evening. Erin had come to the meeting at the end of her shift. It had been a very long day.

"I'm not on duty, sir," she said, taking out her phone and glancing at it. She saw Lieutenant Webb's name on the caller ID. "But I'd better take this. O'Reilly."

"Sorry to bother you at home," Webb said. "But if they call me, I call you."

"Shit rolls downhill, sir."

"It does indeed," Webb said. "I hate to interrupt, but if you're not doing anything important, we've got some police work."

"A body?"

"Three. I'll text you the address."

"Just a second, sir." Erin muted her phone and looked at the others. "Are we just about done for now?"

"Yes," Markham said. "I need to discuss logistics with Captain Holliday and Lieutenant Stachowski, but the rest of you can go."

"Duty calls?" Holliday said.

Erin nodded.

"Lucky you," Holliday said with a faint smile. "I only wish I could join you. On your way, Detective."

Erin returned to her phone. "I'm on my way," she told Webb.

Chapter 2

"Back to base, sir?" Ian Thompson asked.

He fell in step beside Carlyle and Erin, scanning the darkened street for potential threats. He'd been walking the perimeter during the meeting, making sure no uninvited guests crashed the party. The early-December air was chilly and sleet was pelting down, but Ian showed no sign he felt the cold.

"Half a moment, lad," Carlyle said. "Erin's needing to go somewhere else."

Erin checked Webb's message on her phone. "I've got to get to Columbia Street," she said. "Waterfront District. Can you swing by there and drop me off? You don't need to stay; I'll catch a ride north with Vic when we're done."

"Not a problem," Ian said. He paused outside Carlyle's Mercedes, waiting and watching while Carlyle held the door for Erin and Rolf. Only after Carlyle had climbed into the shotgun seat did Ian slide behind the wheel and start the car.

"You didn't bulletproof this thing, did you?" Erin asked.

"It would've played merry hell with the petrol mileage," Carlyle said. "Your own auto's not armor-plated, come to that."

"Most hits don't happen in moving vehicles," Ian said. "Mob guys want to get you, they'll do it in a restaurant, on the sidewalk, something like that. Sometimes at a stoplight, but that's a low-percentage play. Best way to avoid it isn't armor, it's keeping your head on a swivel. Situational awareness."

Rolf settled on the back seat beside Erin, resting his head on her leg. She stroked his ears and watched the pattern of the freezing rain as the droplets spattered against her window.

"Body on the waterfront?" Carlyle asked Erin.

"According to my boss, there's three," she said.

"Columbia Street is O'Malley territory," Carlyle said. "All the way back to Evan's early days in Brooklyn."

"That doesn't mean anything," she said. "We get plenty of homicides that have nothing to do with the O'Malleys."

"True enough," he agreed. "I thought the meeting went rather well."

"Nobody got killed," she said. "And I feel like we're all moving more or less the same direction. But five hundred guys to bring the case home? There's no way we're going to keep this mess secret."

"We needn't keep it completely under wraps," Carlyle said. "So long as most of the lads only see their own wee bit of it, no one will be able to paint the big picture."

"But if Evan hears that all his guys are under surveillance, won't he come to the right conclusion?"

"Most of this won't make it all the way up the chain," Carlyle said. "The Mob isn't a military organization, Erin. They haven't an intelligence-gathering hierarchy. There's no personnel files. Nobody's comparing notes."

"Militaries aren't so great at intel either," Ian interjected. "There's a reason 'military intelligence' is an oxymoron."

Carlyle chuckled. "Excellent point. What you need to remember is, nobody's seeing the whole thing, save you and me and those lads back at the house."

"You hope," she said gloomily.

"I hope," he agreed. "Because if I'm wrong we're... what's that acronym your lads are fond of, Ian?"

"FUBAR, sir," Ian said.

"I know that one," Erin said. "Saw it in a movie. It stands for Fucked Up Beyond All Recognition."

"Affirmative," Ian said.

* * *

Flashing emergency lights made an oddly festive multicolored halo above the crime scene. It was the Christmas season and the blinkers reminded Erin of holiday displays. This scene was illuminated not only by the familiar blue-and-red police flashers, but by golden-orange lights indicating a construction zone.

"Great," she muttered. "Road work."

"Nothing wrong with a bit of urban renewal," Carlyle said. "I'm sure you'd agree Brooklyn can use all the repairs it can get."

"How close you want me?" Ian asked.

"Stop at the first squad car," she said. "I can walk the rest of the way."

"The weather..." Carlyle began.

"Look around," she said. "It's a damn parking lot. The closest roof is that truck depot over there. I'm going to be standing around getting wet anyway. No point putting it off."

Ian pulled the Mercedes to a halt as a uniformed officer waved him to the side of the road. The gray sedan wasn't a police vehicle, so he would've had a hard time getting closer in any case. Erin got out of the car, followed closely by Rolf. The

Shepherd, shielded by his K-9 vest and his coarse outer coat of fur, didn't mind the wet, clinging sleet.

"I'll see Marian has a fine hot toddy waiting for you," Carlyle said.

"What the hell is a hot toddy?" she retorted, but she'd already started closing the car door and didn't hear Carlyle's reply. Ian backed the car into a U-turn and headed back the way he'd come, leaving her to trudge through an inch and a half of slush toward the latest urban atrocity.

She found the rest of her squad standing around a jagged hole in the concrete of the parking lot, accompanied by a half-dozen men in reflective vests and hard hats. The lot was littered with construction equipment. Erin recognized an air compressor and jackhammer, an industrial-sized circular saw, and various hand tools like pickaxes, crowbars, and shovels. Lieutenant Webb held an umbrella; his trademark trench coat and fedora were, as a result, only a little damp. Vic was wearing a wool watch cap and fleece-lined jacket. He looked cold, wet, and grumpy.

"What've we got, sir?" Erin asked.

"You got here fast," Vic said. "There's no way you could've made it so quick from that hole-in-the-wall bar you hang out at."

"The Barley Corner isn't a hole in the wall," she retorted. "It's an upscale Manhattan business. How'd you beat me here?"

"I was visiting my mom," Vic said. "Down in Brighton Beach, just a quick drive."

"I was in the neighborhood too," she said absently. "Maybe I caught the scent of fresh blood."

"Unlikely," Webb said. "There's nothing fresh about these."

"Old bodies?" Erin guessed.

Webb nodded.

"How old?" she asked.

"They're way past their sell-by date," Vic said.

"Doc Levine's on her way," Webb said. "She'll have answers for us."

"You said there's three bodies?" Erin asked.

"At least," Vic said.

"You don't *know* how many?" she asked incredulously.

"Have a look," he said, pointing to the hole. "Utility crew was breaking up the ground. City job, eminent domain. I think they're trying to squeeze it in before the weather gets really nasty. They found these three poor schmucks in the cement and freaked out."

"Wow," Erin said, peering over the edge. Vic aimed a flashlight. The bodies weren't fully unearthed; the work crew must have stopped when they'd realized what they'd found, and no wonder.

"Know what it reminds me of?" Vic said. "What's that place in Italy that got wiped out when that volcano blew up? You know, back in the Roman Empire?"

"Pompeii," Webb said.

"Yeah, that's the one," Vic said. "And the ash cloud rolled down the mountain and cooked everyone right where they were standing. They got basically petrified, and then people dug them out a couple thousand years later. It was like they'd been frozen in time. Freaky shit."

Erin nodded. She felt a cold shiver down the back of her neck, but that might have just been the sleet rolling down her collar. The bodies were only visible up to the shoulders, but one had its hands raised. And she'd noticed something on the hands.

"Take a look there," she said, pointing. "The wrists."

"They're tied together," Webb said. "Looks like a zip-tie."

"That makes it a homicide for sure," Vic said. "As if there was any doubt. It's not like three guys took a dive into cement by accident. And this is a lot thicker than it'd need to be for a parking lot. Somebody dug this hole extra deep and dumped the poor bastards in."

"It's worse than that," Erin said. She swallowed, trying not to think too hard about the implications of what she'd seen. "Hands tied, standing up... these men were still alive when the cement got poured in on them."

There was a brief silence.

Vic broke it. "Okay," he said. "That's pretty friggin' horrible."

"It's murder," Webb said. "If it wasn't horrible, we'd be out of a job. Every murder victim is alive until someone kills them."

"You're a philosopher, sir," Erin said.

"I'm a detective doing his job," Webb said. He turned to the workmen. "Do you guys have something we can use to cover this hole?"

"I got a tarp in my truck," one of the workers said.

"Could you get it, please?" Webb asked. "We don't want the scene getting more contaminated than it already is."

"No kidding," Vic said. He stooped and picked up a handful of gray slush. "You know that song? The one about Bette Davis and her eyes?"

"What about it?" Erin replied.

"There's a line in it about a girl being 'pure as New York snow.' I always got a kick out of that. Look at this shit. You say a girl's pure as this, she's probably turning tricks behind the 7-Eleven for drug money."

* * *

By the time Sarah Levine finally arrived, Erin's teeth were chattering. She, Vic, and Rolf had retreated to the shelter of Vic's Ford Taurus, but it was too late. She'd already gotten soaked to the skin and the sleet had sucked the warmth right out of her flesh. Vic had the heater going full blast, but the only thing that seemed to do was fog up the windows. The car interior steamed and smelled of wet dog.

The Medical Examiner parked her Prius between a pair of squad cars, got out, and walked straight to the excavation, paying no attention either to the weather or the people already on site. Give Levine a dead body, Erin thought, and she wouldn't notice a nuclear explosion in the distance.

"Want to go talk to her?" Erin asked.

"You think she wants to talk to us?" Vic retorted.

"Not really. I think she wants to look at some corpses."

"I say we give her a little quality time with the stiffs," Vic said. "Extra stiff, on account of being locked in concrete for God knows how long. When do you figure they got stashed here?"

"When the concrete was poured," Erin said. "Obviously."

Vic rolled his yes. "I know that," he said, speaking slowly. "I mean, how long do you think the concrete's been here?"

She shrugged. "It'll be in the city records."

"Yeah," he said. "Because I'm sure this was completely legal and aboveboard. You think they went to City Hall and applied for a body-dumping permit? Hey, do they actually have those, you think?"

"Of course they do, Vic," she said. "That's how cemeteries operate."

"What makes a place a cemetery?" he wondered. "It's not the dead bodies. Hell, there's dead bodies everywhere. Half the tenements in the five boroughs would be cemeteries by that definition. That'd make this parking lot a cemetery. It can't be that they're holy ground, because then you'd have no place to dump the atheists. Is it the headstones? 'Here lies So-and-So?'"

"Vic?"

"Yeah?"

"You're being creepy."

"I am?"

"Yeah. Stop it."

"Sorry."

"No you're not."

"So, what were you doing on Long Island tonight?" Vic asked, changing the subject rather than continue addressing his lack of remorse.

"Working," she said.

"We aren't working a case down here," he said. "I mean, we weren't until just now. And I'm pretty sure I saw your sugar daddy's Mercedes driving away."

"That reminds me," she said. "I need a ride back to Manhattan when we're done here. If you call Carlyle my sugar daddy again, I'll kick your ass."

"Love to see you try," he said, grinning. "So, putting two and two together, if you were working, and if your... *distinguished older gentleman* was providing your transportation, that means it was that other thing."

"Distinguished older gentleman?" she repeated.

"Yeah," he said. "I like the acronym."

"What acronym?"

He motioned with his head toward the panting German Shepherd in the backseat. "D-O-G," he said, still grinning.

Erin smacked him on the shoulder. It had no effect whatsoever.

Knuckles rapped on the driver's side window. Vic swiped his hand across the glass, clearing the condensation to reveal Webb. The Lieutenant motioned for them to get out. They complied, Rolf more cheerfully than the other two.

"Let's see what the good doctor can tell us," Webb said. "Then we might as well get indoors. This is a cold case, no doubt about it."

"Cold enough," Erin said, suppressing a shiver. "It's thirty degrees out."

"Ha ha," Webb said.

"I thought you liked getting out of the office onto the street," Vic said.

"As long as the street isn't covered with ice," Erin said.

A pair of unhappy-looking Patrol officers were holding the tarp a few feet above the hole so Levine could kneel there and conduct her initial examination. She'd brought a pair of floodlights and mounted them on either side. The ME was in a pool of bright LED light, surrounded by old corpses, and couldn't have been more at home.

"What've we got, Doctor?" Webb asked.

"Three adult males," Levine said without looking up. "Decomposition is not as advanced as might be expected, due to encasement in concrete."

"So they're mummies?" Vic asked.

"Of course not," Levine said, sounding annoyed. "Mummification requires a process of embalming, including removal of internal organs. These bodies have undergone none of the necessary procedures. They were, however, entombed in a largely anoxic environment. Despite the considerable age of the bodies, soft tissue has not fully decomposed."

"Yeah, we know," Vic said, wrinkling his nose. The smell of death was wafting up out of the hole.

"Cause of death?" Webb asked.

"I have not yet ascertained it," Levine said. "I see no external signs of traumatic injury, but all three will require a detailed postmortem examination."

"What about the age of the bodies?" Erin asked. "Any idea how long they've been down there?"

"Not yet," Levine said. "As I previously stated, decomposition has been retarded by the medium of suspension."

"How about the concrete itself?" Erin asked. "Can you tell how old it is?"

"No," Levine said flatly. "Concrete is effectively impossible to accurately date, except by wear and erosion, neither of which is sufficient for a determination in this case. However, I can determine that the concrete is of fairly high quality and was laid with skill."

"How can you tell?" Webb asked.

"No cracking around the bodies," Levine explained. "The concrete was wet-cured and consolidated."

"Meaning what?" Vic asked.

One of the construction workers stepped forward. He'd been hanging out around the fringe of the site, smoking soggy cigarettes and talking things over with his buddies. "You know concrete, lady?" he asked Levine.

"I understand its chemical composition and industrial applications," Levine said.

"Me too," the worker said. "What she means is, if you want the concrete to set right, you gotta put curing blankets over it after you pour it."

"Explain it to me like I'm an idiot," Vic said. "What's a curing blanket?"

"Like?" Erin echoed very quietly.

"It's a sheet of curing paper or polyethylene," Levine said.

"Yeah, what she said," the worker said. "You put the blanket over top and you keep it wet. You hose it down for a while. That keeps the concrete from cracking."

"How long is a while?" Webb asked.

The man shrugged. "You want it done right, four weeks."

"You're saying the killers came back to hose this place down for a damn month?" Vic said.

"I ain't saying that," the worker said.

"I am," Levine said. "If the concrete had cracked, it would have allowed entry of water and escape of decomposition gases. These bodies would be fully skeletonized, unless they were very recently interred."

Webb turned to the workman. "Do you guys know how long this slab's been here?" he asked.

The man shrugged again. "Years," he said. "Dunno how many, but it's kinda worn down. Concrete gets a look when it's been there a while, y'know? You get a feel for it. I had to guess, I'd say maybe ten, give or take."

"Ten years is a possible timeframe, given the state of preservation," Levine said.

Webb rubbed his temple with one hand, keeping his umbrella above his head with the other. "We've got a mass murderer who buried three guys alive and then visited the grave for a month, just to make sure the bodies were properly preserved?" he said.

"I can't speculate as to the motive," Levine said. "But that is a reasonable hypothesis for the chain of events."

"There's nothing reasonable about this," Webb said.

"Oh, good," Vic said. "It's been a while since we had a total lunatic to chase down. Who was the last? Remember that wannabe serial killer kid?"

"Don't get your hopes up," Erin said. "If this was a decade ago, our perp could be long gone. He could even be dead."

"Nah," Vic said. "This guy was careful. A guy like that doesn't just die. He's still out there. For all we know, he's spent the last ten years putting other dudes in cement. Half the buildings in New York might have dead guys in the foundations."

Erin made a face. "Thanks for that, Vic. I'm sure we'll all sleep better thinking that."

He smiled nastily. "It's what I'm here for."

Chapter 3

"Your dog smells like I feel," Vic grumbled. "I'm gonna have to change my air filters."

"This is a police car, Vic," Erin said. "You've had plenty of worse smells in here. That's why they waterproof the seat cushions."

"You saying I can hose off your mutt?" Vic replied.

"He's plenty wet already," she said.

"Just like the rest of us," Vic said. "As soon as I drop you off, I'm going home. I'm gonna climb in the shower and let it run until the hot water runs out."

"Vic, you live in an apartment."

"So?"

"You'd have to let the hot water run for a week straight."

"Good idea. I'll do that. You can tell the Lieutenant where I went. God, I feel like I'm never gonna be warm again."

"You're Russian. Aren't you supposed to be immune to the cold?"

"Yeah, but I've got the right to bitch about it. That's the great thing about living in a free country. If we were communist, I couldn't complain, so I'd have to drink instead."

"So you're not going to drink?"

"Oh, I'm absolutely gonna drink. Stoli, straight from the bottle. While I'm in my nice hot shower."

"Thanks for that vivid picture."

"No problem. Here you go. The Barley Corner. Hurry up and get out; the meter's running."

Erin opened the passenger door. "Thanks for the lift."

"What, no tip?"

"If you want to come in, I'll get you a drink."

"At the Mob bar with your gangster buddies? I'd rather chug drain cleaner."

"Night, Vic."

Erin slogged through the deepening slush to the Barley Corner's front entrance. She would have preferred to go in the back way, so she could slip upstairs without attracting attention, but that would have required trudging three times as far through the wet, clinging stuff. Her toes were already squelching in her shoes. Even Rolf had lost a little of his perkiness. The Shepherd's ears were laid back against his skull and his paws were dragging.

The light, warmth, and cheerful bustle of the pub were almost too much for her, overwhelming her numbed senses. She paused in the entryway and ran a hand through her hair, spattering the floor with icy runoff.

Carlyle and Corky, with their head start, had gotten to the bar long before. It appeared they hadn't left it since. They looked warm, dry, and cheerful. Erin, damp and bedraggled, pushed through the crowd of patrons and bellied up to the bar next to Carlyle's stool.

He stood up to greet her. "Evening, darling," he said. "It's no fit night to be out and about. Sit yourself here and we'll fetch something to cheer you."

Danny, the bartender, glided over to meet her. “Hey, Erin,” he said. “What am I getting you?”

“I don’t want a hot damn toddy or whatever the hell Corky was talking about,” she said.

“No problem,” Danny said. “Your usual, then?”

She hesitated. Normally she was a straight whiskey girl, but that didn’t feel quite right. Brandy, maybe; something with a little sweetness that would warm up her insides.

Her hesitation gave Corky all the opening he needed. “She’ll have a jackhammer,” he said.

“I will?” Erin asked suspiciously.

“Jack Daniels and amaretto,” Danny explained.

“Fine. But swap out the Jack for Glen D.” Glen Docherty-Kinlochewe was a very high-quality whiskey made in the Scottish Highlands, such a well-kept secret that she’d never seen it in any bar but Carlyle’s. Compared to Glen D, every other whiskey she’d ever drunk was bottom-shelf rotgut.

“Coming up,” Danny said, going to work with his hands. Inside a few seconds, he’d mixed her drink and slid it across the counter. If Danny ever gave up bartending, he could have a good career as a stage magician.

Erin took a sip. The amaretto gave an almond flavor to the whiskey, sweetening the Glen D’s fierce fire.

“Good, aye?” Corky said, watching her drink.

“Yeah,” she said, taking another sip. “That’s not half bad.”

“Corky’s expanding his alcoholic horizons of late,” Carlyle said.

“Is this like that time he tried drinking every cocktail on your menu in alphabetical order?” she asked.

“I’m just thinking what we’d serve at the wedding,” Corky said.

“Who’s getting married?” Erin asked.

“Nobody,” Corky said. “Leastwise, not yet.”

"*You?*" Erin exclaimed incredulously. "That'll be the day!"

Corky kept smiling, but there was a hint of pain at the back of his bright green eyes. "I deserve that," he said.

Belatedly, Erin realized the Irishman had been serious. She felt a little bad for hurting his feelings, but alarm overpowered her remorse. "You're talking about..." she began, stopping short of mentioning the name.

"Aye," Corky said. "It's a foolish notion. Forget I said anything."

He hadn't said the name either, and with good reason. Teresa Tommasino was dead, legally speaking. The Brooklyn schoolteacher was the star witness to a brutal Mafia murder. Erin and Carlyle had faked her death, to appease the Mob and to get Erin in with the Lucarelli Family. Corky had taken the terrified woman under his protection and run off with her. Everything had gone according to plan, right up to the point where Corky had fallen in love with Teresa and tangled with a Mafia assassin. Erin wasn't a hundred percent clear on what had happened to the mobster, but she could guess. Corky had come back to New York to draw attention away from Teresa, but he'd kept in touch with her. Apparently his attachment went even deeper than Erin had known.

"It's dangerous," she said quietly.

Corky grinned, recovering somewhat. "Danger's the salt that gives the dish of life its flavor, love," he said.

"For both of you," Erin said.

Corky's smile faltered again. "I'd do anything in the world for her," he said, "except give her up. I can't do that."

"Well, be careful," she insisted.

"I'm the soul of caution," he lied.

"What've you been about this evening, Erin?" Carlyle asked, deciding it was time for a change of subject.

"Nothing urgent," she said. "Some construction guys dug up a few ten-year-old bodies."

"That's dreadful," Carlyle said. "Poor wee bairns."

"Huh?" Erin didn't understand. Then she got it. "No! I didn't mean the bodies of ten-year-olds. I meant the bodies have been buried for a decade."

"Ah," Carlyle said. "That's better."

"Not much," she said grimly. "They were buried alive. In concrete."

"Jesus," Carlyle said, crossing himself reflexively. "Who were the sorry blighters?"

"No IDs yet," she said. "And they might be hard to identify. But it looks like a Mob murder. I don't suppose you know about anybody who pissed off the O'Malleys about ten years ago and got on the wrong side of some guys in the construction business?"

"I'll ask around," Corky said. "I've plenty of mates in the labor unions."

"Of course you do," Erin said. "You have friends everywhere."

"Better to be surrounded by friends than enemies," he said cheerily. "Which reminds me, I've a call to make. Ta, love. Try not to miss me."

He puckered his lips, kissed the air in Erin's direction, and headed for the exit.

"Sometimes I wish I could hate him," she said. "But I can never quite manage it."

"Aye," Carlyle said, smiling. "He's one of a kind. And he's a good source for you. He knows all the lads in the building trades. How are you so certain they're the ones you're wanting?"

"Because our killers knew concrete," Erin said. "It's important to keep it wet, did you know that? Speaking of which, I'm soaked. I'm going upstairs to get out of these wet clothes. Then a shower and bed."

"I'll be up directly," Carlyle said. "Not to fret. It's been a long night for you, but it's nearly over."

All cops were superstitious, to some degree. Those words should have been a warning for Erin not to tempt fate, but she was too wiped out to notice. She just nodded, gave Carlyle a light kiss on the lips, and went looking for that hot shower.

* * *

A hand was shaking her shoulder, gentle but insistent. It might have been doing it for a while; Erin didn't know. The hand pulled her toward wakefulness. She forced open eyelids that weighed about a hundred pounds apiece. Carlyle's face floated above her in the golden light of the bedside lamp.

"Huh?" she said.

"Sorry to trouble you, darling," he said. "But a lad's come to see you."

"What?" She was waking up a little more and didn't like it. She felt drunk with sleep, and not the good kind of drunk. She couldn't think clearly and her head still hurt.

"It's about the bodies you found," Carlyle said. "Shall I tell him to come back later?"

"Huh?" she said again. "No, I'll... I'll come down. Just a sec. Let me find my pants."

Rolf, who had been curled at the foot of the bed, bounded eagerly to meet her as she sat up. The Shepherd, wrongfully assuming she was getting up because she wanted to, thrust a cold nose against her cheek and panted happily. He didn't mind getting up in the middle of the night; in his experience, that was when some of the most exciting things happened.

"Okay, okay," Erin said, fending the K-9 off with one arm. "*Platz!*"

Rolf sank obediently to his belly, tongue still hanging out, waiting to be told what a good boy he was.

Erin hunted groggily for her clothes, taking two tries to get into a fresh pair of slacks. The sheer number of buttons on her blouses discouraged her, and she was already getting cold outside the comfortable cocoon of her bed, so she pulled on one of her running sweatshirts. It was dark blue with big yellow letters on the front that spelled NYPD.

"A grand thing to wear in my pub," Carlyle said with a wry smile. "Very subtle."

"You may have a bunch of wiseguys downstairs," she said, shaking out her hair and grabbing an elastic band to corral it into a ponytail. "But they already know I'm a cop. How many of them are still around? What time is it, anyway?"

"Quarter of two," Carlyle said. "You've only been asleep a little while." He was still wearing his customary attire; a charcoal-gray suit with a burgundy necktie. He was as well-groomed as if he'd just stepped out of a formal dinner, right down to the pocket square that matched his tie perfectly.

"Great," she muttered. She located her shoes and thrust her feet into them. "I would've done better to stay awake."

"Can I get you anything?" he asked.

"Is there time for coffee?"

"I can ask him to wait."

"Never mind. Let's go get this over with. Rolf, *komm*."

The Barley Corner would close at two o'clock, so the crowd had thinned out considerably. A few of the regulars were still hanging around, sipping their last drinks and talking quietly. The big TV screens were dark. Danny was wiping down the bar. He gave Erin a smile and a nod, then went back to his work.

Carlyle steered Erin to the corner booth, where his contact was waiting. Erin rubbed the last of the sleep out of her eyes and tried to put on her game face. She was a detective, damn it all, and she intended to act like one.

Kyle Finnegan was sitting there, a glass of Guinness in front of him. His hair was uncombed and wild, his entire face slightly askew. The dent in his left temple, where a Teamster had once caved in his skull with a tire iron, gave him a lopsided aspect. His eyes were curiously unfocused, never seeming to look directly at her.

"Oh," Erin said. "It's you."

"Knock, knock," Finnegan said, rapping his knuckles on the tabletop.

"Who's there?" she repeated stupidly, as if the two of them were back in grade school telling silly jokes.

"In the other devil's name?" Finnegan said. "Faith, here's an equivocator, that could swear in both the scales against either scale; who committed treason enough for God's sake, yet could not equivocate to heaven: O, come in, equivocator."

This was pretty typical dialogue from Finnegan. He was utterly insane; everybody in the O'Malleys knew it. Some of it stemmed from his brain injury, but according to Carlyle, he'd always been a little weird. Erin had wondered ever since she'd met him why Evan O'Malley kept him around. Carlyle had explained that in spite of his eccentricities, Finnegan had a razor-sharp brain, a knack for getting results, and a cold-blooded ruthlessness that was always useful to the Mob.

Erin would have felt a lot better if Finnegan was sitting in a padded cell instead of one of Carlyle's booths, but she'd dealt with more dangerous and unsettling men without flinching. She slid into the seat opposite him. Carlyle sat next to her.

Rolf settled on his haunches but didn't relax. The Shepherd kept an eye on Finnegan, his hackles slightly raised. He'd never liked the man. Something about him just smelled *wrong.*

"How's it going?" Erin said.

"Midway between the cradle and the grave," Finnegan said. He took a pull at his drink. "Does this taste a little funny to you?"

"I'm not the one drinking it," she replied. "What's it taste like to you?"

"Broken promises and slow decay," he said. "I was wondering, if nobody hears you scream, is it the same as silence?"

"Are you okay, Kyle?" she asked.

"I'm not the one we should be worrying about," Finnegan said. "And that's all right, because you're not worried about me. You're worried about the dead, which makes no sense. The world belongs to the living."

"But you're alive," she pointed out, trying to keep up with his bizarre ramblings. She wished she was better rested and her head didn't hurt. It really was pounding, as if she was a slab of concrete and a construction worker was going to town with a jackhammer.

"Am I?" Finnegan answered. "You're investigating a multiple murder, and you're investigating me, so maybe I've been murdered. If I'm dead, it stands to reason you'd be interested in your professional capacity. Would you care to check my pulse?"

"I'll take it on faith you're alive," she said. "You came here to talk about the guys we found in Brooklyn. Do you know who they were?"

"Tut, tut, good enough to toss," Finnegan said. "Food for powder, food for powder. They'll fill a pit as well as better. Tush, man, mortal men, mortal men."

"You've Shakespeare on your mind tonight, lad," Carlyle said. "First Macbeth's Porter, now Falstaff?"

"Yond Cassius has a lean and hungry look," Finnegan said, glancing in Carlyle's general direction. "He thinks too much; such men are dangerous."

"Enough screwing around," Erin growled. "Have you got anything for me, or not?"

"You're impatient for knowledge," Finnegan said. "To see a world in a grain of sand and a heaven in a wild flower, hold infinity in the palm of your hand and eternity in an hour."

She gritted her teeth. She hated riddles and had no patience for untangling Finnegan's ball of words, which she guessed was ten percent pretention and ninety percent bullshit. "Okay," she said, starting to stand. "I guess I'm going back to bed."

"I know what you want," Finnegan said, his eyes suddenly locking onto hers with startling clarity. "Justice for the fallen and to lay their spirits to rest."

"You knew them," she said. "Who were they? No games."

"Everything's a game," Finnegan said. "Life's a game, but it's a casino game, so it's rigged in favor of the house. Play long enough and you always get cleaned out in the end. Come for a ride with me. I've got some things to show you and we've got some things to talk about."

"Can't we talk here?" she asked. "It's a miserable night out there."

"It'll be easier if you see for yourself," he said.

Erin had no intention of going anywhere alone with Kyle Finnegan. Carlyle read it in her face before she could think how to reply.

"I've an idea," he said. "Why don't the two of you take Ian with you? The lad's just finishing up for the night. Half a moment and I'll speak to him."

"Sounds good," Erin said.

"You're afraid," Finnegan said as Carlyle walked away. "You think someone's following you? Like one that on a lonesome road doth walk in fear and dread? And having once turned round, walks on, and turns no more his head, because he knows a fearful fiend doth close behind him tread."

"I'm taking precautions," she said. "That's not the same as fear."

"Fear is the flip-side of hope," Finnegan said. "Both look to the future, and both are based on faith. One is heaven, the other is hell."

"This is going to be a long night." Erin said it under her breath, but she didn't really care whether Finnegan heard her or not.

He looked past her face and smiled.

Chapter 4

"So, this is what you drive?" Erin said. "It's... um... nice."

She was just making conversation. The car was a '95 Toyota Camry, painted the off-white that had been so popular back then. No matter how recently it had been washed, it would always look slightly dirty. Rust had eaten into the bodywork around the wheel wells. When Finnegan flicked on the headlights, they didn't match; one was a blue-white halogen bulb, the other a standard golden lamp.

"All visible objects, man, are but as pasteboard masks," Finnegan said. The engine came to life willingly enough; the car was in better condition than it looked. Maybe that was his point.

Erin was riding shotgun, while Ian and Rolf took up the back seat. Ian was behind the driver's seat, where he could put a hole through Finnegan if the mobster did anything crazy. Erin casually double-checked her seatbelt as they pulled out of the parking garage, making sure it was fastened.

"If you knew our victims, you'd have a pretty good idea when they vanished," she said.

"Many and many a year ago," Finnegan said. He handled the steering wheel almost carelessly, using only his left hand. The car's steering was a little loose, as was the suspension. It wobbled on the turns.

"You got a number for me?" she asked, reminding herself to be patient.

"I don't think in numbers," he said. "They're even less real than everything else. I suppose it was when I was in the hospital."

"After those guys from Detroit tuned you up?" she asked.

"Must have been," he said. "Things got cloudy for a while. Then the sun came out and everything turned to a golden glow. I thought I'd died, and maybe there'd been a slip in the paperwork."

"Paperwork?" she repeated.

"Can't imagine I'd get to heaven through normal channels," Finnegan said placidly. He left the garage and turned onto the street. Drops of sleet began spattering the windshield. He made no move to turn on his wipers.

Finnegan's injury had happened ten and a half years earlier. Erin had seen the hospital records, which were also in Phil's files. He'd suffered a severe concussion, fractured skull, and subdural hematoma. He probably should have died, but according to Carlyle, he'd managed to beat all three of his assailants to death with the tire iron they'd used on him. Those bodies had never been found. He'd been hospitalized in Detroit, then transferred to New York to convalesce.

"I'm going to need names," Erin said.

"What's in a name?" Finnegan replied. "That which we call a rose—"

"—by any other name would smell as sweet," she finished for him. "I know that one. I read *Romeo and Juliet* in high school."

"Did it speak to you?" he asked.

"I thought Romeo was a romantic idiot," she said. "If he'd done a better job checking Juliet's vitals, it wouldn't have been a tragedy."

"I suppose you couldn't see your future," he said.

"Nobody sees their future," she retorted. "Are you saying I'm Juliet?"

Finnegan said nothing. The windshield was getting very blurry. Erin thought about commenting on it, decided he wanted her to, and didn't.

"There's no such thing as a happy ending," Finnegan said after a long pause. "Endings aren't happy. They're not sad either. They're just over. It doesn't matter if Juliet lives happily ever after with Romeo. They're characters in a play. The play ends and that's it. They're gone."

"What's your point?" she asked.

"You don't want to be on the stage," he said. "Better to be in the audience. Or better, be the playwright."

"Names," she repeated. "I've got three John Does. Who were they?"

"You'll know by morning," he said.

Erin rolled her eyes and bit back an exasperated sigh. The Camry rolled on through the snowy New York night, heading south.

* * *

Erin knew Finnegan was waiting for her to ask where they were going. She stayed silent. It was probably a tactical error; the first rule of interviews and interrogations was to keep the subject talking. Even a very clever interviewee gave things away. The lies got you closer to the truth.

But Erin didn't understand Finnegan. Either he was totally off his rocker or he was too clever for her to make heads or tails out of what he was saying. She had a nasty suspicion it was the latter. Every now and then she caught bits and pieces of a pattern in his rambling. And in that case, she might be telling him more than he was telling her.

She reminded herself that she was sharing a car with a multiple murderer who'd cheerfully add her to his tally if he so much as doubted her loyalty to Carlyle and the O'Malleys. The way he handled the car looked careless, but he kept in his lane and obeyed all traffic laws.

It wasn't too much of a surprise when the blurred shape of the Brooklyn Bridge appeared in the sleet-spattered windshield. Somehow, Erin's path always led her back to Long Island.

Finnegan finally swiped the wipers, clearing his field of view. He was humming a tune she couldn't place. Ian and Rolf sat quietly in the back seat.

"Your father was a cop," Finnegan said suddenly, around the midway point of the bridge.

"That's right," she said.

"You could've gone the other way," he said. "Crossed over to the dark side of the street."

Erin opened her mouth to say how much she'd always looked up to her dad, how she'd never wanted to do anything but wear a shield. Then, at the last instant, she remembered who she was talking to.

"What the hell do you mean?" she snapped. "What do I have to do to cross your damn street? You remember who you're talking to? Why don't you ask Mickey Connor? Or Siobhan Finneran? How about Conrad Maxwell? Or Teresa Fucking Tommasino?"

"Some people say it's bad to keep score," Finnegan said. "But that's all anybody ever does. What does Daddy think of you these days?"

"You're not my goddamn shrink," she said. "And don't bring up my family again, unless you want both sides of your skull to match."

"That was out of line," he said. "I apologize."

That was the first thing he'd said that night that really surprised her. She stared at him in open, undisguised astonishment.

"Here we are," he said, taking the exit ramp onto Middagh Street. He parked directly in front of a fire hydrant and turned off the motor.

"Seriously?" Erin said. "I'm sitting right here."

"Unless I'm mistaken, you don't have your ticket book on you," Finnegan said.

"I'm not the only cop in town," she said. "You could get towed."

"No I couldn't," he said.

"Why not?"

"It's not my car."

"And then how are we supposed to get home?" she retorted.

"We'll get another one."

Shaking her head, she unloaded Rolf from the back seat. Ian was already on the street, glancing in all directions with his experienced veteran's eye.

"Clear," he said quietly.

"No shit," she said. She was still pissed about Finnegan's questioning. She wasn't used to feeling like she was the one being interrogated.

Finnegan walked to the nearest door, an apartment tower. He entered the atrium and pushed the buzzer for Unit 906. There was a longish pause. Erin fidgeted. Ian stayed just outside, shielded from the sleet by the building's concrete overhang. The former Marine's jacket was unzipped, in spite of the weather, and his hands were open and ready.

The intercom crackled. "Who's there?" a woman asked. Her Brooklyn accent was clearly audible, even through the bad speakers.

"Kyle Finnegan," Finnegan said.

There was another pause. Then, just as Erin was wondering if Finnegan needed to hit the button again, the woman's voice came back on the line.

"Jesus, Mary, and Joseph."

"Finnegan, O'Reilly, and Thompson," Finnegan corrected her. "I hope we haven't come at a bad time. We can wait, as long as it takes."

"No," the woman said. "No, that's fine. Is... is this about Charlie?"

"That's a remarkable guess," Finnegan said. "I'm thinking of a number between one and a thousand."

"What?"

"Can't you see it?"

"Ma'am, may we come up?" Erin asked, deciding to step in before he said anything else weird.

"Sure, yeah," the woman said. There was a metallic click as the door lock disengaged.

"You can stay down here if you want," Erin said to Ian as they crossed the lobby to the elevator. She knew he didn't like elevators.

He shook his head. "Negative," he said. "I stay with you. Mr. Carlyle's orders."

The elevator wasn't in great shape. The walls were dingy and it creaked and groaned all the way up to the ninth floor. Ian, to his credit, didn't seem too nervous. He really was getting better, ever since he'd started seeing Cassie Jordan. Cassie was a rehab nurse, which meant she had a lot of experience dealing with traumatized veterans. She'd been slowly helping him come to grips with his demons.

"Who is this woman?" Erin asked, not really expecting a helpful answer.

"A bonny, bonny lass," Finnegan said.

"Why'd I even bother asking?" she muttered.

Finnegan's hand was poised at the knocker, but the door swung open before he could touch it. A middle-aged woman with straggly blonde hair and tired eyes stood there, sizing him up.

"So," she said. "You believe me now?"

"Truth is a slippery thing," Finnegan said. "And it's a rare man, or woman, who can keep hold of it for long."

The woman looked at Erin, Ian, and Rolf. "Ten years, and now you show up?" she said. "And who're these two? And a dog? What's going on?"

"Ma'am," Erin said. "I'm Erin O'Reilly and I'm with—"

"She's with me," Finnegan interrupted. "May we come in?"

"I guess," the woman said. She stepped back.

The apartment was a typical blue-collar dwelling, one bedroom, the furnishings clean but well-used and worn. Erin reflexively glanced into the corners, making sure nobody was lurking, and knew Ian was doing the same. Rolf, trotting at her side, gave no sign indicating the place held any surprises.

"Am I supposed to offer you coffee?" the woman asked. "Tough, because I got none. Gotta run to the store tomorrow."

"Forget about it," Erin said, reminding herself of the need to play the part of a gangster. "I don't think we've been properly introduced."

"Bonnie Majors," the woman said. She gave Erin's hand a quick, terse shake.

"Ian Thompson, ma'am," Ian said.

"You sound like a local boy," Bonnie said, sizing him up. "And you look young enough to be one of mine. Where you from, kid?"

"Queens, ma'am."

"Well, ain't you polite," she said. "Somebody taught you some manners."

"Marine Corps, ma'am."

"Shoulda guessed, with that haircut. You shouldn't be hanging around guys like Finnegan. He'll get you into all kinds of trouble."

"Thanks for the heads-up, ma'am," Ian said, his face completely expressionless.

"Have a seat if you want," Bonnie said, motioning to a mismatched pair of chairs and a sagging couch. Erin sat at one end of the sofa. Rolf settled next to the couch. Finnegan took the cushion on the opposite end from Erin. Ian placed himself against the wall beside Rolf, where he could see the door, and remained standing.

"So you brought a couple friends with you," Bonnie said, turning her attention back to Finnegan. "And you say this is about Charlie. What gives?"

"Men tend to travel in threes," Finnegan said. "The Magi. Shadrach, Meshach, and Abednego. Learoyd, Mulvaney, and Ortheris."

"Never heard of them," Bonnie said.

"Me neither," Erin said.

"Rudyard Kipling," Finnegan said.

"The *Jungle Book* guy?" Erin asked.

"*Soldiers Three*," Finnegan said. "Same author, different words. Charlie Majors had two friends. He went out with them and didn't come back."

"What two friends?" Bonnie asked. "Charlie left all on his own. You're damn right he never came back. And you said he'd left me for some cocktail waitress in Atlantic City. I told you he never woulda left me, not like that, without even saying goodbye."

"Penny Sizemore," Finnegan said. "I didn't make her up. Charlie was seeing her behind your back."

"And now you're talking about a couple friends of Charlie's? What's that supposed to mean? His best friend was Garth Engstrom, but they was a pair. There wasn't no third guy."

"Garth Engstrom," Finnegan said. "Doesn't ring a bell."

"Of course it don't," Bonnie said. "They was buddies from when they was little kids, growing up together. He didn't have nothing to do with you and Old Man O'Malley. But he's gone too, same night as Charlie. I know, 'cause his wife and me, we was close, too. I called her after Charlie didn't come home, and she said Garth was gone, too."

"Did you file a missing persons report?" Erin asked.

Bonnie gave her a scornful glance. "Like that woulda done any good," she said. "You think the NYPD got nothing better to do than look for a couple knuckleheads who walked out on their wives? They woulda laughed at us. Unless it's some little blonde girl, the cops don't give a shit about missing persons."

Erin didn't have an answer to that, because the woman was largely right. All the NYPD would have done was open a file with Charlie's name on it. "What line of work was Charlie in?" she asked.

"He was a truck driver," Bonnie said.

"Union?" Erin asked.

"Local 813," Bonnie said with a flicker of pride.

"How about Garth?"

"Nah, he wasn't no driver," Bonnie said.

"What did he do?" Erin asked.

"Construction."

Erin blinked. Sometimes a big piece of the puzzle fell right into your lap. "Could Charlie have been meeting with Garth that night?" she asked.

Bonnie shrugged. "He hung out with Garth a lot."

"Hold on a second," Erin said. "Your husband disappeared, the same night as his best friend, and you didn't do anything about it? You didn't tell anybody?"

"I told the guy sitting there next to you," Bonnie retorted. "He's the one who didn't do nothing except give me that bullshit about some cocktail waitress."

"Penny exists," Finnegan said mildly. "At least, she's as real as the people in this room."

"You believe this friggin' guy?" Bonnie said in true Brooklyn style. "So tell me, Mr. Well-Informed Asshole, what happened to Charlie? I figured he was dead, and it was you guys and your bullshit back-room deals got him killed. You here to tell me that?"

"In point of fact, no," Finnegan said, the straightest answer Erin had ever heard him give. He was even sitting up a little more than usual and looking Bonnie in the eye. "Would you believe I thought of Charlie as a friend?"

"Not for a second," Bonnie said. "You don't got friends."

"A trusted associate, then," Finnegan corrected himself.

"And you don't trust nobody," she went on. "Never did."

"A valued associate," Finnegan amended once more. "And his death had nothing to do with me or my organization."

Bonnie's snort was probably loud enough to be heard nine floors down on the sidewalk. "He's dead, then," she said flatly.

"He was lucky, in a way," Finnegan said. "Every man must do two things alone: his own believing and his own dying. Charlie had companions on his journey."

"Garth?" Bonnie said.

Finnegan ignored the question. "What makes a man, without hope, cling to a few more minutes of existence?" he asked nobody in particular. "I wonder how long it's possible to hold your breath under the weight of fresh cement, and if any of them bothered to try."

Bonnie made an involuntary sound, part gasp and part sob, and Erin saw the other woman wasn't nearly as hardened as she'd been acting. Bonnie's hand was at her mouth and her eyes were filling with tears.

"Shut up," Erin hissed at Finnegan.

"What did I say?" he replied, seeming genuinely startled.

"Shut up!" she said louder.

Even a crazy man could see in Erin's eyes when she was dead serious. Finnegan shut up.

"We unearthed three bodies this evening, ma'am," Erin said to Bonnie. "We're working on identifying them now. It sounds like one of them may have been your husband. If that's the case, once the city makes a positive ID, they'll contact you. I'm very sorry for your loss, and for intruding."

Bonnie nodded. "Is... did they... what happened? Did someone really pour cement on... on..."

"We're still working out what happened," Erin said. "But we've taken enough of your time. We'll be going now. Thank you for seeing us."

Finnegan stood up. "If it's any consolation," he said, "I'll bring you a little something. I understand it's customary to bring a dish to the bereaved. I promise you the sweetest morsel to the mouth that ever was cooked in hell."

"Just get outta here," Bonnie said through her tears. "Get out right now, you son of a bitch, and leave me alone."

Chapter 5

Erin waited until they were in the elevator on the way down. Then she turned on Finnegan.

"Damn it!" she said. "What's the matter with you? We were getting information out of her, until you tossed out that shit about her husband suffocating in cement! Now she's pissed at us and we've lost that angle. In addition to looking like assholes."

"She was already pissed at us," Finnegan said. "She's been pissed going on ten years."

"At you, maybe," Erin retorted.

"Splitting hairs. She didn't know anything else."

"You don't know that!"

Finnegan looked at her with his weird, off-kilter stare. "Are you a cop?"

"Of course I'm a cop! You know that!"

"Here? Tonight?"

Erin tried to think what he was getting at. What was the right answer? She chose her next words carefully, trying to ignore her pounding headache and her entirely justifiable anger.

"My squad got this case," she said. "That makes it part of my job. A triple homicide is a big deal, even if it's a decade old. The

Captain's going to be looking over our shoulders on this one, so I have to watch my step. It'd help a lot if you'd lay your cards on the table, so I know what the hell you're doing. I was under the impression we wanted the same thing."

"That's entirely inaccurate," Finnegan said. "Nobody wants the same thing as anybody else. The best you can hope is to be pointed more or less the same direction."

The elevator slowed and stopped, the doors sliding open. Ian stepped quickly out, clearing the doorway and scanning the lobby for threats.

"Feels safer just watching him work, doesn't it?" Finnegan commented. He turned his attention on Ian. "You play soldier a lot growing up, Sergeant Rock? Are you still playing?"

Ian gave Finnegan a slow, silent look. Then he turned away without bothering to reply. Erin, Finnegan, and Rolf exited the elevator and stood in the building's dingy lobby. Ian covered the main door.

"Ian doesn't play games," Erin said. "And neither do I. How did you know Charlie Majors was one of our victims? We haven't ID'd any of them yet."

"I didn't know anything," Finnegan said. "If I knew, what would I be doing here with you? We're in a cave, watching shadows on the wall. Look at the shadows, pick out the patterns, draw conclusions. Isn't that what you do? That parking lot was laid down the night Charlie dropped off the face of the Earth. Charlie was a big guy, never missed a meal. Red hair. The middle body you found was a fat man with red hair. *Quod erat demonstrandum.*"

Erin, surprised to receive a relatively straight answer, was tempted to ask how Finnegan had gotten a physical description of the victims. But that wasn't something she could ask. He obviously had a source in the Department, but chasing after it would only raise his suspicions.

"And now we've got a pretty good idea who victim number two is," she said. "Garth Engstrom. But how about the third man?"

"Harry Lime," Finnegan said. "Oddly apropos. Concrete is largely composed of lime, sand, aluminum oxide, iron, and gypsum. From lime he came, and to lime he returned."

"Okay, who's Harry Lime?" Erin asked.

"A man who faked his death the first time," Finnegan said. "Then he came back, only to be killed again. Orson Welles played him."

"Kyle, what the actual hell are you talking about?"

"*The Third Man*," Finnegan said. "Wasn't that what you asked about?"

"I have no idea what's coming out of your mouth right now."

"Released in 1949," Finnegan said. "It's considered a classic of film noir. You don't know it?"

"So Harry Lime is a character in this movie?" Erin asked.

"All the world's a stage, and all the men and women merely players."

"In other words," she said, holding on to her temper with increasing difficulty, "you have no idea who the third victim we dug up is."

"I have ideas," Finnegan said. "Always more ideas. I think they get in through the weak spot in my skull. You know how it is. A crack in the foundation always lets in the rats. But I don't know, not yet. That's what you're here to do."

"To find out?"

"He was an associate of either Garth Engstrom or Charlie Majors," Finnegan said. "But you suspect that already. That's as much as I know. You're much better positioned to find out who he was than I am. Once we have the identities of Athos, Porthos, and Aramis, we'll be able to discover Count Rochefort. Then we find him, rip the eyepatch off his face, and skull-fuck him straight to hell."

"What?" Erin said, startled by the sudden cold vehemence in Finnegan's voice.

He blinked. "Was it something I said? I'm sorry, I fuzzed out for a moment there. I hope I didn't say anything crazy."

"No," she said. "You were making more sense than usual. At least, I think you were. Are we done here?"

"Where are we?" he asked, looking around the lobby. "This reminds me of East Germany, circa 1985. I've even got a member of the police as an escort, just like then."

"Whatever," Erin said. "It's late, I'm tired, and I'm ready to go home. Are you going to drive me, or do I need to call a cab?"

"That depends on the diligence of your colleagues," Finnegan said.

"How so?"

"If the Camry has been towed, I'll be unable to offer you immediate transportation," he said.

The Toyota was right where he'd parked it, untouched under a thick layer of slushy snow. The sleet had turned to fat, white flakes that drifted down, clinging to every surface. On any other night, Erin would have found it magical and beautiful. Now she just felt cold, wet, and weary. She was tired enough that it didn't even bother her to have a crazy Irishman for a chauffeur. She needed to rest and to think.

The car was quiet on the drive back to Manhattan. Ian stared into the snowy night, on the constant lookout for threats. Erin and Finnegan were each alone with their thoughts.

Erin knew Finnegan had helped her, had given her two probable identities on the victims, together with some other clues. In return, he expected her to read him into the investigation so he could... do what? Exact revenge? But that didn't make sense. Finnegan was a mobster and, crazy or not, mobsters were extremely practical people. They'd kill a man for crossing them, but ten years late? That wasn't good business. It wouldn't serve as an example to others in the underworld. Ten years was a lifetime on the street. In all likelihood Charlie Majors, Garth Engstrom, and the nameless third man had been long forgotten by everybody.

Everybody, apparently, except Finnegan. Erin made a mental note. Wherever else her investigation led her, it was high time she took a much closer look at Kyle Finnegan. She didn't understand him, and on the street, things you didn't understand were things that could kill you.

By the time the battered old Camry pulled up outside the Barley Corner, a blanket of soft, fresh snow had draped itself over Manhattan, shrouding the concrete. Rolf left neat, perfect paw-prints as he trotted to the entrance to the back alley, sniffed at the brickwork, and cocked a leg. Finnegan drove away into the snowy night without another word.

"Everything okay?" Ian asked quietly.

"I have no idea," Erin said. "What's your read on him?"

"Mr. Finnegan?"

"Yeah."

"Wouldn't want him in my squad," Ian said. "He's the dangerous kind of crazy. Kind that gets people around him hurt."

"Thanks for coming with me," she said. "I don't think he would've hurt me. I think he wants my help."

"Not sure he makes a distinction between helping and hurting," Ian replied. "Man with an injury like that shouldn't be on deployment."

"You're right about that," Erin said. "Shit, it's really late. I know you don't sleep, but shouldn't you be getting home?"

"Get you home first," he said. "That's my mission."

"Mission accomplished, kiddo," she said, her hand on the Barley Corner's back door. "I'll take it from here. Goodnight."

"Goodnight, Erin. Need me, you know where to find me."

Erin unlocked the door and slipped in. The pub was dark, empty, and silent. She felt the urge to pour herself a stiff drink and resisted. What she really needed was sleep. Her next shift was starting in less than six hours. It might have been a long night, but the new day was likely to be just as long. She punched in the combination to the keypad on Carlyle's apartment door and led Rolf up to bed.

The apartment was as dark and quiet as the bar. Moving as carefully as a nervous burglar, she eased the bathroom door open, turned on a trickle of water, and brushed her teeth. Then she tiptoed into the bedroom, undressed in the dark, turned back the comforter, and slipped into bed. Rolf walked in a tight circle, did it again, and settled at the foot of the bed with a sigh. Erin lay back and closed her eyes.

"All's well, darling?"

"Damn," Erin said. "I tried not to wake you."

"No fear, darling," Carlyle said. "You were quiet as a wee churchmouse. It's me that's been wakeful, awaiting your return."

She sat up and flicked on the bedside lamp. "Everything's fine," she said. "I had Ian and Rolf watching my back. Anyway, Finnegan's not out to get me. He wants the same guy I do, the one who made those three poor bastards part of that parking lot."

"Was he helpful?" Carlyle asked, rising to a sitting position and maneuvering himself behind her. He laid his hands on her shoulders and began massaging some of the tension out of them.

"Yeah," she said, leaning back into his touch. "I'm as surprised as you are. I've got IDs on two of our victims."

"Anyone I'd know?"

"Charlie Majors?"

"I think I've heard the name," he said, moving his thumbs in small circles at the base of her neck. "Not for years, though that's no surprise, considering. Teamster, unless I'm mistaken?"

"That's the guy." Erin flinched as his hands found a knotted muscle. He applied gentle pressure and she sighed quietly.

"And the other?" Carlyle asked.

"Garth Engstrom. He was in the construction business."

"Can't say I know him," he said. "I'll ask Corky the next time I see him. Corks knows most everyone in that line, provided they're connected."

"What do you know about Finnegan?" she asked abruptly, glancing at Carlyle over her shoulder.

"I've laid out everything I know about his activities," he said. "It's all in Lieutenant Stachowski's files."

"I mean personally," she said. "You've spent a lot of time with him over the years."

"You know about his injury," Carlyle said. "Some ten years back, he was out in Detroit talking to the Teamsters. Some of their lads went for him and cracked his skull. He did for three of them, but he's not been the same since."

"Yeah, I know," she said impatiently. "But what's his deal? He's not as crazy as he acts."

"Nay, he's not," Carlyle said softly. "Evan would've cut loose of him by now if he was half so mad as he seems. Oh, he's not right in the head, no doubt of that, but as he'd say, if this is madness, there's a method in it."

"That sounds familiar," she said. "Are you quoting something?"

"*Hamlet*," he replied. "You've noticed, no doubt, he's a knack for quoting Shakespeare?"

"And other things," she said. "Did you ever see a movie called *The Third Man*?"

"I don't know it. Is it relevant?"

"I have no idea. You know what I think? He plays games with people and he loves doing it. The son of a bitch never gives a straight answer, but he likes tossing out clues. I think maybe he wants people to figure him out, but he doesn't make it easy."

"Maybe you've the right of it," Carlyle said. "He's cut from the same cloth as James Joyce, I suppose. Do you think he's giving you a message?"

"I don't know," she sighed. "I'm too tired to make heads or tails out of him. But can you find out how he's connected to Charlie Majors? I'm pretty sure he wants to kill the guy who killed Charlie, and he wants me to point him at the right target. I don't know if I can stall him long enough for us to take down the O'Malleys, so I'm trying to figure out what to do about him that doesn't end up with someone getting killed."

"I wish I understood Finnegan myself," Carlyle said. "But if he's playing a game, it's a different one from the rest of us and he's the only lad who's read the rules."

"Doesn't it bother you?" she asked. "Not knowing what the hell he's up to?"

"Not so much as it did," he replied. "Now you're watching him, I've no doubt you'll puzzle him out. Then we'll sweep him up with all the other rubbish and clear him off the street."

She leaned back against him. "I wish I had your confidence," she said.

He wrapped his arms around her and kissed her cheek. "You've confidence to spare, darling," he said. "You're just tired. It'll all look better come morning."

She looked at her alarm clock. "Shit, it's practically morning now," she groaned. "I'm going to get three hours, tops, before I have to go back in. You gangsters are lucky. You work all night, just like us, but you get to sleep all day."

"On the other hand, we're much more likely to be murdered," he said.

"There's that," she allowed. "Thanks so much for reminding me, right before I go to sleep."

"Good night, darling." He kissed her again. Then he laid her gently down and curled his arm around her. She nestled against him, enjoying his warmth, and tried to put her worries away for the next few hours.

Ian Thompson had once told her that when the shooting stopped, it was time to go to sleep. That was one smart Marine, Erin thought. Then she didn't think anything at all. She'd been given plenty of fuel for nightmares, so it was a measure of her exhaustion that she didn't have a single dream, good or bad.

Chapter 6

The whiteboard in the Major Crimes office was depressingly blank, mirroring the carpet of snow that had draped itself across New York overnight. The whiteness was blinding, dazzling. Erin squinted at the board. Her headache had diminished to a distant throb, like the underground rumble of the subway, but the brightness wasn't helping.

The board held a few of the photos the CSU team had taken of the crime scene, showing the bodies the way they'd been when the construction crew had unearthed them. That was it. No names, no motive, no time of death, not even a date.

Vic was at his desk with his customary enormous cup of Mountain Dew. Lieutenant Webb was standing at the window, staring out at the monochrome landscape and twirling an unlit cigarette between his fingers.

"Oh," Vic said, looking up at Erin's approach. "It's you."

"Who were you expecting?" Erin replied. "The Giants' cheerleader squad?"

"A guy can hope," he said. "You could totally rock one of those short skirts. Tell you what, I'll get you some pom-poms."

She didn't laugh, didn't even bother slinging a casual insult back at him.

"You all right, O'Reilly?" Webb asked, taking in her face, which didn't have much more color than the whiteboard. It had all drained into the deep shadows under her eyes. She'd thought about masking it with makeup but had given it up as a lost cause.

"I'm fine, sir," she said.

"Of course you are," Webb said. "You're always fine. I don't know why I bother asking."

"Rolf, *platz*," she said, nodding to his blanket next to her desk. The Shepherd stalked over to his accustomed spot, circled, lay down, and tucked his snout under his tail. Then Erin walked to the board and started writing. The other two detectives came over and watched.

"Garth Engstrom and Charlie Majors," Webb said when she'd finished. "Are these lucky guesses?"

"Not confirmed yet," she said. "But both of them went missing the same night, during the summer ten years ago. Majors was connected to the O'Malleys."

"But not Engstrom?" Webb asked.

"Not as far as I know," she said. "But he was in construction."

"And you got these names from...?" Vic prompted.

"A CI."

"Which one?"

"A confidential one," she said. "That being what the C stands for."

Vic rolled his eyes. "One of your O'Malley goons," he said.

"Carlyle's not a goon!" she snapped. "Neither is Corky. Well, okay, Corky's sort of a goon."

"You can't be sort of a goon," Vic said. "It's binary. Either you are or you aren't. For example, the Lieutenant's not a goon, but I am. See how easy that is?"

"How solid is this info?" Webb asked.

"My source is sure of it," she said with a shrug. "But he didn't tell me all his reasons. I talked to Mrs. Majors. The Mob fed her some bullshit story about her husband running off with a cocktail waitress but she never believed it. She figured he was dead."

"How does she know it's bullshit?" Vic shot back. "Guys run off with cocktail waitresses all the time. It's the little skirts they wear and the top two buttons they don't."

"And you're back to short skirts," she said. "Is this a thing with you? But we can check. The waitress is Penny Sizemore and she works in Atlantic City. At least, she did a decade ago."

"Ten years is a long time in that line of work," Webb said. "It's unlikely she's still doing it. But I'll make a call and ask local law to look her up."

"Did you get a DNA sample for this Majors punk?" Vic asked.

"No," she said. "I didn't think to ask. It was two-thirty in the morning. I wasn't at my best."

"After ten years, the woman might not have anything that'd reliably have his DNA on it," Webb pointed out. "If we've got his name, even if he doesn't have a jacket we should be able to run his dental records."

"Does he?" Vic asked. "Have a jacket? You said he's an O'Malley."

"I don't know," she said. "I just got here."

"You could've checked it on your onboard computer last night," he said.

"I wasn't in my car, Vic. I rode down to Brooklyn in a rusted-out Toyota. I slept about three hours. Cut me some goddamn slack."

"Sheesh, you're crabby when you're tired," he said. "Want a sip of my Dew?"

"I'd rather drink battery acid."

"Wouldn't be that different," he admitted. "The pH is about the same."

"Levine's been working on the bodies," Webb said. "O'Reilly, why don't you go down and see how she's coming along?"

Vic grinned. "Enjoy the morgue," he said.

"Neshenko, get started running those names," Webb said. "I want everything you can dig up."

"Didn't we already dig them up?" Vic asked.

He gave it a few beats, but nobody laughed.

* * *

Sometimes the morgue smelled like preservatives. Sometimes the smells were more biological; blood and human waste and fluids that belonged on the inside of the body, not strewn around Doctor Levine's lab. But whatever the smells, they were always unpleasant. Opinions varied on the best way to handle the odors. Some advocated rubbing VapoRub on the upper lip. Erin knew one cop who always ate spicy curry before going in, with the idea the hot food would overload the senses. But Erin had never found a better coping mechanism than just getting it over with as quickly as possible.

She didn't know how Levine could handle the long hours in the cold, fluorescent-lit lab, all metal and tile, with only the dead and the stench for company. But the Medical Examiner never seemed bothered. In fact, she enjoyed it more than associating with the living.

A new smell hit Erin's nose as she pushed through the door into the morgue. It was definitely chemical, but not the formaldehyde stink she associated with the place. This was sharper, more dangerous; the sort of smell that would make you call 911 if you caught a whiff of it coming out of your basement.

Levine had been up all night, but appeared none the worse for it. She was bent over one of the three victims, her lab coat and scrubs showing some disturbing brownish stains. She didn't bother looking up to see who had come in. She had more interesting things to do.

"Good morning, doc," Erin said.

"I believe you," Levine said. "I haven't seen it."

"What is that God-awful smell?"

"Which smell?"

Erin waved a hand in front of her nose. "The chemical one. The really strong one."

"Phosphoric acid and trisodium phosphate," Levine said.

"Okay. That doesn't mean anything to me."

"Then why did you ask?"

Erin took a breath and tried again. "What are phosphoric acid and tri... whatever used for?"

"I used them to dissolve the trace amounts of concrete remaining after breaking the bodies free from the larger pieces," Levine explained. "The process requires careful application in order to avoid damaging the tissues."

"Good," Erin said. "How's your analysis going?"

"I've discovered quantities of cement in the nasal passages and tracheas of all three victims," Levine said. "This, together with the absence of obvious physical trauma, strongly suggests an initial cause of death of asphyxiation due to immersion in liquid cement."

Erin swallowed. She'd suspected as much, but Levine's clipped, clinical words made it undeniably real. She could all too easily imagine being tied up, dumped in a hole, and feeling the thick, watery cement pouring down. The bodies had been standing, she recalled; they'd tried to keep their heads above the surface as long as they could, and the hardening cement had kept them as they'd been in their last moments. Had they screamed? Of course they had. Anybody would have.

"Were they gagged?" she asked.

"Unlikely," Levine said. "I found no traces of fabric around their mouths, and as I said, they had cement lodged in their tracheas. Their wrists and ankles were secured."

"Did you find any identifying features on any of them?" Erin asked.

"All physical features are unique to a given body."

"Right," Erin said, managing not to roll her eyes. "Are the teeth in good enough shape for dental record comparison?"

"Yes."

"What about fingerprints?"

"No. Soft tissue is reasonably well preserved, but not to that degree."

"What about clothing?"

"That's not a complete question," Levine said.

"Did their clothing provide any useful information?"

"I've catalogued everything they were wearing. A full description of every article will be in my report. Their clothing was typical of casual attire worn by middle-class American males between thirty and fifty years of age, which is consistent with my initial analysis of the remains."

"Okay," Erin said. "Thanks. We'll look for your report when it's done."

"It won't be difficult to find," Levine said. "It will be filed through normal channels and procedures."

* * *

"Charlie Majors was a bad boy," Vic announced as Erin came back into Major Crimes.

"What'd he do?" Erin asked, coming over to Vic's desk.

Rolf raised his head and sniffed at her as she went by. She always smelled interesting when she came back from the morgue.

"Labor rackets," Vic said. "You know how it is with crooked unions and mobsters. Majors was suspected of involvement with a hijacking scam. The truckers would tip off the gangsters when they were hauling high-value shipments. You know, electronics and shit. Then they'd get held up by armed robbers who just so happened to know exactly where they were and what they were carrying. And the robberies would just so happen to take place in isolated spots without any pain-in-the-ass eyewitnesses or cops around. The drivers would get their cut and nobody would get hurt, except the owners of the cargo. They'd take it right in the backside."

"That's the oldest trick in the book," Webb said. "Organized crime's been pulling that one since before I put on my shield."

"Wow, that *is* old," Vic said, sounding enormously impressed.

"Did Majors have any convictions?" Erin asked.

"They couldn't make the hijacking rap stick," Vic said. "Lack of evidence. All they had was a pattern of behavior. The city couldn't prosecute and the union wouldn't cut him loose, probably because he was kicking back some of his take to the bosses."

"That's corruption for you," Webb said.

"The Organized Crime Task Force was running something on them," Vic went on. "But then Majors dropped off the face of the Earth and they left it alone. That investigation's been dead for years."

"And nobody thought that was a little too convenient?" Erin asked.

Vic shrugged. "When a lowlife disappears, some cops think of it as a lucky break. We usually figure the schmuck moved to another city and became someone else's problem, or else he got whacked and we don't worry about it until his body turns up. Then he becomes a victim instead of a perp. That's the great thing about these guys. They give us business coming and going."

"What names is he connected to?" Erin asked.

"A few guys I never heard of," Vic said. "But there's two you ought to like: Kyle Finnegan and James Corcoran."

"O'Malley middle management," Webb said. "Corcoran makes sense; he's got Teamsters contacts. But what about Finnegan?"

"He's kind of a wild card," Vic said. "As far as I can tell, Evan O'Malley uses him as some sort of fixer. He's not straight muscle, not like that Connor prick was, and he's not a friendly negotiator like Corcoran. He's something in between, something else."

"Do you know him, O'Reilly?" Webb asked.

Know him? I spent half last night riding shotgun in his car, Erin thought. "We've met a few times," she said. "I don't know him well. I'm not sure anyone does. He's a little weird."

"According to his file, he's got a TBI," Vic said. "Skull fracture and brain bleed, nearly killed him. Happened in Detroit about ten years back. I got a mugshot here from a few years ago and I swear to God, there's a big-ass dent right there in his head. You'd think he would've gotten it fixed. He's one strange-looking guy; he's got weird eyes."

"Everybody looks bad in their mugshots," Webb said. "It's like when you get your picture taken at the DMV for your driver's license, only worse. Half these guys are whacked out on something or other and the rest of them are trying to look tough."

"I'm serious," Vic said, pointing to his computer screen. "Take a look at this dude."

Webb came over and looked at the screen. "Okay," he said after a moment. "I get what you're saying. That's a peculiar individual. Do you think he might've had something to do with his guy's disappearance?"

"He's got a pretty solid alibi," Vic said.

"How can you possibly know what Finnegan was doing ten and a half years ago?" Webb demanded.

"Hospital records," Vic said. "That skull fracture? When it happened, our Organized Crime guys were still running surveillance on Majors. He didn't drop off the grid until a week after Finnegan landed in a hospital bed. Finnegan wasn't even conscious while this was going on."

"You're right," Webb said. "That's an excellent alibi."

"Why did you think he might be a suspect?" Erin asked.

"A mid-ranking mobster who was under surveillance?" Webb replied. "It's not much of a stretch to think his bosses might've seen Majors as a liability. And the timing is interesting."

"What timing?" Vic asked.

"Finnegan's injury," Erin said, nodding. "It'd be quite a coincidence, him getting his head bashed in just a week before these guys got clipped."

"So you think there's a connection?" Webb asked.

"Don't you?" she answered.

"I do," Webb said. "Look into the Detroit angle. See what you can shake loose on the guys who beat Finnegan up. I don't know what we're looking for, but I think we'll know it when we see it. And let's see if we can find out what Majors was doing with this Engstrom character and our John Doe. If they're not Teamsters, something else is going on."

"Like what?" Vic asked.

"If I knew that, I wouldn't be asking you and O'Reilly to look into it," Webb said. "Neshenko, I want you combing the missing persons reports from around that time. Check the full month of June. I want a list of everybody who's close to a match for victim number three. I want a name to go with his face."

"He doesn't really have much of a face anymore," Vic said.

"Then get a name to go with his skull, smartass," Webb said. "I want an ID by the end of the day."

"Do you have any idea how many people get reported missing every month in New York?" Vic said.

"Mrs. Majors never reported Charlie missing," Erin put in. "She didn't see the point. Our guy may not be on the list at all."

"Yeah," Vic said.

"I guess we'll know whether he's on the list after you've combed the list," Webb said. "Thoroughly."

Vic surrendered to the inevitable. "Yes, sir."

Erin took a detour through the break room for a cup of coffee. Next to the coffee machine, to her delight, she discovered a fresh box of donuts. She selected a raised glazed donut for herself, half a cruller for Rolf, and returned to her desk with a little more spring in her step.

"Who brought the food?" she asked.

"I did," Webb said. "Napoleon said an army travels on its stomach, and I don't want you two keeling over at your desks. Don't thank me too much, I expensed it to the Department."

Rolf delicately took the cruller from Erin's hand. Three quick bites and a minimum of chewing transferred it to his belly. He decided no more food was available, and no bad guys had presented themselves to be bitten, so it was time for a mid-morning nap.

And for Erin it was time to figure out what, exactly, had happened to Kyle Finnegan on that long-ago night outside Detroit.

Chapter 7

Talking to out-of-state police departments was a good reminder for Erin that the FBI actually had a reason to exist. An agency that could go across state lines without worrying about jurisdiction could've avoided the delay and red tape that cost her the next two hours of her life. One phone transfer led to another, and another, and another, with long enough hold times in between to make her question all the choices that had brought her to this moment.

Finally, when she was wondering if it might be quicker to jump in her car and drive all the way to Michigan, a secretary said, "I'll patch you through to Detective Heywood." Something about the way the secretary said the name made Erin sit up a little and pay attention. The call went through with no hold music; just two rings and it was picked up.

"Heywood," a man's voice said. It was an older guy, someone who sounded a little like Erin's own dad, down to the Long Island accent.

"Detective, thanks for taking my call," Erin said. "I'm Erin O'Reilly. I'm a detective with the NYPD and I was hoping you could help me out with something."

"New York?" Heywood said. "That's a surprise. I don't get many calls from the old neighborhood."

"You're from here?" she asked.

"You already knew that," he replied. "You been wearing a gold shield long, Detective? You sound like you're fresh outta the Academy. You gotta work on your bullshit radar, or bad guys are gonna pull shit on you all day long."

"I've got twelve years on the Force," she said, a little nettled. "I've had my gold shield a couple years now."

"Only twelve?" he said, whistling softly. "You're young enough to be my daughter. Hold on... did you say your name was O'Reilly?"

"That's right," she said.

"I used to know an O'Reilly," he said. "I was NYPD myself, back in the day. But that woulda been before your time. Hell, it's twenty years now. Patrol guy, down in Queens."

"You're kidding," she said. "That wouldn't be Sean O'Reilly, would it?"

"He your uncle or something?"

"My dad."

Heywood laughed. "Would you believe that! I haven't heard anything from him in years! Good police, glad to know him. How's that old boy doing?"

"Turned in his shield and hung up his sidearm a few years back," Erin said. "He's upstate now, hunting and fishing."

"Good for him! Me, I'm still riding a desk. Gonna get my thirty and then maybe I'll get out. I woulda retired, but I lost my old lady. Heart attack, God rest her. And my kids moved out. One's in California, the other's in Seattle. Don't see much point in sitting around the house all by my lonesome. Figure as long as I'm doing some good, I might as well stay on. Not that the kids round here give me much to do. God only knows why they sent you to me. I hardly hit the street anymore. Knees aren't what they used to be. Is it because I'm from New York?"

"I'm calling about an old case," she said.

"How old?"

"Ten and a half years."

He whistled again. "Maybe that's why Donna tossed you my way. Go back that far, I'm the only guy who was working this department who's still here. All the rest either moved out or moved up, became precinct Captains or Internal Affairs assholes or whatever. What've you got going?"

"We dug up some old bodies," Erin said. "Under a parking lot. I think there might be a connection to some trouble between the Detroit Teamsters and a New York mobster."

"Ten and a half years, you say?" Heywood's voice lost some of its bantering quality and became harder, more businesslike. Erin heard computer keys clacking in the background. "What case you thinking of?"

"A guy got his head cracked open and landed in the hospital," she said. "Bad concussion, brain damage. I heard he killed three Teamsters, but the charges didn't stick for some reason."

"Oh, yeah, I remember that one," Heywood said. "That takes me back. Hell, I was on that case myself. I was the senior guy on my squad, even then. It was weird as hell. There was this one crazy guy, wandered into a truck stop with a bloody tire iron in his hand, giving some sort of wacky speech, if you can believe it. Like he was a friggin' actor in a play or something."

Erin smiled. "I can believe it," she said. "Sounds like my guy. He wouldn't be named Kyle Finnegan, would he?"

"Finnegan, that's it!" Heywood said, snapping his fingers. "Blood all over his face, skull caved halfway in. Scared the hell out of the waitress. Gimme a sec, let me pull up the file."

More computer keys clicked. Erin waited.

"Okay, here it is," Heywood said. "Yup, that's our boy. Kyle Finnegan, Brooklyn native. Had a bunch of priors, but I'm guessing you know all about those."

"I've got his NYPD file," she said.

"Figured," he said. "He was hospitalized, of course. Son of a bitch had a bad brain bleed, probably woulda killed him if we hadn't got him when we did. Near thing anyway. You know how it goes with concussions. His brain started swelling and he went into a coma right as the EMTs got there. So we couldn't ask him any questions. All we had was the blood and the weapon."

"Wasn't that enough to hold him?" Erin asked.

"It got complicated," Heywood said. "The tire iron had blood, hair, and brain matter from four different guys on it."

"Four?"

"One of whom was Finnegan himself," Heywood said dryly. "And fingerprints from two guys, one of whom was also Finnegan. We made a sweep of the area, but that took a lot of time, and we never found any other injured guys, or any dead bodies."

"You should've used dogs," Erin said.

"We did," Heywood said. "Got a genuine Kentucky bloodhound from our search-and-rescue boys. That dog was the one who found the rest of the blood. Not as much of it as you'd think, but our lab matched it to the same four guys on the tire iron, plus a fifth guy we never identified."

"But no bodies?" Erin said.

"No bodies," he repeated. "Somebody else had been there, but we couldn't tell who. It was a vacant lot, all overgrown. Footprints all over the place, cigarette butts, all kinds of evidence, but we couldn't tell what was part of the crime and what wasn't. Hell, we didn't even know what crime had been committed."

"You had bits of brain on a tire iron," she said. "Sounds like homicide to me."

"Some of that brain was Finnegan's, and Finnegan didn't die," Heywood reminded her. "He should've, but he didn't. We had no witnesses, no bodies, and the only guy we had in custody was so brain-damaged we didn't even know if his testimony would be admissible, assuming he ever woke up."

"He did," Erin said.

"Yeah, in New York City," Heywood said. "His lawyer got him moved. Said we could extradite him back to Detroit if we ever thought of a crime to charge him with."

"Which you didn't?"

"We sent the DNA for testing," Heywood said. "Got the answer back four months later. Pretty good turnaround time for that time and place, I gotta say. Matched all three samples on the tire iron to known criminals. Crooked members of the Teamster's Union, all of them Mob-affiliated. Real bad actors. Something like two dozen assaults, one manslaughter, and a bunch of other priors between them."

"Did you look for them?"

"Yeah, but we never found any of them."

"Because they were dead?"

"That's a guess, but I think you're probably right."

"So what did you do?"

Heywood sighed. "What were we supposed to do? You can't get a murder conviction on 'probably.' We could put Finnegan together with those three guys, but given how badly hurt he was, his lawyer could've just claimed self-defense, even if we'd had a pile of corpses. We had no proof any of the three were dead, so even manslaughter would've been tough to sell to the DA, let alone a jury. Besides, we figured Finnegan wouldn't be a problem for anybody, on account of his injuries. Even if we couldn't land him in jail, the guy was gonna spend the rest of his life as a vegetable anyway."

"That makes sense," Erin said.

"So, you think this all has something to do with the bodies you dug up?" Heywood asked. "You trying to close some cold cases, maybe pin them on Finnegan?"

"I'm just trying to figure out what happened," she said. "And Finnegan's definitely involved. Could you possibly send me what you've got on those three missing Teamsters?"

"Happy to," Heywood said. "You still got a fax machine, or do you want me to act like it's the Twenty-first Century and e-mail you?"

"E-mail would be better," she said. "We've got a fax, but it's a little temperamental."

"That's probably because it's been with the Department longer than your dad was," Heywood said. "Say, what did happen to Finnegan? Is he dead now?"

"No, he's very much alive," she said. "And he's not a vegetable."

"Really? What is he, then?"

"I have no idea. You'd to have to talk to a psychiatrist about that. I'm not even sure they've got a name for what's wrong with him."

"If you get the chance, ask Finnegan about those guys," Heywood said. "And let me know. That case is technically open, even though I'm probably the only guy in Detroit who still cares. It's always nice to clear one off the books."

"Will do. Thanks for the help, Detective."

"Forget about it. Thanks for letting me bend your ear. Always good to hear from the old hometown. Take it easy, O'Reilly. Stay out of trouble, and say hi to your dad from Jack Heywood."

"Copy that."

* * *

Erin hung up the phone, stood, and stretched.

"You finally talk to a real person?" Vic asked.

"Yeah," she said. "A guy who used to be NYPD, says he knew my dad back in the day."

"Is that a good thing or a bad thing?"

She gave him a dirty look. "My dad was good police and he'd kick your ass for hinting otherwise."

"Wait a second," Vic said. "Did you seriously just say your dad could beat me up? Are we on the playground? And isn't your dad sixty years old and wearing a spare tire around his gut?"

"So?" Erin retorted. "He's an O'Reilly. We don't lose fights."

Vic thought it over. "Good point," he said. "But I still think I could take him, if I was sober."

"If you two are done swapping macho BS, would you care to tell me what you found out?" Webb asked.

Erin related the conversation. Webb listened, rubbing his chin.

"But from what we know, Finnegan was in a coma in the hospital when his buddies took their cement bath," he said. "How does this help us?"

"I didn't think Finnegan killed them," she said. "But I think there's a connection. Majors was a friend of Finnegan's. Okay, not a friend, maybe, but an associate."

"You think there were two hits," Vic said. "The guys in Detroit tried to take Finnegan out at the same time some of their boys in New York clipped Majors."

"Is that your theory, O'Reilly?" Webb asked. "A mob war between a Detroit organization and the O'Malleys?"

"Maybe," she said. "Right now I'm just looking for pieces that connect."

"I always start with the corners," Vic said. "Then do the edges. After that, you can fill in the middle. God, I hate jigsaw puzzles. I haven't got the patience."

"We're detectives," Erin said. "We spend all night on stakeouts. We do hours of unpaid overtime catching up on paperwork. We're supposed to be patient."

He smiled. "But we're not."

Erin's e-mail box notified her of a new message. It was from username heywoodj in a Detroit city domain and had attachments. She opened it to see a bunch of old files. Heywood had included the case file from Finnegan's incident, along with the rap sheets of three Detroit Teamsters, all of them missing.

"None of these guys are our suspects, right?" Webb said, coming to stand behind her and looking over her shoulder at the computer screen.

"I'm pretty sure all of them are dead," she said.

"They could be zombies," Vic said.

"They're not zombies," Webb said without even turning his head toward the Russian.

"How do you know?" Vic asked.

"Because it's never zombies," Erin said.

"Yet," Vic said.

Erin and Webb ignored him and began examining the documents.

"Some real boy scouts here," Webb said. "Cyrus Pappas... what is that, Greek?"

"It's sure as hell not Irish," Erin said.

"Also known as "Fisherman," Webb continued. "Gideon Drake, AKA "Bible," and Tommy "Two-Foot" Piper. Great, more silly Mob nicknames."

"They could be CB handles," Vic said.

"Come again?" Webb said.

"If these guys were truckers, they'd have CB radios in their rigs," Vic said. "That's how they'd ID themselves on the road."

"Whatever," Webb said. "They're not nice, wherever they got their nicknames. I see known associates in Detroit organized crime, a whole lot of offenses... Drunk and disorderly, assault, aggravated assault, assault with a deadly weapon... Where'd these guys find time to drive their trucks between all the fights?"

"Sounds like they were leg-breakers for the Detroit Mob," Erin said. "They probably had no-show jobs to launder their pay."

"That makes sense," Webb said. "Crooked unions love doing that sort of thing."

"I think we better take a good hard look at the Teamsters," Vic said.

"As long as we're investigating cold cases with them, maybe we can find out what happened to Jimmy Hoffa," Erin said.

"We know what happened to Hoffa," Vic said. "Frank Sheeran killed him in the Seventies. You should be proud, Erin. An Irishman got him."

"That was never proved," Erin said. "They never found the body. Just like these three guys."

"Maybe one of them survived," Vic said. "And he went looking for revenge, but he couldn't get Finnegan, because Finnegan was in the hospital under police guard, so he took out Finnegan's buddies instead."

"That actually makes a little sense," Webb said.

"Except that nobody's seen any of these guys since that night," Erin said.

"As far as you know," Vic said.

"Okay," Webb said. "We've got some new avenues of investigation here. O'Reilly, see what you can find out about the Teamsters. You have contacts with them, don't you?"

"Yeah," she said. "I know a guy."

"I swear, you sound more like a gangster every day," Vic said.

"Roll around in the mud and you end up muddy," Erin said. "Let me make a call. It's time for lunch anyway. I think I'll go down to that Chinese place around the corner. Anyone else want anything?"

"Fried rice," Vic said. "Extra beef and some egg rolls."

"Nothing for me," Webb said unhappily. "I've got a salad in the fridge."

"Doctor's orders?" Erin guessed.

"That's right," Webb said. "I had my departmental physical last week. Blood pressure, cholesterol, weight, the numbers just keep going up. Doc said I have to stop smoking, stop drinking, and eat better. He said it'll add ten years to my life."

"Ten years sober, smoke-free, eating lettuce?" Vic said. "No thanks, Doc. I'll take my chances with death."

"I figured I'd give the salad a try," Webb said. "If I do one out of three, it ought to be good for three years plus change, right?"

"I'm not sure that's how the math works, sir," Erin said.

Rolf welcomed the opportunity to get out of the office for his midday stroll. He pranced happily along the sidewalk at Erin's hip, enjoying the wintry walk. The city had cleared the sidewalks, but snow was piled in various out-of-the-way spots. Rolf liked to stick his snout into the drifts, snort, and shake his head vigorously.

Erin took out her phone as they went. She took a deep breath and dialed Corky's number.

"If it's not the finest lass I've never slept with," Corky said by way of greeting.

"You're saying you've slept with every woman finer than me?" Erin said.

"I'm saying there's only one finer lass walking this Earth," he said, "and she's done me the honor of welcoming me into her arms. But you didn't call to chat about my love life, fascinating topic though it is."

"I didn't, thank God," she said. "I need to talk to somebody with connections to the Teamster's Union."

"You're speaking to him," Corky said. "What is it you're needing to know?"

"I need some info about the Detroit branch of the Union," she said.

"You'll be wanting Wayne McClernand," Corky said at once.

"Wayne?" Erin said. "Great! I know him and he owes me a favor for that thing last year with the State Patrol. Can you put me in touch?"

"I'll ring him and set up a meeting," Corky said. "I'm sure the lad will be delighted, and unless I'm mistaken, he's in the area. Can I give him this number?"

"Sure," she said.

Corky was as good as his word. Erin arrived at the Chinese restaurant, placed her order, waited while it was cooked, and was only halfway back to the Eightball with the food when her phone rang, showing an unknown number.

"Miss O'Reilly?" Wayne's deep, deceptively gentle voice said. Erin heard road noise in the background.

"Hey, Wayne," she said, smiling in spite of herself. Wayne was a trucker with a record, an O'Malley associate who'd done time for a number of crimes. He had jailhouse tattoos, a few missing teeth, and a body as massive and intimidating as the Beast, his beloved big rig. But for all that, he was a nice enough guy who liked and respected her.

"A guy I know said you need some help with something," Wayne said. "You in some kinda trouble?"

"Nothing like that," she said. "But I need to pick your brain. I hear you've done some work around Detroit?"

"Yeah, few years back," Wayne said. "I still go through every now and then, when I'm doing long-haul routes, but mostly I stick to the East Coast these days."

"Are you anywhere near New York?" she asked.

"I'm on my way back to the Big Apple right now," he said. "Coming up I-95 from Trenton. I oughta be there by six. It'd be sooner, but these roads are crap on account of the snow. There's pile-ups and wipeouts all over the place. It's an ice rink out here."

"Take your time," she said. "And you should probably get off the phone and concentrate on your driving. How about I buy you dinner when you get in?"

"Hey, that'd be great," Wayne said. "You got a place in mind?"

"You know the diner on Murray, just off West Broadway?"

"Ricky's?"

"That's the one."

"I'll be there. Six?"

"Sounds good. See you there, Wayne. And be safe."

Chapter 8

It was snowing again when Erin and Rolf left Precinct 8. The Manhattan traffic was even worse than usual. Erin took one look at the gridlock and decided to walk to the diner. She and her dog could use the exercise and they'd get there almost as fast.

They'd left Vic still plowing through ancient missing persons reports. He'd found a few that might be possible matches, and had forwarded them to Levine to compare dental records, but he wasn't optimistic. Neither were the other detectives, but they all knew that sometimes the only thing to do was hammer away at a mountain of data until you pounded loose the nugget of information you needed. Vic had grimly promised to get through the whole list if it took all night. That, he said, was what caffeine had been invented for.

She thought about traffic while she walked. America ran on the internal combustion engine, and it wasn't family cars or yellow cabs that kept everything going; it was trucks. The big rigs were the lifeblood of American commerce. Without them, cargo would pile up on the docks, factories would go silent, cities would starve. Railroads were all very well, but there just weren't enough of them. Truckers carried the whole country in their trailers.

Erin was a union girl at heart. That was how her dad had raised her, teaching her that the labor movement had been responsible for creating the middle class. Like her father, she was a member of the Police Union. She believed in organized labor, which included the Teamster's Union.

But that didn't mean turning a blind eye if a union was involved in something shady. As far as she was concerned, if union guys were using their position to perpetrate crimes, they were the worst kind of parasite. They endangered everything her ancestors had fought for on the picket lines when the Irish workers had taken on the robber barons. Give fat cats an excuse and they'd shut the unions down for good.

She had no idea whether the Teamsters' upper leadership had anything to do with what had happened in Detroit. Probably not; beating a guy with tire irons was pretty low-brow.

But why was she so sure of the connection between Finnegan and the triple slaying in Brooklyn? Was it something he'd said or done? She remembered the way he'd suddenly gotten focused, just for a second, when he'd told her his plans. Just how crazy was he?

"Crazy enough to be dangerous," she muttered to Rolf, who cocked his head at her and listened. When nothing further was forthcoming, he went back to sniffing snowdrifts.

She didn't need to wonder whether Wayne had gotten to Ricky's Diner ahead of her. She saw the Beast as soon as she rounded the corner. It took a special kind of balls to drive a semi cab into downtown Manhattan on a snowy evening, but Wayne had managed it. The truck had shed its trailer somewhere along the way, but it was still a massive piece of machinery. Snowflakes hissed and melted on the hood, the engine still hot from its journey. Erin took a moment to look over the truck, admiring the custom-painted flames that wreathed the hood. Then she went into the diner.

Wayne stood out as obviously as his ride. He was a head taller than anyone else in the place, and even seated at the counter, he took up a lot of real estate. He glanced up when the bell over the door tinkled, and when he saw Erin he gave her a broad smile and a wave. He wouldn't be a bad-looking guy, she thought, if he'd do something with his hair, shave a little more often, invest in some decent dental work, and get some of his jailhouse tattoos removed.

He hopped off his stool and swung his hand out to greet her. Erin's slender fingers disappeared in his big paw. For a second he considered pulling her in for a one-armed hug, but decided against it and let go.

"Miss O'Reilly," he said. "Good to see you again! Been a little while."

"It has," she agreed.

"You got your partner with you, I see," he said, looking down at Rolf. "I still haven't got one of my own. Been meaning to go to a shelter and get one of them rescue dogs, but I been busy. You know how it is. I bet you've been a real good boy, haven't you?"

Rolf gave him a cool look that indicated he was indeed a good boy, but his status didn't depend on Wayne's opinion of him.

"I didn't order yet," Wayne went on. "I dunno what you like."

"I'm buying," she reminded him, sliding onto the stool next to his and signaling the guy behind the counter. She ordered a bacon cheeseburger and a Diet Coke. Wayne asked for two burgers of his own, plus extra fries and what he called "hundred-mile coffee." Erin thought about asking how he intended to eat all that, glanced at his impressive gut, and decided not to.

"It's greasy out there," Wayne said, nodding toward the window. "Don't get me wrong, I'm a good driver. It's those other idiots I'm worried about. Buncha soccer moms in minivans and yuppie assholes cruising around in their trust-fund sports cars. None of them know how to drive on ice. I counted fifteen cars in the ditch since I crossed the state line, you believe it? You're lucky you aren't with the highway patrol. None of them are getting any sleep tonight."

"I'm glad you got here okay," she said.

"The thing I was thinking, all the way up," he said, "is what if some young lady spins out across my lane and I wipe her out, and she's got a baby in the backseat? That's the sort of thing you never get out from under, even if it wasn't your fault, you know? And then, know what I find? Goddamn road work! It's practically Christmas and some jerkoff thinks it's a good time to close down two lanes. Had two miles of pure brake checks, we're talking gridlock. God only knows what they're doing. You can't pour cement in this weather, and blacktop's no good either."

Erin shrugged. She understood Wayne needed to decompress from a stressful drive, so she'd just let him vent. She considered how the construction crew had found their corpses. Everybody in New York was trying to get a little extra work done and the weather had decided to show them who was boss.

"Sorry," Wayne said, a little sheepishly. "You got your own problems and here I am bitching. Sorry about my mouth, too. I don't talk to a lot of ladies."

"Wayne, I'm a cop," she said. "I hear plenty worse every day."

He chuckled. "I forget that sometimes. So what can I do for you?"

"Do any of these names mean anything to you?" she asked. "Gideon Drake, Cyrus Pappas, or Tommy Piper?"

His heavy brow wrinkled. "No, sorry," he said. "Nothing ringing a bell."

"You wouldn't have heard from them in years, probably," she said. "Maybe a decade."

"Nope. I got nothing."

Erin hid her disappointment. It had been a long shot, but worth trying. Then she had a final thought. "How about Bible, Fisherman, or Two-Foot?" she tried.

The lights went on behind Wayne's eyes. "Yeah!" he said, thumping the counter with his hand and making his silverware jump. "I got it now! Bible Drake and Two-Foot Piper! I remember those guys!"

"Really?"

"Hell yes!" Wayne exclaimed, drawing the attention of everybody in the diner.

Erin made a motion with her hand for him to cool it a little.

"Sorry," he said, much more quietly. "Yeah, those guys used to do the run from Motown. Auto parts, mostly."

"So they really were truckers?" she said. "I thought maybe they were no-shows, just drawing checks through the union."

"Nah," Wayne said. "They earned their pay. They did some other stuff, too, maybe. I don't know nothing about that. But they dropped off the grid, geez, it's gotta be years ago. And it's not like I knew either of them real well."

"Do you know what happened to them?" she asked.

He shook his head. "Guys like that, they disappear, you don't ask questions, know what I mean?"

"I heard they got in a scuffle with Kyle Finnegan," she said.

Wayne's eyes got big. "Hold on," he said. "You mean those were the guys in Detroit, the ones who..." He mimed banging his fist against the side of his own head.

"Yeah," she said.

He whistled. "No wonder nobody heard from them."

"You know that story about Finnegan?" she asked.

"Everybody knows that story," he said. "I just didn't know it was guys I knew. Shit, I know Bible's brother."

"Drake has a brother?" Erin asked, feeling a rush of excitement.

"Yeah, kid brother. Well, he's not a kid anymore, I guess. He's gotta be thirty now. He's with the Union, but he don't do long hauls. I run into him every now and then."

"Where was he when Drake—Bible, I mean—disappeared?"

Wayne shrugged. "You got me. But he lives in New York now. Somewhere on Long Island, I think."

"What's his name?" she asked eagerly.

"Let me think. Eddy? No, that's not right. Willy? No. It's right on the tip of my brain."

While Wayne was thinking, the food arrived. Erin dug into her burger, giving him time. Wayne scooped up his first burger, opened his mouth wider than she would have thought possible, and engulfed a third of it at one go. He chewed a few times, swallowed, and did it again.

"Got it!" he announced through a mouthful of food. Then he blinked, swallowed, and cleared his throat. "Sorry. Eli Drake, that's the kid's name. Short for Elias or Elijah or something like that. His CB handle's Chariot. Y'know, like those things they used to ride around in with horses pulling them?"

"Chariot. Copy that."

"Hey, you're not trying to get Finnegan in trouble, are you?" Wayne was suddenly concerned. "Listen, lady, you don't wanna rock that boat. He's nuts, sure, but he's one of us, y'know? Evan ain't gonna like it if you screw around with him. And Finnegan, he don't care if you're a cop or not. If he decides you're gunning for him, he'll hit back and he'll do it hard. Nothing there but trouble."

"You've got me all wrong, Wayne," she said. "I just talked to Finnegan last night. We're on the same page here. Did you know Charlie Majors?"

"Charlie the Tricycle? Of course I knew him," Wayne said, relief all over his face. "Solid guy. Drove an R-model Mack, better than four hundred horses under the hood. Called her the Blue Baby, said she gave the sweetest, smoothest ride you ever had outside an Amsterdam whorehouse."

Erin raised her eyebrows. Wayne went red right to the ears.

"I mean," he stammered, "Charlie had a pretty good rig. I've never been to Amsterdam, so I wouldn't know about that other thing. Sorry, ma'am."

"Forget about it," she said. If Wayne was comfortable enough with her to say off-color things, that was a good sign.

"Anyways, Charlie dropped disappeared a while back," Wayne said. "I heard he ran off with a waitress or something, but that didn't make sense to me."

"Why not?"

"He was making good money in a solid job," Wayne said. "And he had a good thing going with his lady. No fireworks, but he was good to her. So maybe he stepped out on her a couple times, I mean, who hasn't? But he always went home, y'know? And besides, he was making plenty extra on the side."

"Through Evan and his guys?" Erin asked.

Wayne winked and said nothing, starting in on his second burger.

"Yeah, he'd have to be crazy to throw all that away," she said. "Do you remember if he knew a guy named Engstrom? Garth Engstrom?"

Wayne shrugged. "Never heard of the guy."

"What did Charlie have to do with the construction business?" she asked.

"Construction?" Wayne echoed. "I dunno... Wait a sec. Y'know, I ran into him, I clean forgot about it. This musta been ten years back. It only stuck in my head because he was gone, like, the next week. He said he had something lined up, something big. It was gonna make him stacks and stacks, make him a player. I asked if I could maybe get it on it, and he said sure, he'd let me know. It was something with development, down in Brooklyn, but he didn't say what. And I never heard nothing more from him, so I forgot about it till just now."

"Thanks," Erin said. "Say, why did you call him the Tricycle?"

Wayne grinned. "That goes way back," he said. "Charlie was driving a panel truck this one time, making a short run up to Beantown."

"Beantown?"

"Boston. He got jumped by some local boys there, wanted to hijack his cargo. He made a run for it and they rammed him, took out his left back tire. He drove on the rim, these jerks chasing him and shooting at him, clear through downtown if you can believe it. Three good wheels, laying sparks with the fourth one. That's why everybody called him Tricycle. Fifteen bullet holes in his truck, but he made his delivery. That was Charlie. You could count on him. And that's why he never woulda run off with no waitress, you get me?"

"I do," Erin said. "And he didn't."

"You found him?" Wayne asked.

She nodded.

"He dead?"

She nodded again.

Wayne sighed. "That's what I figured. Who killed him?"

"That's what I'm trying to find out," she said. "Hold on, how did you know he was murdered?"

"You're a murder cop, right? Why else would you be asking about him? Besides, if he'd gone down in a crash, he wouldn't have vanished. He woulda been right there in the ditch, like all those losers on the road today, and we woulda had a funeral and everything."

"Anything else you can tell me about him?" she asked.

"No, sorry. It's been years. Right after he disappeared, I got pinched by your boys for my first big trip upstate, so I was out of the loop for a while."

"Sorry about that," Erin said, grimacing.

"Forget about it," Wayne said. "Wasn't you, and I wouldn't take it personal if it was. It's the game, y'know? We run, you chase us. Like lions and those whaddayacallems out there in Africa. Y'know, the big bastards with the horns."

"Wildebeests?" Erin guessed.

"Yeah, maybe. The lions run 'cause they're hungry, the wildebeests run 'cause they don't wanna get eaten. Sometimes it goes one way, sometimes the other." Wayne shrugged. "But everybody's gotta hustle. It's how we're made."

"Yeah," Erin said, feeling a sudden and unexpected wave of melancholy. In a matter of weeks, the NYPD was going to come down on the O'Malleys very much like a pride of lions on a herd of unsuspecting prey. Red meat was going to be on the menu and Wayne himself was one of the beasts who was going to be served up. Would he still be so forgiving?

And would she forgive herself?

Chapter 9

Erin left the diner a little before seven with a full stomach and a dilemma. She could go home at a reasonable hour for once and enjoy a quiet evening with her boyfriend and her dog. The murder case was as cold as they came, ten years plus change, and the bodies weren't going anywhere. It might be nice to relax a little, try to let off some of her stress. The past months had been a constant, relentless hammering. She'd been beaten, shot, nearly asphyxiated and blown up. She'd earned a break.

Or she could follow her next lead and see where it went. Thanks to Wayne, she had another name to investigate. She looked down at Rolf, who looked back, cocking his enormous ears in that endearing German Shepherd way.

"I know what you'd do," she told him. "Give you one sniff of your target and you wouldn't stop for anything."

Rolf kept watching her. He wanted her to know he was listening, though he didn't have the slightest idea what she was talking about.

"Damn it," Erin muttered. She hauled out her phone and placed a call.

"Neshenko," Vic said.

"Miss me?" she asked.

"Oh, did you leave? I didn't notice."

"How're you coming on that third ID?"

"Getting there. I know about three hundred guys it's not. That leaves something like four million possibles."

"Can you run a name for me?"

"Sure, because I haven't been running names through the system all damn day."

"I don't have my car with me, or I'd run it myself."

"Whatever. What's the name?"

"Drake. First name is something that shortens to Eli."

"Drake? Like Gideon? Our mysterious missing Detroit Teamster?"

"His brother."

"You think he's our third corpse?"

"Eli's still alive as far as I know, but he's living in Brooklyn. He's also a trucker, like his brother."

"Hold your horses." There was a short pause as Vic consulted the database. "Okay, I got a hit. Elijah Drake, thirty-one years old. Parole officer lists him at a Brooklyn address. No parents, has a brother... yeah, Gideon. That's gotta be your guy."

"Parole officer? He's a convict?"

"Did eighteen months of a three-year rap for assault," Vic said. "According to the arrest report, he stabbed a guy in the face with a float blade. I got pictures of the poor bastard here. Damn, that's a lot of stitches. What the hell is a float blade? That's no knife I ever heard of."

"I know a guy who knows knives. I'll ask him."

"This guy wouldn't happen to be called Corcoran, would he?"

"No comment."

"Saying 'no comment' is like taking the Fifth. It doesn't prove a thing in court, but everybody knows you're guilty when you say it."

"Corky's not—"

"Now I know you're not gonna say Corky's not a criminal, because we both know that's not true. He's absolutely a criminal."

"Vic—"

"And I'm sure he's a real nice guy. I know, I know. He robs from the rich and gives to the poor. He helps little old ladies cross the street. He farts sunshine and shits rainbows. So let's forget about him. I'm sure he's never done a thing to deserve the loving attention of the NYPD."

"You get really grumpy when you work unpaid overtime."

"Everybody gets grumpy when they work unpaid overtime."

"I'm waiting for you to give me Drake's address."

"You haven't asked me for it yet."

"I'm asking now."

"I'll tell you once we're on our way."

"On the way where?"

"To see the guy, obviously."

"Hold on, Vic. You think I'm going down to Brooklyn tonight?"

"Aren't you?"

She thought about it and realized she'd already made up her mind. If she hadn't intended to go, she would have left it till morning to check the address.

"Yeah, I guess I am," she said.

"Thought so. I'll back you up."

"I don't need backup."

"Not everything's about you, O'Reilly. What about me? What about *my* needs?"

"I don't want to hear about your needs, Vic."

"What I need right now is to get out of this goddamn office before I lose my mind. You want to come in here tomorrow and find me curled up under my desk, sucking my thumb?"

"Now that's a sad image."

"Then it's settled. Where are you?"

"Just a couple minutes out. I'm on foot, coming back to the Eightball to collect my car."

"Then what're you complaining about? I'm on your way so I won't slow you down at all. I'll grab my coat and meet you in the garage."

* * *

"I keep going to Long Island," Erin said. She turned on the wipers and peered through the falling snow.

"It's good to remember where you're from," Vic said. "Even if it just helps remind you why you left."

"I used to think I'd live my whole life in Queens," she said.

"I'm a Brooklyn boy myself," he said.

"I know. Brighton Beach."

"Little Odessa. What a shithole."

"That's a hell of a thing to say about your home."

"My family came over from Russia," he said. "Yours came from Ireland."

"Your point?"

"My point is, America was built by immigrants. You know what an immigrant is? Someone who realizes their home is a shithole and they'd really like to leave. Then they spend all their time in America reminiscing about the old country and how great it was. I got news for you. If it was such a great place, nobody ever would've left. Now we've got more Irish in the Tri-State area than there are in Ireland, so what's that say about the Emerald Isle?"

"If you're going to bash Ireland, you can get out and walk," she said.

"Russia's just as bad," he said. "Worse, probably. At least you didn't have the Czars."

"No, we had the English," Erin said.

"If you're gonna tell me the English were worse than the Czars, you're out of your mind. We actually had a Czar called Ivan the Terrible. You know how bad you've gotta be to get a nickname like that? In *Russia*? It's like in the Mob if they call you Bob the Psycho or something. Oh, that reminds me. I figured out why they called that Drake punk 'Bible.'"

"Enlighten me, Vic."

"His first name's Gideon, right?"

"Right..."

"As in, Gideon Bibles? The ones you find in hotel rooms?"

"And that, Vic, is why they made you a detective."

"Really?" He grinned. "I always figured it was because my ESU commander wanted to get rid of me."

"That, too."

"So, what does this other Drake kid have to do with our case?"

"I don't know yet."

"Why do I want to talk to him?"

"You got bored in the office."

"Okay. Why do you want to talk to him?"

"Because I'm pretty sure Kyle Finnegan murdered his brother. Now here he is, living in the same town where Finnegan's guy got killed right afterward. I don't believe in coincidence, and neither do you."

"You think he killed these guys?"

"I want to know what he knows."

Elijah Drake lived in a small brick row house in a very ordinary blue-collar Brooklyn neighborhood. It was the sort of place Erin knew well; she'd grown up in a similar house in Queens. The tiny patch of yard was neatly kept, the front walk shoveled, the house well-cared-for. Lights glowed in the downstairs windows.

"Cozy place," Vic observed as they got out of the Charger, Rolf hopping out of his compartment to stand beside Erin.

"That's not a bachelor pad," Erin said. "Who else lives here?"

"According to his sheet, he's got a wife and two kids."

"And you're only telling me this now?"

He shrugged. "It wasn't relevant."

"Of course it's relevant! What if we have to arrest him?"

"You don't want to do it in front of the family?"

"I don't want to get in a fight with the wife!" she snapped. "Long Island women are tough. She won't like it if we drag her husband off to jail. I once watched a girl hold off an ESU team with a damn alarm clock. Men are dangerous, sure, but you have to watch out for their women. Those ladies will *disable* you."

"I'll keep that in mind," he said.

"Just don't be belligerent," she said, climbing the front steps.

"If you don't want me to act like me, what'd you want to bring me for?"

"I didn't want to bring you," she reminded him. "It was your idea." Then she rang the doorbell.

A dog started barking; a big one from the sound of it, which was just one more thing to worry about. Erin wasn't scared of dogs; she liked them better than she liked most people. But if there was a scuffle, she might wind up having to shoot the dog and she really didn't want to do that. Rolf could handle aggressive dogs; he'd once taken on a pair of trained attack Dobermans once and come out on top. But that would mean even more headaches, not to mention paperwork.

After a few moments, the door opened a few inches, revealing a woman's face. She was a pleasant-looking brunette, about thirty, with a short, sensible haircut. The woman took in the three of them, paying the most attention to Vic and Rolf.

"Can I help you?" she asked politely.

Erin held up her shield. "I'm Detective O'Reilly, ma'am," she said. "NYPD. This is Detective Neshenko, and this is my K-9, Rolf. Is Mr. Drake in?"

Fear flashed across the woman's face, replaced by a stony wariness. "What's this about?" she asked. The dog was still barking from somewhere inside.

"It's about his brother," Erin said. "May we come in?"

"Who is it, Jen?" a man called from further in the house.

"It's the cops," she called back. "They say they want to talk about your brother."

"Okay," the man said. "Why don't we talk in the living room?"

Jen's mouth tightened, but she stepped back from the door. "Please come in," she said quietly. "And wipe your feet, if you don't mind."

"I hear your dog," Erin said. "Is it okay with other dogs?"

Jen nodded. "Mac's a good boy," she said. "He just sounds tough."

Erin wanted to believe that, but she reserved judgment. For all she knew, Mac was an experienced fighting dog who ate Dobermans and Rottweilers for breakfast. She wiped her shoes on the mat and followed the other woman into the living room, alert for trouble. Vic did likewise.

They entered a snug little room, lit by a Christmas tree in the corner and a blaze in the gas fireplace. A tall, skinny man with dark, spiky hair and a goatee knelt in front of the hearth, one arm around the chest of a square-faced pit bull. The dog was barking fiercely, but Erin knew dogs. This one was wagging its tail so hard its hindquarters were wiggling, its ears were angled forward, and its toes were tapping the carpet. This dog didn't want to attack; it wanted to play.

"Easy there, Mac," the man said. He gave a sheepish smile to the detectives. "Mac's a sweetie, but he comes on pretty strong. Some people are scared of him."

"I get it," Erin said. "I'm a K-9 officer. Rolf, *sitz!*"

Rolf immediately sank back on his haunches. He did his best to ignore the other dog, looking to Erin for further instructions.

"Mac, down," the man said. He reached into a pocket. Mac was instantly aware of the motion. He dropped to his belly, panting eagerly and waiting for the treat he knew was coming. The man's hand emerged with a training treat, which vanished into the pit bull's mouth.

"Sir, I'm Detective O'Reilly," Erin said. "This is Detective Neshenko. Would you be Elijah Drake?"

"That's me," Drake said. "This is my wife, Jenny. You said you're here about my brother?"

"That's right," Erin said.

"Okay, have a seat," Drake said. "Can I offer you a drink?"

"We can't drink on duty, sir," Erin said.

"Oh no, I didn't mean it that way," Drake said. "We don't keep any booze in the house."

"None?" Vic sounded impressed and appalled at the same time.

"Not a drop," Drake said. He put his hand back in his pocket. Erin and Vic both stiffened, but relaxed when he brought it out with a small bronze coin. "Five-year coin," he said proudly.

"Five years sober?" Erin said. "That's impressive. Congratulations."

"I couldn't have done it without Jen," Drake said, smiling at his wife. "It's been five years, three months, twelve... no, thirteen days."

"You're a real solid citizen," Vic said. "I bet you go to church every Sunday, too."

"Trinity Baptist," Drake said. "How about you?"

"I sleep in Sunday mornings," Vic said. "Makes the Saturday-night hangovers hurt less."

"I've got hot cider on the stove," Jenny said in tones of icy politeness. "It's got cinnamon and nutmeg in it, and I guarantee it won't give you a hangover."

"That's very kind of you," Erin said, glaring at Vic. "I'll have a cup, thanks."

"None for me," Vic said. He was staring at Drake as if he could drill holes through the man's skull with his eyes.

"Would you pour me one, too?" Drake said. "Thanks, hon."

Jenny turned on her heel and left the room.

"I don't think she likes us," Vic said to Erin in a stage whisper.

"She probably doesn't," Drake said. "Don't take it personal. It's my fault, mostly. She's had to deal with all the shit... sorry, all the stuff from my past. My PO hasn't exactly been polite. There's been some friction."

Erin's street instincts tingled. Without looking around, she knew she was being watched. Slowly, calmly, she turned her head. A pair of little faces peered down at her between the railings from upstairs.

"Davy, Ruth, you go back to bed," Drake said.

"Heard Mac barking," the girl said. She couldn't have been more than four.

"Mommy and Daddy have grown-ups visiting," Drake said. "We're just talking about boring grown-up things. You go back to bed, and Mac can sleep in your room tonight."

Ruth gave it a moment's thought. "Okay," she decided.

"Go on, Mac," Drake said, ruffling the pit bull's head. "Go to Ruthie."

The pit bull trundled across the room and up the stairs, into the little girl's arms. The children retreated with the dog, out of sight.

"Kids," Drake said, smiling as he said it. There was no mistaking the love in his voice or in his eyes.

"They're good kids," Jenny said from the doorway. "And they're having a hard enough time without the police harassing Eli."

She came in, carrying a tray upon which were two steaming mugs of cider. Erin took one.

"Thank you, ma'am," she said. "And let me assure you, we're not here to harass anyone."

"He's been clean and sober better than five years," Jenny said. "He hasn't broken a single law. He doesn't even drive over the speed limit! What's going to be enough for you people? If you're not going to give him a chance, why'd you even bother letting him out of jail?"

"Jen, please," Drake said, holding up a hand. "They're here about Gideon, not me. Take it easy."

"You're my husband," she said. "This is my house and my life. They've got no right—"

"I apologize for any problems you've been having," Erin said. "I don't know anything about your legal history, Mr. Drake, and it's not why I'm here. I did want to talk to you about Gideon, and about what happened in Detroit."

"I lost my brother, that's what happened," Drake said quietly.

"He died?" Erin asked.

"Yeah," Drake said. "But you knew that, didn't you? That's why you're here."

"We've been assuming it," she said. "But we didn't have any proof. How did you know?"

"A guy told me."

"What guy?"

"A guy who worked with him." Drake met her gaze steadily. "I forget his name."

Erin very much doubted that, but she let it slide. "What else did he tell you?" she asked.

"That Gideon got killed in a fight," Drake said. "He was having a conversation with the guy, it went bad, and the other guy busted his head open. And they were real sorry, but there couldn't be a funeral, because it'd get attention. So he gave me some cash and walked away."

"That's it?" Vic said. "Your brother got killed, so you took a roll of bills off some guy and forgot about it?"

"I didn't forget," Drake said. "I thought about it a lot. Gideon wasn't a bad guy, leastways not all the way bad. He was my big brother and he always looked out for me when we was growing up. When he got in with the Union, he made sure I got my shot too. He was always good to me. But he was into some bad stuff. So was I. I took a fall and did some time for it. But I swore when I got out I was gonna go straight, and that's what I've done."

"You stabbed a guy in the face," Vic said.

"And I did my time for it," Drake repeated steadily, not flinching. "I still see that face, some nights. I wish I could take it back. I'm not proud of everything I've ever done. Are you?"

"Why'd you stab him?" Erin asked.

"I thought you were here about his brother," Jenny interjected.

Drake held up his hand again. "I was messed up for a while," he said. "After Gideon died, I was drinking a lot and I got into pills. Oxy. It screwed with my head. Then, on a job, this guy and I got into it and I just flipped out. I only remember some of it, and it was like watching someone else using my hands. I didn't really mean to stab him. I could've killed him, and it's only by the grace of God I didn't. It was good I went to prison."

Vic snorted.

"I'm serious," Drake said. "It got me clean. I had a chance to think things over. I swore once I got out, I'd do better. And then, when I made parole, I met Jenny, and my whole life changed."

"Eli," Erin said. "Do you know what Gideon was doing that got him killed?"

"Not exactly," Drake said, but his eyes slid away from hers. "Do you know who killed him?"

"We've got a pretty good idea," she said.

"Is he in jail?"

"We can't prove he killed your brother."

"Of course not," Drake said with bitter amusement. "Too bad. Prison might be good for him, too. Rehabilitate him. It doesn't work most of the time, but who knows? It worked for me."

"What've you been doing since you got out?" Erin asked.

"You've read my PO's reports," Drake said. "I've been driving a truck."

"What kind of truck?" she asked.

"Cement truck."

That surprised her. "Not a delivery truck?"

"No," Drake said. "I work for BK Construction."

"Isn't that the same company you worked for when you got arrested?" Vic asked. He'd spent the drive to Brooklyn reading up on Drake's history.

"That's right," Drake said.

"It's a little weird, isn't it?" Vic said. "You getting in a fight on the job, nearly killing a guy, and they give you back your job when you get out? Most places would've fired a guy for shoving a knife down another guy's throat."

"They were understanding," Drake said.

"That reminds me," Erin said. "What exactly is a float knife?"

"It's not really a knife," Drake said. "They called it that on the arrest because it sounds more dangerous than it is. It's a handle on the flat side of this wide, thin piece of metal. We use them to smooth concrete. They don't really cut anything. The edges are thin but they're not so sharp."

"Please, officers," Jenny said. "You're asking about something he's already been convicted of in court. You can't try him again, so unless you've got something else to discuss, I'd like you to leave now."

"They're just doing their job, Jen," Drake said wearily.

"And I'm doing mine," she retorted. "You have to be nice or they'll throw you back in jail; I don't. I'm asking these folks to get out of our house and leave us alone."

Erin stood up. "I'm sorry for disturbing your evening," she said. "Thank you for talking to us, and for the cider. Have a good night."

Chapter 10

"So that's it?" Vic demanded. "Some chick yells at us and we just go? Like a couple of losers?"

"It's her house," Erin said, putting the Charger in gear and pulling away from the curb. "And we didn't have a warrant. She had every right to ask us to leave."

"We were getting somewhere! That punk knows something!"

"We did get somewhere," she said. "BK Construction."

"What about them?"

"They're shady."

"How do you figure?"

"They re-hired a convicted violent felon," she said. "After he assaulted a guy on the clock, with their tools, at one of their construction sites."

"Maybe his wife's brother owns the company," Vic said. "Or maybe he threatened the boss. Or blackmailed him. Tell me you didn't buy that Norman Rockwell, Christmas in New York bullshit back there."

"Vic, are you telling me they bought a Christmas tree and strung tinsel just in case the cops stopped by?"

"No, that's not what I mean."

"And borrowed or kidnapped a couple of little kids?"

"No!"

"Then what are you saying?"

"I'm saying the guy's a violent felon, just like you said. His brother was a leg-breaker for Detroit wiseguys and he gave some other jerk an amateur root canal with a friggin' cement spreader. He's not exactly the salt of the goddamn earth."

"A cement spreader," Erin said. "That didn't strike you as a little strange?"

"It's a lousy weapon. I've seen those things and they're flimsy as hell. You talking about the cement angle? Yeah, I noticed that. You think he's the guy who buried those schmucks under the parking lot?"

"I think it's funny the way cement keeps coming into this," she said. "The brother of one of the guys Finnegan killed just so happens to drive for a construction company? I think we need to look into BK Construction, whether or not Drake himself is our guy. Anyway, he seemed basically okay."

Vic stared at her. "So you did buy the all-American family routine," he said.

"A guy can change," she said. "I spend a lot of time around criminals, Vic."

"So do I. It's one of the perks of our chosen profession."

"Off the clock, too," she said. "I've gotten a sense for them. Drake doesn't feel dirty to me."

"Except he's still working for BK," Vic reminded her. "The company you want to look into."

She sighed. "Yeah, except for that."

"Back to the office?"

"Back to the office," she agreed.

"Can you stop at a gas station on the way? Some idiot ran the vending machine at the Eightball out of Mountain Dew."

"I'm guessing the idiot was six-foot three with a broken nose and a bad haircut."

"Just what are you suggesting?"

"I'm suggesting you might want to talk to somebody about your habit," she said with a straight face. "Chemical dependency is an ugly thing."

There was a gas station at the corner. Erin turned into the lot.

"You're gonna enable me?" Vic asked, smiling.

"Of course I am," she said. "What are friends for? You want to grab me a Diet Coke while you're in there?"

* * *

"Want to know what I think?" Vic asked, once they were back behind their computers at the Eightball and an hour into their research on Long Island's construction industry.

"Not really," Erin said.

"I think you don't want to go home," he said.

"And what's that supposed to mean?" she snapped.

"I'm a detective," he said. "I'm just looking at the evidence. You could be home, cuddling with your sugar daddy right now, and instead you're here with me. Personally, I'd consider that a big red flag."

"I've warned you before. Call him a sugar daddy one more time and I'll feed you your tonsils."

"Sheesh! And you said *I* get grumpy after hours. He's older than you and richer than you. It's an accurate label."

"It's degrading."

"We wouldn't want to hurt the feelings of the former terrorist turned professional criminal. I apologize."

"Your apologies always sound like insults."

"And my insults are compliments," he replied. "Enough about your D-O-G. What've you found about BK Construction?"

"Not a lot," she said. "They've been around about twenty years. Looks like they do the majority of their work in Brooklyn. Commercial development, mostly, but they've done some city projects."

"Who're they connected to?"

She sat back and rubbed her eyes. "Impossible to tell. We'd need a court order, and I don't think we've got enough to get one."

"Not even from Judge Ferris?" Vic asked. "He owes us."

"He does," Erin agreed. "But he won't go around the law. We need probable cause and we don't have it yet."

"How about that parking lot?" Vic asked suddenly.

"The one with the bodies?" Erin replied.

"No, the completely ordinary one five miles away," he said. "The one that's got nothing to do with our case. Yeah, the one with the bodies."

It took a few minutes for Erin to check the public records. "You're right," she reported. "The lot was refinished in June of '05... right around the time Majors and Engstrom went missing. And guess who poured the concrete."

"BK Construction," Vic said. "*Now* can we get a warrant?"

"It's worth taking to Ferris," she said. She checked the time. "Damn, it's late."

"So what? That old guy doesn't sleep. You know him; he's probably got his feet propped up by the fire, sipping his homemade moonshine. No wonder he hasn't retired; he's already living the good life."

Erin picked up her phone. Vic was proved correct. Ferris answered before the third ring, sounding wide awake.

"Good evening," the Judge said. "My phone tells me I'm speaking to the delightful Detective O'Reilly."

"That's right, your honor," she said. "Sorry to call so late."

"Nonsense," Ferris said. "Justice may be blind, but she never closes her eyes."

"Sir?"

"That doesn't make sense, does it?" Ferris said with a chuckle. "I merely meant she never sleeps, so why should her servants? How may I be of assistance, young lady?"

"I need a court order to look into a company's records," she said. "BK Construction, out of Brooklyn."

"Corporate malfeasance is rather outside your normal purview, is it not?" Ferris inquired.

"I think they're Mob-connected," she said. "And there's a good chance they were complicit in a triple homicide a few years back."

"You have my undivided attention," Ferris said.

Erin quickly explained the discovery of the corpses. She had a momentary hesitation about Finnegan and his connection. She trusted Ferris completely, but he wasn't privy to her undercover assignment with the O'Malleys and she was under firm orders not to reveal it to anyone else. She decided to leave out her nighttime journey with Finnegan, simply reporting the connection between Finnegan and the Drake brothers.

"Tenuous," Ferris said when she'd finished. "But I suppose I can expect nothing better from such a cold case. We grasp at straws when we lack firmer handholds. It certainly does sound like this construction company is hiding something, and I think you had best discover what it is. Do you require the warrant immediately?"

"In the morning is fine," she said. "There's no real rush."

"Indeed," Ferris said. "These dead men have waited a long time for justice. A few hours longer should make little difference to them. I'll send the paperwork when I get to the courthouse tomorrow morning."

"How are the repairs coming to your office?" she asked. Ferris's office had been wrecked in an assassination attempt earlier that fall.

"Swimmingly," Ferris said. "However, water damage is pervasive and persistent. I am still working out of the outer office while they finish re-plastering the walls. My secretary has been most accommodating. You remember Miss Lockhart?"

"Of course," Erin said.

"I will give her your regards. Do take care of yourself, Miss O'Reilly."

I'm not the one with a pacemaker and an eighty-year-old heart, Erin thought. "You too, your honor," she said.

* * *

Erin got back to the Barley Corner a little before midnight. It was full of boisterous guys who probably hadn't been up as long as she had. Carlyle looked pretty perky. She knew he didn't normally get out of bed before ten, sometimes later. Ian, standing near the far wall, was wide awake, but he didn't need regular sleep the way most people did.

She'd made it about halfway across the room before she noticed trouble brewing in a side booth. Corky Corcoran was sitting across from Kyle Finnegan. Either man alone needed watching; both together was a dangerous combination. Corky didn't like Finnegan. Sharing a booth with him meant the redheaded Irishman had business with his crazy colleague.

Erin didn't want to talk to them, but Corky had already noticed her. He motioned with his head for her to join them. She wearily changed course and led Rolf over to the booth.

"Evening, love," Corky said. "We were just discussing you. Will you join us?"

"Okay," she said. "But only for a little while. I'm hoping to get some sleep."

"At night?" Corky sounded appalled. "Who'd think of such an unnatural thing?"

Erin briefly considered her options and decided to sit next to Corky. He'd be flirty, but she could fend off his good-natured hands easily enough. Finnegan was too weird for her to relish the prospect of sharing a bench with him. She slid into the booth. Rolf sat on the floor at the end of the table, staring balefully at Finnegan.

"Do I even want to know what you've been saying about me?" she asked.

"Nothing but grand compliments, no fear," Corky said. "Nay, we were talking about your wee problem in Brooklyn. I've talked to some lads, just as I promised."

"And?" she prompted.

"None of them planted any other lads in concrete, if that's what you're asking," he said. "But I did come across something interesting when Finnegan and I compared notes just now."

"What's that?" Erin asked.

"You remember Emerald Isle Estates?" Corky asked.

It took her a moment to place the name, though it was familiar. "Wasn't that the business Evan's nephew was running?" she said.

"Before he made friends with the wrong folk and wound up in a wee concrete room with steel bars on the windows," Corky said. "Tommy Jay O'Malley, aye. You'll not have forgotten him, surely."

"My squad arrested him," she said. "Because he was working with a terrorist who wanted to blow up Police Headquarters."

"Among other things," Corky said cheerfully.

"Emerald Isle was a money-laundering front," Erin said.

"It was more than that," Corky said. "It was a legitimate enterprise. A mite corrupt, I'll grant, but show me a contractor in this fair city that isn't. Evan shuttered the business when his nephew's troubles called attention to it. It's reopened under a new name and new management, of course. It wouldn't do to have all that earth-moving machinery standing idle when it could be making money."

"Of course," Erin said dryly. "What's this got to do with anything?"

"Some ten years back, Emerald Isle was competing for contracts in Brooklyn," Corky said. "It wasn't their usual style. They'd much prefer the sort of contract that was awarded without going through the tedious bidding process, you ken."

"The sort that was awarded by councilmen on the O'Malley payroll, you mean?" Erin said.

Corky made a pained face. "That's a crude way of putting it," he said. "I'd rather say that they had good friends in a position to do favors for one another in a pleasant, unofficial manner. Gratitude, Erin, makes our world go round."

"I hate ingratitude more in a person," Finnegan said, "than lying, vainness, babbling, drunkenness, or any taint of vice whose strong corruption inhabits our frail blood."

"That goes without saying," Corky said. "Who'd hate babbling or drunkenness?"

"Emerald Isle?" Erin said, trying to pull them both back onto the subject.

"At issue was a bit of Brooklyn due to be rebuilt," Corky said. "It was prime real estate; cheap for the asking, but with the right development it'd be worth a fair stack. It had changed hands under dubious circumstances. One of the aforementioned councilmen had tipped off his brother-in-law and that lad had purchased it. That councilman wanted the development done as quietly as possible, to avoid his becoming connected with it. So he was engaged in a negotiation with Emerald Isle to do some of the work off the books, as you might say. Garth Engstrom was the lad with Emerald Isle, as it happens."

"Oh my God," Erin said. "Do you mean the third guy we found under that parking lot was a Brooklyn city councilman?"

"Keep your voice down, lass," Corky said gently. "And of course I don't mean that. A councilman can't simply vanish without a trace. It would've been all over the news. Your lot would've been combing the city."

"For murder, though it have no tongue, will speak with most miraculous organ," Finnegan said.

"Nay, it wasn't the councilman," Corky said. "It was his personal secretary."

"Do you have a name?" Erin demanded.

"James Francis Corcoran," he said, winking.

"The secretary's name," she growled.

"Tracy Chadwick," Corky said. "That's a lad, by the way, not a lass. And so far as either of us can tell, no one's seen poor Tracy since June of ten years ago."

"Which councilman did Tracy work for?" Erin asked.

"Tony Lombardo," Corky said.

"Sounds like an Italian," she said. "Is he connected?"

"Just because a lad's carrying an Italian name, you assume he's with the Mafia?" Corky asked.

"No, I assume he's dirty because you just told me he is," she retorted. "I want to know if he's in with one of the Families, or if he's freelance."

"He's one of ours," Corky said. "Not in Evan's pocket, the lad's far too greedy to belong to one fellow alone, but he's taken a fair bit of Evan's loose change over the years."

That was for Finnegan's benefit. Erin actually already knew that; she'd seen Lombardo's name on Evan's ledger during their recent meeting in Brooklyn, as had Corky. But Finnegan didn't know she knew.

"So this Chadwick went missing," she said. "Didn't anyone look for him?"

"So far as I know, he'd no attachments," Corky said. "No wife, at any rate. And it wasn't in his employer's interest to have people looking for him."

"You think he was meeting Garth Engstrom to talk about this development deal," she said. "And you think someone else killed them?"

"Seems logical, aye?" Corky said.

"Yeah," she said.

"Power is given only to those who dare to lower themselves and pick it up," Finnegan said. "Only one thing matters, one thing; to be able to dare!"

"Okay, you lost me again," Erin said. "Dispatch to Finnegan, please clarify your last transmission."

"You hold power," Finnegan said. "You can easily discover who sabotaged the bidding. We've given you all the tools you need. Now I need you to use those tools to build me a labyrinth."

"A which?" Erin said.

"In the medieval Christian sense of the word, not the classical Greek," Finnegan said, as if that explained everything. "Then we can walk it together, to its heart, where we will find peace."

"Right," Erin said. "Peace. Thanks for getting me the name, Corky. I appreciate it. Now I'll say goodnight."

"Good night, sweet princess, and flights of angels sing thee to thy rest," Finnegan said.

"I'll settle for a shot of whiskey and eight quiet hours," Erin said.

Chapter 11

Erin got her whiskey and seven decent hours of sleep, feeling much better when she woke up. The streets were icy, so she didn't go for a morning run, but she took Rolf to Central Park for an hour of training and play. The K-9 loved every moment of it, taking the opportunity between practice bouts to roll in the snow, kicking all four legs in the air and snorting. Erin hoped no would-be perps were watching; Rolf would have a hard time intimidating anyone who'd seen him acting like an overgrown puppy.

After their outing, they went to the Eightball, pausing on the way to pick up a croissant and a cup of coffee from a café. Erin reflected that she was showing up at a reasonable hour, well-rested and fed, like a regular working stiff. It felt a little weird.

Webb was in the office when she and Rolf climbed the stairs. So, to Erin's surprise, was Vic. Both of them looked tired; Vic because he'd probably been up all night, Webb because he always looked tired. They had their respective caffeinated beverages on their desks and were already working their computers.

"Warrant came through for BK Construction a few minutes ago," Vic reported, holding up a piece of paper. "I love Ferris. If he wasn't male, old, and wrinkly, I'd want to kiss him."

"You do understand, that warrant isn't going to show us where the bodies are buried," Webb said. "We already found the bodies."

"There might be more bodies," Vic said, bringing his own brand of dark optimism to bear.

"It's letting us see the company's financial and personnel records," Webb said. "Which we'll need to go through looking for signs of criminal activity. Over the past decade plus."

"That'll take a while," Erin said.

"Months," Vic predicted gloomily. He no longer looked like he wanted to kiss Ferris.

"I've been asking the Captain to assign us a permanent forensic accountant," Webb said. "Unfortunately, all of them are pretty heavily engaged on existing cases, investigating white-collar crime, and there's no room in the budget to hire another."

"Goddamn bean counters," Vic muttered.

"So the best I could do is get a temporary transfer from the Five," Webb went on. "Apparently they've got someone who's in line for a gold shield, but she's being pulled off the street for medical reasons. I just heard from the Captain that the transfer went through, so we'll be getting a new squad-mate for the next couple of months."

"Great!" Erin said. "We can sure use the extra hands."

"She's more of a street cop than an accountant," Webb said. "So you ought to get on well together. Her CO agreed that this is a good use of her time while she's on limited duty."

"How come we're only hearing about this now?" Vic asked.

"I didn't want to get your hopes up," Webb said.

"I'm Russian," Vic reminded him. "We don't do 'hope.'"

"Besides," Webb said, "I didn't know who was available. I just got the word via e-mail when I got in this morning. I've only known for the past half hour myself."

"Okay," Vic said. "So who is this chick? And what happened to her? She break her leg in an ass-kicking contest, or what? I bet I'm gonna get in fights with her."

"No bet," said a new voice from the stairwell. It was a familiar voice.

"I don't believe this," Vic said.

"Believe it," Zofia Piekarski said. "And if you don't like it, remember this is half your fault." The petite blonde sauntered into the office, making no effort to conceal her obvious pregnancy.

"Zofia!" Erin exclaimed, going to the other woman and shaking her hand with delight. "They pulled you off SNEU?"

"Yeah," Piekarski said, much less happily. "Logan doesn't think I should be running vertical patrols, and unfortunately my doc agrees with him. I could still be out there for another month or two, but I had some little issues. Nothing serious, but—"

"Issues?" Vic interrupted. "What issues?"

"Forget about it," Piekarski said. "It's probably nothing. The doc just says I need to take it a little easier. Something about reducing pre-natal stress. And it looks like I might be getting fast-tracked to Detective one of these days, but my Captain says I need more desk experience. Desk experience! If I wanted to ride a friggin' desk, I would've gotten some bullshit corporate job instead of going to the Academy. But you have to take the bad with the good, I guess, so here I am."

"And we're glad to have you," Webb said. "That's assuming you and Neshenko can work together without undue friction."

There was a pause. Everyone turned to look at Webb. The pause grew longer, becoming awkward.

"What?" Webb said.

"Word choice, sir," Erin said in a strangled voice, trying unsuccessfully to keep a poker face. "Undue friction!" Then she lost it and collapsed into giggles.

"Hey!" Vic said. "We know better than to do any of that on the clock!"

"The NYPD doesn't partner officers who are in a relationship," Webb said. "But since this is a temporary assignment, Captain Holliday doesn't think it'll be a problem. Don't prove him wrong."

"Until the baby's born?" Erin asked, once she'd recovered most of her composure.

"Yeah," Piekarski said. "Then I go out on maternity leave. After that, when I come back on duty, there'll be a nice shiny gold shield waiting for me."

"Congratulations!" Erin said. "You deserve it."

"Yeah," Vic said. "You getting it for taking down those crooked Organized Crime Task Force losers?"

"That's part of it," Piekarski said. "I've been angling for a gold shield for a while. Ever since you and I started going together. I like making street busts, but I think I can do more. Speaking of which, what're we working on?"

"BK Construction," Webb said. "That desk at the back is open, so you can set up there. As soon as they get your computer online, you can get started."

"We think BK is part of a crooked contracting scam," Erin explained. "No-bid contracts through a dirty councilman in Brooklyn. There's the possibility some of their people were responsible for a triple homicide."

"That's a hot potato," Piekarski said.

"More like cold French fries," Webb said. "The bodies spent the last decade under a parking lot. But there's no statute of limitations on murder."

"Oh." Piekarski's face fell. Cold cases were a lot less exciting and a lot harder to close.

"It'll be good experience," Webb said. "You'll get to go through several years' worth of financials. We need to know who's worked for BK, for how long, and who their associates are. We believe there's a connection to organized crime in Detroit, probably through the Teamsters. We also need to know any financial irregularities."

"Wow," Piekarski said. "Anything else? Maybe see if I can develop a new theory of economics while I'm at it, win a Nobel prize?"

"I think you've got enough to get you going," Webb said.

"She's gonna fit right in," Vic said to Erin, grinning. "She can already bitch with the best of them." He turned back to Piekarski. "Why didn't *you* tell me?"

"I like the element of surprise," she said and winked.

Erin figured things were either going to go really well or really badly. She wondered where Carlyle, the professional gambler, would lay the odds, and decided it was a toss-up.

* * *

It was a terrible shame to waste a good night's sleep, Erin thought glumly. Rolf agreed. The K-9 was restless and eager at first, but as the morning wore on and the detectives sat behind their desks, he gradually subsided. Finally, for lack of anything better to do, he curled up and went back to sleep.

Police IT departments were no different from those in the private sector. Piekarski twiddled her thumbs for two hours waiting for a technician to get her computer hooked up. Finally, in disgust, she borrowed Erin's car keys and went down to the garage to use the Charger's onboard computer. No sooner had she done so than the IT guy showed up, requiring her to come back upstairs to set her passwords. The others heard her coming by the barrage of creative profanity echoing in the stairwell.

"Is this a hazing thing?" Piekarski demanded when she got her breath back. "Make the pregnant lady run up and down stairs all day?"

"No," Vic said. "But that's a good idea. Say, would you mind going down to the lobby and grabbing me a Mountain Dew?"

Piekarski threw a ballpoint pen at him.

"You could use the elevator," Vic said.

"Somebody threw up in it," she said. "It smells like cheap beer, puke, and BO."

"And this," Webb said, "is why the NYPD doesn't want couples working together."

"I thought it was so we wouldn't jump in front of bullets for each other," Vic said.

"I'd take a bullet for you, Vic," Erin said. "And not only don't I love you, I don't even *like* you."

"It's so your personal lives don't spill over into the Job," Webb said.

"Yeah," Vic said, giving Erin a very pointed look. "We wouldn't want that, now would we."

"Knock it off, everyone," Webb said. "Or I'm going to ask the Captain to only hire celibate officers."

"How well did that work out for the Catholic church?" Vic said nastily. "Next thing you know, we'd be rolling in abuse lawsuits."

Piekarski and Erin, who were both Catholic, started talking over one another in protest.

"Enough!" Webb shouted. "Shut up! All of you!"

Rolf raised his head and perked his ears, wondering if something exciting was finally happening. But when the detectives got quiet and returned to their computers, he realized it was a false alarm. He heaved a heavy sigh and planted his chin on his paws. There was a wonderful blanket of fresh snow over New York, the city was full of smells to sniff and bad guys to chase, and he was stuck indoors with boring, grumpy humans. He didn't understand them sometimes.

After a few hours staring at bank records, Erin concluded that there was a lot she didn't understand about human behavior, either. She was starting to wish she'd taken an accounting class in college. Back then, it hadn't seemed like something a cop would need to know. Her headache was back with a vengeance, pounding away at the inside of her eyeballs.

"Does anybody know what a brain tumor feels like?" she asked.

"Kinda squishy and rubbery, I think," Vic said. "I'd wear gloves before touching one."

"Ew," Piekarski said, making a face. "I think she's asking what it feels like to have one. Headaches, irritability, that sort of thing."

"Maybe I ought to see a doc," Erin said.

"Don't bother," Webb said. "Headaches and irritability are just part of being a cop. You ought to know that by now. The higher up the ladder you climb, the worse the headaches get, because you end up responsible for people like this squad."

"He's a real ray of sunshine," Piekarski said. "I can already tell your morale is just sky-high."

"We don't have the ready access to drugs you street narcs have," Vic said. "So we substitute with the Lieutenant's pep talks."

"He's a depressant," Erin added. "Prescription-strength. Are any of you having better luck than I am?"

"I don't know," Piekarski said. "I found regular payments to a trucking company. You were talking about the Teamsters, so I figured it could be important."

"BK is a construction company," Webb said. "Paying truckers is something we'd expect to see."

"BK has its own drivers," Piekarski said. "Those are separate."

"What's the company?" Webb asked.

"Black Bull," Piekarski said. "And they're big checks, six figures apiece. We're talking millions of dollars a year."

"That's worth investigating," Webb said. "What do you know about them?"

"Besides the name? Nothing yet. I wasn't sure it was anything we'd be interested in."

Erin typed the name into her web browser. "Got a corporate page here," she reported. "Picture of a big black semi. They're a trucking company all right. Based in Detroit."

"Detroit?" Webb echoed. "That is interesting. Any idea what they haul?"

"Doesn't say," Erin said. "As far as I can tell, they're your ordinary freight company. I expect if you pay, they'll carry it for you, whatever it is."

"Do they have a local branch?" Webb asked.

"Yeah. They're in—"

"Don't tell me," Vic interrupted. "Brooklyn?"

"Brooklyn," Erin confirmed. "Columbia Street Waterfront District."

"Wait a second," Vic said. "That's where those bodies turned up."

"Pretty close," she said, bringing up the address on an online map. "Holy shit. Black Bull's got a truck depot right there. Next door. They probably park their trucks in the lot where the bodies turned up."

Webb's head snapped around. "Really?"

"No joke," she said.

"Get down there," Webb said. "See what you can dig up."

"Do you mean that literally?" Vic asked.

"No," Webb said.

"I asked because there's at least three dead bodies in that lot," Vic said. "And maybe if we start digging more holes..."

"No," Webb repeated. "Not without a warrant. I want the two of you to talk to whoever's in charge at Black Bull. Get a read on the place. But be discreet. You can play it as part of the investigation into the bodies in the lot."

"It *is* part of that investigation," Erin pointed out.

"Yes, but try not to tip them off that we're looking into their company in particular," Webb said. "We don't have anywhere near enough to start getting court orders, and if we spook them they might start destroying evidence and making a nuisance of themselves."

"Copy that, sir," Erin said. She got to her feet. "I guess we're going back to Brooklyn. Again."

Rolf scrambled to his paws, tail wagging. This looked promising.

"Too bad you don't get frequent-driver miles for using your car," Vic said. "You'd have won a trip to Nebraska by now."

"Who'd want to drive to Nebraska?" she asked.

"I'll come, too," Piekarski said eagerly.

"I need you here, Officer," Webb said. "You can keep poking around in BK's records. I think you've got a knack for it. And while you're at it, you can refresh your definition of 'desk assignment.'"

"Yes, sir." Piekarski sulkily subsided. "But if you two have fun without me, I'm gonna be pissed."

"Oh, we're absolutely gonna have fun," Vic said. "You can read all about it in tomorrow's *Times*. Or maybe the supermarket tabloids."

"Read between the lines," Piekarski said, extending the first three fingers of her right hand.

"Ain't love a wonderful thing?" Vic said with a grin. He puckered his lips and blew her an air kiss. She rolled her eyes.

Chapter 12

"So, what do you think of our new squad member?" Erin asked.

Vic stared out the car window at nothing in particular. "I dunno," he said.

"I would've thought you'd be happy," she said. "A lot of guys like working with their girlfriends."

"And office romances always end well," he retorted, rolling his eyes. "It's gonna be different, okay? How many people do you know who'd be glad to hang around each other twenty-four seven? I don't care how in love you are, you need a break from the other person every now and then or you go crazy. Don't get me wrong, I like Zofia. Hell, I like her a *lot*."

"You love her?" Erin asked gently.

"Yeah, that too," he grumbled. "She's the only girl I know who doesn't think I'm an asshole."

"Vic, I hate to break it to you..."

"Okay, okay, she knows I'm an asshole too, but it doesn't bother her. She likes a lot of the same stuff I like. She loves the action. She's fun. But she's got heart, too. That girl is ride-or-die, y'know? When we took down that Maxwell punk and his loser friends, she was all in, a hundred percent. I think she's great."

"But?"

He sighed. "But what if seeing her every day wears it out? There's gonna be days I don't want to be at work. There's gonna be days where everything sucks and I hate the world and everybody in it."

"That's most days, isn't it?"

"Smartass. I'm trying to make a serious point here."

"Okay, okay. Sorry."

"What's it gonna do to our relationship if she's gotta hang around me when I'm like that? We're gonna have more fights. We're gonna get sick of each other. And then what?"

"Vic, you want to know what I think?"

"I got a choice?"

Erin shook her head. "Vic, you're a better guy than everybody thinks you are, including you, but you are so full of shit right now."

"And this is supposed to make me feel better?"

"I'm not trying to make you feel better," she said. "I'm trying to help you."

"Aren't those the same thing?"

"No. My brother's a trauma surgeon, remember? He'd be the first to tell you, sometimes help hurts."

"Point. Okay, oh high and mighty Detective Second Grade O'Reilly, in what way, exactly, am I full of shit?"

"You think you can insulate your love life from all the crap we get into on the Job? You think you won't carry some of it home with you? You think you don't already do that? Vic, if your relationship can't handle seeing each other at your worst, it's not going to last, no matter what you do! And the sooner you figure that out, the better. You saw Zofia when one of her best friends got shot right in front of her. She was a hot mess, and no wonder. Did that make you want to cut loose of her?"

"Of course not! What sort of jerk do you think I am?"

"It's not easy being with a cop. I had a conversation once, talking about this, and I said I couldn't date a cop and I couldn't date a civilian. You know what he said?"

"He said you were screwed."

"No, he said I needed to find myself a gangster."

"Would this guy you were talking to happen to be named Carlyle?"

"He would."

"And I suppose he told you this out of the goodness of his heart, with no personal agenda?"

"No, he kissed me for the first time about ten seconds later."

Vic snorted. "I bet he did. And what did you do?"

"I ran like hell."

"That's a touching story, a real Hallmark moment. What's your point?"

"My point is, I don't think more than five or ten percent of the people out there have the slightest idea what our life is like. They don't know the stress of this job and what it does to us. I'm not saying you ought to find some criminal and try to reform her. I'm saying Zofia gets it. She gets you. She doesn't have any damn illusions to lose, Vic. It's not like she saw your online profile, full of lies about your job, your weight, or the size of your dick."

"I'll have you know—"

She held up a hand. "I don't want to know. I'm sure it's plenty big for whatever you use it for, which I also don't want to know."

"If you don't know how it's used, maybe I ought to have a talk with your boyfriend," he said. "I could give him some pointers."

"Don't."

"Then maybe we should talk about this trucking company. How rough do you want to handle them?"

"Webb said to be discreet."

Vic pouted.

"That means no breaking noses and no throwing guys through windows."

"I know what discretion means," he said. "I just don't usually choose to exercise it. Are you gonna get in trouble over this?"

"How so?"

"With your boyfriend's boss."

She shook her head. "If these guys are anything to the O'Malleys, they're competitors and enemies. I'll be doing Evan a favor if I take them out."

"By 'take them out,' I assume you mean throw their asses in jail," Vic said.

"Yeah."

"Not shoot them."

"No."

"Just making sure. But this stuff all happened ten years ago."

"So?"

"So what if it's all over, and nobody knows anything about it now?"

"All we can do is try."

Vic scowled. "I hate cold cases."

* * *

Erin had seen Black Bull's Brooklyn facility on her first trip to the crime scene, but she hadn't paid any attention to it at the time. That was understandable; it was a forgettable building. The structure was a one-story chunk of cinderblock, all bland rectangles. A big loading dock lined one side. Several semitrailers were parked there, along with a pair of tractor units. All were painted glossy black and emblazoned with the company logo of a snorting, stamping bull. Little white clouds of steam were painted in front of the animal's nostrils.

Two big, bearded guys flanked the building's front door, cigarettes glowing in their mouths. Both had matching gold ring nose-piercings. As Erin and Vic climbed out of the Charger, the men shifted posture slightly. It wouldn't have meant much to most people, but to experienced cops the body language was clear; these men were ready for trouble.

"I'll take the one on the right," Vic said out of the corner of his mouth. "The big one."

"Knock it off," Erin replied in an undertone. "We didn't come here to fight."

She popped Rolf's compartment and the Shepherd hopped down to join her. The men became more uneasy. They'd mix it up with a man Vic's size, their unspoken thoughts indicated, but ninety pounds of bad-ass K-9 was another story altogether.

"Morning," Erin said pleasantly. "Who's in charge of this joint?"

The men glanced at one another and said nothing.

"The lady asked you a question," Vic said.

"Who wants to know?" Thug Number One replied.

"New York Police Department," Erin said, lifting the hem of her jacket to show the gold shield on her belt.

"You got a warrant?" Thug Number Two asked.

"These guys know their Constitutional rights," Vic said. "That just warms my patriotic heart on this cold, snowy day."

"We're not here to search anything," Erin said. "And we're not looking for trouble. We just need to talk to your boss. It's about the thing in the parking lot."

She cocked her head in the direction of the excavation site. The bodies, of course, were in Doctor Levine's morgue, but the hole was still ringed with yellow police tape.

"Nobody saw nothing," Thug Number One predictably said.

Erin resisted the urge to roll her eyes. "You do know those bodies were covered with cement for the past decade, don't you?" she said. "I'm sure neither of you saw anything, because I'm sure you weren't standing on this spot ten years ago. Is this a place of business?"

The men looked at one another again.

"Uh, yeah," Thug Number Two said.

"What are your posted hours?" she asked.

"Uh..." Thug Number One said. From the look on his face, she suspected he hadn't been valedictorian of his high school class.

"Nine to five is customary," Erin said helpfully. "But you might keep longer hours, since I know the transportation business operates overnight. Is that door locked?"

"No," Thug Number Two said.

"Then I'd like to patronize your place of business," she said and walked between them into the building.

They might have tried to stop her, but Rolf was sticking close to her hip and they didn't want to tangle with him. Vic followed, nonverbally daring them to start something. They didn't.

Erin found herself in a bare-bones lobby. A bored-looking, tough-faced woman gave the detectives a quick once-over. A half-full ashtray say on the desk. The woman had a cigarette in one hand and a cloud of cheap tobacco smoke floating around her head. A "No Smoking" sign hung over the woman's desk.

"Yeah?" the woman said in place of a greeting. Her accent was pure working-class Brooklyn.

"Where is he?" Erin asked. She had no idea who she was looking for and hoped the other woman would fill in the blank.

The woman cocked her head to Erin's left, indicating a door.

"Thanks," Erin said. She went to the door and knocked twice.

"Who's that?" a man's voice asked through the door.

"NYPD, sir," Erin answered.

There was the briefest pause. "Okay," the man said. "Come in."

Erin opened the door on a small office furnished with a cheap-looking desk, a laptop computer, a whiteboard on one wall, and a truly hideous pea-green carpet. The carpet was tattered and stained. A smell was rising from it that Erin couldn't quite identify, but which reminded her of how Rolf smelled after making a thorough search of a landfill.

There was no polite way to put it. The man behind the desk was fat. He was tall and broad-shouldered, and fairly muscular, but the muscles were nearly lost in rolls of excess tissue. His thick black beard covered the lower half of his face, so Erin could only guess how many chins he had, but it was definitely more than one. He wore the sort of necktie a man wore when required by a dress code to wear one. It was the same green as the carpet, with burnt orange stripes.

"Maurice Delaney," he said. He didn't stand up or offer to shake hands. "Who are you?"

"Detective O'Reilly, Major Crimes," Erin said.

"Detective Neshenko," Vic said.

Rolf didn't say anything.

Delaney nodded. He waited a moment, like he was expecting something else.

"Sir," she said, "I'm here about—"

"Shouldn't there be music?" Delaney interrupted.

"I'm sorry, what?" Erin said.

"And shouldn't you be in a uniform?" Delaney went on.

"I'm a detective, sir," she said. "Not a Patrol officer."

"I'm still waiting for the music," he said.

"What music?"

"So you can start dancing. Before the clothes start coming off."

Erin blinked at him.

"You still want to play nice?" Vic growled. His hands curled into fists. Two of his knuckles popped audibly.

"This isn't a joke, sir," Erin said to Delaney. "And I'm not a stripper. Neither is my colleague, if that's what you're into. We really are detectives, we really do work for the NYPD, and this interview is not off to a good start. Here's my shield."

She unclipped her gold shield and slapped it down on the desk in front of him. The numbers 4640 gleamed up at him.

"I see," Delaney said. "My mistake. I didn't realize the Department employed such attractive detectives. But I'm sure your boss sees the benefits of the arrangement."

Vic's jaw tightened. He took a step forward.

Erin ignored the crude implication. She'd heard plenty worse. "A construction crew recently unearthed three corpses in the parking lot adjacent to your building," she said.

"Yeah, I heard about that," Delaney said. "It's one hell of a thing."

"We're doing some follow-up on that," she said.

"I'd love to help," Delaney said. "But I don't think I or any of my guys saw anything helpful."

"How long have you worked here?"

"For Black Bull? Fifteen years."

"In this office, I meant."

"Since it opened."

"That'd be in June of '05?" Erin guessed.

"Yeah, I guess."

"Then you might have seen something," she said. "Since that's when the concrete was poured for that lot, and when the corpses were buried."

"Technically, they weren't corpses when they were buried," Vic added. "They were still moving. They didn't become corpses till a couple minutes later."

"Nah," Delaney said. "I didn't see anybody getting buried, dead or alive. But I didn't watch the guys laying the cement. That's none of my business."

"No, I suppose not," Erin said. "BK Construction did the concrete."

"If you say so," Delaney said.

"What is the nature of Black Bull's business arrangement with BK Construction?" she asked, watching his eyes.

He blinked twice but gave no other indication. "Like you said, they did the parking lot for us," he said. "But there wasn't a thing in the contract about burying dead guys."

"Live guys," Vic corrected him. "They didn't die till after they got buried."

"Whatever," Delaney said.

"And that's it?" Erin said. "You don't have any ongoing business with them?"

He shrugged. "I'd have to check the books," he said. "Is that all?"

"Black Bull is a Detroit-based company," she said. "This is a satellite office, correct?"

"Yeah, that's right."

"You're a part of the Teamsters, aren't you?"

"We're truck drivers, aren't we?" Delaney looked proud as he said it, but Erin privately doubted he'd be able to squeeze behind the wheel of even the roomiest big rig. "You're a union girl, I expect."

"That's correct," she said.

"Say," Delaney said, as if the idea had just occurred to him. "After you clock out, you want to get a drink? I know a nice place, just up the road."

"What place is that?" she asked, keeping her tone neutral.

"Sam's," he said. "It's a roadhouse, but it can be real nice if you know the right people. I'm friendly with the guy who runs it. He can get us a private room, get a nice dinner."

Erin gave him what she hoped was a sweetly apologetic smile. "Sorry," she said. "I don't think my boyfriend would like that. And the last guy who pissed him off in a bar got beaten to death with the stool he was sitting on. So I don't think it's a good idea. You have a good day, Mr. Delaney."

Chapter 13

"That was awesome," Vic said, once they were back in Erin's Charger. "Did you see the look on his face? I thought the fat bastard was gonna start shitting bricks right there on the spot."

Erin smiled. "Yeah, I enjoyed that," she said.

"You could've just said you were dating a mob boss," he went on. "But no, you had to make up a juicy story to scare the pants off the son of a bitch. If it was me, I would've just punched his teeth in, and then I'd have another excessive force complaint and the Captain would chew my head off. Your way was better."

"Thanks," she said. What she didn't say was that she hadn't made the story up. Carlyle really had once beaten a man to death with a barstool. He'd been sorely provoked, he had immunity from prosecution, and the other man had truly had it coming, Vic already thought Carlyle wasn't nearly good enough for Erin. He might not understand the finer points of the situation.

"But it was a waste of our goddamn time, driving all the way down here," he complained.

"It got us out of the office," she said. "But I don't think it was a waste of time."

"Yeah? What'd we learn?"

"Delaney's dirty," she said. "Either that or he's so ignorant he has to be reminded to breathe."

"Could be both," Vic said.

"True. But BK is paying millions to Black Bull every year. Delaney's the office manager. That's a sizable operation, but not nearly big enough that a multi-million-dollar contract wouldn't get noticed. There's an ongoing relationship, Delaney knows about it, and he's pretending he doesn't. That means there's something shady going on."

"Okay, it's all connected," Vic said.

"And we know about Sam's Roadhouse," she said. "I think it'd be worth popping in there."

"Why?"

"Because it's going to be a place like the Barley Corner," she said. "Full of goons. We can get a sense of the sort of guys these folks have working for them."

Vic nodded. "Okay," he said again. "I'm hungry and it's lunchtime. Want to pop in for a burger?"

"I was just thinking that," she said. "But you have to promise me something."

"What?"

"You won't start any fights."

"If someone else starts them, am I allowed to finish them?"

"Of course. I'll never say you can't hit back."

"If I punched that Delaney punk, do you think I'd hit anything important before I ran out of arm?" Vic asked. "I figure I'd sink right in to the elbow. It'd be like boxing with a harbor seal, just making the blubber jiggle."

"It's sweet that you wanted to hit him on my behalf," she said. "But I don't need you white-knighting for me."

"I wanted to hit him because he's an asshole," Vic said. "It had nothing to do with you. He's an insult to men everywhere.

But I'm telling everybody at the Eightball you got mistaken for a stripper."

"If you do that, you'd better enjoy that hamburger at Sam's," she said. "Because it'll be the last solid food you'll ever be able to eat. They'll be feeding you through a straw for the rest of your life."

Vic considered this. "It might be worth it," he said. "There's people who live off milkshakes."

"Rolf?" Erin said.

The K-9 poked his head through the hatch between the seats, tongue hanging out, awaiting instructions.

"If Vic tells anybody I look like a stripper, I want you to bring me his balls," she said. "Both of them, left and right. You got that?"

Rolf cocked his head. He didn't understand the order he'd been given, but wanted her to know he was game for whatever she had in mind.

"You're no fun at all, you know that?" Vic said.

"Oh, we're plenty of fun," Erin said. "Rolf loves to play and he's great at fetching. He just needs some new chew-toys."

* * *

Sam's looked like trouble from the moment Erin parked outside. Her Charger was the only sedan in the lot; the rest of the spots were filled with semi tractors, and a row of motorcycles stood against the wall of the building. These were big, black Harley-Davidsons. The building itself was grim and ugly, decorated only by a garish neon sign sporting the proprietor's name.

"This reminds me of that Patrick Swayze movie," Vic said as the two of them walked across the lot. Erin left Rolf in the car, knowing the dog would only attract attention.

"*Dirty Dancing*?" Erin said in utter confusion.

"No! *Roadhouse*, obviously. Sheesh, sometimes I forget you're a girl. Swayze plays this Zen dude who gets hired as a bouncer at this sketchy roadhouse. Then some shit happens, he falls in love, and he beats the crap out of a bunch of bad guys. It's a pretty good flick. He's got this one line, says it to the hot doctor who's falling for him. She sees he's got a ton of scars and asks if he's in any pain. He says, 'Pain don't hurt.'"

"That definitely sounds like your kind of movie," Erin said. "Much more than *Dirty Dancing*."

"Anyway, my point is, this looks like the same sort of place," Vic said. "A dive bar full of lowlifes. Remind me what, exactly, we're doing here."

"Reconnaissance," she said. "We're trying to figure out what Black Bull has going on, and we know their people hang out here. Think about it; that Delaney jerk wanted to take me out to dinner and this is the first place he thought of."

"Real classy joint," Vic said. "You figure he and his buddies come here a lot."

"And Delaney's soft," she said. "If he comes to a place like this, he's got protection. Just remember, we're here to look and listen. That's all."

He rolled his eyes. "Yeah, yeah, I know."

An enormous man was just inside the door, wearing a skintight black T-shirt that showed off bulging muscles. He had a handlebar mustache, a scar over his left eye, and a gold ring in his nose. He glanced at Erin, disregarded her as harmless, and gave Vic a longer look. It was typical goon posturing; one big tough guy glaring at another, two men comparing their manhood through prolonged eye contact. Vic was good at it, but so was the bouncer.

After the stare-down had gone on for almost fifteen seconds, the bouncer curled his lip. "You got a card?" he asked.

"You hiring?" Vic replied. "If you are, you can't ask about union membership. It's against the law."

The bouncer snorted. "We got all the guys we need," he said. "I mean, are you in the Brotherhood?"

Vic shook his head. "I'm Union," he said, "but not Teamsters."

The man shrugged. "Good enough," he said and moved aside.

"You notice he didn't ask me?" Erin said in an undertone as they entered a dimly-lit room. Pool tables were to their left, a bar in front, dining tables to the right. The clientele were almost exclusively large, hairy, and male. The place smelled like beer, fried food, and testosterone.

"He figured you're my date," Vic said. "Otherwise you wouldn't be crazy enough to come to a place like this."

"He saw your gun," she murmured. Vic was openly carrying his Sig-Sauer automatic on his hip. Erin's own Glock was concealed by her jacket. Both of them wore little backup pistols on their ankles, but those were much less conspicuous.

"I figure I'm not the only guy carrying," he replied, steering them to a corner table. Erin took a seat that let her watch the room. Vic sat to her left, keeping his back to one wall. The table sported a very large bottle of ketchup and an only slightly smaller bottle of Tabasco sauce, along with a bundle of cheap-looking napkins and some tattered menus.

"What do you figure is good here?" she asked, picking up the menu. It had only two pages, a front and a back. The back was almost entirely a list of beers.

"I wouldn't order the seafood," he said. "Better stick to beef."

A waitress approached their table. She was almost as muscular as the bouncer. Her left bicep had a tattoo of a skull on it, with a rattlesnake poking its head out of one of the eyeholes.

Her hair was short, spiky, and dyed black. She had a gold ring through the septum in her nose.

"What can I get for you?" she asked.

"Cheeseburger and fries," Erin said. "And a Diet Coke."

"Beef brisket and fries," Vic said. "Bud Lite."

"You *drink* that?" Erin asked quietly, once the waitress had gone.

He shrugged. "I figure I'm not allowed to drink alcohol on duty," he said. "But I'm trying to blend in, so I got the closest thing to water that's on the menu. Let's have a look around."

Erin scanned the room. "I saw three Black Bull rigs out front," she said. "And some other trucks, plus the bikes. I count half a dozen bikers. I can't really tell which guys go with which trucks."

"Really?" Vic said. "I thought it was obvious."

"How do you figure?"

"You notice our waitress's jewelry?"

"Kind of hard to miss."

"Those two guys at the pool table and the one on the right-hand wall all have the same ring in their noses," he said. "Just like the guys out front at Black Bull, our bouncer, and our waitress."

"Delaney didn't," she said, a little nettled that Vic, of all people, had noticed a pattern in jewelry she hadn't.

"He's management," Vic said with a shrug. "But he had a scar on his nose. He used to have one."

"I can't believe you picked up on that," she said.

"I was looking for it after the punks on his doorstep," he said. "I figure it's a calling card. You know, like a gang tattoo."

"Good eye," she said.

They watched the other patrons for a while. Nothing obviously illegal was going on. A couple of bikers returned Erin's look appreciatively, but when Vic scowled at them they turned their attention elsewhere. The waitress brought the food and drinks. The burger was actually pretty good, though a little greasier than Erin liked. The fries were fine once she added a generous squirt of ketchup.

"How's your brisket?" she asked.

"Tastes like roadkill," Vic said.

"And you know this how?"

He shrugged. "Haven't you ever worked Traffic?" He took another bite.

"But you're still eating it?"

"Hey, I didn't say it was *bad* roadkill."

The door swung open again. Erin couldn't see who'd come in, since the bouncer was blocking her view. The newcomer talked to the bouncer for a moment and the guard shook his head. Then the guest handed him something and the bouncer moved aside. Erin guessed it had been a small green piece of paper with the face of a dead president.

Then she saw who the new guy was. "Oh no," she murmured.

"What is it?" Vic said through a mouthful of beef. He turned his head, following her gaze.

Kyle Finnegan walked into the room, feet wandering almost aimlessly. He was as disheveled as usual, his eyes holding their typical vacant, faraway expression.

"It's Finnegan," she said, keeping her voice as low as possible.

"The O'Malley guy?" Vic replied. "Jesus! What's he doing here?"

"I have no idea."

"You didn't know he was coming?"

"No!"

Finnegan let himself fall sideways into an empty chair near the middle of the room. He hadn't even glanced at Erin and Vic.

If he was paying attention to anyone, it was the pool-playing truckers. He started fidgeting with the condiments on the table.

It would have been difficult not to take notice of the odd Irishman. Every eye in the place was watching him. After a few tense, silent moments, the guys at the pool table left off their game and started toward him. They were still carrying their pool cues. The third man with the nose-ring stepped away from the wall and began drifting Finnegan's direction, closing in from behind.

It was like watching a wolf pack surround its prey. The bouncer was watching, but making no move to interfere. Finnegan was the outsider; he'd have to look out for himself.

"Looks like it's on," Vic said softly. "How do you want to handle this?"

"Oh, shit," Erin muttered under her breath. She didn't know what to do.

Chapter 14

The three truckers drew in their ring around Finnegan. The O'Malley boss appeared entirely unconcerned, not even bothering to stand up. The smallest of the truckers outweighed him by at least thirty pounds. Finnegan had no weapon on him that Erin could see. He was clad in a tattered leather jacket and worn corduroys, not baggy enough to hide anything bigger than a small handgun.

"I know who you are," one of the truckers said, stabbing a big, meaty finger into Finnegan's chest. "You're that jerk who runs errands for Old Man O'Malley."

"What're you doing here?" the second trucker demanded. "You think you can waltz in here like you own the place?"

"If you'd like," Finnegan said mildly. "Though I usually prefer a four-count measure."

"Huh?" the first trucker said.

"What do you want?" the second one pressed.

"Doorbells and sleigh-bells and warm woolen mittens," Finnegan said. "Also, the name of the man who stopped Charlie Majors' breath. But mostly I'm here for a drink."

"This guy's whacked," the first trucker said. "He's crazy, coming in here alone. I'm thinking we oughta whip his ass."

"What's he that wishes so?" Finnegan said. "My cousin Westmoreland? No, my fair cousin: If we are mark'd to die, we are enow to do our country loss; and if to live, the fewer men, the greater share of honour."

"Shut up, asshole," the second trucker said. "I'm feeling nice, so I'll give you five seconds to get the hell out of here before I ram this stick up your ass."

Finnegan was unimpressed. "I'd like my drink before I go," he said.

"You're not getting served here," the first trucker said.

"One," the second one said. "Two."

"That's all right," Finnegan said. "I've got everything I need right here."

"Three."

Erin stood up. Vic was right beside her. She didn't know what was going to happen, but she knew things were about to turn ugly. She'd never seen Finnegan fight, but given the size difference and numeric advantage, it looked likely he was about to get seriously hurt.

"Four."

Finnegan nonchalantly popped the cap off the bottle of Tabasco sauce, tilted it to his lips, and took a generous slug straight from the bottle.

"Holy shit," the first trucker said. "Did you see that?"

"Five," the second one said. "That's it. You had your chance, numbnuts."

The third trucker lunged from behind Finnegan, grabbing him around the chest and shoulders, pinning the smaller man's arms to his sides. He hauled his target up out of his chair and held him tightly. The other two raised their pool cues like clubs.

"That's enough!" Vic shouted. He drew his Sig. Nobody paid the slightest attention to him.

Finnegan opened his lips and spat a stream of hot sauce straight into the face of the second trucker. The fiery red liquid splashed directly into the man's eyes. He dropped the pool cue, clapped his hands to his face, and howled.

The first trucker was starting his swing at Finnegan but he faltered at the sound, involuntarily turning his head toward his buddy. The cue went wide, glancing off Finnegan's shoulder instead of clocking him on the side of the head as intended. Finnegan stomped down, jamming his heel into the top of the left foot of the man holding him. His captor cursed but held on tight.

Vic and Erin, despite their experience, were momentarily frozen in surprise. Finnegan twisted like an eel, spinning in the other man's embrace to face him. He crouched, drawing the bigger guy down, then sprang up, driving his forehead into the man's chin. There was an audible clack of bone against bone. The trucker's head snapped back. He let go of Finnegan and went over backward, crashing to the floor.

The bouncer was running toward the melee, pulling out a slim leather bag from his hip pocket. Erin recognized it as a blackjack, weighted with something like ball bearings. Without thinking, she stepped in front of him, pulling open her jacket to show the gold shield at her belt.

"NYPD!" she snapped. "Stop right there!"

The bouncer took no notice of her words. He took a swing at her, the blackjack whistling wickedly. Erin ducked, suddenly wishing she'd brought Rolf in with her. This would've been a great time to have some extra teeth on her side.

Finnegan was in agreement. He spun back toward the first trucker in time to catch another glancing blow from the pool cue. It must have hurt, but he gave no sign of pain. Instead, he stepped in close to the man, opened his mouth, and bit into the guy's cheek.

The trucker screamed, in surprise as much as pain. The scream got louder as Finnegan's jaws clamped shut, tearing a mouthful of flesh clear off. Finnegan's throat bobbed as he chewed and swallowed. The trucker backpedaled, blood streaming from the new hole in his face, flailing with the cue.

Erin didn't have time to worry about the fight at her back. She heard the screams, but she had plenty to deal with in the form of the bouncer, a man twice her size. She let the blackjack sail over her head and came in low, grabbing the man around the waist and twisting her hips.

She was five-foot six and weighed about a hundred and forty pounds. It was a given that most criminals would be bigger than she was, so she couldn't count on raw strength to save her in a fight. She'd learned to use leverage and momentum instead, turning the strength of her opponents against them. The bouncer was still moving forward. She pulled him into and over her hip, making her low center of gravity into an advantage. The big guy's feet left the ground. He sailed into a table, clearing the bottles off it on his way to the floor. Glass shattered around him.

He came up growling, reaching for Erin. She tensed, knowing she couldn't play the same trick twice. She'd have to dodge his next charge and try to propel him into something else. Should she go left or right?

He lunged. She went left. He grabbed at her, catching hold of the lapel on her jacket. She was tugged toward him and she saw the triumph in his face.

The butt of Vic's automatic pistol came down on the back of his head, hammering him down. The bouncer hit the floor again and, true to his job description, bounced once. Then he lay very still, face-down.

"You good?" Vic asked.

Erin nodded. They turned back toward the fight just in time to hear the bitten trucker's screams hit a new register. Finnegan had snaked a hand up, hooking a finger through the man's nose-ring. He hauled on the ring, yanking the poor guy's face down toward his own. As the detectives watched, Finnegan winked at the man, then gave one more hard jerk. Cartilage ripped. Finnegan planted his other hand against the trucker's chest and pushed him away, almost as an afterthought. The man reeled backward, bleeding from two places now, leaving Finnegan wearing a bloody gold ring neatly around his middle finger.

The screaming subsided into wet, choking whimpers from the bloody-faced man and gasps from the guy who'd gotten an eyeful of hot sauce. The third trucker and the bouncer made no sound at all.

Erin and Vic stared at the carnage. Vic was still holding his pistol, but didn't seem to know quite what to do with it.

"Jesus," Vic murmured. It sounded more like a prayer than a curse.

Finnegan turned back to the table where he'd been sitting. He picked up a napkin and dabbed at his lips, wiping away the blood. "Not bad," he said. "The Tabasco definitely adds something to the flavor. How do you say *je ne sais quoi* in Spanish?"

"Christ on crutches," Vic said. "What's the matter with this guy?"

"He's crazy," Erin said quietly. "Didn't you know?"

Finnegan seemed to notice them for the first time. "Once more into the breach, dear friends," he said. Aside from a thin film of sweat on his brow and cheeks, he appeared none the worse for wear.

"You're under arrest," Vic said. "Obviously."

"I claim the right of all creatures to self-defense," Finnegan said. "They came at me with violence. What recourse did I have?"

"You ate a man's face!" Vic exclaimed.

"I needed something to cut the spiciness," Finnegan said. "Besides, I was hungry, and he did say I wasn't allowed to order anything off the menu."

"Vic," Erin said. "You know who he is. I don't know if—"

"He *ate* a man's *face*!" Vic repeated with emphasis. "Right in front of me! I don't care if he's the Pope, I'm taking him in."

"I do perceive here a divided duty," Finnegan said to Erin. "Every subject's duty is the king's; but every subject's soul is his own."

"We'll get this sorted out," Erin said. "But Vic's right. We have to take you downtown. Don't worry, I'm sure you'll be out soon."

"But in the meantime, you're going to jail," Vic said.

"It doesn't matter," Finnegan said. "The mind is its own place and, in itself can make a heaven of hell or a hell of heaven."

* * *

Lieutenant Webb met them in Booking. He was already shaking his head when he got there.

"I looked up the definition," he said. "In Merriam-Webster. 'Discreet. Definition One: having or showing discernment or good judgment in conduct and especially in speech: prudent. Definition Two: unpretentious, modest. Definition Three: unobtrusive, unnoticeable.' Can either of you explain to me how, precisely, what you just did fits any of those definitions?"

"I don't think anybody's ever called us pretentious," Vic said.

"Shut up, Neshenko," Webb snapped. "I was being rhetorical."

"Shutting up, sir."

"You went to Brooklyn to make discreet inquiries into Black Bull," Webb went on. "Next thing I know, there's three Patrol units and two ambulances on their way to some lousy hole-in-the-wall roadhouse to sort out a bar fight. Now I've got two mopes in the hospital, another two in lockup, yet another dirtbag sitting in an interrogation room, and I'm hearing some crazy story about cannibals. Did I miss anything?"

"That's pretty much it, sir," Erin said.

"Did I hear it right?" he said. "Cannibalism?"

"Just the one mouthful, sir," Erin said. "But technically, yeah, he's a cannibal."

Webb rubbed his face. "I should've called in sick," he muttered.

"It wasn't our fault," Vic said.

"Are you whining, Neshenko?"

"No, sir. Stating facts, sir."

"Which one is the cannibal?"

"That'd be Kyle Finnegan," Erin said. "He took a chunk out of one of the truckers after spitting hot sauce in another's eyes."

"He spit hot sauce?" Webb said.

Erin nodded.

"That's creative," Webb said.

"I thought he was gonna get his ass kicked," Vic said. "They had him three on one, but he wrecked them. I gotta admit, I'm impressed."

"Is this guy out of his mind?" Webb asked.

"Yes, sir," Erin said. "Traumatic brain injury."

"Right," Webb sighed. "I'd forgotten about that. Who started the fight?"

"The Black Bull guys went straight for Finnegan when he walked in," Erin said. "They knew him on sight. They told him to leave, he refused, then he swigged the Tabasco, one of them grabbed him, and it was on. Vic and I tried to break it up, but it happened really fast."

"The bouncer was coming in on the truckers' side, I think," Vic said. "But he took a swing at Erin, so I cold-cocked him with my Sig. That's all I did, I swear. One good hit."

"Is that the guy who's in the hospital right now with a level two concussion?" Webb asked.

"Probably," Vic said. "But none of us bit anybody. Hell, the dog wasn't even inside."

"That's a welcome change of pace," Webb said. "But what was Finnegan doing there in the first place? He must've known he was *persona non grata*. Did he just happen to show up, hoping to get in a bar fight?"

"He's crazy, but he's not stupid," Erin said. "He's up to something."

"Then let's find out what," Webb said. "You and me, O'Reilly. Neshenko, find something useful to do."

"Rolf, help Vic," Erin said.

Rolf gave her a mournful look.

Finnegan was sitting in the interrogation room, hands neatly folded. If not for the handcuffs on his wrists, he would have appeared completely relaxed. His clothes were slightly askew, but that was typical. A small smear of blood lingered at the corner of his mouth. He wasn't exactly smiling, but Erin thought he looked vaguely pleased with himself.

"Kyle Finnegan," Webb said, sitting down in one of the chairs across from the man. Erin took the other.

"No," Finnegan said. "I'm Kyle Finnegan. You're Harold Webb. Wherefore art thou Harold Webb? Deny thy father and refuse thy name."

The usual problem in interrogations was how to get the subject to start talking. With Finnegan, as Webb was now learning, the problem was a little different; he'd talk plenty. The question was how to get him to make any damn sense.

"That's right," Webb said. "Lieutenant Webb, NYPD Major Crimes. You know my associate, Detective O'Reilly."

"I don't know her," Finnegan said. "I wonder if I could hear the cock crow through these walls."

"You went to Sam's Roadhouse earlier today," Erin interjected. "Why?"

"It's amazing how much trouble a man can get in just for wanting a drink," Finnegan said. "It's like Prohibition all over again."

"A drink of hot sauce?" Webb asked.

"I hadn't ordered yet," Finnegan explained. "The bottle was already on the table."

"So you just took a gulp?"

He shrugged. "It was that or ketchup. And who do you know who drinks ketchup? The texture is all wrong. It's like a lukewarm tomato milkshake, or a teetotaler's Bloody Mary."

"It wasn't a coincidence I was there," Erin said. "Were you following me?"

"Were you already there?"

"Yeah, I was."

"Then it's impossible for you to have been following me," Finnegan said. "I must, therefore, have followed you. Impeccable logic."

"What's your problem with Black Bull?" she demanded. "Why don't you like them?"

"'Tis death to me to be at enmity," Finnegan said. "I hate it, and desire all good men's love."

"Could you give me a straight answer?" she shot back. "Just once? To prove you can?"

"To crooked eyes truth may wear a wry face," Finnegan said. "You might as well ask yourself what you were doing there."

"My job," she said.

"Ah, the Nuremberg Defense," Finnegan said, nodding. "I was under the impression we were united in purpose, you and I. You had to bring me here, naturally. Appearances are truth, after all. Don't worry, I bear you no ill will. I do not know that Englishman alive with whom my soul is any jot at odds more than the infant that is born tonight. I thank God for my humility."

* * *

"You see what I have to put up with?" Erin said.

She, Webb, and Vic were in the observation room, watching Finnegan through the one-way glass. Rolf had positioned himself next to Erin and was leaning gently but insistently against her leg.

"He's... interesting," Webb said.

Vic snorted. "That's one word for it."

"He's not as crazy as you think," Webb said. "And he's extremely well-read."

"How do you mean?" Erin asked. "I know he quotes Shakespeare sometimes."

"Among other things," Webb said. "I'm sure I missed some of his references, but I caught *Richard III*, *Romeo and Juliet*, the Bible, and something else that sounded familiar."

"The Lord of the Friggin' Rings," Vic said.

"What?" Erin said. "You mean the movie?"

"No, the book," he said. "I haven't read it. Tried once, years ago, got bored and quit. I looked up the quote on the Internet while I was watching your little discussion."

"What's the context of the quote?" Webb asked.

"What does that matter?" Vic replied.

"It matters because it tells us about his state of mind," Webb said.

"I have no idea," Vic said. "I told you, I didn't read the damn thing!"

"The bit about denying your father and refusing your name is from that balcony scene in *Romeo and Juliet*," Erin said. "I read the play in high school. Juliet's pissed because Romeo belongs to the other family, the one that hates Juliet's family, and she wants him to disown them."

"So she can boink him without their families getting pissed," Vic said.

"Yeah," Erin said.

"So... Finnegan wants to boink the Lieutenant?" Vic said, wrinkling his brow.

"No!" Erin and Webb said in unison.

"Thank God." Vic looked relieved.

"He wanted to know if I'm a dirty cop, I think," Webb said thoughtfully. "He thinks Erin's malleable and was wondering whether I could be bought. That may be the most roundabout way anyone's ever tried to bribe me in my whole career."

"Bribing a cop's a felony," Vic said, brightening.

"Good luck proving that one in court," Erin said.

"A jury wouldn't even understand it," Webb agreed. "And our boy in there is very fond of quoting Richard the Third. The character, that is, not just the play."

"What does that tell you?" Erin asked.

"Richard the Third is a chess-master, a sort of Shakespearean super-villain. He betrays everybody in order to become king."

"This is giving me a headache," Vic said. "I'm having flashbacks to freshman English class. I swear, I've had nightmares about conversations exactly like this one."

"Either he's going out of his way to give us coded messages," Erin said, "or he's trying to confuse us and laughing at us."

"If this is madness, there is method in it," Webb said.

"Huh?" Vic said.

"That's from *Hamlet*," Webb said.

"Good God, it's contagious," Vic said. "Now he's got the Lieutenant doing it. Can't we just lock this asshole up? Preferably in a soundproofed cell?"

Webb shook his head. "He'll be out in two days, maybe less," he said. "We can hold him on assault, but he didn't start the fight. His lawyer will say he defended himself against an unprovoked attack by three huge guys. At best, it gets knocked back to some pitiful little disorderly-conduct misdemeanor. At worst, charges get dropped and he walks. Either way, he'll make bail without breaking a sweat."

"He ate a guy's face!" Vic protested.

"A guy who was trying to crack his head open with a pool cue," Erin said gently. "The Lieutenant's right, Vic. We can't hold him."

"Not for long," Webb said. "But I think we'd better keep him as long as we can before charging him. That'll give you a head start."

"To do what, sir?" Erin asked.

"To solve the case," Webb said. "You heard the man. He thinks he's working the same case you are. You led him to Black Bull. It's a safe bet that now he knows about them, he'll keep pressing. Unless you want to try solving a ten-year-old case while trying to stop the O'Malleys going to war with the Teamsters, I think keeping Mr. Finnegan off the street as long as possible is in everybody's best interests."

Erin nodded slowly. "That's probably a good idea, sir," she said. "But I don't think he'll be happy."

"Looks pretty happy to me," Vic said. Finnegan was staring down at his own hands, tapping the fingertips together in a complicated rhythm. He appeared to be humming to himself.

"He said something about that when you cuffed him," she said. "About making a heaven of hell or something."

"Milton," Webb said absently. "*Paradise Lost*. It's something Satan says."

Vic rolled his eyes. "So now he's quoting the Devil. What is this, paranoid schizophrenia meets Oprah's Book Club? No wonder he doesn't care if we throw his ass in jail. It'll just give him more time to catch up on his reading."

Chapter 15

"So we've got a shady construction company burying people alive," Webb said, glancing at the whiteboard in Major Crimes. "They're connected to an equally shady trucking company, under whose parking lot they dumped the victims. The truckers lead back to the Detroit branch of the Teamsters, which is linked to the flesh-eating lunatic currently inhabiting one of our holding cells. The aforementioned lunatic is, in turn, a part of the O'Malley gang, who've been at the middle of half the big cases we've handled in this office. Agreed?"

"Accurate, sir," Erin said.

"What else do we have?" Webb asked.

"We've tentatively identified all three victims," Erin said. "Charlie Majors was with the Teamsters, Local 813. He was friends with Garth Engstrom, who worked for Emerald Isle Estates. Emerald Isle was competing with BK Construction for a contract. A councilman, Tony Lombardo, has been implicated. His personal secretary, Tracy Chapman, is likely our third victim."

Vic shrugged. "So it's a mob killing," he said. "BK took out a member of their competition and sent a message to the councilman by whacking his secretary at the same time."

"Is Lombardo still on the City Council?" Webb asked.

"District Thirty-Five," Vic confirmed. "He's been there practically forever."

"I'm confused," Webb said. "If Majors is a Teamster, and so are the guys in Black Bull, why would he be working with BK's competition?"

"Maybe he was trying a side hustle," Erin said. "It wouldn't be the first time a guy went behind his bosses' backs."

"What's the O'Malley stake in this?" Webb asked.

It was Erin's turn to shrug. "I have no idea."

"There has to be something," Webb said.

"Yeah," Vic said. "Otherwise, Hannibal Lecter's got no business chowing down on truck drivers."

"Emerald Isle was shut down last year," Webb said. "Even if the O'Malleys are still in the construction business, why are they fighting with Black Bull?"

"I think this is personal," Erin said. "It's not about the O'Malleys; it's about Kyle Finnegan."

"Vendetta?" Vic guessed.

"He's out to get the guys who killed Charlie Majors," Erin said.

"Why?" Webb asked.

The others looked at him.

"Revenge," Vic said.

"After ten years?" Webb retorted. "How many associates of Finnegan have gone down since then? Has he avenged every one of them? The street's got a short memory. Even if Majors was Finnegan's buddy, he wouldn't bother now. These guys aren't exactly known for their undying loyalty."

"Well, he is crazy," Vic said.

"No!" Webb snapped. "Stop that!"

"Stop what?" Vic said, bewildered.

"Stop saying that like it explains everything," Webb said. "Insanity isn't random. Even schizophrenics have patterns. People have reasons for what they do. Those reasons may not seem good to you, or even rational, but they exist. If you're not willing to go looking for them, you're just being lazy. And the city of New York pays you too much for you to be lazy."

"We don't get paid *that* much," Vic grumbled.

"You're right, sir," Erin said. "Finnegan is the key. He killed those guys in Detroit around the same time as the killings here. Three kills each place. Finnegan couldn't have done any of the killing in New York; he was in the hospital. I think they were retaliation."

"Which means our victims were important to Finnegan," Webb said, nodding. "But he must have known when they vanished that something had happened to them. Why did he wait this long to hit back?"

"He didn't know," she said. "Not for sure. He suspected Majors was dead, but he didn't know who the other victims were. He's only figuring this out now."

"Because of us," Vic growled. "That son of a bitch is piggybacking on us. He's not a cannibal. He's a goddamn leech. I bet back in grade school, he was that one kid who lets everyone else do all the work on the group project and takes all the credit at the end. I hate those little jerks."

"We need to find out what deal our victims were working on," Webb said. "The Teamsters, the City Council, and Emerald Isle were all involved. If we pull on all three threads, something might come loose."

"I don't think the Teamsters are gonna want to talk to us," Vic said. "Somebody might've told them we helped beat up their guys."

"O'Reilly, talk to your contact," Webb said. "I'll go see Councilman Lombardo. Neshenko, take a look at Emerald Isle's records. We've got them in Evidence from when Tommy O'Malley went down. Pull the files and start digging."

"Can't I just go to prison, drag Tommy O'Malley out of his cell, and beat the information out of him?" Vic asked.

"That's not a terrible idea," Webb said.

"It's not?" Erin blurted out.

"Beating information out of a convict is an absolutely terrible idea," Webb said. "I meant the part about talking to Mr. O'Malley. Where's he locked up?"

"He's still at Riker's, I think," Erin said. "He's appealing his conviction."

"Excellent," Webb said. "That means it's only a short drive. O'Reilly, do you think your connection with the O'Malleys can help open up our friend Thomas?"

"Maybe," she said.

"All right," Webb said, glancing at his watch. "You've still got time to run up there before visiting hours are over. See what the two of you can get out of him."

"If I can't beat the shit out of him, can I at least play bad cop?" Vic asked.

"No," Erin said.

"Why not?"

"Because when you do it, it's not playing. You're just being yourself."

He grinned. "That's more like it."

* * *

The last time Erin had seen Thomas J. O'Malley, the Irishman had been wearing an executive suit. He'd had a corner office in a Manhattan high-rise, a pretty secretary, money to burn, and the world at his feet.

The man who shuffled into the visiting room at Riker's Island bore little resemblance to that successful businessman. His red hair was shaggy and poorly trimmed, his body stuffed into a shapeless orange prison jumpsuit. He looked tired and irritated.

"Mr. O'Malley," Erin said.

The look he gave her in return was half apathy, half weary recognition.

"How're you handling things in here?" she asked, sliding into a chair across from him.

"How do you think?" he replied, slumping into the opposite seat. "I'm seriously considering leaving a one-star review on the Riker's website. Not that you care. You're making small talk to get me relaxed. Forget about it. What do you want? Did you come here to gloat? Is that what gets you off?"

"Hey now," Vic said. "Watch your mouth, buddy."

"I remember the two of you," Tommy said. "Where's the dog? He didn't catch a bullet in the teeth, did he? That'd be a shame."

"Rolf's fine," Erin said, forcing a smile through her own clenched teeth. "They don't let K-9s into this place. They don't want the impression of police brutality. It's bad enough they let Vic in."

Tommy glanced at Vic. "You bring this meathead to watch your ass? Afraid of seeing me on your own?"

"Your case is up on appeal," she said. "I bet your lawyer would love it if one of the detectives who built that case lost their cool and smacked you around while you were in prison. It'd give you a decent shot at getting your conviction overturned, if you could prove misconduct."

Her words were aimed at Vic as much as at Tommy, warning him to keep his temper in check. The last thing they needed was to get hauled in for a disciplinary hearing while the legal system spat Tommy O'Malley back out onto the street.

"We're not here to beat the shit out of you," Vic said. "You're not worth it. And I've seen kiddie cartoons that scared me more than you do."

"Then why are you here?" Tommy asked. "Wasn't it enough to take my whole life away? I lost everything because of you."

"You lost everything because of choices you made," Erin retorted. "You hired a terrorist to come to New York and then you lost control of him."

"And you came out of it pretty well," Tommy said bitterly. "You and Cars climbed right over me to get what you wanted. I hope you're enjoying it, because someday somebody just like me is going to strip it away from you. Yeah, I know all about you and your jerkoff boyfriend. He keep you nice and warm at night? Or do you need a little freshener from that knucklehead you brought with you?"

"See, Erin?" Vic said. "This is why you don't tell them to their face that you're not gonna hit them. Then they think they can disrespect you."

"Garth Engstrom," Erin said, ignoring the back-and-forth.

"Is that supposed to mean something to me?" Tommy replied.

"He worked for Emerald Isle," she said. "And he was making development deals under the table."

"So what? I hate to be the one to tell you this, since you're a sworn officer of the law, but there's this little thing called the statute of limitations. A deal under the table sounds like bribery of a public official, which would be what you call a class B felony. The statute on those is five years. So, hypothetically speaking, if this Garth Engstrom had been doing what you say, he would've had to do it within the past five years for it to matter to a judge. And here's the kicker; nobody's seen anybody by that name in twice that long."

"I know," Erin said. "That's because he was under a parking lot in Brooklyn."

Tommy blinked. "Since when?"

"Ten and a half years," she said. "We dug him up a couple nights ago."

"Shit," Tommy said quietly. "I liked that kid."

"As you've just pointed out," Erin said, "you've got nothing to lose talking about him. And you're up for appeal. If you can help us on this, I can put in a good word with the appeals court. Cooperating with us will look awfully good on your record. Even if your conviction stands, you could see a reduction in sentence."

"Time served?" Tommy asked, suddenly becoming energetic as hope rushed through him.

"Maybe," Erin said, though she would have been extremely surprised at that outcome. The New York courts took a dim view of terrorists and their associates.

"What do you care what Garth was doing?" Tommy asked. "That was years ago and it's over now."

"I'm trying to close a case," she said. "It'll be good for the NYPD and your uncle. Evan will want the guy who put his people in the ground to go down hard. I don't care if you hate me. This isn't personal, it's good business. You want to look really nice to the Court of Appeals, the NYPD, and the O'Malleys? This is your big chance, maybe your only chance."

He considered her. She held her breath. Then something shifted in his eyes and she knew, even before he spoke, that she had him.

"I'd need protection," Tommy said. "Rats don't do well in here."

"Nobody's gonna know," Vic said. "Quit bitching and start snitching."

"He's got a real way with words," Tommy said. "You know what? The hell with it. Like I said, this was years ago, and I swear you're the only two people in New York who care."

Erin and Vic leaned forward, listening. The moment when an interviewee cracked and started spilling was always interesting.

"The construction business is pretty cutthroat," Tommy said. "A lot goes on behind the scenes. You have to have contracts for everything. Materials, transportation, labor. Then there's the permits. You wouldn't believe the amount of red tape. But you know what cuts through all that tape?"

"Money," Erin said. "And connections."

"Give the lady a cigar," Tommy said, snapping his fingers and pointing to her. "If you get the right guys on your payroll, all that bureaucracy just disappears. That's what bureaucracy is there for, right? To make sure everybody gets their cut."

"Capitalism and corruption," Vic said.

"They go together like beer and pretzels," Tommy said. "Now, there was this big city development project going on down in Brooklyn, this would be ten years ago. Millions of dollars on the line. We thought we had an in. Everything was lined up. Except for those goddamn Teamsters."

"Union troubles?" Erin guessed.

"Right again," Tommy said. "Somebody got to them. Next thing we knew, all our shipping contracts were falling through. And not just on the Brooklyn job. Our other projects were getting shut down."

"What did you do?" Erin asked.

"We tried a couple things," Tommy said. "We sent a couple guys to Detroit to try to hash something out with the Teamsters, but that didn't go so good."

"One of your guys ended up in the hospital," Erin said. "I don't know about the other. But you should've seen the three Teamsters."

"You heard about that," Tommy said with a smile. "It could've been worse, I guess, but it still didn't help our position. But then Garth came to me. He said he knew some guys who could help. One was in the Teamsters and he was willing to come over, if the money was good enough. The other was a city government guy. I told him to set up a meeting and see what he could find out."

"And he never came back from that meeting?" Erin guessed.

Tommy shook his head. "Not a sight of him, not a word," he said. "And that kid had promise. He was going places."

"Places like a Brooklyn parking lot," Vic said. Nobody paid him any attention.

"His Teamsters contact and the Councilman's secretary died with him," Erin said quietly. "We were wrong; this wasn't a revenge hit. It was a business transaction."

"That's the construction biz," Tommy said, shrugging. "Sometimes you end up in the penthouse, sometimes you end up part of the foundation."

Chapter 16

"I wasn't expecting you until evening," Carlyle said. "Is something the matter?"

"Maybe I just needed a drink," Erin said. She'd left Vic at the Eightball to work on Emerald Isle's records, and brought Rolf back to the Barley Corner. The early supper crowd hadn't had time to get drunk after work, so the atmosphere was calmer than it would be later.

"On duty?" Carlyle replied, raising an eyebrow. "You can get Diet Coke out of the machines at your station house."

"Okay, what if I wanted to see you?"

"I'm flattered, but skeptical."

She smiled and kissed him on the cheek. "You're also, what's that phrase you use, 'too bloody clever by half,' you know that?"

"Guilty as charged, darling. So what does bring you here before five o'clock on a work day?"

"I need to talk to Corky. It's about the Teamsters."

"You're in luck," Carlyle said. "He just came through the door a few minutes ago, with a fine colleen on his arm."

"He what?" Erin exclaimed. "But what about—"

She caught herself before blurting out Teresa's name. Carlyle shrugged.

"You'd have to ask him," he said. "The lad's in the third booth by the window."

"I'll do that," she said grimly. She turned on her heel and stalked toward the booth in question, Rolf pacing beside her. The Shepherd, sensing the sudden shift in her mood, became tense and alert. His hackles bristled in expectation of sudden violence.

Corky's back was to her, so she saw his female companion first. The woman was a brunette with a model's build, tall and willowy. Her hair and clothes were stylish and, though the faint lines at the corners of her eyes hinted she was on the far side of forty, she retained a slender, striking beauty. She had truly remarkable blue eyes, so bright that Erin suspected colored contact lenses.

Those eyes slid from Corky to Erin, taking in the detective and the K-9. The woman blinked once.

"Can I help you?" she asked.

Corky turned to see who his companion was talking to. His own eyes lit up. "Erin!" he said. "Just the lass I was hoping to see!"

"I can't say I'm surprised," Erin said dryly. "You lasted longer than I thought you would."

"That's what all the lasses say," he replied cheerfully. "Never underestimate an Irishman's stamina, love. But you've a rare scowl on your face. Come, sit and have a drink with us. It'll cheer you up, I promise."

"Aren't you going to introduce me to your *friend*?" Erin said, laying harsh emphasis on the last word.

"Of course!" Corky said. "Erin, this is Penelope Vanderbeek. Penny, this is my dear friend Erin O'Reilly. Perhaps you've heard of her; she's been on the national news."

"Pleased to meet you," Penny said, offering a hand, which Erin shook. Penny was wearing several rings that all looked expensive.

"Likewise," Erin said. "And I'm sorry to pull your date away from you, but I need to borrow Corky for a few minutes."

"Date?" Penny repeated. She darted a sidelong look at Corky. Both burst out laughing.

"What's so funny?" Erin asked. She was more confused than angry, but the balance was rapidly shifting in favor of anger.

"Erin, love, Penny's married," Corky said.

"That makes her exactly your type, as I recall," Erin shot back in dangerous tones.

"I deserve that," he said, having the decency to lower his eyes for a moment. "But it's not why Penny's here. And Vanderbeek isn't the name she was born with. She was Penny Sizemore once upon a time. I've been scouring Atlantic City to find her, for your good I might add. It wasn't easy tracking her down, took me all day, but I've done it. I come back with her, tired and thirsty, and this is the thanks I get?"

"Penny Sizemore?" Erin said. "Penny the cocktail waitress?"

"Not for a few years," Penny said with a smile. "That's a young woman's racket. When I married Niles, I got out of it. Those short skirts, dark clubs, and flirty gamblers weren't really my scene anymore."

"Do you still want to drag me away from dear Penny's company?" Corky asked with a twinkle in his eye.

Erin sat down next to Corky, trapping him in the booth. "I'd like to talk to Ms. Vanderbeek first, if that's all right," she said.

"Of course," the other woman said. "But it's Penny, please."

"How did Corky convince you to come all the way up here?" Erin asked.

"He said it was important," Penny said. "That it was about Charlie."

"So you did know Charlie Majors?" Erin asked.

"Of course I did," Penny said, smiling at the memory. "Charlie was a sweet guy. He was kind of an idiot, but sweet. He was a dreamer. He had all these big plans, all these great things he was going to do one of these days."

"Were you romantically involved with him?"

"What do you think?" Penny answered. "We had a thing going for a while. It was never going to lead anywhere. I was one of his dreams, you see. He liked to come down to Atlantic City for long weekends. He'd tell his wife he was working a long-haul gig, then he'd play out this whole fantasy. He'd pretend he was this big-shot high-roller and we were having this grand, forbidden love affair."

Penny laughed quietly. "It was kid stuff, really," she said. "We were too old for it, but maybe that was part of the point. He was stuck in his dead-end truck-driving job, I was a thirty-year-old waitress, and we were going nowhere, except in our minds. It was an escape. But it was never anything more than that. He'd always go home to his wife every Monday."

"Did you know what happened to Charlie?" Erin asked gently.

Penny shook her head. "He just didn't turn up one Friday night," she said. "I thought he was coming, but he didn't show. I figured maybe he'd finally woken up and decided to get on with his life. I called him a few times, but he didn't answer. I left some messages, but when he never called back, I realized it was time to let him go. That's the thing about dreams. Sooner or later, you have to wake up from them. And I met Niles. He's not a dreamer; he's a doer. He knows what he wants and he goes for it."

"What does Niles do?" Erin asked.

"He's a hedge-fund manager," Penny said.

"That's rather like a gambler," Corky said. "Except they gamble with other lads' money instead of their own."

Penny laughed again. "You're right," she said. "But he's good at it. We've got a good life and I've got no regrets."

"When were you expecting to see Charlie?" Erin asked. "Do you remember the date?"

"June Tenth," Penny said. "I don't know why the date stuck in my head, but it did. Why?"

"Do you know why Charlie didn't make your rendezvous?"

Penny nodded, the smile dissolving on her lips. "Corky told me," she said. "Charlie's dead."

"I think he would've come to see you if he could," Erin said. "If that's any consolation."

"It's always nice to feel wanted," Penny said. "Just tell me one thing. Was what happened to him because of me? Because of us?"

"No," Erin said, quickly and firmly. "Absolutely not. The people who killed him also killed a couple of his associates. We think it was because of a business deal he was trying to make. You said Charlie was a dreamer. Did he ever talk about his dreams with you?"

"All the time," Penny said. "I always told him, the good thing about cloud castles is you don't have to pay property taxes on them."

"Can you remember the plans he was making right before he disappeared?"

"I think so, yes. This is a long time ago, so I may not have the details right, but he was going on about how he wanted to split off from the Teamsters and start an independent trucker's association. They'd be able to get around the Union on construction jobs. He had a friend in construction, who knew a guy in the city government up here. Together they'd know about all the good jobs that were coming in. They could get contracts before anyone else even knew they were up for bidding. It was all pretty complicated, and I couldn't really follow what he was saying, but Charlie loved talking about it."

"I can't imagine the Teamsters were happy when they heard about that," Erin said.

"They weren't supposed to hear about it," Penny said. "But I always thought it was just another of Charlie's big plans. There was this one plan he had, about smuggling watermelons. It was absolutely ridiculous, but he was sure it would work. And another time he was working this idea about getting Chinese imports across the Canada border to avoid customs duties. I think that was probably illegal, but if all you do is talk about it, you're not breaking the law, right?"

"That's right," Erin said. "So Corky tracked you down? How'd he manage that?"

"I know people, love," Corky said. "I managed to find Penny's former employer. From him, I learned she'd quit her job some years ago. He didn't know why. But he did know a lass who'd been friendly with Penny on the job. Ellie Gillian was her name. But Ellie didn't work for him anymore, either. I found Ellie in an unfortunate situation."

"Ellie was an old friend of mine," Penny said. "She learned she could make a lot more as an escort than as a waitress."

"Through her, ah, employer, I was able to pin Ellie down," Corky continued, enjoying the story. "I discovered her in the throes of passion with a gentleman. Despite the awkwardness of the moment, she was willing to tell me about her dear friend Penelope. More importantly, she knew Penny's married name. After that, it was child's play to find her."

"Corky?" Erin said. "Did you really barge in on a call girl while she was turning a trick?"

He shrugged. "It's nothing I've not seen before. Both she and her client were eager to be rid of me, as you can imagine, so they were quite forthcoming with information."

"You've got absolutely no shame, you know that?"

He grinned. "When it's a choice between shame and results, which would you rather?"

"And you agreed to come up to New York with this guy?" Erin asked Penny.

"Like I said, he told me it was important," Penny said. "I liked Charlie. It's a damn shame what happened to him, and I'd like to help sort things out if I can. It's hard being the mistress in this situation. I can't exactly go to his widow and offer my condolences, can I?"

"I can't see that going well, no," Erin said, thinking of Bonnie Majors. Charlie's widow would probably take a frying pan to this stylish, classy woman.

"I hope I've been helpful," Penny said.

"You have," Erin said. "If you think of anything else, here's my card. You can reach me at this number any time."

"Niles is traveling," Penny said, taking the card and stowing it in her purse. "He won't be home for a week, so he won't miss me. We've got no children, and my neighbor's son is taking care of the cats. I'll be in town for a few days. Corky's promised to show me the city."

"Make sure that's all he shows you," Erin said, giving Corky a hard stare. "You're married and he's spoken for."

"Erin!" Corky protested. "I'll have you know I've been a perfect gentleman thus far, and I plan to be on my very best behavior."

"That's what I'm worried about," she said. But she winked as she said it, softening her words a little. Maybe, just maybe, Corky really had turned over a new leaf. But she still wouldn't completely trust any woman alone with James Corcoran, particularly a pretty one.

"Now, what is it you wanted to talk to me about?" Corky asked.

"Kyle Finnegan and what happened in Detroit," she said.

"If you'll kindly excuse us, love?" Corky said to Penny. "I'll be back in two shakes."

Erin took Corky into Carlyle's back room, the one with the card table. Corky slid easily into one of the chairs. Erin took a seat across from him.

"Sorry about earlier," she said. "When you're a cop, you learn to assume the worst of people."

"Think nothing of it, love," Corky said. He began toying with a stack of poker chips, flipping them into the air and catching them in one hand, three at a time. "People have been assuming the worst of me for the past forty years and more. I'm used to it."

"Thanks. For finding Penny."

"My pleasure. I'd not been down to Atlantic City for some time. I try to get there every year or so, to remind myself what a dreary, depressing place it is. It makes me happier to be where I am. Though I'll confess I'm finding New York rather bleak these days, come to that."

Erin peered closely at him, remembering the way he'd looked when he'd come back to the big city, sporting a deep suntan. "You wouldn't be thinking of a warmer, sunnier place, would you?"

"I would, now you mention it." Corky smiled sheepishly. "I thought I missed my life here, when I was there. But I ought to have known better. Terry told me."

"What did she tell you?"

"She said this life was no good for me," he said. "She was afraid I'd fall back into my old habits. Terry's the only woman I've ever known who's believed the best of me. I'd hate to disappoint her."

"You're doing well," Erin said. "I mean, you're still drinking like a fish and hanging out with dangerous people. I'll bet you risk your life about twice a week, and I'm sure you're committing petty crimes all over the place, which I don't want to know about. But Penny's the first pretty woman I've seen you hanging out with since you got back, and you tell me there's nothing going on there."

"There isn't!" he insisted. "Word of God, Erin, I've not taken a lass to bed since I came back from Mexico."

"So that's where you were?" Erin said. She hadn't known for sure; he'd been careful not to tell anyone where he'd taken Teresa.

Corky cursed. "Bloody coppers," he muttered. "You can't have a civil bloody conversation with them without giving the game away."

"It's fine," she said quickly. "You know she's in no danger from me, and Mexico's a big damn country. But don't let that slip to anyone else. Not even Carlyle."

He nodded. "I'm dreadfully sorry," he said. "And you're right. It'll not happen again. Now what did you want to know about Finnegan?"

"I know how he got that dent in his head," she said. "And I know who gave it to him. But I don't know who was behind the attack on him. Who did he go to Detroit to talk to? Was it the president of the Teamsters?"

"Lord love you, no," Corky said. "He'd never dirty his hands meeting with a lad like Finnegan. You do know the head of the Union is Jimmy Hoffa's son, don't you?"

"Really?" Erin said.

"Oh aye," Corky said. "The lad's quite popular. But so far as I know, he'd nothing to do with this business. No, Finnegan was supposed to meet with a scunner called Courtney. Leroy Courtney. Back then he was just a convention delegate, but a lad with a great deal of pull. Now he's a vice president."

"So he takes over if Hoffa dies?"

Corky laughed. "There's twenty-two vice presidents in the Union, love," he said. "Nay, he's simply a regional leader. Though it might be worth mentioning, his region includes the great island of Manhattan. He made the move from Detroit a few years back. The lad lives in Midtown these days, in quite a grand apartment."

"That is interesting," Erin said. "So Finnegan was supposed to talk to Courtney?"

"Aye. He was trying to hammer out some sort of arrangement. We'd been having a spot of trouble with the Teamsters."

"I know," she said. "I just talked to Tommy O'Malley about that."

"And he was willing to talk to you?" Corky was surprised. "I'd have thought he'd be carrying a bit of a grudge."

"Because my squad got him thrown in jail?"

"That sort of thing does upset some lads, aye."

"I convinced him he'd be helping Evan and improving his chances for early release."

"You appealed to his greed and personal well-being, in other words. That could well turn the trick."

"So what went wrong in Detroit?"

Corky shrugged. "Difficult to say," he said. "Finnegan took one other lad with him, Dan Collins. But neither of them was in any position to explain what happened. Finnegan had his head caved in, as you know, and poor Dan was in an even worse way."

"I'd thought Finnegan was alone," Erin said. "I've been hearing hints of this other guy, but nothing definite."

"It makes no real difference," Corky said. "Poor Dan vanished without a trace. I knew his da; he was a fine lad. Good dancer, grand tenor voice, absolutely reliable. He'd have gone places, had he lived. But that's the Life."

"Was Leroy Courtney behind the Teamsters when they tried to undercut the O'Malleys?" Erin asked. "Or was he just a gatekeeper or negotiator?"

"I don't know," Corky said. "I'm not certain anyone does."

"Whoever it was," Erin said, "they apparently had Dan Collins killed along with Charlie Majors, Garth Engstrom, and Tracy Chadwick. When did Courtney get the VP job in New York?"

"A short while after the unpleasantness," Corky said. "I agree, the timing's a mite suspicious."

"I need to talk to Courtney," she said.

"Take care when you do," he said. "This lad's possessed of an unlovely reputation. I get on well with most of the Teamsters, but not him."

"How come you didn't go to Detroit instead of Finnegan?" Erin asked. "You're a better public-relations guy than he is."

"If it'd been an amiable negotiation, Evan would've sent me, no doubt," Corky said. "But these lads were being obstreperous. Evan doesn't think I'm the best lad when things turn nasty."

"I wouldn't know," Erin said. "I've never seen you in a serious fight." But she had seen him hold a live explosive device, powerful enough to take out a building, in bleeding hands. He'd been scared and hurt, but he hadn't flinched, hadn't twitched a muscle. Corky had speed, skill, and guts to spare. Erin privately thought she could do a lot worse than him for backup if the knives came out.

"I'm more of a people person, you ken," Corky said with a smile. "And I value that reputation. There's plenty of rough lads in the Life if you need leg-breakers, but not many like me for smoothing troubled waters. I'm the reason the O'Malleys get on so well with the Teamsters now."

"You are?"

"Aye," he said. "I'm the one made the peace after Finnegan's troubles. We hashed out an agreement. Nobody got everything they wanted, so I suppose it was a fair compromise. We made a new contract with them for Emerald Isle's business and they resumed their trade with our other interests. It made me something of a gangland statesman, and put me in Evan's good graces."

"I'm glad to hear it," Erin said. "How can I get in touch with Courtney?"

"I know a lad," Corky said, as she'd known he would. "I'll set up a meeting. Just remember, the lad's a snake. Keep your eyes on him and don't trust him one bloody inch."

Chapter 17

"Finnegan's dangerous."

Erin said it into the dark of the bedroom, talking to a man she couldn't see.

"He's that, aye," Carlyle replied. "You did know he was a gangster, didn't you?"

"Well, yeah," she said. "But I always thought..."

"You thought he was a funny, harmless lad, a bit touched in the head?"

"Something like that. Then I watched him fight three guys at once, all of them bigger than he was, and it wasn't even a fight! It was more like watching one of those nature programs. You know, the ones with hyenas eating zebras alive. He chewed those bastards up, and I mean that literally! I've fought dozens of criminals, but I've never seen somebody fight that way."

"He frightened you?"

She didn't want to admit it. "Yeah," she finally said. "A little. Not the way Mickey Connor did. Mickey was a son of a bitch, but he was *human*. I understood him. Finnegan's different."

"No fear, darling. He'll be off the street soon enough."

"I know. We're counting the days now. It's going to be strange, once this is all over. I won't know how to act anymore."

"Of course you will," he said. "You're what you've always been, a copper. And a damned fine one. It's me will have to make adjustments."

"Who knows?" she said, rolling over and putting an arm around him. "You might like being respectable."

"I rather think I will," Carlyle said.

"I think even Corky likes the idea," she said. "You know he brought a woman, a good-looking one, into the Corner for dinner and didn't even try to get her in bed?"

"I knew we'd had snow," Carlyle replied. "But I'd no idea it was that bad. Hell's frozen over, has it?"

Erin laughed quietly. "You've known him a lot longer than I have. Has he ever been like this about a girl before?"

"Not to my knowledge," he said. "Perhaps you've appealed to his better nature."

"I don't think it was me," she said.

"Miss Tommasino must be a truly remarkable lass," Carlyle said. "And it must hurt Corky terribly to be parted from her."

"It's temporary," she said. "Only until she testifies and we shut the O'Malleys down. After that, they can go wherever they want—together."

"Have you thought it might be better to let this business with the Teamsters be?" he said. "Until after we've concluded our affairs, that is."

"I don't know if I can," she said. "Finnegan's hot on the trail. He stirred up the Black Bull guys on purpose. Maybe he wanted to shake something loose, or maybe he just thought it'd be fun. Either way, they know I'm onto them. Worse, they know Finnegan is, and he doesn't give a damn about due process. If I don't get this wrapped up fast, somebody else is going to get killed."

"That's an excellent point," Carlyle sighed. "The road's laid out in front of us, darling. All we need to do is walk it."

"Corky promised to get me together with Courtney, the Teamsters guy. Do you know anything about him?"

"Nay, Corky's the one to talk to on that count. I'm just a publican, a gambler, and a money-launderer."

She swatted his shoulder. "Knock it off. You're just going to be a pub owner soon. We'll bury all this crap in the past, where it belongs."

"And hope nobody comes along and cracks open the tomb," he said.

They lay in silence for a few moments. Erin laid her hand on his chest, feeling his slow, steady heartbeat through her fingertips.

"I'd been wondering whether Finnegan really was crazy," she said at last. "I'd thought maybe it was an act, to keep people off balance."

"If it is, he ought to be treading the boards on Broadway," Carlyle said.

"No, he's crazy all right," she said. "But he's more complicated than that. I think he *knows* he's crazy. And he likes it. It's something he can use to throw everybody off. It gives him an edge. I think if somebody was able to cure him, and offered him the treatment, he'd turn it down."

"That's an interesting thought," Carlyle said.

"It's a scary one," she replied. "What sort of guy would want to be insane?"

"A madman?" Carlyle guessed.

"A guy who's so far out of control, he doesn't even want self-control," she said. "And he's smart. He's a lot smarter than I thought. Everything he says, everything he does, it's all got meaning to it. It's a pattern. If he wasn't crazy, he'd be a damn genius. Like I said, he's dangerous. I think he's one of the most dangerous men I've ever met."

"Then it's a good thing you're here to put him away," Carlyle said.

"Yeah," Erin said.

But later, as she tried to get to sleep, the thought crept into her head that she might not be able to stop Kyle Finnegan. What if he was smart enough to anticipate her reactions, her own thoughts and plans? What if he'd taken them into account? He'd manipulated her and Vic into leading him to Sam's Roadhouse.

Nobody was that smart, she told herself.

But how could she be sure?

* * *

Finnegan was gone by the time Erin got to the Eightball the next morning. Walsh, the O'Malley attorney, had come and taken him away. The lawyer had timed his visit well; none of the Major Crimes detectives had gotten to the office yet, and the desk sergeant had been a substitute. Brendan Malcolm, an old friend of Erin's dad, had been called away by a family emergency. Malcolm knew all sorts of useful delaying tactics, and would have at least gotten Webb on the phone before letting Walsh prance out with the prisoner. But the newly-minted sergeant who'd sat in for him, stripes still bright and fresh on his sleeve, wasn't wise to the tricks of the trade. Walsh had flummoxed him with legalese, befuddled him with jargon, and now Finnegan was back on the street, presumably looking for more truckers to chew on.

Erin didn't bother getting mad at the sergeant. It wouldn't do any good, and if word got back to Evan O'Malley it would make her look bad. So she went upstairs and straight to work.

Maybe her squad could get to the perps before the mad Irishman did.

When Webb arrived, Erin told him about Finnegan's release. Webb sighed and shook his head.

"Lawyers," he muttered. "Wouldn't it be nice if they gave us radio tags, like game wardens have? Then we could clip one to his ear and we'd at least know where he was."

"He might just cut his own ear off," Erin said.

"Like Vincent van Gogh?" Webb replied. "You're probably right. Where are we with this mess?"

Erin laid out what she'd learned from Tommy O'Malley, Penny Vanderbeek, and Corky. Webb listened carefully, nodding.

"Good work," he said when she finished. "I wish I had better news from my end, but Lombardo had nothing to say. He was polite enough, but I would've had more luck squeezing a block of concrete. Speaking of concrete, as soon as Neshenko arrives, I'm sending the two of you to BK Construction. Piekarski uncovered some more financial irregularities. Judge Ferris signed the warrant late last night."

"What're we looking for?" Erin asked.

"Evidence of criminal activity," Webb said. "What'd they teach you at the Academy?"

"I've done a lot of stuff they never taught at the Academy," she said.

"Isn't that the truth," Webb said.

The sound of angry voices echoed in the stairwell; one male, one female. Erin recognized the man's voice, and the woman's was familiar enough that she wasn't surprised to see Vic and Piekarski come up the stairs a moment later.

"—do you ever clean it?" Piekarski was saying.

"Yeah!" Vic protested. "I cleaned it a while ago."

"Things are *growing* in there!"

"It's not so bad."

"Yeah, compared to third-world hospitals, meth labs, and autopsy rooms! Oh, wait; autopsy rooms are sanitary!"

Webb cleared his throat. "Excuse me," he said. "Am I interrupting something?"

"Not a thing," Vic said. He shot Erin a look that said he'd told her this sort of thing would happen. Erin replied with a don't-look-at-me shrug.

"I've got a warrant here," Webb said, brandishing the piece of paper. "In case you wanted to do some police work. Get over to BK Construction right away. I'll have a CSU team follow up. Get files, computers, flash drives; all the records you can find. Start sifting data. We're looking for money from Black Bull, or from anyone else affiliated with the Detroit Teamsters. I want names and dates."

"What's this got to do with our dead guys?" Vic asked.

"BK did the initial work on the parking lot," Webb said. "Either somebody put one over on them, or they dumped the bodies themselves. And if they did, they're murderers and conspirators."

"We're on it, sir," Erin said, reaching for the warrant.

Webb didn't let go of it. "Now that I think about it, we should all go," he said. "There's no reason for me to hang around here, and Piekarski can start looking at the files as soon as we have them."

"All right!" Piekarski said, her scowl disappearing. The prospect of field work, however tedious, energized her. "I'll ride with Vic."

"You'll ride with O'Reilly," Webb corrected her. "I'll ride shotgun with Neshenko. It'll give you two a chance to cool off."

* * *

"Cool off!" Piekarski huffed. "Like it was my fault in the first place!"

"What happened?" Erin asked, steering the Charger on a too-familiar course toward Brooklyn. Rolf poked his head through the hatch between the seats to see where they were going. Unlike Erin, he was excited at the prospect of another long car ride.

"It's what didn't happen that's bugging me," Piekarski said. "Do you know he doesn't clean his toilet? Like, at all? I've been in public restrooms in tenements that were cleaner!"

"So, you stayed over with Vic?" Erin asked, dodging the subject of bathroom hygiene.

"I'm sort of living there," Piekarski said. "We're trying it out to see if it works. For the kid's sake."

"What do you mean?"

"We think it'll be better if both of us are around. More stable, you know? It's not like we're going to be some sort of apple pie, all-American bullshit family or anything. But Vic's got this idea if it's a boy, his dad ought to hang around. And he's right, damn it. But Vic's such a bachelor! He's never lived with a girl, you know that?"

"I didn't," Erin said. "But it doesn't surprise me."

"Vic's sort of like fentanyl," Piekarski said.

"You're going to need to explain that," Erin said.

"In small doses, he can be fantastic," Piekarski said. "But it's really easy to overdose on him."

Erin laughed. "Yeah, I can see that. But he's a solid guy. He's really a sweetie if you dig down deep enough."

"I know," Piekarski said. "But that studio apartment isn't going to work. It's not even big enough for the two of us. Add number three and we'd all go crazy, the kid included. But you know what apartment-hunting is like in New York. Could you keep your eyes open and let me know if you find anything? A two-bedroom would be great, but we can manage with one. It's just got to have more than one room, so we can get away from each other. If we don't, you're going to get another homicide case one of these days."

"Which one of you is going to kill the other?" Erin asked.

"Flip a coin," Piekarski replied. "Thank God I'm getting out of the office. Maybe if we're lucky somebody will start a fight. Beating up some construction guys would make me feel a lot better."

"I thought your doctor said you should take it easy."

"He also said I should watch my blood pressure, and Vic's sending it through the roof. I love him, but... argh!"

* * *

BK Construction was a brick one-story building next to a fenced-in lot packed with earth-moving machines. Erin saw bulldozers, dump trucks, front-end loaders, road graders, and steamrollers. Little Bobcat construction vehicles were lined up in front, as if they were the bigger machines' kids. A backhoe's arm craned above, reminding her of the neck of a dinosaur. No wonder little boys loved dinos and construction equipment; there was an odd similarity. All the machines were coated with a layer of bright white snow.

Vic brought his Taurus alongside Erin's Charger. The four cops, plus one K-9, lined up and took a moment to look the building over.

"I hate crooked construction guys," Vic said. "I ever tell you about the undercover guy I knew who was busting up the rackets?"

"Yeah," Erin said. "When we were digging up that foundation with that woman buried under it."

"Oh, right," he said. "You know what he told me? He said the rackets raised the average cost of a Manhattan building by twenty percent. You believe that? It's like the whole city's paying a criminal tax. Bastards. No wonder they get on so well with the City Council."

"No kidding," Erin said.

"Are these guys gonna give us any trouble?" Vic wondered aloud. He cracked his knuckles expectantly. "I hope they give us trouble."

"I doubt it," Webb said. "But if they do, that's why we brought you."

The front door was unlocked, which made sense; it was a little past nine in the morning, normal business hours. But the lobby was deserted. Nobody was sitting at the counter. The cheap-looking table and chairs were empty, except for a few well-thumbed back issues of magazines like *Esquire* and *Harley-Davidson*.

"Huh," Vic said, disappointed. "I guess nobody's home."

"Nonsense," Webb said. "They're open. Somebody's here. They're probably in back. Hello!"

His call received no response.

"NYPD!" Vic called, his voice carrying much better than Webb's. "Get up here. We want to talk to you!"

The hairs on the back of Erin's neck were standing up, an evolutionary legacy of the days when humans had raised their hackles. "Something's weird here," she said quietly. Without fully realizing she was doing it, she pushed back the flap of her jacket to clear her holster.

"You're right," Piekarski murmured. "I've got the heebie-jeebies."

No experienced street cop ignored the warnings whispered by their subconscious. Intuition was how you stayed alive. When that little voice talked danger, you listened. Even Webb, burned-out old gumshoe that he was, knew the feeling. Without further discussion, the four cops spread out, drawing their guns, the weapons angled toward the ceiling. Rolf, picking up on the sudden change in mood, became alert and attentive. He stayed within inches of Erin, staring up at her, ears perked for instructions.

"Anybody here?" Webb shouted.

Silence answered him.

"I saw a car and a pickup in the lot," Vic said. "Either they hoofed it, or they're still here somewhere. They just don't want to answer."

"Or they can't," Erin said. Her throat was suddenly dry. She felt the familiar hot rush of adrenaline. She stepped to the counter and looked behind it. An office swivel-chair stood unoccupied. A cell phone lay on the counter, unattended.

"Let's secure the building," Webb said. "O'Reilly, you take lead with your K-9. Neshenko, you're next. Then Piekarski. I'll take rear."

That wasn't cowardice on Webb's part. He knew perfectly well that Erin and Vic were best suited to go first. Vic was a former ESU door-kicker and Erin had Rolf with his nose and teeth. Piekarski was in the safest spot; if anyone attacked from behind, Webb would cover their collective asses.

Only one door led from the lobby into the interior of the building. Erin tried the handle and found it unlocked. She went in quickly, clearing the bottleneck in the doorway, and found herself in a hallway. Doors branched off to either side. She and Vic split left and right, trying knobs.

The first two were locked. Nobody answered their knocks and calls. The second door on the left led to a break room. A water cooler stood against the wall next to a soda machine. The room was decorated with posters of pinup girls. A table held the most recent *Sports Illustrated* swimsuit edition, open to a particularly curvaceous photograph. Next to the magazine lay a Coke can on its side. A pool of brown liquid had soaked into the pages of the magazine.

"Somebody was sitting here," Erin said. "Looks like something startled him."

"Spilling pop on the swimsuit edition," Vic said, looking over her shoulder. "That's just not right. It's sacrilege or something."

It was a sign of how spooked Piekarski was that she didn't elbow him or make a sharp remark. "Where is the guy, then?" she asked, her voice pitched slightly higher than usual.

"We'll find out," Erin said. She holstered her gun, pulled on one of her gloves, picked up the can, and held it in front of her dog's snout. "Rolf! *Such!*"

Most humans saw the world primarily through their eyes; dogs used their noses the same way. Every animal had a scent unique not only to its species, but to the individual. When animals experienced intense emotions like fear, anger, or lust, their glands gave off stronger scents than usual. If Rolf could have explained, he would have told his partner the can was soaked with pheromones indicative of fear and anger. The can practically glowed with emotional odors, which etched their specific signature into the dog's olfactory receptors. The path his target had taken out of the room was fresh. It could not have been clearer.

Rolf snuffled eagerly and pulled. The detectives followed hard on his heels, the K-9 leading the way down the hall to the metal door at the far end. He scratched at it and whined, just in case his partner couldn't tell where he was going. He loved Erin and trusted her completely, but humans were awfully dense sometimes. It was almost like they couldn't track a scent themselves. Fortunately, he was there to follow the smell, like the good boy he was.

Erin nodded toward the door. "Ready?" she asked.

"Ready," Vic said. His Sig-Sauer, held in both hands, was trained on the door.

"Ready," Piekarski said in a small, tight voice.

"Go," Webb said.

Erin grabbed the handle, twisted it down, and shoved the door open. She yanked out her Glock and went left. Vic went right, gun ready.

"NYPD!" Vic shouted. "Show me your hands!"

The cops poured into a big, concrete-floored room full of tools and machinery. Bright fluorescent lights gave a cold, wintry radiance to the space. Erin's nostrils filled with the smells of metal and motor oil.

Rolf tugged toward the side of the room, where the wall was lined with metal cabinets and racks of tools. Erin saw a workbench with something on top of it. The shape was lumpy and odd, but somehow disquieting.

The thing on the bench moved slightly.

"Oh, Jesus," Erin murmured. Then, louder, "Over here!"

She ran toward the bench, Rolf forging ahead of her. The Shepherd barked twice, indicating he'd found his quarry.

Erin stopped a few steps short of the bench. Nausea swelled up in her like an incoming tide, threatening to spill out over her teeth. She didn't fully understand what she was looking at. From the waist up, it was definitely a man, but something was so wrong with the legs that she couldn't figure out what had happened. There was blood, though not as much as at many crime scenes. It was the shape that was off.

Webb and Piekarski hurried up behind her. Vic was clearing the rest of the room, scanning for threats, covering his comrades. The Lieutenant moved to Erin's side.

"What've we got, O'Reilly?" he asked. Then, more quietly, "Oh my."

Piekarski took one look, made a liquid sound of dismay, turned aside, and threw up on the floor.

Erin recovered somewhat. Looping Rolf's leash around her wrist, she snatched out her phone and called Dispatch.

"This is O'Reilly, shield four-six-four-oh," she rattled off. "I need a bus to BK Construction forthwith. Got one civilian, both legs badly broken, in shock."

"Copy that, O'Reilly," Dispatch replied. "Bus is en route. ETA ten minutes."

The man on the bench moaned softly. He tried to curl in on himself, but his wrists were tied to the bench, forcing his arms wide. His ankles were also tied to the opposite legs of the bench, but his legs weren't capable of movement regardless.

"You're going to be fine," Webb said to the man. "It's okay. We're the police. An ambulance is on the way. We'll get you to a doctor."

The man whispered something.

Webb bent closer. "What's that?" he asked. "'Me?' What about you?"

"Mia..." the man said. His lips were trembling.

"Mia," Webb repeated. "Who's that? Your wife?"

The wounded man shook his head feebly. He was shivering from shock. "Mia... here..."

"Someone else is here?" Webb asked sharply. "A woman?"

"Help..." the man whispered.

Piekarski ran a hand across the back of her mouth. She had herself back under control now, cheeks flushed with embarrassment. She holstered her sidearm, took a quick look around, and ran to a white box with a red cross on it. She popped the box open and grabbed the first-aid kit that was inside, rushing back to assist Webb.

Erin turned her attention outward. "Vic!" she called. "We think there's another civvie in here! A woman!"

"Copy that," Vic said. "We know her name?"

"Mia," Erin said.

"Mia!" Vic yelled. "Can you hear us?"

"We're cops!" Erin called. "You're safe! Come out!"

There was no answer.

"Rolf, *such!*" Erin said once more. This would be trickier for the dog; she didn't have a scent to put him on. She had no way of knowing whether he'd follow the correct trail.

Rolf cast about, nostrils twitching. This room was full of fascinating smells. He smelled sweat, fresh blood, and all the strange mechanical odors of humans and their big metal toys. He discounted the artificial smells; the "search" command always meant he was looking for a human. But lots of humans had been here. Their scent trails crisscrossed the room; some fresh, some old and faded. Which one did Erin want him to follow?

He decided to ignore the freshest, bloodiest one. That was the one he'd already successfully followed. That player was out of the game. His partner probably wanted another fresh smell, one that stank of fear, excitement, and blood. Those were the easiest to follow. He found such a trail. It was worth pursuing. If he located this second person, maybe Erin would remember to give him his rubber Kong ball. She'd forgotten the first time. Humans really had no sense of what was important.

Rolf set off on his new trail. Erin's heart sank. He was leading her back toward the workbench.

"Not that one," she told Rolf. "You already found him."

Rolf veered abruptly back the way they'd come, toward the entrance to the room.

Erin thought maybe he was confused. Was he tracing back along the path taken by that poor guy with the broken legs? She considered bringing Rolf up short, correcting him and resetting him on a new course. But she'd learned to trust her K-9. She gave him his head and let him run.

Rolf scratched at the metal door, which Erin pulled open. The dog slithered through the gap and went immediately to the first door on his left. He scratched at it and whined.

Erin tried the door. It was locked.

"Anyone in there?" she shouted. "This is the NYPD! Open up!"

Silence met her call.

Rolf scrabbled at the door again, insistent.

"Mia?" Erin tried. "Are you in there? Are you okay?"

After a moment a faint, desperate voice, interrupted by hiccupping sobs, was audible.

"Is he gone?"

Chapter 18

"You're safe, Mia," Erin said. "I'm a police detective. We've got cops all over the building. Nobody can hurt you."

"What about Howie?" Mia asked.

Erin guessed Howie was probably the guy in the back room. "We're taking care of him," she said. "Are you alone in there?"

"Yes." More sobs.

"Okay. I need you to unlock the door for me. Do it slowly and carefully."

There was a short pause. Then the bolt clicked open. Erin heard sirens approaching; one sounded like a squad car, the other an ambulance. That was good news. They could use all the extra hands they could get.

The door swung open a couple of inches to show a red-rimmed blue eye and a tear-stained cheek.

"Mia?" Erin said. "My name's Erin O'Reilly. Are you hurt?"

"No," Mia said. "Well, a little. I think... I think I'm okay." Her eye caught movement at Erin's side and widened at the sight of Rolf.

"It's okay," Erin said. "He's a trained police dog. He won't hurt you. He helped me find you. Take a step back, please."

Mia retreated. Erin pushed the door the rest of the way open and tucked her Glock back into its holster. Mia was a small, slight brunette who looked to be in her early twenties. Her eyes were very large, made even bigger by fear. She had pale skin, covered by a blue silk blouse and dark gray slacks. An angry red mark stood out sharply on the flesh of her right cheek.

"Rolf, *platz*," Erin said.

Rolf settled to his belly and awaited further orders. He was wondering whether he ought to remind Erin, but there was no need. She took his Kong ball out of her jacket pocket and dropped it in front of his snout. He grabbed it eagerly and started making wet squeaky sounds of delight, his tail sweeping back and forth.

Erin was gratified to see the faintest hint of a smile at the corner of Mia's mouth when she saw Rolf chomping on his favorite toy. "What happened, Mia?" she asked.

"A man came in," Mia said. She clutched her own elbows and shivered. "He asked me who was in charge. I told him Howie was. He told me to get Howie. I told the guy to wait while I called him. But when I picked up the phone he... he grabbed me."

Mia rubbed her wrist, presumably where she'd been grabbed.

"Then what?" Erin asked.

"He told me to take him to Howie. I tried to twist free, but he grabbed my face with his other hand and said he'd..."

"What did he say?" Erin asked gently.

"He said he'd peel my face off," Mia whispered, hiccupping again. "Right off my skull. He didn't... he didn't sound angry, or excited, or anything. He just... said it."

Erin nodded, her jaw tightening. She had a pretty good idea who'd attacked Mia and a cold fury was slowly building inside her.

"I was scared," Mia whispered. "He had me unlock the door and he went behind me, holding the back of my blouse. By the collar. I knew Howie was in the break room. He always has a Coke there in the morning when he clocks in."

"What's Howie's full name?" Erin asked.

"Howard Manterville," Mia said.

The door to the lobby swung open and banged against the wall, revealing a pair of uniformed cops. Mia flinched and retreated further into the room. Erin, giving the officers a quick glance, unclipped her shield and held it toward them.

"Where's the injured guy?" one of the officers asked.

"In back," Erin said, cocking her head. "We've got three more detectives there. The area should be secured."

"Copy that," the uniform said. The officers hurried past, followed closely by two paramedics pushing a stretcher.

Mia shuddered and drew in on herself. "Howie's dead, isn't he," she murmured.

"No," Erin said firmly. "He's hurt, but he's getting help. What's your last name, Mia?"

"Kozlowski," Mia said. "I... I can spell that if you need me to."

"Not right now," Erin said. "Keep going with what you were telling me."

"I went to the break room," Mia said. "I didn't want to. I didn't want him to do anything to Howie. Howie's always been nice to me, ever since I started here. But I was scared. I thought if I did what he told me, maybe everything would be okay. I know it was stupid, but I hoped maybe... it was some kind of joke."

"Was Howie in the room?"

Mia nodded. "He was sitting there, reading a magazine and drinking his Coke. When he saw us, the other man gave me a shove. I… I fell forward and Howie stood up to catch me. When he did, the other man came in close and hit him."

"With his fist?"

Mia shook her head. "With a stapler."

"I'm sorry, what?" Erin said.

"A stapler," Mia repeated. "He must have gotten it off my desk. He had it open, in his hand, and he slapped it against Howie's face. I… I saw the staple… in there. It stuck. Howie screamed. So did I. Then *he* put a hand on my shoulder and said if I wasn't quiet, he'd make me scream until I coughed up blood. He said he didn't want to hurt me and I shouldn't make him.

"Howie was trying to get up and fight him, but he hit Howie two or three more times with the stapler; once in the face, then a couple times in the arm when he tried to block it. Then he dropped the stapler and grabbed Howie by the throat. He squeezed a little and said he'd… rip it out. Then he told me to come with him."

"So you did?" Erin asked.

"I didn't know what else to do," Mia said miserably. "I thought he'd hurt Howie if I didn't do what he said. We went into the shop. The other man got some rope and… and he made me…"

"He made you tie Howie to the bench?" Erin guessed.

Mia nodded again. "He said he had some questions and he expected the truth. He said something weird in some other language. The last word sounded like *veritas*, I think."

"*In vino veritas?*" Erin asked. She didn't know much Latin, but she knew that phrase. Carlyle, as a pub owner, was fond of it. "In wine is truth?"

"Sort of like that, but not quite," Mia said. "He didn't say *vino*. He said something like 'dollar.' Maybe he was offering Howie money. But then he started looking at the tools on the racks. He picked one up and… and he was *whistling*."

"What did he pick up?" Erin asked.

"A hand jackhammer," Mia said. "He hooked it up to the air compressor and he kept on whistling some kid's tune. I think it was the one that goes, 'I've been working on the railroad.' Howie was trying to talk, saying he'd tell him whatever he wanted to know. Then the other man..."

Mia trailed off into silence. She started crying again.

"Mia," Erin said gently. "I need to hear this. Please. It's important."

"He put the jackhammer on Howie's foot," Mia whispered. "And turned it on."

Erin flinched slightly. She steeled herself not to show the horror that was trying to break through her calm façade.

"Howie screamed," Mia murmured. "He screamed and screamed and... I ran. I ran and I hid. I don't know if the man even noticed. I have the keys to the building, so I went through the first door I could find and I locked it. I should have called for help, I know I should, but my phone was at the front desk and this room doesn't have one and I was too scared to go back outside. So I just... I put my fingers in my ears and... and I waited."

"Mia, you didn't do anything wrong," Erin said. "You were trying to stay alive. And you succeeded. If you'd tried to do anything to this guy, he would've hurt you too. When did this happen?"

"Eight-thirty, maybe," Mia said. "It might have been a little earlier. I don't know."

"What time did he leave?"

"I don't know," Mia repeated. "I was trying not to listen. Howie... Howie just kept screaming. And then he couldn't scream anymore, and that was worse."

"Do you know where the other guy went?"

Mia shook her head. "I was hiding."

"You saw the man's face? When he first came in?"

Mia nodded.

"Would you recognize him if you saw him again?"

Mia shivered. "I don't want to see him ever again," she moaned.

Erin nodded. "I'm going to show you some pictures," she said. "In a little while. If one of them is the guy who attacked you and Howie, I'll need you to point him out."

But she already knew whose face it would be.

* * *

"There's truth in dollars?" Vic said. "What the hell does that mean?"

"Maybe he meant money talks," Erin guessed.

The detectives were watching the CSU team combing the BK building for clues. The unfortunate Howard Manterville was on his way to the hospital. Piekarski was taking Mia's statement, which Webb said would be good practice on her way to wearing a gold shield.

"I blame our school system," Webb said.

"Huh?" Vic said.

"They don't teach Latin anymore," Webb said. "Or German, apparently. The word 'dollar' isn't Latin. I'd think you might know the German at least, O'Reilly. In German it's 'thaler,' because there was a silver mine called Joachimsthal, or something like that, and the word got shortened and used for silver dollars that came from those mines."

Vic stared at his commanding officer. "Sir," he said in awestruck tones, "why would anyone ever know that?"

"It was in a book I read once," Webb said. "That's beside the point. My point is, the word 'dollar' wouldn't be in a Latin phrase. I think what our witness heard was 'dolor.'"

"That means pain," Erin said. "I feel like an idiot."

"Why?" Vic asked.

"Because I may not have learned Latin in school, but I've heard some of it in church," she said. "That word shows up in hymns."

"In pain is truth," Webb said. "That's a reasonable thing to say if you're about to torture information out of someone."

"There's nothing reasonable about taking a jackhammer to some poor bastard's legs," Vic said. "Those bones weren't broken, they were splintered. I hope your brother earns overtime, Erin, because he's gonna be working on that schmuck all day and all night. They won't be able to pin the things together. I doubt there's enough whole bone to fit a pin through. It'll be like the jigsaw puzzle from hell, a regular Humpty Dumpty situation."

"You're sure it was Kyle Finnegan?" Webb asked.

Erin nodded. She'd shown Finnegan's mugshot to Mia, but that had been nothing more than a formality.

"Then let's go get that son of a bitch," Vic said.

"We'll put out a BOLO," Webb said. "And assuming Mr. Manterville regains consciousness, his testimony plus that of Ms. Kozlowski should be plenty to put him behind bars for a good long while. He can't possibly claim self-defense this time. O'Reilly, you know this guy. What's going on in his head?"

"He knows BK Construction was behind our triple homicide," she said. "And he knows Black Bull is connected. He's chewing his way up the food chain."

"I wish you wouldn't put it that way," Vic muttered. "I can still see him chowing down on that trucker's face."

"He's being reckless," Erin went on, "but not completely. He could've hurt Mia, too, but he didn't."

"He held her hostage and threatened to mutilate her," Vic said.

"But he didn't actually hurt her," she replied. "By his standards, that qualifies as self-control. He doesn't want to hurt the wrong people."

"And Manterville was the right people?" Webb asked.

"Apparently," Erin said. "But he didn't kill him either. He left two living witnesses."

"One of whom is never gonna walk again," Vic said. "You ever hear a jackhammer being operated? Those things are *loud*. If that girl could hear him screaming over that, you know how loud he must've been yelling? Why not finish the job while our guy was at it? Why not just plant the hammer over his sternum and pound it straight into his heart?"

"Because Howie talked," Erin said quietly. "Finnegan wanted information. He must've gotten what he came for. At that point Finnegan didn't have any further use for Howie, so he left him there and walked away."

"This guy's nuts," Vic said.

"I think we've established that, yes," Webb said dryly. "But what's he going to do next?"

"He's going to follow up on whatever Howie told him," Erin said.

"Which is what?" Webb asked.

Erin shrugged helplessly. "I don't know."

"And we can't ask him," Vic said. Manterville had slipped into deep shock even before the paramedics had gotten to him. He'd been unconscious when they'd loaded him into the ambulance. It would be hours before he came out of surgery, and even then he'd be coasting on so many narcotics that Erin wasn't sure he'd recognize his own mother. Any reliable testimony would have to wait a day or two, maybe longer.

"Do you think Ms. Kozlowski knows anything?" Webb asked.

"Maybe," Erin said doubtfully. "But she's only worked here about three years. She was in high school when those guys were murdered. And she doesn't strike me as the gangster type."

"You'd recognize that, wouldn't you," Vic said.

Erin gave him a dirty look. "And you wonder why people don't like you."

"No, I know why people don't like me," he said. "I just don't care. If the Kozlowski chick knows anything, Zofia will get it out of her."

"And if not, we'll have to hope we get something off the computers or the files," Webb said. "Which, let me remind you, are why we came here in the first place."

"That'll take time," Vic said gloomily. "Meanwhile that fruitcake is running around New York ripping pieces off people."

"If you have any bright ideas, this would be a good time to share them," Webb said sharply. "O'Reilly, can you try to get in touch with Finnegan?"

"I can work my contacts," she said. "Maybe someone can put a leash on him."

"Do it," Webb said. "He hasn't killed anyone so far, at least that we know of, but I don't expect that to continue."

"Copy that," Erin said. She stepped away and pulled out her phone. Then she hesitated. Carlyle would still be asleep. She hated waking him up, but there might be lives on the line. If anybody could stop Finnegan's rampage, it would be Evan O'Malley. And she didn't have Evan's direct line.

As she made her decision and aimed her finger at the screen, it lit up with an incoming call. She jumped and nearly dropped the phone. The number was unidentified, which meant either gangsters or solicitors.

"O'Reilly," she said cautiously into the phone.

"You sound unhappy," Corky's unmistakable voice said by way of greeting. "I've just the thing to cheer you up. I've talked to a lad I know and he's set up a meeting for you. Mr. Courtney will be expecting you for brunch. Villard on East 50th, ten-thirty."

Erin checked the time. "That's in half an hour," she said.

"Is that a problem, love?"

She did some quick calculations of driving times. "No, I can make it. But I need you to do something for me."

"You've but to name it."

"Talk to Evan."

"And what is it I'm to tell him?"

"Tell him Finnegan's going berserk. He's stirring up all kinds of trouble. He's got the NYPD after him, and maybe the Teamsters too. There's no way I can keep a lid on this thing by myself. Evan's got to get Finnegan under control right now, or I can't be responsible for what happens."

"I'll pass your news along," Corky said. "And you're in a hurry, clearly, so I'll not keep you. Ta, love."

Erin hung up and led Rolf back to Webb and Vic. "I've got to go," she said.

"Where?" Webb asked.

"Manhattan. Looks like I have a lunch date with the Teamsters' VP."

"Where?" Webb asked again.

"Villard. In Midtown."

"You need backup?" Vic asked hopefully. His stomach growled.

"It's just a conversation," Erin said. "I don't want to spook him."

"We have plenty to do here," Webb said. "You're staying, Neshenko. But be careful, O'Reilly."

"It's a Manhattan restaurant," she said, trying not to think of a murder she'd witnessed in an Italian restaurant on an otherwise peaceful Sunday. "What's going to happen?"

Chapter 19

Erin had left Rolf in the car, curled in a furry ball in his compartment with the Charger's heater draining the battery. When she saw the dining room at Villard, she was glad she'd left the dog behind. It was like stepping into a Nineteenth Century ballroom, or maybe a fancy church. The ceiling arched high overhead, decorated with a mural showing a quartet of young women in diaphanous robes. One end of the room even had a balcony with a balustrade, backed by bas-relief sculptures. Gold leaf was everywhere.

"Excuse me, ma'am," said an elegant, gray-haired maître d'. "Do you have a reservation?"

"I'm meeting someone," Erin said, feeling underdressed in her plain blouse, slacks, worn leather jacket, and comfortable shoes.

"And the other party's name?"

"Leroy Courtney."

The maître d's face lit up. "Ah, of course! And you would be Ms. O'Reilly?"

"That's right."

"This way, please."

He led her to the far corner of the room, in the angle of the balcony and a gigantic stained-glass window. Sitting at the table, flanked by a pair of guys built like football players, was the biggest man Erin had ever met.

The largest man she'd encountered prior to this moment had been Mickey Connor. Mickey had been a former heavyweight boxer, six and a half feet of physical danger; a brutal force of nature from his size sixteen shoes to his broken nose and empty, pale eyes. Mickey had affected Erin on a visceral level, tapping into a primal fear of male violence she supposed all women shared.

Leroy Courtney, when he got to his feet to greet her, was a couple inches taller than Mickey, just as wide in the shoulders, and slightly overweight. The hand he extended to her was scarred and callused, gold rings decorating every sausage-sized finger. Erin saw the muscles in that arm, but his smile was open, honest, and friendly. His eyes were warm and bright, sparkling in a way that reminded her of James Corcoran.

"Erin O'Reilly!" he exclaimed, his accent pure Midwest. "I've been wanting to meet you for a long time!"

"You have?" she blurted, taking the offered hand. It was warm and strong, engulfing her own slim fingers.

"Of course! You're quite the local celebrity."

"I'm just doing my job, sir," she said.

"Of course!" he said again. "Please, sit down and join us. I'm Leroy Courtney, obviously, but most people just call me Roy. This is Chad Pohlman and Lee Briggs."

"Meetcha," Pohlman said. He barely glanced at her before returning his attention to the room at large. *Bodyguard*, Erin thought, reading his body language. She noticed the bulge of a shoulder holster under his arm.

"How's it going?" Briggs asked. He was a dark-skinned guy with a shaved head, a diamond earring in his left ear, and a gold tooth that gleamed when he grinned at her. "You a football fan?"

"Baseball, mostly," she said.

Briggs's face fell. "Then I guess you wouldn't know me," he said.

"Lee played half a season with the Lions," Courtney explained. "Offensive Tackle. He was good, but he got unlucky."

"Knee injury," Briggs said and shrugged. "It happens."

"And now he works for you?" Erin asked.

"And now he works for me," Courtney said.

A waitress approached their table. "Are you ready to order?" she asked Courtney.

"We've been waiting for you," Courtney said to Erin. He turned back to the waitress. "Yes, I'd like the steak and eggs, medium rare, extra peppers. Lee here will have the same. Chad wants the smoked salmon, and Miss O'Reilly will have the Villard omelet."

It wasn't the first time a sketchy man had ordered on Erin's behalf. It annoyed her, but she'd learned to roll with it. Like most of what these guys did, it was a power play, intended to assert control over her and the situation. She'd save her energy for the real battle and ignore the preliminary skirmishes.

"Thank you," she said, giving the waitress a sweet smile. "Can I get a cup of coffee, too? Cream, no sugar."

"Coming right up," the waitress said.

"You're going to love the omelet," Courtney said. "And their roast potatoes are fantastic. You come here much?"

"I don't get into this area often," she said. "My squad works out of South Manhattan. We see a lot of action on Long Island, too. I grew up in Queens."

"Is that so?" Courtney said. "What'd your dad do?"

"He was a cop."

"Detective?"

"Patrolman."

"And you're in the family business, just like dear old Dad? I like it." Courtney grinned. "My dad was a Teamster, and so was his, and so on, back to when they were using horses. That's why we're called the Teamsters, you know. Because we used to drive teams of horses."

"Yeah, I know about that," she said.

"There were people who were scared of gasoline engines," Courtney said. "They thought those newfangled things were going to take their jobs. But what they learned was, you have to change with the times. An old job goes away? Okay, you learn how to do a new one. Like Lee here. He wrecked his knee, but he found himself another job he could do. He still gets paid, he's still a team player. Aren't you, Lee?"

"Damn right," Briggs said.

"You've been hurt a couple times in your line of work, haven't you, Detective O'Reilly?" Courtney said.

"Once or twice," Erin said. She'd had concussions, cracked ribs, cuts, contusions, and plenty of other hard knocks, but she wasn't about to list them for this guy's benefit.

"But you play through the pain, you come back, and you keep going," Courtney said. "I respect that. You've got one hell of a work ethic, I can tell. That's what makes this country great, am I right?"

"Absolutely, sir," she said.

"When I heard from this guy I know, a great guy, absolutely fantastic, that Erin O'Reilly, *the* Erin O'Reilly wanted to see me, I jumped at the chance. And let me say, you do great work for New York."

"Thank you, sir," she said, remembering Corky's words: *keep your eyes on him, and don't trust him one bloody inch*. Courtney seemed open, friendly, and forthright, but he was a politician, and Erin knew honest politicians were an endangered species.

"So here we are," Courtney said. "Enjoying a great brunch—my treat, by the way, no need to mess around with those expense reports—and having a good talk. Are you married, by any chance?"

"No," she said, feeling herself tense up.

"But you're seeing someone," he said with a knowing gleam in his eye. "Is he a good guy? Is he treating you right?"

"We're very happy," she said, relaxing slightly. At least he wasn't clumsily hitting on her.

"Good, good! If you haven't got a good home life, it doesn't matter how good you've got it at work, you're going to be miserable. See this?" He pointed to a fat gold ring on his third finger. "Twenty-three years. There's guys who like to roam around. Not me. I like the home field advantage. My Julia, she's something else, putting up with me all these years."

Erin nodded politely. She wanted to cut through the bullshit and get down to business, but sometimes you had to let these guys talk. She waited and listened and tried not to grind her teeth.

One advantage of breakfast food was that it didn't take long to cook. Their meal arrived, hot and steaming.

"Good, huh?" Courtney said, slicing a strip of meat off his steak and chewing with relish.

"Very," Erin said. In truth, she would've preferred a homemade omelet with ham and cheddar, or maybe bacon. The Villard's omelet was some weird French cheese, Gruyère or something like that, and held no meat at all; just spinach and tomatoes. But it wasn't the worst thing she'd ever eaten, and as he'd said, the roast potatoes were excellent. It wasn't worth the price tag, but then, how many Manhattan restaurant meals were?

"It's because of us, you know," Courtney said between bites.

"What is?" Erin asked.

He spread a hand to indicate the table. "All of this. Eggs, meat, potatoes. The Teamsters make it all happen, bring it all into the city. Without us, New York starves."

"You do good work," she agreed.

"And so do you, so do you," he said cheerfully. "So what is it I can do for you, Erin? Can I call you Erin?"

"Of course, Roy." She'd learned how to smile with only the lower half of her face, the way mobsters did it. "I'm working a case right now. It's a cold one, from a while ago. You remember Charlie Majors?"

Courtney's face was a blank, innocent mask. "Can't say I do," he said. "How long ago are we talking? I used to live in Detroit, so if it was before I moved here..."

"He was in Local 813," she said. "He was murdered about the same time you came here. I'm sure you would've heard about it."

"I definitely would have heard about a murder of one of our members," Courtney said.

"You didn't hear anything around your organization?" she pressed. "Charlie was stepping out of line. He was going behind the Union's back, trying to strike out on his own. That's the sort of thing that gets noticed."

"I'm sorry to hear it," Courtney said. "And sorry if he suffered the consequences of betrayal. Unions exist from the knowledge that working men are stronger when they stand together. When they're betrayed from within, unions fall apart. It sounds like this Charlie fellow thought he could do better on his own than by standing with his brothers. It's an understandable choice, but the wrong one, as he must have found out."

"The Teamsters are connected to other labor organizations, aren't you?" Erin asked.

"We're the friends of working men everywhere," Courtney said, flashing his charming smile once more. "That includes the Police Union, by the way."

"And BK Construction," Erin said.

Courtney nodded. Then he hesitated and his broad politician's smile flickered briefly. Uncertainty flitted across his face. He hadn't said anything, but he hadn't needed to.

"You're a very clever policewoman," he said after a moment. "And you have a remarkable reputation, as I'm sure you're aware."

It was Erin's turn to nod.

"Your rep is that of a reasonable woman," he went on. "You understand how things work in this city. You know how the sausage gets made. You know that as long as there's sausage in the end, nobody really wants to look too closely into the meat-grinder. Besides, we're talking about ancient history here. It's not like you're investigating some fresh-faced coed, some attractive, innocent girl who'll play well on the nightly news and the tabloid covers. From what you say, you're looking into a decade-old disposal of a piece of human garbage. I think we can all agree, whatever Charlie Majors was like in life, New York is a better place without him."

Erin stared at Courtney, trying to control her reactions. He was still smiling broadly, having recovered his composure. He looked as pleasant and friendly as ever. But hiding at the back of his eyes was something cold and reptilian.

If she hadn't had her prior experience with guys like Evan O'Malley to fall back on, she might have said or done something stupid. She would have flared up, or shied away in revulsion, or come up with a smartass remark. Instead, thinking of all those evening poker games with Evan and his henchmen, when she'd had to smile in the faces of psychopathic killers, she just nodded again and let one corner of her mouth quirk up in what might have been a chilly smile of her own.

"If you know my reputation, you know how I play the game," she said. "You also know who I work with. You say Corky Corcoran is a solid guy. Do you agree that whatever bad blood was between you and his people is in the past?"

"Dead and buried," Courtney said, the smile lingering on his lips.

"Here's the problem," she said. "One of Evan's people isn't willing to let it stay buried. He's cutting his way through everyone in his way. It's making a lot of work for me and a lot of trouble for you and yours."

"That sounds like something you'd want to take care of internally," Courtney said.

"That's easy for you to say," she said. "Have you actually met Kyle Finnegan?"

The name got a bigger reaction. Courtney blinked twice. He started to say something, paused, cleared his throat, and continued.

"I've heard of him," he said.

"I know he'd been scheduled to meet with you," Erin said. "It was a long time ago, but I'm sure you remember. Bible, Fisherman, and Two-Foot stood in for you."

"You're very well-informed, Miss O'Reilly," Courtney said. He was speaking much more quietly now.

"How's everything tasting?" the waitress asked, choosing that moment to walk up to the table.

"We're fine," Courtney said sharply, without taking his eyes off Erin. "Scram."

The waitress opened her mouth, decided not to say anything, and beat a hasty retreat.

"Finnegan," Courtney said to Erin. "What does he know?"

"He knows guys at BK took care of Charlie Majors," she said. "He was there this morning."

"What did he do?"

"Broke every bone in Howie Manterville's legs with a jackhammer."

"Is Howie dead?"

"He's in the hospital," Erin said, noting that Courtney hadn't even tried to pretend he didn't know who Manterville was. "I think he'll pull through. But you have to assume Finnegan knows everything Manterville does."

Courtney nodded. "What's it going to take to make this go away?" he asked.

"How do you mean?" she asked.

"Finnegan is a problem," he said. "I'd like to solve that problem. I understand you're a woman who can take care of this sort of thing."

A cold spike shoved itself into Erin's gut. She knew exactly what he meant. She'd just wanted him to spell it out for the benefit of her recording wire, which was humming merrily away under her blouse.

"That's going to be a little sticky," she said.

He shrugged. "I've always found money to be a great lubricant in sticky situations. Can you give a ballpark figure?"

She shook her head. "I can't do that for you," she said. "Not to one of the O'Malleys."

"Can't? Or won't?" His eyes no longer held any warmth at all.

"You want this taken care of that way, you need to talk to Evan," she said. "I can't freelance."

"And what am I supposed to do in the meantime?" he demanded.

"That depends," she said. "How much did Howie know? How much damage can that info cause? Where's Finnegan going to go next?"

"What's his goal?" Courtney replied.

"He wants to find the guy who took Charlie Majors out," she said.

Courtney leaned forward. "I tell you this, you need to get that crazy bastard under control," he said. "If you don't, I'll find someone who will."

She leaned in to meet him. "Give me a name," she said in a low voice.

"Elijah Drake."

Erin knew her face was showing too much, but the familiar name startled her. She hadn't expected someone she'd already met. "You're sure?" she asked, trying to cover her reaction.

Courtney settled back in his seat. He folded his hands in front of his big belly. "I'm counting on you to take care of this," he said. "And you'd better hurry. I don't think you have a lot of time."

Erin pushed her chair away from the table and shot to her feet, leaving half an expensive omelet on her plate. "You're right," she said. "I don't. Thanks for brunch. You have a good day, Mr. Courtney."

"It was very pleasant meeting you, Miss O'Reilly," he said, but he was talking to her back. Erin was walking out of the restaurant. By the time she got through the front door, she was running.

Chapter 20

"How did the meeting go?" Webb asked.

"Never mind that!" Erin said into her phone. "Where are you and Vic?"

"We're still at BK Construction," Webb said. "Collecting evidence. Are you okay? Do you need backup?"

"You need to get to Elijah Drake's house right now!"

"O'Reilly," Webb said slowly. "You do understand we have a chain of command in the NYPD, and I'm your superior officer, don't you? I give you orders, not the other way round."

Erin threw the Charger in gear and stomped the accelerator. The car slewed out into the street, slid on a patch of black ice, and narrowly missed sideswiping a taxi. The cabbie honked irritably, but Erin ignored him.

"Yes, sir," she said, fighting down her exasperation and impatience. "But this is important. Drake killed Majors and the others."

"And you know this how?" Webb asked.

"The Teamsters VP gave me his name!" she snapped. "He's our guy."

"Okay, we'll pick him up," Webb said. "It shouldn't be too complicated. We know where he is, and—"

"Finnegan knows too!" she interrupted. "He's probably on his way there right now, if we're not already too late!"

Webb didn't waste any more time. He took his head away from his phone, but Erin could hear him as he started talking fast.

"Neshenko," he said. "You're going to Elijah Drake's house, fast as you can. Have Dispatch send two Patrol units; they'll get there ahead of you. Have them secure the house and get some protection on the family. Once you're on scene, take charge and get Drake in custody. He's a suspect, but he's also in danger. O'Reilly says Finnegan may be after him."

"Copy that," Vic said. "I'm gone."

"Where are you now?" Webb asked, coming back on the phone.

"On my way south from Midtown," Erin said. "It'll take me some time to get back to Brooklyn."

"I'll wrap up here and meet you at the Drake house," he said. "How good is your intel on Drake and Finnegan?"

"I think it's solid. I can explain when I get there."

"I'll look forward to it."

* * *

Erin was halfway across the East River when the call went out on the police-band radio.

"*Attention, all units in the Seven Eight. We have a possible home invasion and a 10-24K. 635 Baltic. Two Patrol units on scene, bus en route.*"

"Shit," Erin said. That was the Drake family's address. The 10-24K code stood for an assault with a knife. She grabbed her radio handset. "Dispatch, this is O'Reilly, Major Crimes. Responding to call to 635 Baltic. ETA ten to fifteen."

"Copy that, O'Reilly," Dispatch said.

"Shit," Erin said again. "Shit, shit, shit." She put on the siren and stomped the gas.

Some dogs hated loud noises, but Rolf liked the siren. It was the sound of the chase. It meant speed, and often bad guys at the end. He thrust his muzzle next to Erin's ear and let out a low howl, harmonizing with the siren's wail.

It was usually enough to make her crack a smile, but not now. She was thinking of the family in the little Brooklyn house, of their Christmas tree and the kids upstairs. She was also remembering rushing into another family's house and finding her niece and nephew huddled under the bed, her sister-in-law taken by a crazed killer. Dispatch hadn't said anything about a homicide. She clung to that thin thread of hope and willed the Charger to go faster.

When she was about five minutes out, her phone lit up with Vic's name. She snatched it up and whipped her thumb across the screen.

"Talk to me, Vic," she said.

"I'm at the Drake house," he said. Sirens were audible in the background. "It's a mess, Erin. Some asshole came in and trashed the place."

She gripped the phone tightly, forcing her next question through a clenched jaw. "Is anybody dead?"

"Not yet, not as far as I know."

Erin let out a breath she hadn't known she was holding. "How bad is it?" she asked.

"That Drake mope got worked over pretty good," Vic said. "We got a couple uniforms doing first aid and a bus on the way. He's lost a lot of blood and he's gonna need surgery. Where are you?"

"A few minutes out. I'm coming as fast as I can."

"I just talked to Webb. He's on his way, too."

"What about the wife and kids?"

"They're okay, more or less."

"More or less?"

"One of the kids, the boy, has a broken finger."

"That's not so bad."

"Yeah." But Vic's voice sounded a little funny. If Erin hadn't known the big Russian so well, she would've thought he sounded shaken.

Erin wedged the Charger between a pair of NYPD blue-and-whites, jumped out, and unloaded Rolf. An ambulance had arrived just ahead of her. The paramedics had already gone in. Two Patrol officers flanked the front door of the Drake house, staring stonily out at the neighborhood. Erin flashed her shield and they stepped aside.

As she pushed the door open, a wave of memory swept over her with astonishing force. She froze in place, mind reeling. She felt herself running through another door, her brother's, screaming the names of her family, certain she'd find nothing but blood and tiny broken bodies.

The echoes of her own voice chased her back into the present. She had one hand on the doorframe, leaning against it. She was breathing hard, almost panting. For a second she thought she might throw up.

"Detective?" one of the uniforms asked. "You okay?"

"I'm fine." The familiar lie spilled easily from her lips. Erin straightened her shoulders and walked inside.

The EMTs were busy in the living room, in front of the Christmas tree, which lay on its side. The two paramedics were working feverishly. Erin could see the lower half of a man's body. The guy was strapped to a stretcher. His feet were twitching fitfully and he was making a sound that made Erin very glad she couldn't see the rest of him. Jenny Drake stood a short distance away. Her son was crying against his mother's leg. The boy's left hand had a white splint on the index finger. Jenny's daughter was clutched in her arms. Jenny herself was sheet white. She was visibly trembling, but appeared physically unharmed. Two more Patrol officers took up space against the wall, looking uncomfortable and awkward.

"Vic?" Erin called.

Vic came out of the kitchen, pulling the door shut behind him. "There you are," he said. "What a clusterfuck this turned out to be."

"You've got blood on you," she said.

Vic looked down at his hands and sleeves. They were smeared dark red. "Oh, this? Forget about it, it's not mine."

"What were you doing back there?" She looked past him at the kitchen door.

He sidestepped, barring her path. "You don't want to go there," he said quietly.

"Why not? Vic, what the hell is going on?"

He sighed and rubbed the bridge of his twice-broken nose, leaving bloody fingerprints on both cheeks. "The dog's in there, Erin," he said.

"Mac?" Erin remembered the happy, friendly pit bull she'd seen on her last visit to the house.

"That asshole killed him," Vic said heavily. "I guess he tried to defend his family and... shit. I've been hanging around you too long. Dead people don't bother me, but seeing that... I dunno. I found a towel in the bathroom and put it over him. I hope that doesn't screw up the scene for CSU. I just couldn't leave the poor guy lying there."

She put a hand on his massive shoulder. "Vic, tell me what happened," she said.

He shrugged the hand away. "What do you think?" he said. "A guy came to the door, and when the wife opened it, he asked to talk to Eli."

"Why wasn't Eli at work?"

"Beats me. I didn't have time to get into particulars. Eli was in the kitchen, helping get lunch ready. Our boy followed Ms. Drake into the kitchen and got hold of a butcher's knife out of the knife block. He held it on the woman. The dog went for him and he stabbed the dog. Then he tied up the guy. He used Christmas lights, can you believe it? Goddamn Christmas lights off the tree! Then he started asking Drake questions."

"Jenny told you all this?" Erin asked.

Vic nodded. "He tied her up too," he said grimly. "Then he used his knife to get answers. But Drake wasn't talking. He said he was out of that life and wasn't going back. Then, in the middle of things, his kid came downstairs. He must've heard the ruckus. And our jerkoff home invader grabbed the kid and started breaking his fingers. Right in front of Mom and Dad."

Erin shuddered. "Jesus," she murmured.

"That was enough for Dad, like you'd expect," Vic said, scowling. "He started talking, spilling everything. But in the middle of it, our first batch of uniforms showed up. The perp went out the back way in a hurry. The unis were too busy giving first aid to pursue, so that jerk could be anywhere by now."

"I can set Rolf on his trail," Erin said.

"What's the point?" Vic replied. "He'll have gotten in a car by now. He's gone. Besides, we all know who it was."

"Yeah," she said. "I guess we do. What did Drake tell Finnegan?"

"I don't know," Vic said. "The medics have him pretty well drugged up now. Besides, I don't think he'll want to tell us."

"I was thinking we should talk to the wife. She heard it."

"Oh. Yeah, good call. I didn't get her detailed statement yet, just a quick run-down. Want to wait for the Lieutenant?"

Erin shook her head. "Finnegan's one step ahead of us," she said. "The longer we delay, the more damage he causes. Maybe if we find out what he knows, we can guess where he's going. I'm surprised he didn't kill Drake."

"He didn't have time," Vic said. "It's a damn good thing the cops showed up when they did. The medics even think they might be able to save his eye."

"His what?" Erin stared at Vic.

"You heard me," he said. "I can go into more detail if you want."

"No thanks."

"That's what I thought."

* * *

In spite of Erin's impatience, they had to wait until Elijah Drake was loaded into the ambulance and driven away. Jenny absolutely refused to give her attention to anything else while her husband was bleeding in front of her. Then the detectives needed to get her upstairs, away from the bloodstained living room and kitchen, and calm her down enough to talk. Vic's initial interview had been hurried and slapdash, but now they needed details, and for that they needed a witness with a clear head.

The cup of hot chocolate had been Vic's idea. He'd seen the mix in the kitchen and made six cups; one each for Jenny and her kids, the other three for the detectives. Webb had arrived just a few minutes behind Erin, but he'd sent Piekarski back to the Eightball to start sifting the data CSU had recovered from BK's computers.

Now the six of them were in the upstairs den, a cozy little room with a soft old sofa and a couple of beanbag chairs. Webb was squeezed onto the couch next to Jenny and her kids. Erin had sunk into a beanbag and wasn't sure she'd be able to get back out without help. Vic elected to remain standing next to the door. Rolf lay beside Erin, his chin resting on the beanbag.

Jenny was still pale, but she wasn't shaking anymore. The steaming mug of cocoa in her hand helped a little. Her daughter was asleep, as often happened to kids after a bad fright, but little Davy's finger was bothering him and he was fretting. Jenny continually laid one hand on top of his head, stroking his hair and soothing him, almost unaware she was doing it.

"Eli's not a bad guy," she said.

"Nobody's saying he is," Webb replied.

"I know what you think," Jenny said. "Eli had a record. He did time. You look at him and you see a thug. But he's not like that. That's who he was, not who he is. People can change."

Erin caught the roll of Vic's eyes out of the corner of her own. She shot him a warning glance, hoping he'd have the sense and decency not to say anything.

"You think I'm just a stupid woman, that I've got a blind spot for the man I love," Jenny went on. "I'm not blind. I know what he did. I know what kind of people he hung around with. And I'm telling you, he doesn't do that sort of thing anymore."

"What do you mean?" Webb asked gently.

"That fight," Jenny said. "The one that got him sent to jail. When he hit that guy in the face."

"How about the others?" Erin asked. "The three guys in the parking lot, ten years ago?"

Jenny shuddered. "He used to have nightmares," she said in a near-whisper. "For years. He talked in his sleep. He dreamed about getting smothered. He'd kick the covers off and wake up gasping. I knew about all of it. He told me everything. We don't have any secrets."

"And you didn't tell anyone?" Webb asked.

Jenny's eyes flashed angrily. "For what? So you guys could haul him back to prison? So my kids would have to grow up without their dad? Eli didn't make any of this happen. It wasn't his idea. He didn't have a choice!"

Erin swallowed and looked at the carpet between her feet. Some of this was hitting a little too close to home. She knew something about Carlyle that the rest of the NYPD didn't. When a murderer wore the face of someone you loved, it was different.

"What did Eli tell you about that day?" Webb asked.

"It wasn't day," Jenny said. "It was night. He was just finishing work for the evening. His boss called him over and said there was a special job for him. Overtime. Eli had a reputation as a guy who could do jobs that weren't exactly..."

"Legal?" Vic guessed.

Jenny nodded. "He'd been in trouble before. He'd done some stuff. But I don't want to talk about that. I don't want him to get in more trouble."

"Lady," Vic said harshly. "Your man's on his way to the hospital. He got his face broken, his friggin' dog killed, and his kid's hand broken. Just how much more trouble do you think it's possible for him to be in?"

Jenny flinched. "You don't know what those guys at his company are like," she said.

"Actually, we do," Webb said. "I just came from BK Construction. It's a crooked company that's connected to the Mob. It's got guys working there who'll break legs and even kill people, but we've got their number and we're shutting them down. We can protect you."

"But the more you tell us, the better we can look after you," Erin said. "We need to know what the people at BK made your husband do."

"There was a parking lot," Jenny said quietly. "It was being resurfaced, replacing the blacktop with concrete. They told Eli he needed to help pour the cement. It was a rush job and had to be done overnight."

"What night was this?" Webb asked.

"It was before I met him," she said. "June twenty-third of '05."

Webb made a note. A lot of detectives used an app on their phones to take notes, but Webb was old school and preferred an actual paper notepad and pencil.

"When he got to the place, some other guys were already there," Jenny went on. "Two of Eli's work crew and some others. Two management types from BK and four big guys with nose rings."

"Black Bull truckers," Erin said.

"That's right," Jenny said. "They had a truck with them and Eli heard banging inside it. The truck drivers got in the back of the truck and pulled three men out. They were tied up, begging to be let go. The BK boss said, 'Relax, I'm not going to shoot you.'"

"That's true enough," Vic muttered.

"The other two construction workers had already dug the hole," Jenny continued in a low voice. "They'd made it deeper than the rest of the lot. The boss said to one of the tied-up guys, 'This is what happens when you go behind our backs. Think about that.' Then he snapped his fingers and the truck drivers tossed the men into the hole.

"Eli was the cement guy, the one who knew how to mix the stuff and lay it nice and smooth. The boss said he wanted this patch of lot to look just the same as the rest of it. Eli didn't do anything, so the boss asked why he was just standing around. Eli didn't want to do it, he was scared. He'd never done... anything like that before. But he was more scared of what the others might do to him. He told me there was plenty more room in the hole."

"So he filled it in?" Erin asked.

"He still sees their faces," Jenny said. "He can still see the look in their eyes. He goes to church, he tries so hard to be a good man, but he can't get away from it. And he had to keep going back there, day after day, for weeks."

"To cure the concrete," Erin said, nodding.

"That's right," Jenny said. "He kept thinking about them, under his feet. But what could he do? They were already dead."

"He still works for BK," Webb said. "Why?"

Jenny looked at him like he was crazy. "You think he could leave after something like that?" she demanded. "They'd never let him go."

"I bet the money was good, too," Vic said in an undertone.

"It wasn't worth it," Jenny said bitterly.

"Ms. Drake, this is important," Webb said. "What were the names of the other men who were at the parking lot that night?"

"Al Higgins and Dickie Fox were the construction guys," Jenny said.

"Are they still with BK?" Webb asked.

"I think so."

"What about the suits?" Vic asked.

"Suits?" Jenny looked blank.

"The management guys," Erin translated.

Jenny hesitated.

"If they're behind bars, they can't hurt you," Webb said.

The woman shook her head. "I've got a family," she said, curling her arm protectively around her children. "And their dad's going to be in the hospital and then prison. They need me."

"Jenny, think what this secret did to Eli," Erin said, speaking as softly and gently as she could. "It's been chewing him up inside for ten years. The only thing you can do with a secret like that is let it out. It's like draining a wound. It'll let off the pressure. It's the best thing you could possibly do for your husband and for yourself. It'll come out one way or another."

"Eli didn't know one of them," Jenny said slowly. "But he heard one of the others call him Roy."

Erin's heart skipped a beat. "Was Roy a big guy?" she asked. "Unusually big? Tall, broad shoulders?"

"Eli called him the big man," Jenny said. "I thought he meant it was because he was the big boss. But maybe."

"And the other one?" Webb asked.

"Micah Fielder," Jenny said.

Webb nodded. "He's BK's Personnel Director," he said. "His name is all over the documents we got."

"Finnegan," Erin said. "The man who was here, I mean. Did Eli tell him all this? Including the names?"

"Not all of it," Jenny said. "That man seemed to know most of it already. All he wanted was the names."

"What names did Eli give him?" Webb asked.

"The ones I told you," Jenny said. Micah, Al, and Dickie. And Roy."

"Then that's where he's going next," Erin said. She sprang to her feet. "We need to get to them before Finnegan does."

"They won't be at BK," Vic said. "The whole building's sealed off. We've got so many cops there, I bet a donut shop's already open next door."

"Then they'll go home," Erin guessed. "Or hide. Or maybe link up with their bosses."

"Like the guy you just met with?" Vic replied.

"Maybe," she said. "He's probably the Roy Eli ran into that night. Shit, there's too many places they could be."

"Fortunately, we've got the NYPD in our corner," Webb said. "And there's a lot of us. O'Reilly, you're going back to Midtown. Find your pal Roy and stick to him like glue. I'll get you some uniforms in case you need any extra bodies. Neshenko, grab a unit and go to Fielder's home address. If he's there, get him in protective custody. If he's not, set up camp and wait for him. I'll coordinate with Patrol Division and send units after Higgins and Fox."

"Where'll you be, sir?" Erin asked.

"Right here," Webb said. "I'll finish taking Ms. Drake's statement and supervise CSU. I'm getting a lot of practice at it."

"Copy that," Erin said. "Rolf, *fuss*."

The Shepherd hopped up and positioned himself at her side, ready for action.

"And watch yourselves," Webb warned. "There's no telling what this guy's going to do."

"Finnegan's not going to kill cops," Erin said, pretty sure she believed it.

"He hasn't killed anybody yet," Webb replied grimly. "But he's dishing out a lot of pain. Make sure you're not in line if he's got more to hand out."

Chapter 21

"Drive to Brooklyn," Erin growled. "Drive to Manhattan. Back to Brooklyn. Back to Manhattan. I'm not a cop, I'm a goddamn shuttle service."

Rolf panted happily.

It was snowing again. This wasn't the magical, fluffy white flakes that had blanketed the city. This snow was chilly, wet, and clinging. It was more like congealed rain. Erin had her wipers going full tilt. Even though it was only a little past noon, visibility was terrible. She was craning her neck and straining her eyes, expecting to see crashed cars and stalled traffic any moment.

Her expectations were fulfilled. By the time she made it to the East River, she'd already seen three fender-benders and two spin-outs. The roads were coated with hard-packed slush that was at least as slippery as solid ice. The Charger had excellent tires and good handling, but she still fishtailed a couple of times.

Traffic wasn't as bad as she feared, but that was only because a lot of New Yorkers were being sensible and staying off the streets. It still took her half again as long to get back to Midtown as it had taken to drive to Brooklyn, and she had a few hair-raising calls on the way. By the time she got to her destination, she estimated she'd shaved about a year and a half off her life.

Leroy Courtney's office was on the top floor of a twelve-story building on the Upper East Side. As VP of a major trade union, he rated a corner suite. The building was sleek and modern, all steel and mirrored glass. The police space outside was already occupied by an NYPD blue-and-white.

"The backup got here early," Erin said. "That's a nice change of pace. But I guess they didn't have to come nearly as far."

Rolf wagged his tail and barked once. Car rides were great, but he'd been in the Charger quite a while. It was about time they found some bad guys and got the teeth in them.

She took a moment before going in to double-check Rolf's vest and to strap on her own Kevlar. When you were on a protection detail, it was a lot easier to take a bullet for some other guy if you were wearing body armor.

The lobby was manned by a stony-faced man who looked more like an extra from a Mafia movie than a receptionist. Erin saw the scar on his cheek and the look in his eye and was immediately wary. His hands were hidden by the front desk and she didn't like it.

"Something you need?" he asked, sounding like he didn't care one way or the other.

"I'm here to see Leroy Courtney," she said, unclipping her shield with her left hand and laying it on the desk in front of him. "My name's O'Reilly. I don't have an appointment." She kept her right hand open and near her gun. It was crazy paranoia and she knew it; nobody was going to whack an NYPD detective in the lobby of a Manhattan office building in the middle of the day. Besides, she hadn't called ahead. The only people who knew she'd be here were the cops Webb had asked Dispatch to send.

"Just a sec," the man at the desk said. He picked up his phone and punched a number. "Yeah, I got some lady cop at the desk, says her name's O'Reilly. Okay, gotcha."

He hung up and looked back at Erin. "Take the elevator up to Twelve," he said. "They'll be waiting for you."

"Thanks," Erin said. "Rolf, *fuss*."

The two of them went to the elevator. She hit the button for the top floor and tried to relax. Her nerves were jangling. She'd projected a certainty to Webb that she didn't feel. Inwardly, she was quite sure Finnegan was willing and able to kill cops. There wasn't a single thing she'd put past him. But at the same time, she had a hunch he didn't want to kill her. On some odd level, he liked her. Or at least he found her interesting, which for Finnegan came to the same thing.

Her uneasiness, she decided, was mostly due to not understanding what was going on. Why was this one act of revenge so important to Finnegan? What did he hope to gain out of it? Mobsters, even the crazy ones, were practical people at heart. They didn't embark on vigilante rampages just for the hell of it. And where was he going? He might not be targeting Leroy Courtney. He might not even have made the connection she had with the name "Roy." For all she knew he was still in Brooklyn, or on his way to New Jersey, or maybe California or Arkansas or God only knew where.

"Relax," she said as the elevator hummed to a stop.

Rolf cocked his head curiously at her. He wasn't sure what she meant. When he was wearing his vest it was time to be tense and alert. Relaxation was for boring paperwork in the office.

The elevator doors slid open. Two enormous men filled the hall outside, blocking her in. She was staring down the barrels of a pair of automatic pistols. The holes in the ends of the guns looked like black, empty eye-sockets.

A jolt of pure panic shot down Erin's spine. Her own gun was in its holster at her belt, about as much use as it would've been on her nightstand at home. Ian Thompson's view of elevators, that they were ready-made kill-boxes, echoed in her mind. Her entire body tensed, expecting to feel bullets slam into her.

Then she recognized the men. Chad Pohlman and Lee Briggs, Courtney's bodyguards. "Put those things away," she snapped. "Don't you know it's me?"

The men lowered the pistols but kept them in hand. "We had to be sure," Briggs said. "C'mon, the boss is this way."

He took the lead, the slight hitch in his stride serving as a reminder of the knee injury that had ended his football career. Pohlman brought up the rear. They walked on thick, plush carpet much nicer than an office cubicle farm would have. The walls were lined with bold, stark modern paintings that appeared, to Erin's untutored eye, to be random blocks of solid black and red.

"Pointing a gun at a cop is a good way to get shot," she commented. "You ought to be more careful."

Pohlman snorted. "She thinks we were the ones who almost got shot," he said to Briggs.

"Don't worry," Briggs said. "We got cops here already."

"Then why are you so jumpy?" Erin asked.

"Because there's some crazy bastard running around busting guys up," Briggs said. "That's why you're here, isn't it?"

"Yeah," she said.

The hallway rounded a corner and ended at a door that was real hardwood, not paneling. An engraved brass plaque proclaimed it the entrance to Leroy Courtney's office. Briggs knocked. The door swung open and Erin saw the face of an NYPD Patrolman.

"I got Miss O'Reilly here," Briggs said.

"The more the merrier," the uniform replied. "C'mon in."

They trooped in past the cop.

"Officer," Erin said.

"Detective," he replied.

It was the swankiest office Erin had ever been in, including Evan O'Malley's private office and Carlyle's upstairs sanctuary. It even smelled like money. The desk was mahogany, the carpet even thicker than outside. The windows overlooked the eastern edge of Central Park, the view currently blurred by the fast-falling sleet.

Leroy Courtney sat behind his desk in a very comfy-looking black leather swivel chair. The desk held a laptop computer, a thumb drive plugged into one side. Another Patrol cop stood by the wall, a donut and a cup of coffee in his hands. On a side table sat a platter of assorted pastries, a coffeepot, and a cluster of ceramic cups.

"Detective O'Reilly," Courtney said, getting to his feet with his charming, false smile. "I wasn't expecting to see you again so soon. Welcome to my humble place of business."

"Thank you, sir," she said, baffled. To be met by drawn guns at the elevator, followed by baked goods and hot coffee a moment later, was disorienting.

"When your colleagues arrived, I took the liberty of having some refreshments brought up," Courtney said. "Help yourself. Are you hungry?"

"I'm good, thanks," she said. "Sir, do you know why we're here?"

"I understand it has something to do with a threat to my personal safety," Courtney said. "But don't worry, I'm sure we're all quite safe here."

"Sir, don't underestimate this guy," Erin said. "He's dangerous."

"No doubt," Courtney chuckled. "Which is why I'm grateful to have so many representatives of New York's Finest here, in addition to my own private security. And, of course, there's you, the notorious Erin O'Reilly. I could hardly be safer in a vault in Fort Knox. So make yourself comfortable. I'm sure there's nothing to fear. Please, try one of the Danish pastries. I have them delivered fresh every morning. There's a really excellent bakery just up the street. And the coffee is to die for. It's Jamaica Blue Mountain, fresh-brewed."

"It's really good," the cop by the wall added. "Officer Jenkins, ma'am, from the One-Nine. It's an honor to meet you."

"Officer Burkhardt," the other cop introduced himself. "We've heard a lot about you, ma'am."

"That's way too many 'ma'ams' for one day," Erin said. "You're making me feel like my mom."

This was met by good-natured laughter. "I'll have some more chairs brought in," Courtney said. "I'm afraid you're in for a boring afternoon."

"I'll stay standing, thanks anyway," Erin said. She didn't take him up on his offer of coffee, either. The little voice in the back of her head warned against getting too comfortable. She might need to move fast.

What was the matter with her? She'd been hanging around too many dangerous people for too long. Finnegan wasn't coming, she told herself again. This whole business was a waste of time. The other cops were obviously bored. Pohlman was yawning. Even Rolf looked bleary. The dark, cold, dreary day was sapping everyone's energy. Courtney was the only one doing anything useful. The man was on his computer, doing the job the Teamsters paid him to do.

Time dragged. An hour passed. The donuts on the platter slowly diminished in number. Rolf went to sleep.

Erin called Webb. "Anything going on, sir?" she asked when he picked up.

"Not a thing," he said. "We've got protection details on everybody."

"Any sign of Finnegan?"

"That's a negative. Everything all right where you are?"

"Yeah. I'm just hanging around with the subject, his hired goons, and a couple guys from the One-Nine."

"Reliable guys?"

"How would I know that, sir? It's two uniforms, Jenkins and Burkhardt. I don't know them."

"Okay. Keep me posted if anything changes."

"Copy that, sir."

She hung up. Burkhardt shook his head.

"I don't like how you call us that," he said.

"What?"

"Uniforms. Sounds like we're empty suits, interchangeable parts."

"Sorry," she said. "I don't mean anything by it. I was a Patrol cop not that long ago myself."

"Right," he said. "Even if we're not all glamorous gold-shield folks."

"It's not that glamorous," she said. "Besides, I called Briggs and Pohlman goons, and they don't seem to mind."

"That's because that's what we are," Briggs said, grinning. A gold tooth glinted in the middle of his smile.

Erin glanced at Courtney, who was engrossed in his work. "Mr. Courtney?"

"Hmm?" he said, looking up.

"Can you call down to that guy you've got at the front desk?"

"Why? Is something the matter?"

"It's a routine perimeter check," she said, thinking of Ian again and wondering what the former Marine would have done if he'd been in charge of protecting Courtney. He'd probably have three guys with assault rifles on site and he'd be camped across the street with a sniper rifle, ready to put holes in any suspicious characters. Finnegan wouldn't make it within twenty yards of the front door. Too bad the NYPD wasn't allowed to do that.

Courtney shrugged. "If it'll make you happy," he said. He picked up his desk phone and dialed an extension. He paused, listening. Several seconds passed.

He shrugged again and hung up. "It's just ringing," he said. "I guess Ed went on break."

"You mean nobody's watching the front door?" Erin asked sharply. Rolf, hearing the sudden change in her tone, perked up his ears and raised his head.

"I'm sure it's just for a minute or two," Courtney said.

"You don't know that," Erin snapped. She turned to the others. "We need this floor secured now. We need to check the elevators and the stairs."

Courtney might be right, nineteen times out of twenty he would be, but she was suddenly sure he was wrong. The hard-faced man she'd seen at the front desk hadn't struck her as the kind of guy who'd just wander off, not when there was potential danger.

"I'll check the stairwell," Pohlman volunteered. "It's right next to the elevators."

"I'll go with him," Jenkins said.

"I'll stay here and cover the principal," Burkhardt said.

"Me too," Briggs said. "I don't move so fast."

Pohlman and Jenkins hurried out of the office. Erin wondered if she was overreacting and quickly decided it didn't matter. If she had to be wrong, she'd rather be over-cautious. She turned to Burkhardt.

"Call Dispatch," she said. "Get two more units here."

"You sure that's necessary?" he asked.

"No. But what if it is?"

"Copy that," he said. "I'll call it in."

Erin nodded. Then she took Rolf and followed Jenkins and Pohlman out into the hall, letting the door swing shut behind her.

She went around the corner, walking briskly back the way she'd come. As she went, she felt her certainty draining away. If she was wrong, she'd look awfully silly. She was just stirring up confusion and imagining trouble. It was because she felt partially responsible for Finnegan. If she'd moved faster against the O'Malleys, he might already be behind bars. Then two men wouldn't have been maimed, a little kid wouldn't have been hurt, and she wouldn't be wasting the afternoon babysitting a crooked union official instead of doing real police work.

She was just in time to see the stairwell door swing shut behind Pohlman. Officer Jenkins was standing outside the bank of elevators, shaking his head.

"What are we doing here, Detective?" he asked as she came up next to him.

"Our job, Officer," she said.

"I hate protection details," he muttered.

"Isn't being a cop one great big protection detail?" she replied.

He blinked. "Y'know, that's a good point," he said. "I never thought of it that way. Nothing happening with the elevators. One of them is two floors down, the other's in the lobby."

Erin's phone buzzed. She took it out and saw Webb's name. "Excuse me," she said to Jenkins, raising the phone to her ear. "O'Reilly."

"Who did you say was with you there?" Webb asked. No preliminaries, just straight into the questions.

"Courtney, his hired muscle, and two cops," she said, bewildered. "Jenkins and Burkhardt. Listen, sir, we've got a situation here and—"

"You listen, O'Reilly," Webb interrupted. "There's something you need to know. Piekarski was going over BK's financials and—"

A short, sharp exclamation sounded behind the stairwell door, followed by a muffled thump.

"What was that?" Jenkins wondered aloud.

"Hold that thought, sir," Erin said. She turned toward the stairwell and shifted the phone to her left hand, looping Rolf's leash around her wrist, freeing up her gun hand. Webb kept talking, but she wasn't listening.

Jenkins stepped toward the door, drawing his sidearm. It was a Glock 18, identical to Erin's own.

"Jenkins, get back!" she ordered, but it was too late.

The stairwell door flew open. A long loop of something tan-colored whipped through the air. It fell around Jenkins, pulled tight, and yanked him off his feet. The officer gave a startled yelp and went down hard, his pistol skittering across the floor.

Erin had time to register the makeshift lasso as a length of emergency firehose from the stairwell. She saw the heavy bronze nozzle with odd clarity. Then Kyle Finnegan stepped through the doorway, hauling the hapless Jenkins toward himself like a kid playing tug-of-war. He wasn't even bothering to look at the fallen cop. Instead, his eyes were fixed on Erin. He had a casual, almost pleasant half-smile on his face.

"Mistress, what cheer?" he said by way of greeting. Without looking away, he stooped and picked up Jenkins's pistol with one hand, the other still holding the hose.

Erin's answer was directed at Rolf and was only one word.

"*Fass!*"

Rolf's claws dug deep into the expensive carpet. He launched himself across the intervening space without even touching the floor, ears laid flat against his skull, mouth open.

Finnegan didn't have time to raise the gun or dodge; he hardly had time to blink. Then Rolf's jaws snapped shut on his forearm. Ninety pounds of German Shepherd dragged at the limb.

Erin had only known one man who could still use an arm once Rolf had it in his mouth, and Finnegan was no Mickey Connor. The pistol hit the floor for the second time in ten seconds. But Finnegan didn't go down. Rolf bit down harder, teeth shredding the man's tattered jacket sleeve. Erin saw blood on the arm. The K-9 growled ferociously, tail lashing with excitement, but Finnegan's expression didn't change.

"Stop fighting my dog!" she ordered, snatching out her Glock and taking two-handed aim at the man's center of mass. She'd dropped her phone. Webb's name still showed on the screen, his voice emanating plaintively, talking to nobody.

"Am I fighting him?" Finnegan replied mildly.

The sheer absurdity of the question made Erin blink. This was outside her experience; Rolf's too. The dog was used to opponents who fought back or, more typically, curled into screaming balls of panic. A man who didn't fight, but didn't surrender either, was something he had no idea how to address.

Rolf fell back on his training. His partner had told him to bite this man, and he'd been trained to hold on until she told him to let go, so that was what he intended to do. He growled louder and began whipping his head from side to side with increasing vigor, trying to shake a more normal reaction out of his victim.

Finnegan let his arm move with the dog, watching it with detached interest. At his feet, Jenkins started struggling free of the hose. Casually, almost nonchalantly, Finnegan took hold of the end of the hose with his free hand, a few inches below the nozzle, and brought it around in a short, businesslike arc. The nozzle crashed down on top of Jenkins's head. He crumpled in a heap.

"Jesus Christ!" Erin burst out. "You just assaulted a cop!"

"No, I didn't," Finnegan said.

"What're you talking about? I just watched you smack him on the head!"

"That's not a cop," Finnegan said. "And neither are you."

"Shut up!" she shouted. "Of course I am! Get down on the floor or I will shoot you!"

"Pluck up thy spirits," he said. "Look cheerfully upon me. Here, love, thou seest how diligent I am."

"Enough!" Erin was still shouting. "That is enough, God damn it! No more games, no more damn cryptic quotes, no more Finnegan bullshit! This ends here!"

Rolf snarled through a mouthful of Finnegan, agreeing with Erin. He clawed at the man with his front legs but couldn't get a good purchase, so contented himself by continuing to immobilize the arm. That was what a good dog was supposed to do, and Rolf was a very good dog. His tail wagged a little more uncertainly than usual, but it still wagged.

"You're right," Finnegan said. "It ends here. But we're at an impasse, would you agree? I'm unarmed, I'm not resisting, so you can't shoot me and still be what you claim to be."

"I don't *want* to shoot you," she retorted. "I will if you make me."

Rolf was continuing to thrash back and forth with Finnegan's arm, which was making Finnegan a difficult target. Erin didn't want to hit her dog, but she also didn't want to tell him to release. Finnegan had already shown how dangerous he could be, even without a weapon.

"Backup's on the way," she told him. "There's going to be a bunch more cops here any minute. Give it up now, before this gets any worse."

"Drop it!" someone said behind Erin. It sounded like Courtney.

Erin knew better than to take her eyes off a suspect, but Rolf had him more or less under control. She spun around. At the corner of the hallway stood Lee Briggs, Leroy Courtney, and Officer Burkhardt. Briggs and Burkhardt held guns in their hands, aimed and ready.

Chapter 22

"Drop the gun!" Burkhardt shouted. To her disbelief, the officer was pointing his pistol directly at her.

"What're you doing, Burkhardt?" she asked, but the creeping cold in her stomach told her she already knew the answer.

"Now!" he said.

Erin didn't see a choice. She could do the blaze-of-glory thing and try to shoot him, but he already had a bead on her. Both of them were wearing Kevlar vests, so she'd have to go for a head shot. That was chancy at the best of times. And even if she got him, Briggs would probably get her.

"We're all on the same team here," she said, slowly crouching and laying her Glock on the floor. She considered going for her ankle gun, but it would take too long to draw. "*Pust,*" she added.

Rolf, on hearing his "release" command, finally relaxed his jaws and dropped his front paws to the carpet. His hackles bristled and he stared balefully at Finnegan for a moment, then trotted to Erin's side to be told what a good boy he'd been and hopefully get his toy. Finnegan, bleeding from his right arm, leaned against the wall next to a fire extinguisher box. He looked suddenly very tired.

"If only that were true," Courtney sighed. "Why couldn't you just shoot that crazy Irishman? He's broken into the building, he's assaulted multiple people, including a police officer. That's plenty of justification. It would've been simple to do the paperwork. But you never intended to get rid of him."

"What the hell are you talking about?" Erin demanded.

"I had my suspicions when Corky Corcoran set up the meeting," Courtney said. "Evan O'Malley's pet detective, wanting to talk to me? About a case nobody cares about? Please. Everyone knows what you are. Junkyard O'Reilly, the attack dog with a badge. But when I offered you a chance to take care of Finnegan, you ducked out."

"I appreciate that," Finnegan said.

"Forget about it," Erin said without taking her eyes from Courtney. "It was business. I don't even like you."

"I never thought you did," Finnegan replied.

"I came here to protect you," Erin told Courtney.

"Bullshit," Courtney said. "You've been working with him this whole time."

"What kind of sense does that make?" she snapped. "What possible reason would I have?"

"I assumed he was paying you," Courtney said, shrugging. "I pay enough for my own police protection. I told you I was connected with the union."

Erin glared at Burkhardt.

"Don't you go getting high and mighty on me," the Patrolman said. "You do the same thing, lady."

"So you'd kill another cop?" she spat.

"I told you," Finnegan said. "There are no cops here, just killers behind shields."

"Why'd you come?" she asked. "What was the damn point? And don't feed me that revenge line, or any bullshit about Charlie Majors being your best friend. I think we're past that."

"He didn't tell you?" Courtney asked in surprise. "I guess that makes sense. Then he wouldn't have to share."

"Share what?" Erin asked.

"The money, of course."

"What money?" That startled her enough to glance Finnegan's way.

The Irishman was sane enough to offer her a slightly sheepish smile. "Would you believe me if I told you I'd always intended to offer you a fair share?" he asked.

"No," she said.

Courtney chuckled. "Why don't you tell her the truth?" he said. "So she understands what's at stake."

"And we can do business?" Finnegan replied. "Do you think she'll ope her lap to saint-seducing gold?"

That quote sounded vaguely familiar to Erin, but she couldn't place it and didn't care. "I think I can guess," she said. "Charlie Majors was meeting Garth Engstrom and Tracy Chadwick. I'd been assuming it was a negotiation, to set up a crooked real-estate development through the City Council. But that doesn't make sense. Tracy was a nobody, a clerk. He had no power to negotiate anything. I think the agreement had already been reached. That meet wasn't a discussion; it was a payoff. Tracy was getting money from Charlie and Garth."

Courtney clapped his hands slowly. "Give the lady a cigar," he said. "Go on, tell us the rest. You're doing great."

"I would've guessed cash," she said. "But a briefcase full of money would be long gone by now. You would've taken it off them when you snatched them."

"Me?" Courtney asked, feigning innocence in an utterly unconvincing manner.

"Yeah, Big Roy," she said. "You were there, fresh from Detroit. I'm guessing you left a few guys you trusted to take care of Finnegan out there, while you handled the crooked branch of your union's little problem here in New York. But Finnegan turned out tougher than you thought, and the money wasn't where you thought it was."

"Oh, it was there," Courtney said. "We just couldn't lay our hands on it."

"An encrypted thumb drive?" she guessed. "With account information?"

"Right again," Courtney said. "You're good at this."

"I'm a detective," she said dryly.

"We couldn't open the thing," Courtney said. He laughed. "Maybe we snuffed Majors too quickly, but he didn't give up the password. None of them did. And the really funny thing is, neither did the intended recipient."

"Councilman Lombardo," Erin said.

"Oh, we talked to him," Courtney said. "Years ago. He would've loved to be part of an arrangement. It really was a sizable payout. Five hundred large, even split two ways, is worth going after. But he didn't have the password! Why do you suppose that is?"

"It was insurance," Erin said. "Sort of like an escrow account. Once the deal was finalized, he'd get the password and be able to access the money. But if he didn't have it, and neither did the guys who gave him the drive..."

"Then someone else did," Courtney finished. "Somebody in charge of the operation."

Everyone looked at Finnegan.

"The good gods assuage thy wrath," he said. "And turn the dregs of it upon this varlet here—this, who, like a block, hath denied my access to thee."

"Do you have any idea what this lunatic is talking about?" Courtney asked Erin.

"Not usually," she said.

"Well, here's my proposition," Courtney said. "You give me the password, Mr. Finnegan, and in return, I won't kill either of you."

"Lord, Lord, how subject we old men are to this vice of lying," Finnegan said.

"Okay, that one I understood," Erin said. "He's calling you on your bullshit. You can't leave me alive, because I'm a cop, and you can't leave him alive, because he's a batshit maniac who'll hunt you down and kill you."

Courtney sighed. "All right. There's still a few different ways this can go. You're absolutely right, Finnegan doesn't walk out of here. You might recall, I was perfectly willing to have him taken out of the picture. Then that thumb drive would be just a really expensive paperweight, but getting rid of him would've been worth it. That's the problem with having a reputation as a homicidal nutjob. People don't trust you, and you're too dangerous to keep around. But Miss O'Reilly, you can still walk away. I'd really rather not deal with the headache of killing a decorated detective. It would raise all sorts of questions."

"I was wondering how you were planning on explaining it," she said. "Especially when more backup will be arriving any second. I doubt the whole One-Nine is on your payroll."

"They're not," Courtney said placidly. "So it's a good thing no backup's on the way."

"I never called it in," Burkhardt said. "Sorry."

"I see," Erin said.

"So it's really not that hard to explain," Courtney said. "I can see the headlines now: heroic detective dies defending New York citizen from murderous assault. I've got two officers to swear to my version of what happened."

"One officer," Finnegan corrected, nudging Jenkins with his foot. "I think this fellow's gone the way of that lad who went up the hill to fetch a pail of water."

"Whatever," Courtney said. "Lee, I'd like you to convince Mr. Finnegan that if he holds out on us, what's left of his life will be very painful. Officer Burkhardt, if Detective O'Reilly or her dog tries to interfere, please kill them both."

Briggs started down the hallway toward them. Burkhardt advanced alongside, keeping his pistol trained on Erin.

"Thanks for all that," Erin said.

Courtney gave her an odd look. "For what?"

"Confessing," she said.

"You're not wearing a wire," Courtney scoffed.

"No," she agreed. "But look on the floor, by the elevators. What do you see?"

Briggs looked. "It's a cell phone, boss," he reported. "Oh, shit. The line's open!"

Erin didn't know how much Lieutenant Webb had heard over the open phone line. She didn't know if it would matter; Courtney, with nothing to lose, might very well decide to kill everyone in the hallway and run for it. What mattered was that she and Finnegan had a second's worth of distraction and she intended to use it.

"*Fass!*" she yelled at Rolf as she charged Briggs.

Burkhardt reflexively fired at her, but she'd deliberately sidestepped as she rushed Briggs, putting the big ex-football player's body between her and the crooked cop. The bullet didn't come anywhere close. Briggs was twice her weight and much wider than she was, which made him a great human shield but a terrifying close-combat opponent. He reached for her with enormous hands.

Erin ducked and kicked him in the side of his bad knee as hard as she could. The toe of her shoe connected with the joint.

Briggs gave a remarkably high-pitched cry of pain. His leg buckled and he started to fall.

Erin knew Burkhardt would shoot her as soon as the big man was out of the way. She went in low, grabbing Briggs by the belt buckle and collar, pulling to add force to his fall. She rammed him headfirst into the wall. His head smashed through the plaster.

Another two gunshots echoed overhead. Rolf yelped. Then there was a hissing sound and the hallway disappeared in a cloud of white vapor.

Briggs was momentarily stunned. Erin gave a mighty heave, rolling him over and planting a knee in his stomach. She couldn't see a thing, but she heard Rolf snarl, followed by a cry of alarm and the thud of a falling body. A pistol fired again at God only knew what.

A shape ran past her. She caught a glimpse of Finnegan out of the corner of her eye. He was carrying a fire extinguisher, which explained the white cloud. The cloud had a strong ammonia smell and made her eyes water.

Erin had no idea where her Glock or phone were, but Briggs had dropped his own pistol right next to her. She grabbed the semiconscious thug, rolled him back onto his belly, and quickly cuffed his hands behind his back. Then she scooped up his gun and did a quick chamber check, verifying it was loaded. It was a Browning nine-millimeter and appeared to be in decent shape. Holding the confiscated gun ready, she went into the smoke, following the sound of Rolf's growl.

Rolf hadn't been a hundred percent sure he was biting the right guy. The situation had changed more quickly than he was accustomed to, and Erin hadn't given him very specific information. He'd briefly considered going back to the first guy he'd bitten, but that one hadn't been fighting his partner anymore. He'd started for the big human Erin had attacked, but then a bullet smacked his vest just behind the shoulder, nearly taking him off his feet, and he locked on to a new target.

This new opponent was quick; he got two more shots off as Rolf charged. One of the bullets thudded into his chest, right over his heart. The ballistic vest stopped the bullet cold, as it had the first one, but it still hurt. Rolf didn't like being hurt; it made him mad. His yelp of outrage rapidly turned into a furious snarl. He was going to enjoy this.

Rolf's second target was much more satisfying than Finnegan had been. When his jaws came together on the human's arm, this human did what they were supposed to; he screamed and fell over. Rolf ended up on top, enthusiastically gripping the arm, relishing the sounds his victim made. It was almost more fun than the rubber Kong ball.

Erin stumbled over Burkhardt and Rolf. Burkhardt wasn't screaming by the time she got there. The breath escaped him in a low hiss of pain and exertion as he tried, and failed, to extricate himself from the K-9's teeth. Rolf didn't seem to be seriously injured, so Erin kicked Burkhardt's gun down the hallway and left him to the dog's tender attentions. Finnegan and Courtney were still unaccounted for.

As she reached the bend in the hallway, she heard a shout and the crash of breaking glass. She stepped clear of the drifting haze from the fire extinguisher and saw the door to Courtney's office standing open. The sounds of a struggle came from within.

"Freeze!" she shouted, moving through the doorway, Briggs's gun leveled.

Courtney had Finnegan by the neck. The enormous Teamster was standing by the window, which showed a dizzying pattern of cracks. High-rise glass usually had a protective layer of plastic inside it, Erin thought distractedly. The glass itself was tempered, so if it broke it would come apart into little pebbles rather than big, jagged shards, but the plastic layer was holding the pane together. Courtney was banging Finnegan's head against the window. Finnegan hung limply in his grasp, head lolling. His eyes were closed.

"Drop him!" Erin ordered.

Courtney turned his head toward her. He smiled, but it no longer looked friendly. "You really should choose your words more carefully," he said. He rammed Finnegan against the window one more time. The plastic flexed and bent. Broken glass cascaded into the falling snow like sparkling bits of ice. Courtney pushed and let go.

Finnegan's eyes flew open. One hand came up and seized Courtney's necktie even as he tumbled out into space.

Courtney gave a startled squawk and lurched forward. He flailed at the window frame and caught it with one hand. He hung on desperately, even as Finnegan's full weight dragged at his neck.

Erin tossed the pistol away and sprinted across the room. Finnegan was dangling by one hand, his other hand scrabbling for grip at the base of the window, lacerating his fingers on the pebbles of glass that remained lodged in the frame. Both men were about to fall. She might be able to save one, both, or neither. Finnegan's hand slipped on the necktie, sliding down almost to the end. Courtney struck at the dangling man with his free hand, landing a glancing blow on his skull.

If she braced Courtney, he'd just use the opportunity to knock Finnegan loose. To save Courtney was to kill Finnegan. But if she relieved him of the weight at his neck, he might not fall and just maybe everybody would survive. Erin made the best choice she could.

She dropped into a slide, skidding on her ass across the carpet, her feet fetching up against the intact window just to the right of the broken pane. She reached down with both hands, her right going across her own body, and grabbed Finnegan's left wrist as tightly as she could. She took a breath and hauled him up, thanking God he wasn't a big man.

Finnegan came up, but he didn't let go of Courtney's tie. As he ascended, he planted a knee on the window frame. Then he made a quick twist and pull, bracing himself against Erin's arms.

The twisting motion caught Courtney by surprise. The Teamster's hand slipped on the frame. His center of gravity was in his big, broad shoulders, which hung outside the building. He toppled forward.

Erin, practically touching the man's leg, couldn't do a damn thing. Even if she'd let go of Finnegan, she had about as much chance of holding the big man up as she did of lifting a fully-loaded semitrailer. All she could do was watch as Courtney pitched out into the fast-falling sleet.

It was twelve stories to the street. The fall took about two and a half seconds. He screamed all the way down.

She let go of Finnegan and took a moment to collect herself. He got to his feet, a little shakily, and leaned on Courtney's desk, resting his hands next to the man's computer.

"NYPD!" someone shouted in the hallway. Several voices were talking at once. They all sounded upset.

"In here!" Erin shouted back. "Don't touch the dog!"

There was a rush of running footsteps. Half a dozen uniformed officers swarmed into the office, guns in hand. They stopped, staring at Erin, Finnegan, and the shattered window.

A Patrol sergeant with the tough, lined face of a veteran cop stepped in front of his colleagues. He lowered his pistol. "What in God's name is going on?" he demanded.

Chapter 23

"It doesn't matter what the weather report says," Webb said wearily. "Whenever this squad gets going, there's always a shitstorm."

"I took a look outside," Vic said. "No shit falling out of the sky. Just snow and crooked union guys."

"Not funny, Neshenko," Webb said. He pulled his trench coat tight around himself and shivered. He'd grown up in Los Angeles and had never gotten used to New York winters. The draught from the broken window was making Courtney's office very chilly.

The top floor of the building was overrun with cops. Burkhardt, Briggs, and Finnegan were on their way to holding cells. Jenkins, Pohlman, and Ed from the front desk were on their way to the hospital. Courtney was well beyond either incarceration or medical attention. CSU techs were beginning the lengthy process of gathering evidence.

"Thanks for coming," Erin said.

"What choice did we have?" Webb said unhappily. "One moment I'm trying to warn one of my detectives that a couple of cops' names have shown up as taking organized crime payoffs, the next I'm listening to bad audio of what sounds like World War Three. Of course I called more backup, and of course we got here as fast as we could."

"So that's what you were trying to say," Erin said. "You found out about Burkhardt and Jenkins."

"Zofia did," Vic said proudly. "That girl's gonna make one hell of a detective."

"Which is good, considering the chances you people take," Webb said. "At what point, exactly, did you decide to throw our prime murder suspect out a window?"

Erin sighed. "I didn't. Finnegan pulled him. Sort of. I was holding Finnegan at the time, and Courtney was trying to chuck him out."

"Did Kyle Finnegan, or did he not, murder a man right in front of you?" Webb asked.

"It's complicated."

"Not for Courtney," Vic said. "All his problems came down to one patch of New York sidewalk. They'll be cleaning him up for a while."

Erin shuddered. She could still hear his terrified scream. That sound would follow her into her nightmares. "I didn't want him to fall," she said.

"Lay this all out for me," Webb said. "You've solved the case, haven't you?"

She nodded. "For what it's worth."

"It's your job, as well as your sworn duty," Webb reminded her. "As is obeying orders. So as your superior officer, I'm ordering you to enlighten me."

"Okay," Erin said. "Ten years ago, Charlie Majors wasn't happy working for the Teamsters. He was planning to branch out from the Teamsters and go to work for the O'Malleys. He had a friend, Garth Engstrom, in the construction industry, who was already connected. One of them knew a buyable councilman. Together, they hatched a plan to set up a crooked business. They were planning to pay the councilman a half-million dollars in exchange for lucrative contracts for Emerald Isle Estates. You remember them; the O'Malley construction company. The O'Malleys would make out like bandits, and so would Majors and Engstrom.

"The Teamsters got wind of what was going on. I don't know how; word gets around in the underworld. The truckers weren't happy about it and were already making noises against the O'Malleys, so Evan O'Malley sent Kyle Finnegan to sort things out."

"He's a shitty peacemaker," Vic observed.

"If all Evan wanted was peace, he would've sent Corky," Erin said.

"Finnegan is the Mob equivalent of gunboat diplomacy, I take it," Webb said.

"Exactly," she said. "Finnegan was supposed to apply pressure. But Courtney had already decided to make his move. He was supposed to meet Finnegan in Detroit, but he sent a crew of henchmen in his place and came to New York to deal with the Majors situation in person. The henchmen got Finnegan's assistant, but they underestimated Finnegan. He killed all three of them."

"Jesus Christ," Vic said. "Why isn't this guy already warming a cell?"

"The Teamsters got rid of the bodies and hushed it up," Erin explained. "They didn't want the questions four corpses would've raised. There was no murder investigation in Detroit."

"And there wasn't one in New York either," Webb said, "since those bodies disappeared too."

"But the half-million dollars didn't," Erin said. "That's why Courtney wanted to handle Majors himself. I don't think he wanted to share the payoff with his bosses. He'd found out about the meeting between Councilman Lombardo's assistant and the other two. He had his buddies at Black Bull snatch them and take them to that construction site in Brooklyn for disposal. But he guessed wrong. No cash changed hands that night; what they had was an encrypted thumb drive with the account info on it. And none of the guys there knew the password."

Vic snickered. "I'd love to have seen the look on his face," he said. "It's like that scene in that movie *Dead Presidents* when the demolition guy blows up the armored car and all the money catches fire. All that dough and he couldn't lay his hands on it."

"Finnegan was the only man who knew the password," Erin said. "And Finnegan had brain damage thanks to getting smacked with a tire iron. Courtney couldn't get at him; first he was in the hospital, under police guard, and then he was back with the O'Malleys. Besides, there was no telling he'd remember the password at all.

"But Courtney kept the thumb drive, just in case he ever got the chance to get the password out of Finnegan. You never know, right? And anyway, he'd taken care of the traitor and removed the competition for those fat city contracts. Emerald Isle Estates never really recovered, and now they're gone."

"That's right," Webb said. "They got shut down last year after the City Center thing with Tommy O'Malley."

"Then we dug up the bodies and things got complicated," Erin said. "Finnegan never knew exactly what happened to Majors and his buddies. The O'Malleys told Charlie's widow he'd run off with a girl in Atlantic City, and I guess it was possible. They might've taken the money and run; it's the sort of thing gangsters sometimes do. But once we had the bodies, Finnegan started trying to learn what had happened to the money."

"He told you about the money?" Vic asked.

"You think he'd want to share with me?" Erin said. "No, he played it as getting revenge for what had happened to his dear friend Charlie, but Finnegan doesn't have friends. He piggybacked on our investigation, finding out what he could. He got to BK Construction and beat Elijah Drake's name out of poor Howie. Then he went to Drake's house and got an ID on Big Roy. After that, he came here to get his money back."

"How'd he know Courtney kept the drive?" Vic asked doubtfully. "Ten years is a long time to sit on something like that."

"If you had something worth five hundred grand, would you throw it away?"

Vic shrugged. "Good point. But how'd he know it was here?"

"He didn't," Erin said. "And he doesn't. Neither do I. Maybe it's not. CSU hasn't found it yet. I think Finnegan intended to torture the information out of Courtney, the same as he did with the other two guys."

"He's nuts," Vic said.

"We've been over that," Webb said.

"No, seriously," Vic said. "This place was full of armed guards and that asshole thought he could just walk in, by himself, and take them all out?"

"It worked, more or less," Erin said. "Finnegan's a pretty tough son of a bitch."

"I'll say," Vic said. The first responders had found Ed behind his desk, unconscious and bleeding from the face. Their best guess was he'd been head-butted in the nose hard enough to break it and drive fragments of cartilage into his brain. He'd need a neurosurgeon. Pohlman was luckier by comparison; he'd just been tossed down two flights of stairs, breaking both collarbones, an ankle, and his right arm. Officer Jenkins had a fractured skull and a concussion, courtesy of the fire hose nozzle.

"It's a miracle only Courtney was killed," Webb said. "What about Burkhardt and Jenkins?"

"We called them in," Erin said. "They were on duty and close to the building, so they responded to Dispatch and volunteered. Nobody but Piekarski knew they were on Courtney's payroll. Damn it all, he even bragged to me about being in with the Police Union."

"I can imagine what the union rep's gonna say," Vic said.

"Let the Captain worry about that," Webb said. "That's way above your pay grade."

"Thank God for that," Vic said.

"You're telling me there's a bank account out there with five hundred thousand dollars in it," Webb said. "And nobody knows how to get it?"

"Looks that way," Erin said.

"So this whole thing was for nothing," Vic said. "I guess it's true; crime really doesn't pay."

"Crime pays pretty well," Webb said. "That's why there are so many criminals."

"At least we got that bastard Finnegan," Vic said with irritated satisfaction. "He needs to be in jail. Remember, he—"

"Yeah, yeah, we know," Erin said. "He ate a guy's face. Leave it alone already."

"You're right," Webb said. "We ought to have enough to take him off the street for a good long time."

"Yeah," Erin said. But she had a sneaky feeling it might be a little more complicated than the Lieutenant thought.

* * *

Ian Thompson made eye contact with Erin the moment she walked into the Barley Corner. The time was just before four o'clock. She was actually a little early; after Courtney's death, Webb had decided that even though she technically hadn't killed him, she'd still been directly involved. He'd sent her home once CSU had the scene well in hand.

"Afternoon," Ian said. "Mr. Carlyle's in back. He's waiting for you with—"

"Don't tell me," she interrupted. "Evan O'Malley?"

"And Mr. Pritchard," Ian said.

"Have they been here long?"

"Arrived about half an hour ago."

Erin nodded. "Thanks."

She briefly considered going upstairs to grab a quick shower and change, but decided not to. She was in the middle of what Ian might call a "fluid situation," and that didn't mean the kind of hot water that came out of a shower. It called for speed and adaptability.

Evan had come about Finnegan. There was no other possible reason. And Erin didn't want to talk about Finnegan. But undercover work was rarely based on personal preferences. So she held off on her after-dinner drink, sucked in a deep breath, activated the recording device hidden in her underwire, and led Rolf into Carlyle's back room.

Carlyle and Evan were seated at the card table, directly across from one another. Carlyle had a glass of Guinness in front of him, apparently untouched. Evan was sipping from a glass that contained either clear liquor or—more likely—water.

Erin nodded to Evan. She was too tired and shaken by the day's events to be overly polite, even to the O'Malley chieftain. "Mr. O'Malley," she said. "Thanks for coming. I assume the Snake's behind me, checking out my backside."

"Nothing personal," Gordon Pritchard rasped from the dark corner behind the door. Erin believed him; "Snake" Pritchard was a creepy son of a bitch, with his damaged vocal cords and horrible scars, but he was really just Evan's version of Ian Thompson. He was a bodyguard and a trained killer, not a voyeur.

It still took all her self-control to stand still and listen to that rough voice sending unpleasant tingles up and down her spine. Pritchard was armed and ready for trouble. If Evan suspected her of treachery, neither she nor Carlyle would leave this room alive.

But to show nerves would be to invite suspicion, so she ignored Pritchard and took a seat on Carlyle's right. "Did I miss anything important?" she asked, keeping her tone as light as she could manage.

"Not at all," Evan said. "In fact, it's you I've come to see, Miss O'Reilly. I've just been filling the time with everyday business matters."

"Okay," Erin said. "Here I am. What is it you're wanting from me?"

"I understand you've taken Mr. Finnegan into custody."

"Yeah. That'll happen when somebody chucks another guy out a twelfth-story window right in front of a cop."

"You were the only witness to the alleged defenestration?"

Erin had to fight to keep her poker face. It was the first time she'd ever heard that word used in an actual conversation. It was such an oddly specific word, making it unintentionally amusing. Did the English language really need a word that meant "the act of throwing someone out a window?"

"That's right," she said. "The backup arrived a few seconds later."

"And you were not wearing a body camera?"

She shook her head. "Detectives usually don't."

Evan smiled thinly. "So you and Mr. Finnegan must, of necessity, be the arbiters of the truth of this event."

"You want me to doctor my report," she said. "So Finnegan doesn't go down for murder."

"A crude way of putting it," Evan said. "I would say it would be helpful to instill reasonable doubt into the proceedings against him."

"Finnegan's out of control," Erin said bluntly. "He went totally off the rails. He's left a trail of busted-up bodies from here to Brooklyn. Most of his targets were in the Life, but not all of them. A little kid got hurt and he killed the family dog. I can't sweep all this under the rug."

"No one is asking you to," Evan said. "Don't worry about minor peripheral issues. Just give me your assurance he will not be charged in connection with Mr. Courtney's unfortunate accident."

"What about the rest of the guys who were there?" she replied. "Courtney's bodyguards and those two cops?"

Evan's shoulders moved in the slightest hint of a shrug. "They're not in my employ," he said. "What happens to them is immaterial."

"And the thumb drive?" she pressed.

"What thumb drive?" Evan asked blandly.

"The one with the bank info," she said. "The one that gives access to five hundred grand in O'Malley money."

"Long gone, I fear," Evan said. "I wrote that off as a bad investment years ago. The organization has moved on."

"So that's it?" she said. "Get Finnegan off the hook? And then what? He needs to lie low. He can't just go around New York breaking legs. He's lucky to be alive, let alone free and clear. He almost got me killed, too."

"My apologies," Evan said. There wasn't the slightest hint of warmth in his icy stare. "I didn't realize you were so sensitive."

"Just guarantee me this is over," she said. "Finnegan followed that damn drive all the way up the chain, and that chain just got broken. No more revenge, no more beating the crap out of kids in front of their parents."

"I may be misunderstanding you," Evan said. "But it sounds like you're giving me orders."

"Of course not," she said quickly, before Carlyle could open his mouth to protest. "I'm giving you advice, sir. Good advice, based on my years of experience in the Department."

"Understood," Evan said. "Don't doubt how much I value your knowledge and position. Good afternoon."

He stood up. Pritchard, emerging from the shadows like a vampire in an old black-and-white horror movie, favored Erin with a nod of professional respect. Then they left.

Erin buried her head in her hands. Carlyle laid a hand on her shoulder.

"This is the last time," she said, knowing she was making herself a promise she might not be able to keep.

"Let's hope so, darling," he said. "No fear, he'll get what's coming. It's not far off."

"It's too damn far. The sound that guy made... Finnegan *murdered* him. And I was right there."

"And he'll pay for it," Carlyle said.

"I should've let him fall, too," she said bitterly.

"So you could be a murderer as well?" he asked quietly. "I've killed when I didn't have to, Erin. It leaves a stain on the soul. I'd not have you so tainted."

"But I am," she said. "I helped him, don't you see? I didn't mean to, but I did it. He used me, that bastard!"

"That's what people in the Life do," he said. "They use those around them."

"This is the last time," she repeated.

Chapter 24

"This is your report?" Webb asked.

"Yes, sir," Erin said. She'd come in at noon, per Webb's request, and had filed the falsified report. She'd written another report too, a genuine one, but that was under lock and key until the O'Malley situation was resolved.

"You understand what's going to happen," Webb said. "Without the murder charge, Kyle Finnegan was looking at a number of assault charges. He could easily make bail on those. He'll be out on the street by the end of the day, tomorrow at the latest."

"Was?" Erin asked.

"Keep up with the times," Vic growled.

"What happened?" she asked.

"Nobody's pressing charges," Webb said with weary disgust. "People are changing statements, refusing to make positive IDs. Take the attack on BK Construction. Howard Manterville is recovering from the first of what promises to be several invasive, painful surgeries. His legs have more pins in them than a bowling alley. But he says everything's all a blur, on account of the pain. I showed him a picture of Finnegan. Nothing."

"What about Mia? The receptionist?"

"Sudden-onset amnesia," Vic said. "All of a sudden she doesn't remember a thing."

"Then there's the Drake family," Webb went on. "You'd think Mrs. Drake, at least, would want the guy who assaulted her son locked up, wouldn't you? Except she went in to see her husband at the hospital. Nobody knows what they talked about, but when she came out, she'd forgotten the face of her home invader. Her husband's singing the same tune."

Erin sighed. "The O'Malleys got to *all* of them?"

"There's still Briggs, Pohlman, and Villiers," Webb said.

"Who's Villiers?"

"Ed Villiers," Vic said. "The guy in Courtney's lobby."

"But they all have records," Webb said. "They're known enforcers for the Detroit mob. Their word doesn't carry much weight in court, and Finnegan's lawyer will point out all the assault charges they've racked up between them. Then he'll show them Finnegan, who's all of a hundred sixty pounds dripping wet and wouldn't make half of Briggs or Pohlman. You think a jury's going to make assault charges stick?"

"And Finnegan wasn't armed," Erin said.

"Hard to prove premeditation if a man doesn't bother bringing a weapon," Webb agreed. "He could even claim Courtney invited him there to talk about some kind of deal and then ambushed him. We've got no forced entry to the office. CSU says the glass fragments they took from Finnegan's hair indicate he was shoved through the window."

"And that's it," Vic said. His face twisted angrily. "He walks. After everything he did. He walks the hell away! What are we even doing here? Because we're sure as shit not serving the goddamn public trust!"

"That's enough, Neshenko," Webb said sternly. "You know the drill. We don't win all of them."

"You're damn right that's enough!" Vic snapped. "That's it. I'm done."

"What do you mean, done?" Webb demanded, but he was talking to Vic's retreating shoulders. The Russian was leaving the Major Crimes office in long, angry strides.

"Get back here!" Webb called. Vic took no notice.

"I'll go after him, sir," Erin said. "Rolf, *fuss!*"

The two of them chased Vic down the stairs, catching up to him at the stairwell door that led to the parking garage. He was way too angry to wait for the elevator. He stomped each step so hard that Erin almost expected to see boot prints hammered into the concrete.

"Vic," she said. "Wait a second!"

"What the hell for?" he retorted. "That's all we do around here, is wait."

He flung open the door and marched across the garage to his Taurus. He fumbled in his pocket for his keys and dropped them on the floor.

"God damn it!" he burst out. He kicked the keys. They skittered across the garage and disappeared under another parked car.

Erin, Vic, and Rolf stared after the keys. Vic measured the vehicle with his eyes, as if considering whether he could pick it up and toss it away.

"Well, that's just great," he said, shaking his head.

"Rolf, *bring!*" Erin ordered, pointing to the car.

Rolf sprang forward eagerly. He loped to the parked car, ducked his head, and wriggled his way under it. All that was visible was his tail, which was enthusiastically wagging. After a moment, he backed out from under the car and trotted proudly to Erin's side, Vic's keys in his mouth.

"Good boy," Erin said, ruffling the base of his ears. "*Sei brav.*" She pulled out his Kong toy and offered an exchange.

Rolf figured he was getting the better side of the deal. He dropped the keys and went for the rubber ball. Erin scooped up the keys.

Vic held out his hand.

"Just a minute," she said. "What's eating you?"

"You know damn well what," he said. "That asshole belongs in prison."

"And he'll be there in the end," she promised, uncomfortably aware that last night she'd been on the opposite side of this same conversation.

He shook his head. "Not soon enough. I've had it."

"So what're you going to do?" she asked. "Take your ball and go home?"

"Something like that, yeah. I'm gonna put in for a transfer."

The last word hung on the air between them. Erin stared at him in disbelief.

"You don't mean that," she managed to say.

"I don't? Then why don't you tell me what I do mean."

She sighed. "Vic, we can't talk about this here."

"Because other cops might hear," he growled. "Yeah, I know. Goddamn secrets and lies. I'm so fucking sick of them."

Erin unlocked the Taurus. She opened the rear door.

"Oh, no you don't," Vic said. "That mutt's just been under a squad car. He's gonna get oil and all kinds of shit on my seats."

"Your back seats are washable," she reminded him. "Guys throw up in there. Rolf, *hupf!*"

Rolf hopped up into the car, still clutching his precious toy. He settled on the seat and got down to some serious gnawing and slobbering.

"He's drooling," Vic complained.

Erin ignored that and slid into the passenger seat. Vic, still grumbling, got behind the wheel. Once all the doors were closed, providing some noise privacy, Erin turned to face him.

"Look, Vic, I get it," she said. "You think I'm not sick of this? I know you think I've gone native, that I'm too sympathetic to gangsters, but hanging around these guys is wrecking me. I feel like little pieces of me are flaking off every day. I have to hold on with both hands or I'll forget I'm a cop. Do you know how easy it'd be for me to just straight-up murder Finnegan? And do you think it hasn't crossed my mind?"

"You're choosing to go through with this," he said, pointing his finger at her face. "Don't try playing the victim card. We know what real victims look like and there's none of them in this car."

"Is that what you're worried about?" she asked. "Other victims?"

"Yeah," he said. "Erin, that jerk doesn't just kill bad guys. He's a danger to everybody around him. He's an unstable psycho just looking for an excuse to go off! You know why he doesn't carry a weapon? Because everywhere he looks, he sees weapons! And that's the way he likes it! You gonna try to tell me he doesn't like hurting people? Because what I see is a goddamn sadist who gets off on pain."

She sighed. "That's what you see because that's what he is," she said. "I don't like him. He gives me the friggin' creeps. But I need to buy a few more days of goodwill with the O'Malleys. We're *this* close. But we have to move carefully."

"Why?"

"Because of cops like Burkhardt and Jenkins, that's why."

"Oh."

"Exactly."

"I liked it better when I knew who the bad guys were," he said.

"If it was always obvious, they wouldn't need detectives. And you're a great detective, Vic. I mean it. You may not like thinking outside the box, but you're good at it. We need you."

He shook his head. "I just don't know if I can do it anymore," he said.

"Why not?"

"It's a boy."

Erin blinked. "I think I missed something here."

"The kid. Our kid, Zofia's and mine. We were gonna wait to find out, but then we talked about it and we figured we're cops, and what do cops hate?"

"Surprises?"

"Surprises," he agreed. "I'm gonna have a son, and that ought to make me happy, but every time I think about it now I see that little boy, Davy Drake, and I think about that bastard breaking his fingers. If that'd been my kid, I'd have told that prick everything he wanted to know to get him to stop. And then I would've grabbed a tire iron and gone to work on him, and I wouldn't have stopped with the legs. I would've broken every bone in his body, toes to skull, in that order."

"It's getting too personal, isn't it," she said quietly.

"Yeah, I guess it is," he said. "It's getting real. Zofia's due in March. This is actually gonna happen."

"It's going to be great," Erin promised, laying a hand on his arm. "You're going to be one hell of a dad."

"At least when my kid's in kindergarten and tells the other boys 'My dad can beat up your dad,' he'll be telling the truth."

Erin giggled. "No kidding," she said. "I'm just trying to picture you at parent-teacher conferences. There'll be some skinny little teacher sitting across from you, and you'll be leaning across the table playing bad cop, telling her she'll be lucky if she pulls twenty to life."

The tension broke. Vic chuckled. "Yeah," he said. "That'll be something, all right."

"Don't transfer," she said. "You want your kid to be safe? Keep doing what you're doing. Tell you what; you want to be the one to slap the cuffs on Finnegan when the time comes? We ought to be able to swing that."

"Really?" His face lit up. "Okay, you got yourself a deal. And I can make them as tight as I want?"

"Just don't make his hands fall off."

"Are you gonna give me my keys now, or do I have to beg?"

"What're you going to do with them?"

"I'm gonna put them in my pocket. Then I'm gonna go back upstairs and grab a Mountain Dew from the vending machine, unless it's out. If it's sold out, I'm gonna put my foot through the machine. Then I'm gonna get back to work. Those DD-5s aren't gonna file themselves."

"I wish," she said.

And they went back to their desks to finish closing the case.

* * *

Erin avoided courthouses whenever possible. Courts were full of a cop's two least favorite types of people; criminals and lawyers. They also usually had a few of the third least popular category; reporters. And on three separate occasions, she'd gone to court and either witnessed a murder or nearly gotten killed herself.

But this was Finnegan's arraignment, held two mornings after his arrest. He'd have bail set, he'd pay the bail, and he'd walk out free. She needed to be there when it happened, not because she wanted to, but because it was important for her underworld image as his benefactor. So she went through the metal detectors, handed over her guns, and took Rolf to a bench near the back of the courtroom.

Arraignments were usually pretty dull. The defendant pled either guilty, not guilty, or no contest. He also had the option not to say anything, but Erin didn't expect Finnegan to exercise that option. Bail was set or refused. Then the defendant went home, if he'd been able to post bail, or back to Riker's Island if he hadn't. The whole thing usually took only a few minutes.

The most startling thing for Erin was seeing Finnegan in a suit instead of his usual attire. Even though he was wearing everything on the correct body parts, he somehow managed to look off-kilter and disheveled, as if he'd slept in the clothes. His hair was uncombed and he sported a five-o'clock shadow, in spite of the early hour. He looked around the courtroom with mild interest.

Finnegan had drawn Judge Ferris; bad luck for the Irishman. Ferris was old school, a hard-nosed octogenarian whose sense of duty had managed to keep his advancing age at bay. The Judge didn't like criminals one bit.

Once Ferris was seated, the list of charges against Finnegan was read out. He'd been charged with multiple counts of assault, but murder and attempted murder were conspicuously absent and the assault charges were weak. Erin had talked to the DA the night before and he'd agreed not to charge Finnegan for Courtney's death. There was some small stuff, too, like trespass and disorderly conduct, but nobody really cared about those.

"How do you plead?" Ferris asked.

Finnegan didn't appear to have heard the question. He wasn't even looking at the Judge.

Ferris rapped his gavel sharply against his lectern. "If it's not too much trouble, I'd appreciate the defendant's attention."

Finnegan blinked. "Of course," he said, turning his eyes on Ferris.

"Well?" Ferris asked. "How do you plead?"

"Thieves are not judged but they are by to hear," Finnegan said. "Although apparent guilt be seen in them."

There was a short pause. "You can plead guilty, not guilty, or *nolo contendere*," Ferris said. "Those are your only options. Or you can keep spouting nonsense, in which case I'll hold you in contempt of court so fast you'll pick up a speeding ticket on top of your other charges."

"In that case, your Honor, I plead not guilty," Finnegan said.

"Very well," Ferris said. "Bail is set at fifty thousand dollars."

"I applaud your honesty, sir," Finnegan said. "Many men would be more circumspect. What denomination of bills would be most convenient for your use?"

Ferris scowled. "You're not paying me," he said sternly. "You're paying the court a bond, which will be returned to you when you stand trial, or when the charges are dismissed. I don't want your filthy money."

"It's not filthy," Finnegan replied. "I understand it's been well laundered."

Erin could practically hear Ferris's teeth grinding. "Get out of my courtroom," he growled, "and out of my sight."

* * *

Erin and Rolf were waiting for Finnegan when he walked out. He was accompanied by Walsh, the lawyer Evan O'Malley kept on retainer for his people.

"My client has nothing to say to the NYPD," Walsh said automatically. Then he registered her face as well as the shield on her belt. "I'm sorry, Detective O'Reilly. I didn't mean to be rude."

"Forget about it," Erin said. "I was just hoping to have a quick word with Mr. Finnegan. It'll only take a moment."

Walsh nodded doubtfully. He obviously wanted to get his client as far from the courthouse as possible, before Finnegan said something else and got himself thrown back behind bars. He stepped to one side of the hallway.

"You can go a bit further, counselor," Finnegan said. "That way you'll remove the temptation to eavesdrop."

"Whatever you say, Mr. Finnegan," Walsh sighed. He walked away, putting his hands in his suit pockets and whistling a tune he'd probably learned from Corky.

"I thought that went rather well," Finnegan said.

"You nearly got held in contempt," Erin said.

"Horseshoes and hand grenades," Finnegan said placidly.

"Whatever," she said. "You may not be on the hook for taking Courtney out, but those are still serious charges. You've got a record, so they'll throw the book at you. If Ferris is running the sentencing, you could be looking at a decade plus. I hope you have a plan."

"The first thing we do, let's kill all the lawyers," Finnegan said.

"Ha ha," she said dryly. "What're you going to do? Seriously."

"I don't need to do anything," he said. "The road will lay itself before my feet. You know you're on the best possible path when obstacles move themselves out of your way."

"You think the charges are going to be dropped," she said. She already knew, from Vic and Webb, but she wanted to hear Finnegan say it. Admitting to witness tampering would be one more nail in his coffin.

"The pieces are already moving," Finnegan said. "Eyewitnesses are so very unreliable. Glaucoma is a serious condition."

"Glaucoma? What the hell are you talking about?"

"The human eyeball is very susceptible to pressure," he said.

"I see," she said. "And maybe you're right, maybe you'll beat these charges. But let's get one thing straight. Are you listening to me?"

"Always," he said absently, looking at something just over her left shoulder.

"I've smoothed things out for you as well as I could," she said. "Because it's what the boss wants. But I've got a line you do not want to cross. You do what needs doing, but you keep it in the Life. If you ever touch an innocent civilian like that little boy again, I'm going to be there, and Evan O'Malley won't be able to help you."

She had his attention, his vacant, watery gaze fixed on her. "Now you're the one speaking indirectly," he said.

"You want direct?" she retorted. "If you hurt another kid, you won't see the inside of a courtroom. You won't even make it to a damn holding cell. You got that?"

Something flickered in Finnegan's eyes, something she wouldn't have noticed in anyone else's face. It was something entirely normal, entirely sane. Sane... and impressed.

"Copy that," he said, and the moment was gone. "Now, if you'll excuse me, the process of justice in this city, reminiscent as it is of the workings of a sausage-grinder, has left me nauseated. I feel the need to prostrate myself before the porcelain altar."

He walked past her into the nearest men's room. Erin shook her head.

"Translation," she said to Rolf. "He's sick to his stomach and is on his way to puke. He may be a weirdo, but that's not an unusual reaction to the food at Riker's."

She suddenly felt a little sick herself. Had she really just done that? Threatened to murder a man? And she hadn't been bluffing. If her behind-the-scenes machinations got another kid injured, she'd never forgive herself. If Finnegan went nuts again and started hurting the wrong people...

Did that mean there were people it was perfectly okay for him to hurt? The *right* people? She wasn't thinking like a cop. She was thinking like a gangster. She had to get away; from the O'Malleys, from undercover work, from this big, clean, well-lit hall of justice.

The fresh, cold outdoors revived her a little. The sleet had washed away some of the snow, leaving a more typically gray, gritty, slushy New York in its wake; less magical but more solid, more real. She breathed in the brisk December air and watched Rolf prancing happily at her side. It was time to put Finnegan out of her mind. His time would come. She only wished she could be waiting outside that bathroom with cuffs in hand.

Something was still bothering her. Erin slowed, then stopped. Rolf cocked his head at her, one paw poised, ready to continue their walk.

"He ate a guy's face," she said quietly. "Raw. With hot sauce. That guy doesn't get sick to his stomach. Not on prison food, not on anything. If he's throwing up, it's because he wants to. But he doesn't have an eating disorder, at least I don't think so."

She slapped her own forehead. "Damn it! We searched him when we arrested him. The only way he could've gotten anything out of that office would be inside his own body. He got the drive! He was walking around with half a million dollars in his gut! He must've put it in a plastic bag, like a drug mule with a bag of cocaine. How did I miss it?"

Rolf kept listening. She hadn't said anything he understood yet, but he wasn't giving up.

"Shit," she went on. "He had his hands on the desk. The drive was in Courtney's computer. It was right in front of me!"

Erin turned back toward the courthouse. She'd walked a full block. She could run back, but Finnegan would already be gone. He could move very fast when he wanted to.

"Okay, you son of a bitch," she said, knowing he couldn't hear her. "You win this round. Enjoy the moment and the money, because I'm coming for you."

His time would come. Erin O'Reilly was counting the hours. She was going to enjoy taking him down.

Here's a sneak peek from Book 23: Frostbite

Coming 3/25/24

"The National Weather Service has issued a winter storm warning for the greater New York City area, with predicted snowfall in excess of ten inches. Temperatures are expected to plummet well below zero, with a wind chill in the negative double digits. All residents are advised to remain indoors and refrain from unnecessary travel."

The weatherman's face was grim and serious. "We're not joking, folks," he continued. "This is going to be a nasty one. Stock up on food, make sure your heating is working, and hunker down."

A chorus of groans and boos met the man's words. Someone threw a crumpled-up napkin. It ricocheted off the big-screen TV that hung on the Barley Corner's wall. Several anonymous voices expressed unflattering opinions of the weatherman's appearance, personal habits, and sexual preferences.

"At least the kids can look forward to a snow day," Erin O'Reilly said, swirling the half-empty glass of Guinness in her hand. She was sitting at the bar next to her boyfriend Morton Carlyle, reformed gangster and friendly local pub owner.

"But not you poor blighters," Carlyle observed. "Neither snow nor sleet nor gloom of night..."

"That's the Postal Service," she said. "But you're right, the NYPD never closes. I'm just glad I'm not working Traffic. Those guys are going to have a nightmare."

"I'd imagine that's what's got these lads all in a tizzy," Carlyle said. "Two-thirds of them are truckers. They've cargo to move and their living to earn, whatever the weather boffins say. Have you ever tried handling an eighteen-wheeler on an icy highway?"

Erin shivered. All this talk of snow and ice was making her feel cold. "No," she said.

"Nor I," he said. "But according to Wayne McClernand, it's an experience best avoided. Are you sure you're going out tonight? Wouldn't you rather put your feet up with another bowl of Marian's Irish stew?"

"You know I would," she said, looking regretfully at the empty bowl on the bar in front of her. "But it's not up to me. This is an important meeting. You know why."

Carlyle nodded. "I'd be happier if you could do it over the phone, but I understand."

Erin shrugged. "It's the Job," she said, standing up.

Rolf uncurled himself from the base of her stool. The German Shepherd stretched and yawned, opening his jaws amazingly wide. Then he positioned himself at Erin's hip and stared up at her, waiting to see what would happen.

"Call me when you start for home," Carlyle said.

"I'm meeting my people, not yours," she said quietly. "I'm in no danger."

"Not from your folk, perhaps," he said. "But there's the weather to consider. There'll be widows made on the roads tonight, I've no doubt."

"In that case, you've got nothing to worry about," she said, grinning at him.

"And why's that?" he replied.

She leaned in and kissed him on the cheek. "Because we're not married," she said. Then she winked and left the pub.

* * *

"We've got to stop meeting like this."

It was cliché, but the only thing Erin could think of to say. She was still tense from driving through the snow, and meeting with her undercover handler wasn't exactly relaxing. Neither was the venue. Phil liked to meet in parks and other outdoor locations, preferably under cover of darkness, but the weather had wrecked that plan. So now they were standing on a subway platform, pretending they didn't know one another, while Rolf hung out next to Erin and waited for something interesting to happen. The station was otherwise deserted, except for a homeless guy who sat against the far wall with his upturned hat in front of him, a silent receptacle for the charity of strangers. He appeared to be asleep.

"How was the drive?" Phil Stachowski asked. He didn't look like an NYPD Lieutenant. He looked like a down-on-his-luck community-college professor, maybe one who taught English Literature to bored freshmen. He was balding and slightly overweight. His mild, pleasant face was screened by wire-rimmed eyeglasses. He was wearing a shabby topcoat, and Erin knew if she looked under it she'd find an equally shabby tweed jacket with leather elbow patches and a pair of corduroys. If he even bothered wearing a gun, she'd never seen it.

"A little rough," she said. "Not as bad as I thought. Most of the other drivers listened to the news and they're staying home. I'm surprised the subway isn't busier."

"The city's shutting down," Phil said. "The snow's coming pretty hard."

"It's as bad as I've seen it," she said. "My niece and nephew are going to love it. The governor's already closed the schools."

Phil smiled. "Christmas comes a little early this year," he said. "My girls are happy, too. When I left, they were already planning a whole family of snowmen."

"How old are they?" she asked.

"Nora's ten and Grace is twelve," he said. "I'm trying to enjoy the pre-adolescence as long as I can. I just know if I blink, they'll be into boys and wanting to borrow the car."

"So what'd you want to talk about?" she asked.

"We're putting pieces in motion," he said. "Finally. We're going to be setting up surveillance on the O'Malley leadership, round the clock. I've got a team of guys from my house."

Since Phil had just been talking about his family, his reference to his house confused Erin for just a second. Then she realized that of course he was talking about his police precinct. The cold must be slowing her wits.

"Are they solid?" she asked.

"I've worked with them for years," Phil said. "And they're discreet. They've all worked undercover assignments for me, so they know the drill."

"What do they know?" she asked. Paranoia was tickling the back of her neck and she didn't like the feeling.

"Nothing about you," he assured her. "All I've told them is that we're setting up a watch on the O'Malleys. I didn't tell them about the upcoming arrests, and I haven't breathed your name, or anything else that would compromise you. As far as they know, this is just a watchdog detail, gathering information."

"What's the real purpose?" she asked.

"To track their movements," Phil said. "When we come down on Evan O'Malley and his buddies, we need to make sure we get all of them at once, or as many as we can. You know what'll happen as soon as we start making busts."

"Everyone else will scatter," Erin said.

"Right," he said. "We'll have a fair amount of manpower on this, but it's unavoidable. Don't worry, it's compartmentalized. Like I said, you haven't been mentioned, or even suggested."

"You're known for running undercover operations," Erin said. She knew she was probably borrowing trouble, but she couldn't stop herself. "Won't they suspect you've got an informant in the O'Malleys?"

"Possibly," Phil said. "But your position is rock solid. You've killed for them, remember."

"But what about Carlyle?" The worry showed in her eyes.

"Erin, it's natural to feel some nerves at this point," he said. "I'd be lying if I said there wasn't any risk, but I don't think either of you is in any more danger than you were a week or a month ago. This is just the next step."

"I don't like it," she grumbled. "You may trust these guys, but I don't even know them."

"They're good police," he insisted.

"They'd better be," she said. "You could be betting my life on them."

"It'll be okay," Phil said. "I'm going to talk to some of them in person tonight. If anything feels off, I'll take care of it. Remember, you can call me if anything comes up; anything at all. I've got your back, Erin. No matter what."

* * *

The drive back to the Barley Corner was worse. The snow was really coming down now, whipping across Erin's windshield in lines of brilliant white. She couldn't see more than a few yards. She went at a crawling pace, wondering if she might not be better off leaving the car somewhere and walking. Even though most of the other drivers were also being sensible and driving slowly, she still lost count of how many times she squeaked through close calls and near misses.

A big SUV tried to take a turn too tightly in front of her and spun out clean across the intersection, only narrowly avoiding wrapping itself around a lamppost. Two taxis had somehow managed a head-on collision on a one-way street, though they appeared to have been going slow enough that no one had been hurt. An NYPD Patrol car was already on scene, two cops trying to separate the taxi drivers. Erin passed them, their muffled argument filtering through her window.

When she finally saw the Barley Corner's lights through the swirling blizzard, she breathed a sigh of relief. It had taken her almost an hour for a drive that normally took twenty minutes. She steered into the parking garage across the street from the pub and eased the Charger into its designated space. Then she sat back in her seat and rubbed her hands. Her knuckles ached from gripping the steering wheel so tightly.

"That's it," she told Rolf. "I'm not going anywhere else tonight. I don't care if Canada declares war on us. I don't care if it's the second coming of Christ Himself out there. It can wait till tomorrow."

Rolf nosed her cheek and panted happily. He didn't know what the big deal was. He loved snow.

Erin climbed out of the car, adjusted her jacket, and hurried across the street toward the warm welcome promised by the pub's glowing windows. She was already thinking about a hot shower, or even better, a long soak in Carlyle's tub. Maybe she'd forget about her usual evening glass of whiskey and have a cup of hot cocoa instead. Carlyle would be happy to give her a nice, relaxing back rub. Then they could curl up on the couch together and...

She opened the Corner's front door and her happy train of thought went right off the rails. Waiting just inside was a wiry, dark-haired Irishman with a black glove on his right hand and horrible, puckered scars on the right side of his face. His eyes, so dark brown they looked black, zeroed in on her like a pair of pistol barrels.

"Snake," she blurted, reflexively using the man's Mob nickname. "What're you doing here?"

"O'Reilly," Gordon Pritchard rasped. His vocal cords had been permanently scarred by the same gasoline bomb that had ruined half his body. "The boss is in back. We need to talk. We got a problem."

Erin followed Pritchard to the back room, trying to hold down a sudden surge of uneasiness. She wished she was wearing her special bra, with its recording microphone stitched into the underwire. But she hadn't expected an encounter with Evan. The O'Malley chieftain ought to be at home, riding out the storm like a sensible human being. Something really important must have happened.

She glanced down at Rolf. The dog padded along beside her; solid, warm, and reliable. He was a comfort.

The back room at the Barley Corner was a place for private card games and meetings. It was small, dimly lit, and dominated by a heavy wooden card table topped with green baize. At the table, facing the door, sat Evan O'Malley. He was alone.

"Evening, sir," Erin said, speaking as lightly as she could.

"Good evening, Miss O'Reilly," Evan said. "Please sit down." He spoke politely, but he remained seated, hands clasped on the tabletop. His eyes were midwinter blue, holding no hint of warmth or humanity.

"Rolf, *sitz*," she said, giving the K-9 his German "sit" command. She slid into the chair opposite Evan, though it put her back to the door and to Pritchard, neither of which made her comfortable.

"It's an unpleasant night for traveling," Evan said. "Where have you been tonight?"

"Police business," she said, giving what she hoped was a casual shrug. "Just meeting a contact. Who else are we waiting on?"

"Nobody," Evan said.

She blinked. "What about Cars?" she asked.

"Mr. Carlyle is otherwise engaged," Evan said. "It's you I've come to see."

Erin schooled herself to stay calm. It didn't mean a thing. There might be any number of things Evan would want to talk to her about. But he had to at least suspect whatever he said to her would be repeated to Carlyle. The two of them were a unit as far as the O'Malleys were concerned.

"What can I do for you?" she asked.

Evan's cold-eyed stare drilled into her like twin icicles, sucking the heat out of her heart. "You can tell me about Philip Stachowski," he said.

Ready for more?

Join Steven Henry's author email list
for the latest on new releases, upcoming books and
series, behind-the-scenes details, events, and more.

Be the first to know about new releases in the Erin
O'Reilly Mysteries by signing up at
clickworkspress.com/join/erin

Now keep reading to enjoy

Screwdriver

A Vic Neshenko Story

Screwdriver

A Vic Neshenko Story

Steven Henry

Clickworks Press • Baltimore, MD

Copyright © 2023 Steven Henry
Cover design © 2023 Ingrid Henry
Cover photo © 2023 under license from Shutterstock.com (Credit: Dmitry Kalinovsky/Shutterstock)
Additional cover photo © 2023 under license from Shutterstock.com (Credit: CynthiaL04/Shutterstock)
All rights reserved

First publication: Clickworks Press, 2023
Release: CWP-EORVN1-INT-P.IS-1.0

Sign up for updates, deals, and exclusive sneak peeks at clickworkspress.com/join.

This is a work of fiction. Names, characters, places, organizations, and events are either the products of the author's imagination or used in a fictitious manner. Any resemblance to actual persons, living or dead, is purely coincidental.

Screwdriver

Fill a highball glass with ice. Add 1.5 oz. vodka. Top with orange juice, preferably fresh-squeezed, and serve.

Chapter 1

"Viktor Neshenko!"

The high-pitched voice, female and angry, using his full first and last name, jolted Vic straight past waking and clean back to high school. For a sleep-dazed moment he was a teenager again, groggily trying to think what he'd done that had pissed off his mom. His eyes snapped open.

He was lying in bed staring at the ceiling, but it wasn't the ceiling of his childhood home in Brighton Beach. Disoriented, he wondered where he was and just how much he'd had to drink last night.

A hand came into his field of view. It was holding a cardboard carton. The hand was Caucasian, with a slenderness to it that suggested it belonged to a woman. The hand shook the carton. Inside it, liquid sloshed back and forth.

"Huh?" Vic said. It was the most intelligent thing he could come up with.

A face followed the hand into his vision. It had blue eyes, a perky nose, and slightly rounded contours. It was framed by a tousled mass of blonde hair. The face would have been pretty, even beautiful, if it hadn't been spoiled by an angry scowl.

"I can't believe you did that!" the woman exclaimed.

"Oh, hi, Zofia," he said, remembering where he was with a surge of relief. He was lying in his own bed, in his own apartment, looking up at Zofia Piekarski, his own girlfriend. Everything was okay, more or less.

"What do you mean?" Zofia snapped. "Were you expecting someone else? Do you get call girls delivered straight to bed? You can do that now. I've talked to some of the Vice cops. This shit happens all the time."

"Huh? No!" Vic spluttered. "What're you talking about? I haven't slept with a call girl! At least, not since Tatiana, and that was before I even met you. Besides, I didn't know she was a hooker till later."

The look on Zofia's face suggested not only that he wasn't climbing out of his hole, but that he was, in fact, digging it deeper.

"Explain this," she said, shaking the carton at him again.

"It's orange juice," he said.

"And...?" she prompted in dangerous tones.

His thought processes still weren't entirely up and running, so he hadn't caught up yet. "Where'd it come from?" he asked.

"The fridge," she said. "*Your* fridge."

Realization dawned. "Oh," he said. "Right. Yeah, there's some Stoli in there, too."

"You poured vodka in your OJ and then stuck it right back in the damn fridge?!"

"It's not that surprising!" Vic retorted. "The bottle was almost empty! I just figured I'd dump it in the carton!"

"I can't drink hard liquor!" she snapped. "You know that!"

"If you'd asked—" Vic began.

"I'm not a goddamn psychic!" she interrupted. "Normal people don't do that!"

"Lots of people drink vodka and OJ," Vic said. "Everybody knows what a screwdriver is. It's the most common highball in the world."

"I'm pregnant!" she hissed. "With our baby, in case you'd forgotten. We're living together. I get it, this isn't easy for you, you've never lived with a girlfriend before."

"I've never had a pregnant girlfriend before, either," he added.

"And I've never been knocked up before, so isn't that something," she said. "My point is, you can't go spiking drinks and not tell me! All I wanted was breakfast! Toast, scrambled eggs, and a glass of orange juice! And now I'm going to have a baby with FAS and it'll be your fault! He'll probably come out with three eyes or something!"

"Wait, what?" Vic said. "Is that a thing? Fetal Alcohol whatever giving you three-eyed babies?"

"No! Not that you'd know, since you don't know the first thing about babies!" Zofia threw her arms in the air in exasperation. The carton of juice slipped from her fingers and described a slow, graceful arc across the room. It hit the wall. If it hadn't been open, it probably would've fallen to the floor intact, but a mixture of slightly fermented orange juice and vodka sprayed out the top, soaking into Vic's cheap carpet.

"Whoa, take it easy," Vic said, sitting up and trying to think how to tell her to calm down without saying those words. In his admittedly limited romantic experience, telling your girlfriend to calm down was a good way to get punched in the face. And Zofia Piekarski might be petite, barely five foot three, but she'd spent the past few years on the Street Narcotics Enforcement Unit, and SNEU had taught her to throw a mean right hook.

"We have to get out of here," Zofia said. She gestured with both hands, encompassing Vic's entire studio apartment.

Vic liked his apartment. It had seemed plenty big enough for him. His weight equipment went in one corner, his game console in another, separated by the used pleather sofa he'd gotten for ten bucks. The couch wasn't much, but it was better than the one in the Major Crimes break room at Precinct 8, so why be picky? The kitchenette was tiny, but Vic ate takeout half the time, and he barely fit in the shower, but that just meant less surface area to clean. What was the problem?

The problem was that even as things stood, it wasn't big enough for both Vic and Zofia, and in less than four months, they'd have a third resident. Vic tried to imagine where they'd even put the crib and came up with nothing. There just wasn't space.

"You're right," he said. This was a pretty safe thing to say to an angry girl. Maybe the only safe thing. Zofia's face unclenched slightly, which was a good sign, so he said it again. "You're right. The lease is good for another two months. We'll find a new place by then, I promise."

"Two months," she said, considering.

"It's the best I can do," he said. "You know how Manhattan rents are. I can't afford to walk out on the lease early, and it was a six-month thing."

"Okay," Zofia said. "Good. What is your plan for finding a new apartment?"

"I'll get right on it," he promised.

"Good," she repeated. "I've got a couple possible places lined up. We've got a visit scheduled for nine-thirty."

"What day?"

"Today."

"But it's my day off!"

"It's *our* day off," she corrected. "Isn't it great working the same squad? One of the benefits of my transfer. And if you can come up with a way you can visit apartments and work Major Crimes cases at the same time, I'd love to hear it."

"We actually go to a lot of apartments," Vic said.

"Yeah, that people have been murdered in!"

"Which means they have vacancies in the building," he said.

"*That* was your plan?" Zofia said in disbelief. "To wait for a two-bedroom apartment to open up on account of the residents getting murdered?"

That had, in fact, been Vic's plan. He'd been proud of it. That was the sort of clever plan a detective would think of.

"There's a little more to it than that," he said defensively.

"Nine-thirty," Zofia said in tones of absolute finality. "That's forty-five minutes from now, and it'll take us twenty minutes to get there. You've got time to get dressed and eat something, but then we've got to get going."

"Okay, okay," Vic said. "You told me you were making eggs and toast. Did you make enough for two?"

Zofia froze. At that moment, Vic identified the scorched smell that had been creeping into his nostrils for the last couple of minutes.

"You did take the eggs off the stove," he said slowly. "Right? Before you came over here to yell at me?"

* * *

"It wasn't so bad," Zofia said.

Vic, sitting as far on the other side of the back seat of the taxi as he could, sulked and said nothing.

"Once the pan's soaked for a few hours, the burned bits will come right off," she said.

Vic continued to say nothing.

"And the smell will dissipate," she went on. "It'd be quicker if we could open the window, but this is December. It's too cold and the radiator might explode."

Vic tried to loosen the muscles in his jaw. Cohabitation, he was discovering, was difficult for a man of his temperament. *Calmness and caring*, he reminded himself. *You love this girl. Don't screw it up, like you did with the last one.*

The last one was working with Russian Mafia human traffickers, his internal voice reminded him. *They tried to murder you and she helped.*

Okay, bad example. But the point was, his relationship history was sort of like the history of the Middle East; nasty little squabbles over resources, occasionally spilling over into full-fledged crusades and jihads.

"It's not a big deal," he said.

Zofia reached out and took hold of his hand. She squeezed his fingers. "Don't worry," she said. "We're house-hunting as a family! This'll be fun!"

"There'll be no booze, no fistfights, and no felony collars," he said. "How fun could it be?"

But he smiled as he said it, enjoying the sparkle in Zofia's eyes. He felt a warm tingle in his gut. He really loved this woman. It astonished him every time he thought it. Would he ever get tired of that feeling?

Vic didn't know, but he hoped not. She was more likely to get tired of him.

* * *

Two hours and three apartments later, the warm tingles were gone. Vic had all the headache of a hangover, without the fun of being drunk. Zofia was trying to be optimistic and upbeat, but Vic was a detective. He was used to people pretending, and he could see right through her forced smile and constant chatter.

"The discoloration on the ceiling wasn't *that* bad," she was saying as the taxi pulled up to the fourth stop on their increasingly awful journey through Manhattan real estate. "It's probably just from the minerals in the water. I bet it isn't mold."

"I looked in the bathroom," Vic said. "Something was climbing out of the shower drain."

"Just a house centipede, probably," Zofia said. "They eat other bugs, you know. Having them around is a good thing."

"It was big enough I could've put handcuffs on it," he said. "And I didn't have enough pairs for all those legs."

"It was better than the last one," she said desperately.

"Yeah," he agreed. "Because the last one had that smell."

"I think it was from the old incinerator across the air shaft."

"It reminded me of the time a tire shop caught fire in my old neighborhood. Can we give this up for today?"

"Just one more," she said. "I've got a good feeling about this one. It's an old building, from all the way back in the 1840s, but it's getting renovated."

"That means it's falling down around their ears," he said gloomily.

"But if they're doing major work, they'll have to bring everything up to code," she shot back. "It'll have all the charm and character of an old building, but with brand-new appliances, wiring, and plumbing. Best of both worlds!"

"Can we afford it?"

"If you cut back on the liquor store bills a little."

Vic glowered. "Just when this day couldn't get any worse," he muttered.

"Just keep an open mind," she said. "I know you don't like doing this, but I promise I'll make it worth your while."

"And just how are you planning on doing that?"

She grinned impishly. "You know what you have to do when you move into a new place with someone?"

"What?"

"You need to make love in every room. Dispels the bad energy."

He nodded. "We don't want any bad energy around," he agreed soberly. "But won't that upset the realtor?"

She smacked him on the shoulder. "Not while they're around. After! Guys always want everything right away."

The taxi pulled to the curb. They climbed out.

The building certainly had character. Vic wasn't so sure about charm. But it was old enough. It was a converted brownstone, one of the classic New York homes that'd started as a one-family dwelling and been broken up into three or four separate apartments when the housing market had gone nuts. The stone was weathered and pockmarked by all the history that had swept around it over the hundred seventy-odd years it had stood.

Vic paused outside, probing the stonework with a finger. "You know," he said thoughtfully, "that looks an awful lot like a large-caliber bullet hole."

"Don't you ever stop being a cop?" Zofia asked.

"He's right," a woman said from the top of the front steps. She was obviously the realtor; Vic bet they all bought their clothes from the same online catalogues, wore the same shoes, and went to the same hair stylists. Everything about her was professional, pleasant, and perky. She was attractive in a completely unapproachable way, her makeup covering her face like the visor on a helmet.

"Beg pardon?" Zofia asked.

"It's a bullet hole," the woman said, advancing down the stairs and extending a hand. "You'd be Ms. Piekarski, am I right?"

"That's right," Zofia said, shaking hands.

"Lauren Haskell," the woman said. "I'm with Fairlawn Realty. We spoke on the phone. And you are?"

"Vic Neshenko," Vic said. "NYPD."

"So am I," Zofia said.

"A blue couple," Lauren said with a bright, professional smile. "That's lovely! Neighbors often like having someone in law enforcement living nearby. It makes everyone feel safer. If you'd like to step inside, I'll show you the place."

"Hold on a second," Vic said. "You said this was a bullet hole?"

Lauren laughed. "Yes, but it's nothing to worry about. It's ancient history. That bullet was fired from a Civil War musket."

"There weren't any Civil War battles in New York," Zofia said.

"No," Lauren agreed. "That shot was fired during the Draft Riots, probably on July 14, 1863."

"I've heard of those," Vic said. Anything involving firearms interested him.

"Me too," Zofia said. "But just the name. I don't think we covered them much in history class."

"We're near the Midtown Docks here," Lauren explained. "During the 1850s, as there was an influx of black longshoremen, the Irishmen who'd been working those jobs started to resent them. There was a lot of racial hatred bubbling just under the surface. It erupted just after the Battle of Gettysburg into a full-fledged race riot."

"How come?" Zofia asked. "We're in the North. Weren't we fighting to free the slaves?"

"That's just the point," Lauren said. "A lot of Northern soldiers were fighting to preserve the Union, not to free the slaves. They were often just as racist as their opponents, and when President Lincoln instituted the national draft, the working-class folks in New York thought they were being forced to fight and die for the dark-skinned people who were taking their jobs. Even worse, when they heard you could buy your way out of the draft, they figured the poor were dying in a rich man's fight."

"That's nothing new," Vic said. "Some things never change. So there was a street fight here?"

"There was an exchange of fire between Union soldiers and rioters," Lauren said. "If you look closely, you can see several bullet holes in the building. The rioters dispersed and the soldiers kept moving, restoring order."

"You know a lot about this," Zofia said.

"It helps to understand the history of your properties as a realtor," Lauren said. "Everyone likes to know what's happened in their house."

"Anyone ever die here?" Vic asked eagerly.

Lauren blinked. "I'm not sure," she said. "But since this house is almost two centuries old, someone probably has."

"Vic's a detective," Zofia explained. "He solves murders for a living, so he tends to see them everywhere he looks."

Lauren's smile was just a little more brittle than before. "I see," she said. "Now, would you like to come in?"

The entryway was surprisingly elegant. The staircase on the right-hand side of the front hall sported a fancy carved bannister. The plasterwork was obviously old and worn, but still showed the faded glory of the house.

"This home was originally owned by a man named Jessup," Lauren said, starting up the stairs. "Arthur Jessup. He was a very successful manufacturer of locomotive boilers. Mr. Jessup was actually killed in the riots we were just talking about."

"Right out front?" Zofia asked.

"No. His factory was attacked by looters and burned to the ground. He was killed in the confusion, while trying to defend his property. His widow sold the house and moved west to Chicago. Then the house passed through a succession of owners..."

They climbed past the second floor and up to the third story as Lauren recounted the history of the building. "And now here we are," she finished. "Here's the open unit. We're working on remodeling the bathroom. What did you say your timeframe was?"

"My lease is up at the end of next month," Vic said. "We were thinking to move around the start of February."

"Perfect," Lauren said, opening the door and stepping inside. "All the work should be finished by then. Try to overlook the mess and the noise. They're working very hard to get everything ready."

The apartment was nice, Vic had to admit, even under the canvas drop-cloths. He could tell the floor was quality hardwood, holding up well in spite of its age. The rooms were nicely proportioned, much more spacious than his cramped studio unit.

"Oh, Vic," Zofia said, putting a hand to her mouth. "I just love it! Look at that bay window on the south facing!"

Vic glanced at Lauren and could practically see the dollar signs in the realtor's pupils. He made himself scowl. Lease negotiations were like police interrogations. It paid to have a good cop and a bad cop, and Vic was very good at playing bad cop.

"You said the bathroom wasn't done yet?" he asked in neutral tones, edging toward slight hostility.

"Right this way," Lauren said, motioning them on. "We are redoing all the plumbing, of course, since there wasn't originally a kitchen or a bathroom in this part of the house. Here's the spare bedroom, perfect for a growing family."

Had she noticed Zofia's belly? Vic wasn't sure, but he wouldn't put it past her.

"And here's the master bedroom," Lauren went on. "It's a suite, so it connects directly to the bathroom. We're expanding the bath to include a large, built-in tub and shower unit. Our workmen may be here, or they may be on lunch. I'd better knock, so we don't startle anyone."

She rapped on the bathroom door. "Hello?" she called. "I've got a couple of clients here. May we come in?"

There was no answer.

Lauren shrugged. "I guess they've gone out to eat," she said. She turned the knob and opened the door, resuming her sales pitch. "We had to add more tile for the shower, but we've tried to get tiles that match the rest of the décor as closely as possible, to retain that nineteenth-century ambience. The pipework is almost done and—"

Her voice cut off so suddenly that Vic wasn't sure what had happened. Lauren Haskell had frozen in place, staring into the half-finished bathroom. Vic, much taller than the realtor, stepped forward and looked over her shoulder.

A hole gaped in the back wall, showing a dark crawlspace. The roof sloped steeply down, making a little triangle of dusty, cobwebby wood. A handful of tools lay around the hole. But that wasn't what had grabbed Lauren's attention.

A man in dusty coveralls lay slumped on the bathroom floor. He lay very still. More importantly, the handle of a large screwdriver protruded from his left ear. Half a foot of the screwdriver's steel had been driven straight through the eardrum into his brain. It didn't appear to be a survivable injury.

"What is it?" Zofia asked. She was craning her neck, trying to see past Vic's bulk.

"You were talking about bad energy earlier?" Vic replied. "We've got a little problem here."

Chapter 2

"You should sit down for a bit," Vic said. "Do you feel dizzy?"

"Stop it," Zofia said. "I'm pregnant, not helpless. I'm a Street Narcotics cop, remember? You think that's the first body I've seen? Some beats I've walked, you practically trip over them."

"Oh my God," Lauren Haskell said. It was at least the sixth time she'd said it since Vic had basically manhandled her out of the bathroom. The realtor was very pale under her protective layer of cosmetics.

"Sorry," Vic said. "That's just me being a stupid macho guy."

"I know," Zofia said, squeezing his arm. In spite of her words, she looked a little shaky. "What do you think happened?"

"You know how people say a guy's got a few screws loose in his head? Everyone talks about it; he *did* something about it."

Zofia laughed. Vic wasn't surprised; dark humor was what got cops through their day.

"You figure he fell on his own screwdriver?" she asked.

"Not likely," he said. "The angle's weird. But I guess it might not have killed him right away. Maybe he rolled over. But I'd expect more blood spatter if he'd thrashed around. It'd show up great on that white tile."

"Who was he?"

"One of the workmen, I guess."

There was a rush of running footsteps on the stairs. Vic and Zofia both knew the sound very well. They were already facing the door and holding up their own shields when a pair of NYPD Patrol officers, both women, burst in. Vic's fingers were wrapped around a gold shield. Zofia's was silver; while she was temporarily detailed to the Precinct 8 Major Crimes unit, she wasn't officially a detective yet.

The Patrol sergeant nodded to the two of them. "Detective," she said. "Officer. I thought we were first on scene. What were you, off duty and in the area?"

"Sort of," Vic said. "We're the ones who found the body."

"We're viewing the property," Zofia explained. "With the realtor."

"Hi," Lauren said weakly, managing a wave with one hand. The other was over her mouth. She looked like she was about an inch from throwing up on the floor.

"If you've gotta hurl," Vic advised, "do it out here. Don't go to the bathroom; you'll mess up the crime scene."

"Sergeant Kirkland," the patrolwoman said. "This is Officer Rockford."

"Detective Neshenko," Vic introduced himself.

"Officer Piekarski," Zofia said. "Don't see many two-woman units."

"The brass doesn't like it," Kirkland said. "We make the boys look bad. You said the bathroom's where the body is?"

"Yeah," Vic said. "Looks like a homicide. We need the scene secured."

"Copy that," Kirkland said. She nodded to her partner. "C'mon, Peaches."

"Peaches?" Vic said. "If I called a lady cop that, she'd tear my nuts off and make me eat them."

"Damn right I would," Rockford said, grinning. "*You* can call me Officer Rockford, Detective. Nickname privileges have to be earned."

Kirkland donned a pair of gloves and nudged open the bathroom door. "Whoa," she said. "That's something you don't see every day."

"Looks like a Phillips to me," Rockford said. "But it could be a flat-head. We'd have to pull it out to make sure."

Kirkland looked at her. "What possible difference does it make what kind of screwdriver did this?" she asked. "Never mind. Call it in. We need detectives."

"Seriously?" Vic said. "I'm standing right here!"

"You know what I mean," Kirkland said. "Homicide dicks. From our own house. I've heard of you, Neshenko. Aren't you down with the Eightball in South Manhattan?"

"That's us," he said proudly.

"Then unless this gets kicked up to Major Crimes, all you get to do is observe and advise. Rockford will take your statement in a minute."

* * *

Lauren was over by the bay window, one hand holding her phone, the other cupped around her opposite ear. She was talking to her boss, finding out what to do. Vic didn't think corpses in the bathroom were covered in realtor training. Vic and Zofia were in the middle of the living room, talking. That is to say, Vic was grumbling. Zofia was still trying to be upbeat.

"In a minute," Vic said, mimicking Kirkland's voice. "I'm gonna get interviewed, as if I was a friggin' civilian, by somebody called Peaches. Peaches! How do you get a dumb-ass nickname like that?"

"It's because of her last name," Zofia said.

"I don't get it," Vic said. "I mean, if her name was Del Monte or Dole, I could maybe see it."

"There was a women's professional baseball team," Zofia said. "During World War II. The Rockford Peaches. Didn't you ever see the movie *A League of Their Own*? About female ballplayers?"

"Does that really sound like my kind of movie?" Vic asked.

"No," Zofia admitted. "Not nearly enough explosions or special-forces jargon."

The apartment door opened again. Vic glanced up, expecting more cops.

A guy in coveralls came in, carrying a plastic bag in each hand. He was big-shouldered, but a bulging gut indicated he didn't hit the gym nearly as hard as Vic. He stopped short in surprise, staring at Vic and Zofia.

For an absurd moment, Vic was convinced this guy was some sort of mobster or assassin. The dude was going to whip out a submachine-gun and start laying waste to the apartment. Vic reached for the gun he should've been wearing. Then he realized he hadn't even brought his off-duty piece with him. He almost never left home without it, but his spat with Zofia had distracted him and he'd forgotten.

He realized it didn't matter. This was obviously the other workman, partner to the poor bastard in the bathroom. Vic took out his shield for the second time and held it up.

"NYPD," he snapped. "Show me your hands!"

"Jesus!" the man yelped. He dropped the bags, which thumped to the floor. His eyes went really wide. He couldn't have looked more terrified if Vic had remembered his Colt Delta Elite and brandished the .45-caliber hand cannon in his face. The guy raised his hands.

"Knock it off, Vic," Zofia said. "Stop scaring the poor guy!"

The workman's knees were actually knocking together. Vic had heard of this happening, but had never seen it on the street. He stifled a chuckle.

"Identify yourself, sir," Zofia said to the man. "This is an active crime scene."

"Bruno," the man said. "Bruno Gallo. What're you doing here?"

"She just told you that," Vic said. "We're cops. I'm Detective Neshenko, Major Crimes. Who's the guy in the bathroom?"

"What guy in the bathroom?"

Vic tried not to roll his eyes. Why did people always lie to cops? It was a reflex, probably stemming from their teenage years, taking Mom's station wagon out for a spin and getting pulled over with a case of beers in the passenger seat. He wished that once, just once, everybody he met in a given day would tell him the truth. In the movies, when a guy lied to the cops you knew he was the guy you wanted. Not on the street; out there *everybody* lied, all the time. They did it to make themselves look good, or feel better, or maybe just out of sheer force of habit.

"The guy wearing clothes that look just like yours," he growled. "The guy that second bag of takeout is for, I'm guessing. Your partner. What's his name, dumbass?"

You could get in trouble these days for calling people "dumbass." The correct term, according to the Department, was "person of interest," but you couldn't very well call a guy that to his face, could you? You'd sound like a bureaucratic jerk and you'd lose all your street credibility. Besides, labels were only really out of line when they weren't true, and Vic would bet a week's salary the term "dumbass" could accurately be applied to the man in front of him.

"Pedro," Gallo said. "Pedro Gesualdo."

"What's in the bags, Mr. Gallo?" Zofia asked.

"Sub sandwiches," he said. "From Lenny's Deli. Roast beef and Swiss. Lettuce, tomatoes, mayo, and onions."

"How long were you gone?" Vic asked.

"I don't know," Gallo said. "Half an hour, maybe? It might be a little longer. What time is it?"

"Going on noon," Zofia said.

"About half an hour, then," Gallo said. "We stopped working at eleven-thirty."

"Then what was Pete doing in the bathroom?" Vic asked.

"Taking a dump?" Gallo suggested.

Vic gave him a look.

"I don't know, man!" Gallo said. "Why don't you ask him?"

"I can't ask him," Vic said, watching him for a reaction. "I can't ask him because he's got a screwdriver in his ear canal. Why do you think someone would do something like that?"

"Pete's dead?" Gallo asked.

"I never said he was dead," Vic said. "I said he had a screwdriver in his ear canal, which could mess with a guy's hearing."

"I guess I assumed," Gallo said. "A screwdriver? Really?"

"Yeah. We're still working out whether it was regular or Phillips. Let's stay on the subject here. Did you see anybody else in this house today?"

"That lady over there." He pointed to Lauren. "She's been walking around, looking at stuff. She had a couple other folks with her."

"What other folks?" Vic asked.

"A guy and a chick. They were checking the place out."

Vic turned to Lauren, who'd gotten off the phone and was listening to their conversation. "We're gonna need the names of that couple," he said.

"Why?" she replied. "I was with them the whole time. And everybody was still... still alive when they were here."

"We're establishing a timeline," Vic said. "And we need to know who had access to this building. When did you show them the place?"

"Eleven o'clock," Lauren said. "They didn't stay long; it wasn't what they were looking for. They were gone by eleven-twenty. My God. This is so horrible."

"Do I still need to be here?" Gallo asked.

Vic scowled at him. "You got somewhere else to be?"

"Well, no... I mean, if there isn't anything else you need from me..." the workman said.

"You're gonna take a seat right there on that drop-cloth," Vic said, pointing to the far corner of the living room. "And you're gonna stay there until somebody wearing a shield tells you to go home. In the meantime, don't touch a damn thing. You get me?"

"Okay, sure," Gallo said. "But I got work to do."

"In the bathroom?" Vic said. "You're shit out of luck, buddy. That room is off limits. Hey, Sergeant?"

Kirkland's head popped around the corner. "Yeah?"

"Can you or Rockford grab some yellow tape from your unit? We came by taxi, so we don't have our stuff."

"Copy that. Peaches, take a run downstairs. Any word on the Homicide boys?"

"They caught a body on the dock," Rockford said. "Dispatch says they'll be here when they can."

Vic watched Rockford hustle out the door. Then he walked to the bathroom. The door was ajar. He hip-checked it open, being careful to avoid touching any surfaces. CSU would dust for prints and he didn't want to smudge anything.

"Vic," Zofia said, nudging his arm.

"What?" He was looking at the mortal remains of Pedro Gesualdo.

"What are we doing?"

"We've got a probable cause of death," he said. "And a time window; between eleven-thirty and noon. We've also got a preliminary ID on the victim. Now we need to see if we can zero in on a motive."

"No, I mean, what are we doing investigating this?" she asked. "You heard Sergeant Kirkland. This isn't our case."

Vic smiled at her. "Why do dogs chase squirrels?" he replied. "This is who we are."

"That's true," she said, and that sparkle was back in her eye. "But you're going to get in trouble when the Homicide boys get here."

"Nah," he said. "I'm just doing some of their legwork for them. They'll appreciate it. I promise, I'll turn over everything we get and make sure it goes through the proper channels."

"You hate the proper channels."

"Of course I do. But that doesn't mean I don't understand them. Okay, let's see what we've got here."

The bathroom was much larger than Vic's tiny half-bath. It was easy for both of them to avoid stepping on the body.

"Hardly any blood," Zofia commented.

"That's because our killer left the weapon in the wound," Vic said. "The steel's keeping the blood in. If our victim here had been shanked in the chest or neck, he might still be alive. Hell, even getting one in the brain isn't always a death sentence. I don't see any other injuries."

"Nope," she agreed. "Looks like he only got stabbed the once."

"And no defensive wounds on the hands and arms," Vic added, peering at Gesualdo's hands. They were a workman's hands, callused and covered with little nicks, scratches, and scars, but none of them were fresh enough to have come from the time of death.

"Maybe he got stabbed from behind," she suggested. "Never saw it coming."

"Maybe," Vic said. "But that'd mean our killer's a southpaw."

"How do you mean?"

He pointed. "The screwdriver's in his left ear. If the killer came from behind, the stab would've come from his left."

"So the killer would be left-handed," Zofia said. "But you're right-handed and you could stab a guy with your left if you wanted."

"Yeah, but I wouldn't," Vic said. "If I'm trying to kill a guy quick and quiet, I'm gonna use my good hand to do it. If our killer misses just a little, say an inch high, he might bounce it off the skull. A screwdriver's sharp enough, I guess, but it's not like an ice pick or a stiletto. Then instead of falling down dead, this guy starts screaming and probably fighting back."

"So we figure on a lefty taking him out from the back, or else someone he knew from the front," Zofia said.

"Exactly," Vic said. "Someone he wouldn't expect to kill him."

"Like his buddy?" She cocked her head back toward the living room.

"Or the real estate broad."

"Lauren? Really?"

He shrugged. "Women kill guys too. Toughest guy I ever saw got taken out by a woman."

"You're talking about Erin O'Reilly and Mickey Connor."

"Damn right I am."

"Are you seriously comparing Erin to Miss Professional Catalog out there? Erin would eat her for breakfast and spit out the bones."

"I dunno," Vic said. "Those professional ladies can be cold, hard bitches."

"You ever go to bed with one?"

"I tried. Passed out from hypothermia before I could seal the deal."

She smacked him. "You made that up!"

Vic grinned and returned his attention to the body at their feet. "Why a screwdriver?" he wondered.

"It's what was handy," Zofia said. "There's tools all over the floor."

"That's just what I'm saying. This wasn't planned ahead of time. This was a spur-of-the-moment thing. A guy plans on stabbing someone, he brings a knife."

"Crime of passion?" she guessed.

"Maybe. Hey, maybe both of them were banging the real estate lady and they had a fight over her."

Zofia rolled her eyes. "This is my fault," she said. "I put your mind in the gutter."

"That's my mind's natural habitat," Vic said. He crouched down and peered into the hole in the bathroom wall. "I didn't bring my flashlight," he grumbled. "Or any other damn thing. Not even my gun!"

"What're you looking for?" she asked, bending to look over his shoulder.

"If I knew that, I wouldn't need to look," he said. "I'm just wondering what's back here."

"You really should wait for CSU," Zofia said.

"Sorry, didn't copy," he said. "I get deaf when people tell me what I should do."

He stuck his head through the hole, trying not to inhale the floating particles. The space behind the wall was thickly coated with mouse droppings, dust, and cobwebs. Obviously, nobody had been back here for a very long time, maybe not since the house had been built.

"I can't see a damn thing," he muttered.

"Here." Zofia thrust something into his hand. His fingers closed around the familiar shape of a cell phone.

"Flashlight app?" he guessed.

"Don't you have one?" she asked.

"I don't install extra crap on my phone."

"It's already on there. You scared of technology?"

"Nope. It's just annoying when I have to replace the phone. Mine tend to get broken, or dunked in puddles, or lost. The whole thing's one big hassle."

"Here," she said in exasperation. "I'll do it." She reached down and poked the screen. Brilliant light flared from the phone. Vic squinted and panned the light around the cramped, dirty crawlspace.

"See anything?" Zofia asked.

"No," he said.

"Oh well," she said. "It was worth a look, I guess."

"I saw a very specific nothing," he said, straightening up and handing the glowing phone back to her. "Take a peek."

Confused, she shone the light back into the hole. "Nothing," she said. "Just bare boards."

"Take a closer look," he said. "Just a few inches inside."

"Vic, I'm telling you, nothing's there." Zofia was getting annoyed.

"I agree."

"Being smug isn't a turn-on," she said.

"Sorry." But he still felt the smile on his own lips. He was feeling very clever and wanted to savor the moment. "Look at the dust. What do you see?"

"If this is your idea of humor..." she began. Then she stopped short and he knew she'd seen it too. "Something was here. I can see the outlines. Looks like a rectangle, maybe eight by ten inches. There's no dust."

"I'm thinking a box," Vic said. "It was back here, hiding behind the wall. For a very long time. And now it's gone."

"What was it?" Zofia wondered.

"I have no idea," Vic said. "But I'm guessing it was worth killing for."

Chapter 3

"Hey, Bruno!" Vic called as he came back into the living room. "Got a couple more questions for you."

Gallo didn't answer, probably because he wasn't in the room. The only person in sight was Lauren Haskell.

"Where'd he go?" Vic demanded.

"Out," she said, pointing to the front door.

"Where's the other cop? Sergeant Kirkland?"

"She got a call on her radio and went downstairs."

Vic knew several excellent words for situations like these. He used a few of his favorites as he ran for the stairs. Zofia trailed him, keeping pace. She might be almost six months pregnant, but she was also a street cop, and street cops knew how to move their feet. The two of them made it to street level without touching half the steps. They burst out the front of the brownstone to see Kirkland and Rockford's squad car, lights flashing, and the two Patrol officers inside it, but no sign of Gallo.

Vic stormed down the front steps and banged his hand on the hood of the car. Kirkland looked up. She opened the door of the vehicle and got out.

"Don't do that again," she said, quiet menace in every word.

"I won't," Vic said, "if you can explain why you let our number-one suspect waltz right out of the building, and left the crime scene unsecured."

"I left the building to try to light a fire under the homicide dicks," Kirkland retorted. "They're all hot and bothered about that homicide on the docks. They think it's gangs or terrorists or some damn thing. Rockford said they're not coming until six, maybe later."

"Six?" Vic echoed in disbelief. "That's hours away! What're we supposed to do until then? Sit on our thumbs?"

"And if you'd bothered to tell me that guy was a suspect, I could've had him in cuffs in the back of our car right now," Kirkland went on. "But you didn't. You didn't give me any orders at all; not that you were authorized to anyway, since this isn't your friggin' crime scene! You're off duty and out of jurisdiction."

"Just one goddamn minute," Vic said. "Either I'm a cop or I'm not. I can't be both at the same time. So either I'm off duty, in which case you left the scene of a murder unattended by an on-duty cop, or I'm an authorized detective, in which case I'm the ranking officer here. So which is it?"

Kirkland glared at him. "You're a pain in the ass, is what you are," she said.

"And you just met Vic," Zofia said. "Usually it takes people at least an hour to figure that out about him."

"Okay," Kirkland said. "What do you want us to do, *Detective?*"

"Now that we've got that cleared up, where'd that Gallo punk go?" Vic asked.

"Beats me. I wasn't watching him."

Vic reminded himself that calmness was a good leadership trait. He thought of Erin O'Reilly's K-9 and the rubber ball the dog loved so much. If he had a rubber ball to squeeze, or better yet to chew on, he might feel better. He'd have to remember to ask Erin where he could get one.

"Look him up in the system, please," he said, marveling at how cool and collected he sounded. "I need to know his address and phone. Also check to see if he's got a jacket, any priors, that sort of thing. Got it?"

"Copy that," Kirkland said in more professional tones.

"What should I do?" Zofia asked.

Vic tried to think. Delegating was hard, particularly when some of the subordinates on a scene were being difficult. He felt like a piece of chewing gum getting stretched three ways at once. He could feel another headache coming on and really wanted a slug of Stoli. Too bad Zofia had spilled the ready-mixed screwdrivers he'd had back at his place.

God, is this how Lieutenant Webb feels all the time? Vic thought. No wonder the old bastard smoked and drank so much.

"Kirkland," he said. "Can you get your buddy Peaches out here to listen to this?"

"I heard that," Rockford said from inside the car. She glared, but Vic was used to people glaring at him and it didn't bother him. He could match anybody in New York stare for stare. He waited until she got out of the car and joined them. Then he started talking.

"Here's what we're gonna do. Over half of all murders are solved in the first forty-eight hours."

He wasn't a hundred percent sure of that statistic, but he'd heard it somewhere and it sounded good. Anyway, the other three cops were listening, and that was a good start. Vic forged ahead.

"These hours are really important. Since the boys in Homicide left us hanging, it's up to us to bring this one home. Here's what we know. Pedro Gesualdo got stabbed to death by a screwdriver to the brain. It happened about an hour ago, either right before or right after his buddy Bruno Gallo left him. So either Gallo killed him, or someone else snuck in and did it. Either way, the perp wanted something Gesualdo found behind the bathroom wall. I'm thinking buried treasure."

Rockford snorted. Up until that point she'd been on board, but now she was laughing at him. "Seriously?" she said. "Buried treasure? Like what, pirate gold? Pieces of eight?"

"Something like that, yeah," Vic said, irritated. "People hide money in houses, Officer Peaches. Sometimes they don't trust banks, sometimes they don't want people to know about their income. Maybe it's drug money, maybe something else off the books. We need to know what Gesualdo found."

"Why?" Kirkland asked. "What difference does it make? Just get a warrant and search Gallo's house."

"On what evidence?" Vic replied. "And what're we looking for? The murder weapon's still at the scene. If his fingerprints are on it we're golden, but I wouldn't bet on it. All we've got right now is suspicion, and that's thin."

Good God, he thought. *I'm even starting to sound like Webb.* He unconsciously rubbed his forehead, making sure his buzz cut was intact and his hairline hadn't started receding.

"How do we figure out what was there?" Zofia asked.

"That'll be our department," he said. "Kirkland, once you get Gallo's address, I want you and Rockford to go to his house and set up camp. Make it inconspicuous, but I need to know if he shows up there."

"What about the crime scene?" Kirkland asked.

"I'll stay here and get more units on site," he said. "But give me a roll of tape and I'll seal it off."

"What do we do while we're here?" Zofia asked. "Where do we start?"

"We start by talking to the realtor," Vic said.

Lauren was pacing the living room nervously. Vic cursed himself. He'd left her outside an active crime scene, unsupervised. If she was the perp, she could've destroyed evidence. Even if she wasn't, she might have accidentally contaminated it.

"Ms. Haskell," he said. "Did you go in the bathroom while we were out?"

"No," she said and shuddered. "I don't even want to go near it. He's really dead, isn't he?"

"He's about as dead as it's possible to get," Vic said. "I need to know some things about this building. You said you're good on its history, right?"

"Yes." Lauren laughed with an edge of hysteria in her voice. "What are you worried about? Ghosts?"

"Not exactly," he said. "Has that bathroom been remodeled before?"

"Once, back in the Forties," Lauren said. "That was when they ran the modern pipes in. There was no shower, just an old claw-foot bathtub. I've seen the pictures."

"Did they tear open the back wall?"

"I... no, I don't think so."

"You don't think so, or you know for sure?" he pressed. "This is important."

Lauren collected herself a little. "No," she said more firmly. "They tore up the floorboards and put in tile, but they didn't touch the wall."

"Okay, good," Vic said. "Now tell me about the Jessup family."

"What about them?"

"How rich were they?"

"Very. Before the riots, Arthur Jessup was one of the richest men in New York."

"And after?"

"He was dead," Lauren said. "I told you that."

Vic reminded himself to be patient. "What about his money?" he asked. "Where was he keeping it?"

"A lot of his wealth was tied up in his factory," Lauren said. "He'd just expanded it to meet wartime demand. Unfortunately, the insurance company went under. There were just too many fire claims, on account of the widespread destruction, and the insurers went bankrupt. The factory was a total loss. He didn't have much in the way of ready money. One reason his widow moved away was that she needed cash. That was why she sold the house."

"So what happened to his cash?" Vic asked. "He must've had at least some liquid assets."

"I don't know," Lauren said.

"Did he have kids?" Zofia asked.

"Yes, a son and a daughter," Lauren said. "The son died in the war the following year, outside Petersburg, Virginia. But the daughter survived, as far as I know. I wasn't able to trace the family history any farther, and besides, it didn't have anything to do with the house at that point."

"What was the daughter's name?" Zofia asked.

"Priscilla."

"And the mom?"

"Margaret."

"Okay," Zofia said. "Do you have a computer handy?"

"I've got a laptop," Lauren said.

"You told me this building was rigged for wi-fi when we talked about renting," Zofia said. "You told me it was brand-new, with great bandwidth."

"That's right," Lauren said, falling back on her realtor experience with relief. "Broadband internet access."

"Great," Zofia said. "Can I borrow your computer? Official police business."

"Um, sure," Lauren said.

Vic wanted to ask what Zofia was up to, but restrained himself. He'd let her surprise him. In the meantime, he had to coordinate with the local precinct house and get some more bodies on scene, and he had a door to slap yellow police tape all over. He hoped he wasn't forgetting anything important.

For the first time in his life, he wished Lieutenant Webb was supervising him. The thought scared him.

* * *

While Zofia banged away on the realtor's computer, Vic brooded. Now that he had temporary control of the crime scene, he wasn't sure he wanted it. This was supposed to be his day off, a nice relaxing break from police work. But it'd all gone wrong from the start. The argument with Zofia, the mind-numbing tour of Manhattan apartments, and now the poor schmuck with the screwdriver through his brain pan.

He was going to get in trouble. That was inevitable. Vic was a Detective Third Grade and that was all he was ever going to be. He was radioactive to the NYPD's high command. It didn't matter how many perps he put away, how many cases he closed, how many lives he saved; he'd always be Vic the surly Russian. He had rips on his record for insubordination, excessive force, more insubordination, alcohol abuse, and more minor Patrol Guide infractions than he could remember.

He could only imagine the shitstorm in store when the news of the day worked its way up the chain. He'd basically hijacked a homicide investigation out from under the proper investigators. He'd probably already made a dozen procedural errors that could taint the case. Lieutenant Webb would be hearing from whoever was in charge of Midtown Homicide. Maybe Captain Holliday, too. There'd be a waiting list of NYPD brass wanting to yell at him.

Vic decided he didn't care. If he was going to step in shit no matter what, he might as well be wading through it toward a worthwhile goal. He was going to figure this out, and then he was going to find an apartment where he and Zofia could live happily, if not ever after, at least for a while. And no NYPD red tape or bureaucrats were going to stop him.

Red tape was a funny name for it. The only tape he ever saw the police use was the yellow stuff he'd just finished stringing across the bathroom door. But nobody ever talked about cutting through the yellow tape.

The worst part of being a detective was the paperwork and bureaucracy. The second-worst thing was the waiting. Vic waited a very, very long time. He wondered if Webb's cigarette habit helped the time pass more quickly.

God, but he could use a drink right now.

"Bingo!" Zofia said. Vic and Lauren jumped.

"What?" Vic asked, hurrying over to her. For a glorious moment he thought Zofia must have everything sorted out; this case, the mysterious missing box, the secret of life itself maybe.

"I've got Arthur Jessup's great-great-great grandkid," she said triumphantly. "And he's in New York! Just a few blocks away!"

Vic blinked at her. She looked expectantly back at him. An awkward moment passed.

"Um," Vic said, looking for something positive to say. "Is he a suspect?"

"No," Zofia said impatiently. Then she paused. "Maybe, I guess. I don't know."

"Zofia, what are you talking about?"

"See, the problem with tracking him down was the name," she said. "Jessup had one living kid, according to Ms. Haskell."

"That's right," Lauren said. "Priscilla Jessup."

"Exactly," Zofia said. "But I figured Priscilla probably got married. In the Nineteenth Century there's no chance she would've kept her maiden name. And I didn't know her married name. So I looked up the marriage records in Chicago. Fortunately, Priscilla Jessup wasn't the most common name, even back then. I found one marriage. She got hitched to a guy named Bartholomew Cousins in 1879. So I tracked the Cousins name through the next few generations via public records and..."

Vic held up a hand. "Okay, okay, let's cut to the chase," he said. "Let's assume I believe you, because you're good at this, and you've tracked down his great-great-whatever. Which is great, by definition. Why'd you do it?"

"Because if anybody would know what was hidden in Jessup's old house, it'd be his family," Zofia said, as if it was the most obvious thing in the world. Which, Vic supposed, it was.

"Kind of a long shot," he said.

"But it's the best one we've got," she replied.

"Okay, what's this punk's name?" Vic asked.

"Charles Cousins the Third," Zofia said. "It was actually kind of easy tracking the name after the first couple generations."

"He sounds like an asshole," Vic said.

"Don't be prejudiced."

"I'm not. I speak from experience."

"You know the guy?"

"No, but the last guy I met who had 'the Third' tacked onto the end of his name was a date-rapist, a murderer, and most definitely an asshole. We locked him up after chasing him on an Amtrak. Good times."

"That doesn't mean everybody who's named after his granddad is like that," Zofia said.

"No, but families that pull crap like that tend to be pretentious."

"Whatever." Zofia gave up. "I've got his phone number and address. I've also got his job. He's—"

"Let me guess," Vic said. "Hedge-fund manager?"

She blinked. "How on Earth did you guess?" she asked.

He grinned. "With that name, he had to be either that or a lawyer. I gave him the benefit of the doubt. I hate lawyers."

"You hate Wall Street types, too."

"Well, yeah, but not quite as much. So he's got an office on Wall Street?"

"Yeah."

"As soon as I get a couple uniforms to babysit the corpse, let's you and me go talk to him."

Chapter 4

To Vic's annoyance, Charles Cousins III turned out to be a cheerful, friendly, likable young man. He didn't have a fancy corner office or wear expensive suits; he had a cramped cubicle and wasn't even wearing a tie. Vic wanted to hate him on sight, but Cousins's manager was the real asshole in the office. The manager kept whining about lost productivity and disruption of the workplace.

In the end, Vic threatened to shut down the entire office with a court order. That was bullshit, of course, but the manager didn't know it. By the time the chastened mid-level drone brought him and Zofia to Cousins's desk, Vic had developed a certain sympathy for the kid. Maybe he was getting soft.

The manager led them to a conference room, not out of courtesy or respect for the kid's privacy, but to prevent the dreaded workplace disruption. The room was one of the dreariest corporate chambers Vic had ever seen. The table was fake wood, the décor nonexistent. There wasn't even a coffee machine.

Vic didn't waste any time. "I'm Detective Neshenko," he said, showing his gold shield. "This is Officer Piekarski. We're with NYPD Major Crimes."

"Wow," Cousins said, smiling a little nervously. "Am I in some kind of trouble?"

"Are you?" Vic couldn't resist replying. It was amazing what people would confess to if you left the door open. For all he knew, Cousins might be a budding serial killer, or he might be embezzling millions from his employer. On closer inspection, Cousins looked tired. He had dark circles around his eyes and pale skin. He looked overworked and under-rested.

Zofia shook her head. "Mr. Cousins, we're not really here about you," she said.

"I don't understand," Cousins said.

"We're here about your great-great-great... um, maybe another couple of 'greats' granddad," Vic said. "Arthur Jessup."

"Oh!" Cousins's face cleared. "Yeah, he was my great-great-great grandfather. But he's been dead a really long time. I'm pretty sure whatever he did, the statute of limitations ran out about a hundred years ago."

"Do you know about the old family home?" Vic asked.

"What, the brownstone in Midtown? Yeah, I've even been by there a couple of times. I never went inside, though. Just took some pics of the exterior to send to my dad. He's sort of the family archivist. I guess every family's got one of those."

"A man was killed there this morning," Vic said bluntly.

"Whoa," Cousins said. "Really? No joke?"

"For real," Vic said. "Somebody stabbed him in the head."

"I guess that's why you're here," Cousins said. "Wait a second, do I need an alibi?"

"Do you?"

"I can tell you where I was," Cousins said. "I've been here since seven this morning. We work long hours. Trading doesn't start until nine-thirty, but we have a lot of prep work. I'll probably be here until nine or ten. There's got to be fifteen guys who can vouch for me. I swear, I wasn't anywhere near the old house. I haven't been there for months."

"I'm just screwing with you," Vic said. "What do you know about Arthur and his wife?"

"Margaret," Zofia added helpfully.

"Arthur died in 1863," Cousins said. "He was killed in the Draft Riots. Nobody ever knew who did it; probably just a stray bullet. There was a lot of shooting and a bunch of people died. Margaret sold the house and moved."

"Yeah, we know all that," Vic said. "We heard she had to sell the house because she couldn't find Arthur's money."

Cousins grinned good-naturedly. "Oh!" he said, with the air of someone sharing a private joke. "So you know about his missing gold?"

"Gold," Vic repeated, trying to sound like he knew what the hell the kid was talking about.

"Yeah," Cousins said. "It's an old family legend. Dad showed me Margaret's diary once. She was complaining about it. See, on the first day of the riots, Arthur panicked. He was worried a mob was going to storm his bank and burn it down, maybe break into the vault and make off with his life savings. No FDIC insurance back then, you know? If robbers got into your bank and got your money that was it, the money was gone. So he withdrew everything he could. Greenbacks were getting popular, but he didn't trust them, so—"

"Hang on," Vic said. "Greenbacks like these?" He took out his wallet and showed Cousins a few dollar bills.

"That's right," Cousins said. "Paper money really started catching on during the Civil War, because the war was so expensive and there wasn't enough gold and silver to go around. But it caused really bad inflation, especially in the South. Did you know toward the end of the war in Richmond, if you bought a dollar's worth of gingerbread, the baker would actually cut around the dollar bill? So you got exactly a dollar of the stuff?"

"Truth in advertising," Vic said, trying to pretend he cared. He saw the kid was interested in money, which made sense given his career choice. "You were saying?"

"Anyway, Arthur didn't hold with paper money," Cousins said. "So he made his withdrawal in gold. Double eagles, twenty-dollar gold coins."

"How many?" Vic asked.

"Opinions vary," Cousins said. "According to the family, he had ten thousand dollars in gold."

"That's... uh..." Vic tried to do the math in his head.

"Five hundred coins," Cousins said helpfully. "They weighed a little less than an ounce apiece, so it worked out to a little over thirty pounds of gold. Each coin would be worth about twelve hundred dollars today, just going by weight of metal. To a collector, of course, they'd be worth much more."

"Six hundred grand," Vic said, getting the multiplication this time. He whistled.

"What happened to the gold?" Zofia asked. "According to the family legend?"

"Nobody knows for sure," Cousins said. "That's what Margaret was complaining about. She searched the whole house before she sold it, but eventually she decided he must have been carrying it with him when he went to his factory that day. Looters must have grabbed it off his body, because he didn't have a cent on him when the police brought him back to the house. Even his pocket-watch and wedding ring were stolen."

"What if he'd hidden the gold in the house?" Vic suggested. "Maybe behind a wall, in a crawlspace."

Cousins shrugged. "Then I guess it'd still be there," he said. Then he saw the look on Vic's face. "Wait a second. Are you saying somebody actually found the gold? It exists? I always thought it was just an old story."

"Can your family prove it's theirs?" Vic replied.

"I don't know," Cousins said. "I'd have to ask my dad. He's got all the old records."

"How much do you get paid here?" Vic asked.

"Not as much as you'd think," Cousins laughed. "Everybody thinks us hedge-fund guys are all millionaires, but most of us are just cube monkeys, like in any corporation. I couldn't afford to live in the old family house, not even now that it's chopped up into a bunch of little apartments. I've got a cheap studio in the Bronx and I ride the subway to work. In this office we hustle all day, because we don't draw a salary. It's all commission, all the time, and they're not big commissions either. The big players grab all the big accounts and guys like me get the leftovers. It's like they say; the job sucks, but at least the hours are long. And that reminds me, I really ought to get back to my desk. I'm falling behind."

"Don't sweat it too much," Vic said. "That's the thing about the rat race. Even if you manage to win it, you're still just a rat."

* * *

"Now what?" Zofia asked. They were on the street outside the hedge-fund office, bundled in their jackets.

"We could stake out pawnshops and gold brokers," Vic said doubtfully. "It's not like our guy can pay his grocery bill with a stack of gold coins. He's gotta turn the loot into modern money."

"Maybe that's why those gold buyers advertise in checkout lines," Zofia said. "In case you've got an empty checking account but a big pile of gold."

"It's because they're bottom-feeders," Vic said. "One step up from payday loan guys and pawnbrokers. They're the people you go to when you're desperate and you have to hock the family jewels. They're also the people you go to when you've got hot gold and don't know a good fence."

"And you think our guy doesn't?"

Vic shook his head. "This wasn't a professional burglary," he said. "And he's not a career criminal. This is a guy seeing more money than he's ever seen in his life and getting greedy and stupid. Now he's got thirty pounds of gold he doesn't know what to do with."

"Won't he just sit on it for a while, until the heat dies down?"

"Why would he? As far as he knows, he's the only guy in New York who knows it even exists. And he wants to get rid of the evidence. No, we've got two ways we can go on this. We can try for a warrant, which we may or may not get, or we can shadow Gallo until he tries to offload the loot. And if we wait for the warrant, he'll ditch the gold."

"So you're sure it's Gallo?"

"Absolutely."

"Why?"

"Sandwiches."

Zofia's brow wrinkled. "What do you mean?"

"Remember the sandwiches he was bringing?"

"Yeah. He said he'd gone to pick up lunch for himself and his buddy."

"Right. And that seemed weird to me, but I couldn't put my finger on it right away. It's a little strange he went alone and left his pal on site. Maybe that would happen, but workmen like to take breaks together. That's not enough by itself, but do you remember what the sandwiches were?"

Zofia shrugged. "Roast beef, I think."

"If you're gonna be a detective, you gotta pay attention to detail," Vic said. "Every detail of those sandwiches was the same. They were exactly identical."

"So?"

"So when's the last time you saw two grown men order the exact same sandwich, down to every condiment?"

"Wait a sec," Zofia said. "You're saying he bought the extra sandwich as camouflage? To cover up the fact that he'd already killed his partner?"

Vic nodded. "And he got two of the same sandwich because it's one he'd like to eat. I'll bet it's his favorite. I'll bet even more that if we check his fridge tonight, we'll find the leftover sandwich there."

She thought it over. "I guess that makes sense," she said. "But I don't know if a judge would go for it."

"Not even Judge Ferris," Vic agreed. "And Ferris likes us. So we need to go to plan B, which is why I told Kirkland and Rockford to keep a low profile. I don't want Gallo arrested yet. I want him to show us where he's got the treasure."

"You've been planning this the whole time?"

"I'm mostly making it up as I go and getting lucky."

"You know, you could've pretended to be smart and taken the credit."

Vic grinned. "I don't want to lie to you," he said. "We've gotten this far by being who we pretend to be. If I'm not good enough for you, I'm not gonna fake being better just to impress you."

"Vic Neshenko, that's adorable," Zofia said. She went up on her tiptoes and kissed him lightly on the lips. "You're my musclebound idiot and I love you for it. You're also not as dumb as everybody else thinks."

"And that's the sweetest thing you've said to me all day."

Chapter 5

Vic had his phone to his ear almost before it finished the first ring. "Neshenko," he said.

"This is Kirkland. We're at Gallo's place. His van just pulled into the basement garage."

"I copy," Vic said. "We're on our way. If he moves, follow him. Otherwise, sit tight. Good work."

He hung up and turned to Zofia. "Let's roll," he said.

"Great idea," she said. "On what wheels? Your car's back at the apartment. So is mine. We took a cab to get here, remember?"

Vic cursed. "I guess we'll get another taxi," he said.

They flagged down a cab and set off. Gallo's apartment, oddly enough, wasn't far from Vic's own; just four blocks up the street. So Vic told the cabbie to take them to his place instead. That way they could pick up his Taurus and get a little freedom of movement.

"What'd you think of the apartment?" he asked as the taxi rolled through the Manhattan streets.

Zofia stared at him. "You're seriously asking that? Vic, a guy got murdered in the bathroom!"

"It's fate," he said. "Destiny, serendipity, kismet, whatever the hell you want to call it. I'm a murder cop and that's what you're gonna be too. Think of it like a christening, like when they smash a champagne bottle on a ship when they launch it."

She made a face. "Except it's blood instead of champagne."

"They'll clean up the blood. It's not like there were pools of it lying around, and it was in the bathroom, on tile. Stains come right out of that stuff. Forget about the corpse for a second. What'd you think of the rest of the place?"

"I liked it," Zofia said. "It had character and charm."

"Now it's got more character and a little less charm," he said. "Look, this is an old city. People have died on pretty much every acre of Manhattan at one time or another. If you believe in ghosts, you'd better move somewhere else, because New York must be chock-full of them."

"You're right," she said. "How're you feeling about this whole thing, anyway?"

"What, moving?"

"Yeah, that," she said, taking his hand and laying it against her belly. "And this."

"A little freaked," he admitted. "Kind of like I'm feeling about this head detective gig I fell into. It's a lot, and I'm not sure I'm ready for it, but I'm gonna do the best job I can. And if that's not good enough? Fuck it, I gave it my best shot."

"I think your best shot is pretty damn good," she said, squeezing his hand.

* * *

Back at the garage next to his apartment, Vic slid gratefully behind the wheel of his Taurus. He twisted the key and felt the familiar throaty hum of its powerful engine. The car rolled out onto the street and he set a course for Gallo's apartment. He felt much more in control of the situation, until he remembered something he should've fetched from his room as long as they'd been there.

"Damn," he said.

"What?" Zofia asked.

"Forgot my guns."

"What do you call that?" She pointed a thumb at the rifle rack, upon which rested Vic's M4 assault rifle.

"That might be overkill in this situation," he said.

Zofia put a hand out on his forehead. "Funny," she said. "You don't feel feverish. Are you feeling okay?"

"I'd feel better if we had some pistols, that's all."

"It'll be fine," she said. "Kirkland and Rockford will be with us and they'll be carrying if things go sideways. If it's important to you, we can turn around and go back."

He sighed. "No. We don't want to waste more time. I'll be fine."

"Some kids have security blankets or stuffed animals," she said with a smile. "You've got your emotional-support pistols. It's kind of cute."

"Shut up."

"You could probably get plush holsters for them. Then you could cuddle them at night."

"You think you're funny, but you're not."

She giggled.

Vic grinned in spite of himself. "Here's Gallo's address," he said. "You ever wonder how many murderers live within a four-block radius of us?"

"I try not to," Zofia said. She picked up the car's radio handset. "Sergeant Kirkland, come in. This is Neshenko and Piekarski."

"Kirkland here," the answer came. "Where are you?"

"Passing Gallo's place right now. Where are you?"

"At the corner, half a block away, keeping a nice low profile. Wait, I think I see you. Black Taurus?"

"That's us," Zofia said.

"Watch your six. See that van that just pulled out?"

Vic checked his rearview. "I see it," he said. "Is that our guy?"

"That's affirmative," Kirkland said.

"Great, just great," Vic said. "He's following me. That's a little tricky. Get on his ass, Kirkland. But not too close."

"Will do," Kirkland said.

Vic considered his options and did the simple thing. He moved into the rightmost lane and drove annoyingly slowly, drawing honks from other New Yorkers. Sure enough, the other cars started moving around him, including a white van with badly rusted bodywork.

"That's the most child-molester van I've seen in a long time," Zofia commented. "Creepiness way off the charts."

"Now who's prejudiced?" Vic replied. "Just be glad it's nice and conspicuous."

"Where do you suppose he's going?"

"If I knew that, there'd be no point chasing him. I'd just go there and wait. Isn't this exciting?"

"What?"

"Your first car chase as part of Major Crimes."

"Eh. I've had better."

"No guy likes to hear that."

"Even when it's true?"

"Especially when it's true."

* * *

Vic had to admit, as car chases went it was a pretty lame one. No desperate slalom between civilian cars, no driving the wrong way down one-way streets, no clever PIT maneuver to disable the suspect's vehicle. They just moseyed along through the Manhattan traffic, trying not to get so close they got noticed, or so far behind they lost the van. It was depressingly like being a commuter.

Vic yawned.

"Bored?" Zofia asked.

"A little."

"Careful," she said. "In SNEU, Sergeant Logan would smack anybody who wished for more excitement. He said it was a sure recipe for something bad to go down."

"Do you miss it?"

"What kind of a question is that? Don't you miss kicking down doors with ESU?"

"Yeah," he said. "It's funny, though. I thought I'd miss the adrenaline, and sometimes I do. Sure, we get in gunfights every now and then in Major Crimes, and we beat the shit out of plenty of bad guys, but ESU serves high-risk warrants practically every day. Mostly I miss the simplicity."

She nodded. "You knew exactly who the bad guys were and what you were supposed to do about it," she said.

"Yeah. Being a detective is so damned complicated."

"But you're good at it."

"I'm as surprised as you are."

"Would you go back to ESU?"

"I almost did."

"You what?!"

"I was gonna transfer."

"Why? Because of me? And the baby?"

"No! Because... because of stuff I can't talk about."

"Ooh," she said. "Top secret, need-to-know stuff?"

"Something like that."

"What sort of stuff? Is this about Erin O'Reilly?"

"The sort of stuff I can't talk about. Because it's top secret, need-to-know."

Zofia pouted.

Vic would've loved to tell her, but he wasn't even supposed to know it himself, let alone spread it around. It was an undercover operation, a long-running op involving Erin O'Reilly. She was pretending to be a crooked cop who took contracts from the Mob. She'd gathered enormously valuable information on the Irish Mob, enough to take down their entire leadership and cripple the organization. She might be able to wipe the O'Malleys out altogether. But she'd had to make compromises along the way, and they'd gotten harder and harder for Vic to swallow.

"Forget about it," he said in classic Long Island style. "The transfer didn't happen. I'm not going anywhere."

"No," she said, pointing through the windshield. "You're not."

"Shit!" he grunted. The stoplight ahead was in the last second of its yellow stage. Gallo's van was tootling merrily on, oblivious.

Vic gritted his teeth and put his foot down, but not on the brake. The Taurus leaped forward. He swerved around the car in front of him, which had come to the opposite conclusion and decided to stop. He rushed into the intersection just after the light flicked red. A chorus of honks from the cross-street let him know exactly what his fellow drivers thought of him.

"Nice and subtle," Zofia said. "I can tell you've got lots of experience at stealthy shadowing. You think he saw us?"

Vic's radio crackled to life, sparing him the need to reply.

"This is Kirkland. We lost you at that last light."

Of course they had. Nobody else could've made it across after Vic. He picked up the handset.

"Copy that," he said. "Come when you can."

Gallo abruptly turned onto a side street. Vic considered driving past and circling back, or maybe trying to run a parallel route, but it would be too easy to lose the other vehicle. He decided to risk following. There'd been three cars between them and he didn't think Gallo had made them yet, in spite of his last-minute stoplight blitz. He brought the Taurus around the corner and saw the van parked curbside. Gallo was already getting out.

"Lucky bastard," Vic muttered. Gallo had gotten the last available spot.

"Let me out," Zofia said. "I'll get him."

"Like hell," Vic said. He wasn't letting his pregnant girlfriend go it alone against a murderer, especially when she was unarmed and not wearing body armor.

"He's getting away!" Zofia complained.

"Watch where he goes," Vic said. He guided the Taurus down the street, looking for a police space. He found one at the end of the block. Taking it would blow whatever cover he still had, but he intended to take the chance.

"He went into a store," Zofia reported. "I think it's a pawnshop."

"Beautiful," Vic said as he brought the Taurus to a stop. He threw it into park and jumped out. "Call Kirkland and let her know where we are."

"Hey! Wait up!" Zofia protested, but Vic wasn't listening. He was already on the move.

Vic walked briskly, arms swinging. He'd left his rifle in the car, mainly because he was already a pretty conspicuous guy. Hauling an M4 around on the sidewalk would attract all kinds of attention and might tip Gallo off before he got close. Besides, backup would be there any minute.

The pawnshop had the run-down, sleazy look those places always seemed to have. The windows were thick, double-paned glass, screened by metal bars. The evil red eye of a security camera glared at Vic as he reached the door. He glared back and shoved the door open.

"Hi!" he said cheerfully. "I'm looking for some gold coins, Civil War vintage. Got anything like that?"

Gallo and the pawnbroker stared at him. The broker was behind bulletproof glass. On the counter between the men was a rectangular wooden box.

"Oh, sorry," Vic said. "You're in the middle of a deal. That's fine, I can wait. What were you about to offer him, Mr. Gallo?"

Gallo was at a loss for words. His mouth flopped open and closed, reminding Vic of a landed fish he'd seen on the Brighton Beach shoreline as a boy. The air Gallo was gasping in was about as much good to him as it'd been to the fish. He'd gone suddenly very pale.

"You remember me, don't you?" Vic asked, walking closer. "Detective Neshenko. The guy who's investigating your partner's death. Pedro Gesualdo, dead of a screwdriver in the brain. We've got a theory about the death. See, it wouldn't be an ordinary home invasion or burglary, since he was in a vacant apartment. No furniture, nothing worth stealing. But your buddy Pete found something behind the wall in the bathroom; a box that'd been hidden for more than a hundred years."

The pawnbroker's eyes flicked down to the box on his counter. So did Gallo's.

"It was heavy," Vic went on. "Over thirty pounds. Imagine his surprise when he popped it open and found hundreds of gold coins. Some antiques look like junk; it'd take a collector to know what they're worth. But every little boy knows what a chest full of gold looks like. He had hundreds of thousands of dollars, money nobody else knew was there. It would've been his lucky day if he'd been alone. But he wasn't.

"You were there too, Bruno. The really sad thing is, the two of you could've split it fifty-fifty. Nobody would've been the wiser and you both could've made out like bandits. But maybe you fought over it, or maybe you just got greedy and wanted it all. The result was the same. You grabbed a screwdriver out of your toolbox and stabbed him. Then you took off with the money."

"That's not..." Gallo began.

Vic waited politely for him to finish the sentence. He didn't.

"You knew you had to get the cash out of there before the cops arrived," Vic said after a moment. "And you wanted to set up your own alibi. So you went to order and pick up lunch. But you slipped up and made me suspicious. First, you ordered the wrong thing. Pedro didn't like the same sandwiches you did."

"How did you know that?" Gallo demanded. "He never told you what he ate!"

"I didn't, not for sure," Vic said with a grin. "But you just confirmed it. And then you forgot about the dust."

"What dust?" the workman demanded.

"That dust," Vic said, pointing to the box. "It left an outline in the crawlspace. I'll bet every dollar I've got against every coin in that box, if we take it back to the apartment, it'll match the clean outline perfectly."

"What if it does?" Gallo said, having recovered somewhat. "There's lots of boxes this size. These coins could've come from anywhere."

Vic sighed. "Before I was a detective, that might've stumped me," he said. "But now, since I've been hanging around CSU, I know about this little thing called transference. What that means is, everything that comes in contact transfers bits of itself. So the box left traces in the crawlspace, and the dust from there got on the box. And not all dust is the same, buddy. CSU, they've got all sorts of tests and weird chemicals and shit. They'll run those tests and they'll be able to tell if it's the same dust. And if it is, you're gonna have some serious explaining to do."

"It was an accident," Gallo said weakly. "I didn't mean to."

"Of course it was," Vic said. "I accidentally stab guys in the skull all the time. You wouldn't believe how often it happens. Okay, here's the drill. You're under arrest for the murder of Pedro Gesualdo. You've got the right—"

Gallo might or might not have understood his rights, but he wasn't about to stand around and listen while Vic informed him of them. He shoved a hand into the pocket of his coveralls and came out with a flat-head screwdriver. The handle looked to be from the same set as the one currently decorating the late Mr. Gesualdo's ear. He lunged, stabbing at Vic's stomach.

Vic pivoted, bringing his left foot back and swinging his torso, letting the thrust go past him. He cupped his left hand around his right fist and drove his right elbow into Gallo's face. Vic heard a muffled crunch from Gallo's nose. The screwdriver clattered across the floor. Gallo stumbled back against the counter with a wet, bubbly sound of distress. Blood was squirting from his nose.

"All right," Vic said, more annoyed than anything. "Let's try this again."

Gallo reached back, grabbed the wooden box, and heaved it at Vic, who reflexively caught it.

That was a mistake. The box, as he'd said earlier, weighed over thirty pounds. Vic was plenty strong to lift it, but thirty pounds of gold had significant momentum. It slammed against his torso, a corner of the box digging into his solar plexus.

Vic grunted and doubled over. He dropped the box, which crashed to the floor and broke apart. A glittering shower of coins bounced and rolled in all directions, thousands of dollars carpeting the concrete. Every coin made a high-pitched but surprisingly loud ringing sound as it struck the hard floor.

Gallo seized his chance and made a run for it. Blood streaming from his face, he sprinted past Vic, snatched at the door handle, and yanked it open. Looking back over his shoulder to see if Vic was coming after him, he ran out onto the street.

Zofia's arm caught him just under the chin in a classic football-style clothesline. His feet went up and out and he came down flat on his back, the breath leaving his lungs in a single emphatic "Oof!"

Vic straightened up and walked over to the downed man. Zofia scowled at both of them.

"You could've waited for me!" she snapped at Vic.

"All part of the plan," he said. "You were my backup in case he did a rabbit. You were perfectly positioned."

"That was sheer dumb luck and you know it," she said.

"If it works, nobody cares if it's luck," he replied. Then he slapped his forehead. "Damn it!"

"What?" Zofia asked.

Gallo groaned and tried to sit up. Vic absentmindedly grabbed him by the hair and threw him back down again. His head thudded against the concrete and he decided to stay down this time.

"I don't have my cuffs," Vic said. "Didn't think I'd need them for looking at apartments."

"No problem," Zofia said. She looked past him at the pawnbroker, who was staring at the spilled gold with eyes like dinner plates. "Hey buddy, you got any handcuffs?"

"Sure, ma'am," he said. "You want the fur-lined kind or the regular ones?"

Chapter 6

"This is how you spend your days off," Lieutenant Webb said. He shook his head and sighed.

"It's not like we asked for this to happen," Vic said. "All I agreed to do was look at some apartments."

"Did you find one?" Erin O'Reilly asked.

"Hell yes," Vic said. "We're moving into the old Jessup place when my lease comes up."

They were back at work in the Major Crimes office of Precinct 8, the morning after the infamous apartment visit. Vic and Zofia had just finished filling the other two in on the events. Erin was amused. Webb didn't even seem surprised. He expected his squad to get into crazy situations by now.

"After all that, you're taking the apartment?" Erin said, raising her eyebrows.

Zofia shrugged. "We got a break on the rent," she said.

"We ran the old good cop/bad cop on the realtor," Vic said. "I convinced her to knock ten percent off the asking price, on account of the bad publicity."

"And the public service we'd done by getting the murderer," Zofia added.

"Who gets credit for the bust?" Webb asked.

"We do," Vic said. "As long as we get all the paperwork to the Homicide boys in Midtown. They finally showed up around six-thirty. We'd had time to get most of the arrest reports and DD-5s filled out in the meantime, and we delivered the perp to them. Practically gift-wrapped."

"They said it was the first time they'd had a guy handed over wearing leopard-print handcuffs," Zofia said.

"I wanted the plain ones, but Zofia insisted," Vic said.

"I expensed them to the Department," she said.

"You should put Sergeant Brown's name on the expense form," Erin suggested. "It's probably not the first time Vice has paid for something like that."

"So we get the credit, but we don't get paid for the overtime," Vic said.

"You know all departmental overtime needs to be approved in advance," Webb said wearily. "I'm sorry, but that's the rules."

"That's okay," Vic said. "It was fun. Anyway, I learned some stuff."

"Such as?" Erin asked.

"I don't want your job, sir," Vic said to Webb.

"That makes sense," Webb said. "Neither do I, most days."

"What happens to the gold?" Erin asked.

"It goes into Evidence," Vic said. "And it stays there until the trial, if there is a trial. I'm guessing there won't be."

"He'll plead out," Zofia predicted. "If he hadn't confessed to Vic and then attacked him, he might've thought he had a chance to beat the rap, but now he's screwed and he knows it."

"Screwed," Vic snorted. He was thinking about construction tools.

"And after Gallo goes up the river?" Erin asked.

"Then it's between the current owner of the house and the Cousins kid," Vic said. "I'm not real up on property and inheritance law, so I don't know who the rightful owner is. The lawyers will sort it out. I guess there'll probably be a settlement. Maybe the building owners keep fifty or sixty percent and give the rest to the kid. That'd be nice; he wouldn't have to keep hustling on Wall Street."

"You just said nice things about lawyers and a stock broker," Erin said. "You're either getting soft in the head or the heart."

"Vic's really a big softy once you get to know him," Zofia said.

"Hmph," Vic grumbled. "You know, I could've had that guy even if you hadn't nailed him."

"Of course you could," Zofia said soothingly. "But I didn't think you wanted to hog all the fun. It was generous of you to let me get a shot in."

She took a long drink from the cup on her desk and winked at him.

"What're you drinking this morning?" Erin asked.

"Orange juice," Zofia said. "*Pure* orange juice. You ought to try it sometime, Vic. It's good for you."

"I'll stick with screwdrivers," Vic said.

About the Author

Steven Henry learned how to read almost before he learned how to walk. Ever since he began reading stories, he wanted to put his own on the page. He lives a very quiet and ordinary life in Minnesota with his wife and dog.

Also by Steven Henry

Fathers

A Modern Christmas Story

When you strip away everything else, what's left is the truth

Life taught Joe Davidson not to believe in miracles. A blue-collar wood-worker, Joe is trying to build a future. His father drank himself to death and his mother succumbed to cancer, leaving a broken, struggling family. He and his brother and sisters are faced with failed marriages, growing pains, and lingering trauma.

Then a chance meeting at his local diner brings Mary Elizabeth Reynolds into his life. Suddenly, Joe finds himself reaching for something more, a dream of happiness. The wood-worker and the poor girl from a trailer park connect and fall in love, and for a little while, everything is right with their world.

But suddenly Joe is confronted with a situation he never imagined. What do you do if your fiancée is expecting a child you know isn't yours? Torn between betrayal and love, trying to do the right thing when nothing seems right anymore, Joe has to strip life down to its truth and learn that, in spite of the pain, love can be the greatest miracle of all.

Learn more at clickworkspress.com/fathers.

Ember of Dreams

The Clarion Chronicles, Book One

When magic awakens a long-forgotten folk, a noble lady, a young apprentice, and a solitary blacksmith band together to prevent war and seek understanding between humans and elves.

Lady Kristyn Tremayne – An otherwise unremarkable young lady's open heart and inquisitive mind reveal a hidden world of magic.

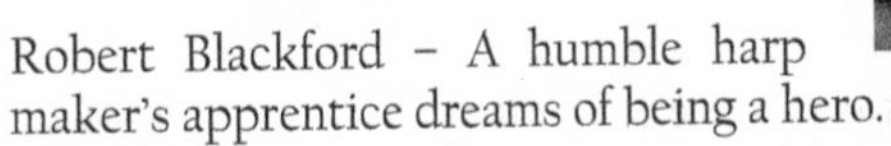

Robert Blackford – A humble harp maker's apprentice dreams of being a hero.

Master Gabriel Zane – A master blacksmith's pursuit of perfection leads him to craft an enchanted sword, drawing him out of his isolation and far from his cozy home.

Lord Luthor Carnarvon – A lonely nobleman with a dark past has won the heart of Kristyn's mother, but at what cost?

Readers love *Ember of Dreams*

"The more I got to know the characters, the more I liked them. The female lead in particular is a treat to accompany on her journey from ordinary to extraordinary."

"The author's deep understanding of his protagonists' motivations and keen eye for psychological detail make Robert and his companions a likable and memorable cast."

Learn more at tinyurl.com/emberofdreams.

More great titles from Clickworks Press

www.clickworkspress.com

The Altered Wake

Megan Morgan

Amid growing unrest, a family secret and an ancient laboratory unleash long-hidden superhuman abilities. Now newly-promoted Sentinel Cameron Kardell must chase down a rogue superhuman who holds the key to the powers' origin: the greatest threat Cotarion has seen in centuries – and Cam's best friend.

"Incredible. Starts out gripping and keeps getting better."

Learn more at clickworkspress.com/sentinel1.

Hubris Towers: The Complete First Season

Ben Y. Faroe & Bill Hoard

Comedy of manners meets comedy of errors in a new series for fans of Fawlty Towers and P. G. Wodehouse.

"So funny and endearing"

"Had me laughing so hard that I had to put it down to catch my breath"

"Astoundingly, outrageously funny!"

Learn more at clickworkspress.com/hts01.

Death's Dream Kingdom

Gabriel Blanchard

A young woman of Victorian London has been transformed into a vampire. Can she survive the world of the immortal dead—or perhaps, escape it?

"The wit and humor are as Victorian as the setting... a winsomely vulnerable and tremendously crafted work of art."

"A dramatic, engaging novel which explores themes of death, love, damnation, and redemption."

Learn more at clickworkspress.com/ddk.

Share the love!

Join our microlending team at
kiva.org/team/clickworkspress.

Keep in touch!

Join the Clickworks Press email list
and get freebies, production updates, special deals,
behind-the-scenes sneak peeks, and more.

Sign up today at clickworkspress.com/join.

Printed in the USA
CPSIA information can be obtained
at www.ICGtesting.com
LVHW090826221223
767141LV00013B/597

9 798889 000150